THE AMULET

ANN BENNETT

Andaman Press

For Siobhan

1

LARA

Northamptonshire, 2000

Lara Adams had always been curious about her mother's childhood. Being brought up by nuns in an orphanage on Singapore Island seemed to Lara both exotic and tragic. It lent her mother an air of mystery which set her apart from the other women in the nondescript village in the Midlands where Lara herself was raised.

Not that Nell ever spoke about it, other than on the odd occasion when she let her guard drop. 'Sister Xavier used to take us to the market to buy fresh mangoes on Saturday mornings,' she'd exclaimed when the first fruits appeared in Sainsbury's. Her eyes took on an uncharacteristic, dreamy look as she paused with the trolley to squeeze an unripe mango between expert fingers. Lara had been eager to hear more, but her mother had pursed her lips and the shutters came down again.

The faded green certificate that Lara unearthed from the drawer of Nell's desk a few days after her mother's death, was the first concrete proof that the orphanage had been anything more than a myth Lara had dreamed up to fit the fragments of gleaned information into a coherent story.

Lara had come home to the old stone cottage on the village green to be with her father. It was strange to be back in the old place after such a long absence, but the low-ceilinged rooms with their gloomy, old-fashioned furniture were just the same; clean and orderly as Nell had always kept them. Even the familiar smell of the lavender polish she used still lingered.

It was four days after the funeral. George Adams would sit at the kitchen table for hours at a time, staring into the void. Lara had tried to help him through those dark days, but she knew it would take time and patience. He went through the motions of his daily routine, hardly eating, rarely speaking, and when he did speak, he would often pause mid-sentence as silent tears spilled down his lined face.

She hovered by the door, wondering how to tell him that she had to go back to London the next day.

'Is there anything you need me to do, Dad?' She couldn't bring herself to say, 'before I go'.

He turned to look at her, his eyes vague. 'I haven't a clue. Everything's done, isn't it? Nellie took care of the house.'

'What about bills? Do you need me to pay the electricity? Order more coal?'

He shrugged. 'You could check. She kept all that stuff in the desk.'

In the dining room, beside the inglenook fireplace, stood Nell's bureau. Nell herself stared out from a silver framed wedding photograph on the polished surface, severe and upright even on that day. Lara was tempted to turn the photo round to face the wall. She could feel Nell's presence, right there in the room where the smell of soot and old wine mingled with the odour of fading chrysanthemums. It made her nervous. As she opened the desk drawers one by one, she felt her mother behind her, ready to rap her knuckles with a ruler as she had each time Lara had transgressed her strict code of conduct, by helping herself to a biscuit without asking first, or getting into trouble at school.

Lara carefully eased the neat folders of household bills out of the top drawer and checked the payments were up to date. Nell's steady handwriting showed the date and amount of each cheque. In the next drawer down, Lara's own certificates from school were stacked in date order: pianoforte, grades 1-5, ballet, swimming. She leafed through them, remembering the pain and tears that had accompanied the gaining of each one.

In the bottom drawer, she found a thin brown folder that she had never seen before. Again, the neat handwriting on the sticky label: "Nell Joseph – personal papers". Lara hesitated. It seemed wrong to violate her mother's privacy, but the tug of curiosity was strong. Even so, her hands shook as she eased the contents out. Nell's old Singaporean passport lay on top. Inside the dark green cover was another photograph of the unsmiling young woman, this time in a starched nurse's uniform. The passport was long expired. Once Nell had reached England she'd never left its shores, not even for a holiday. There was her certificate of nursing, issued in Singapore in 1962, and finally there it was, the pale green paper with a crest at the top and a sketch of the Virgin Mary under an arch of roses.

"Convent of Our Lady, Bukit Timah, Singapore". Underneath that was a simple entry. "December 1942. Baby Girl, approx 3 months old. Brought from Chinatown by a local woman. Baby named Cornelia Joseph by the Sisters."

Lara stared at it, mouthing the unfamiliar place-names

silently. They seemed so strange and remote. So unconnected with her practical mother, who, despite her dark hair and oriental looks dressed just like the other women in the village, spoke perfect English and led what seemed to Lara a boring middle-class life. Lara tried to imagine what the Convent of Our Lady in Bukit Timah might have been like, and why baby Nell had been taken there. She could hear her mother's voice now, if she'd been asked: 'Oh, questions, questions. It's not worth dwelling on the past, Lara my girl. What on earth's the point of that?'

Lara went to her father's bookcase and took down the *Times Atlas of the World*. Bukit Timah was a suburb of Singapore city now. She looked at it for a long time, trying to picture what it must be like there. Was that where Nell had been born? To an unmarried mother in a native village somewhere outside the city perhaps, who had taken her to the orphanage for fear of being cast out of the community? Or to a family so poor that they couldn't afford to feed a new-born baby? As she stared at the map, she realised how remote from her own life her mother's beginnings were, and at the same time the thought struck her forcefully how little she really knew about the woman who'd brought her into the world.

She picked up the folder to slip the certificate back in and something rattled in the bottom. She turned it over and a silver chain dropped out. Lara picked it up and examined it, holding it up to her eyes. From the chain dangled a pale-yellow stone that glittered in the light from the window. It was set within a silver surround. On the back was an inscription. Just two words: *For Suria*.

'Lara? What are you doing?' Dad's voice came from the kitchen. She hastily slid the atlas back into the bookcase and pushed the folder and papers back into the drawer.

'Just checking the bills.' She went back into the kitchen. 'Shall I make you another cup? That one's gone cold.' He looked at her, the trace of a smile on his lips. 'That would be nice.'

'Everything seems to be OK for the time being,' she said, 'there's nothing to pay until next month.'

'That's good. She was so efficient, Nellie. I don't know what I'll do...'

Lara put her hands on his shoulders.

'I'm here to help you Dad.'

'You will stay for a bit longer won't you?' he asked, clasping her hand. His palm was cold and dry.

Sympathy for her father flooded through her. It was disconcerting to see him like this. He'd always been so strong and resilient. For Lara's entire life he'd taught history at the comprehensive school on the edge of the local town, where the kids from the London overspill estates had little or no interest in the Tudors or the Russian revolution. At best they would sit through his lessons staring at him as if he was bonkers, and at worst they would throw missiles from the back of the class and call him names. But she'd never once seen him lose faith or enthusiasm for his task. The slightest spark of interest in a pupil would give him hope, and if his fifth formers managed to scrape a few GCSEs between them, he would come home from school in celebratory mood.

He's lost without her, Lara thought. She was always there to organise him, cook the meals, do the washing. He had lived in awe of her all the same, skirting round her moods, fearful of igniting her temper by saying the wrong thing, avoiding confrontations, striving for a quiet life. But now that quiet life had suddenly arrived, he was adrift.

'I'll have to go tomorrow, I'm afraid, Dad. They need me

at the shop. But I'll come back at the weekend.' She felt his shoulders tense up under her hands, but he didn't protest.

Instead he said, 'I wouldn't have blamed you if you hadn't come, you know.'

'I came for you, Dad. You know that.'

'She loved you, Lara. She found it hard to show it sometimes, but it was because she loved you that...'

That she refused to speak to me for the past two years? Lara didn't say the words, but they hovered in the air between them.

'Your mother had some rigid views. But that didn't mean she didn't care.'

Lara turned away and busied herself at the sink, a lump in her throat stopping her from swallowing or even speaking. The pain of grief and the anger of her estrangement from her mother suddenly felt overwhelming.

She turned back towards her father, tears in her eyes.

'Come here,' he said, holding out his arms.

Later she went up to her childhood bedroom, changed into some old pyjamas and slid between cool sheets. It felt luxurious compared to the lumpy mattress in the studio flat in the crumbling Victorian mansion block in Holloway Road, where lorries thundered up the A1 and rattled the dusty windows into the small hours. Despite the peace of the village, or perhaps partly because of it, she had not been able to sleep properly since she'd come back.

Lying awake and staring at the light from the street lamps playing on the ceiling, she thought back over the past week. She relived the shock of the news that Nell was in hospital with pneumonia, and the panic of rushing to see her, unconscious and surrounded by monitors. Then the strained days that followed, when she'd paced the hospital corridors for hours, talking to the doctors and helping her anguished father to cope. When the end finally came, the feeling of emptiness, and the bitterness and frustration of all those wasted months and years had overtaken her. That empty hollow feeling had persisted until now, leaving her unable to cry, or even feel.

At the funeral, people had come up to her and hugged her and squeezed her hands. They were the same people from the village who, years ago, had teased her and made her life a misery because her mother was different. They had all said how sorry they were for her loss and what a wonderful woman Nell was. And Lara had smiled and accepted their condolences and their unspoken apologies, expressed only in the anguished looks on their faces.

'Hypocrites,' she muttered into the dark. But she quickly banished this thought as the pale green certificate lying in the bureau floated into her mind. And with it floated the image of a shimmering city on a tropical island, surrounded by a turquoise sea, where gleaming buildings rose from a palm-fringed seafront.

2

LARA

London, 2000

The flat felt damp and cold as Lara let herself in. It smelled of stale cooking and town gas. She'd left in such a hurry she hadn't had time to wash up after her last meal. The frying pan was still in the sink filled with greasy water. She dumped her bag, crossed the darkened living room and pulled back the curtains to stare down at the lanes of traffic crawling past in the autumn drizzle of the late afternoon.

Outside the newsagents on the other side of the road the Romanian woman sat on a camp stool selling the Big Issue. She was always there, rain or shine, bundled up in a dark shawl, saying the same words over and over to everyone who went into the shop. She had been sitting there when Lara had taken Dad's telephone call ten days ago. Lara wondered how many times the woman had said 'Big Issue, madam? Big Issue, sir?' in the intervening days. In those days, Lara's own life had changed irreversibly, but everything here went on just as before.

As she turned back into the room she noticed a note on the coffee table scribbled on the back of a torn brown envelope. On top of it were some keys. Her gut squirmed as she recognised the writing.

Came to fetch my Bob Dylan albums. Helped myself to some beer. Where are you? Thought you might as well have the keys back. Call me sometime, Joe.

Joe. The source of all the pain. Beside the note, a dented beer can with a cigarette butt stubbed out on the top. She screwed the note into a ball and threw the empty can across the room. The can just missed the kitchen bin and ricocheted off under the table.

She pictured him sitting here on her sofa, feet up on the table, smoking and drinking. He'd probably flicked the TV on to watch some daytime soap, and when he'd finished the beer, he would have had a good poke round the flat, checking her post, looking in the wardrobe to see if there were any male clothes, turning on her computer. Did he still know her passwords? Her breath quickened with irritation. No, she couldn't think about him now, not when she was feeling like this.

She put some coins in the meter and lit the gas fire, huddling close to get some warmth. Then she turned on her laptop and, kneeling with it on the floor in front of the fire, tried to find something about "the Convent of Our Lady, Bukit Timah". But after half an hour of searching all she had managed to unearth was a single page from the Catholic historical society of Singapore, saying that the Convent had been closed in 1943.

The green certificate was in her bag. She'd felt awkward about simply taking it away, so had said to Dad before she left,

'I found something in the desk drawer when I was

looking for the bills. It was something from an orphanage in Singapore. Where Mum was brought up, I think. It looks like a registration certificate.'

'Oh, I haven't seen that for years. I'd forgotten it was there.'

'It's funny that she hardly ever mentioned it, isn't it?'

'She didn't want to look back. I don't think she had a very happy time there, you know. She wanted to put it all behind her.'

'But she didn't really put it behind her, did she?'

His face fell, and Lara wished she hadn't said that. They both knew what she meant. Nell's toughness and self-denial, her refusal to compromise and her almost fanatical self-discipline must all have been imbued in her in that orphanage. As must her ruthless treatment of Lara, her constant pushing for academic success that had eventually driven them apart, and her refusal to back down, even if it meant estrangement from her only daughter.

'Do you mind if I borrow it?' Lara broke the awkward silence, 'I'd like to try and find out a bit more about it.'

He paused for a second and then said, 'Of course not. By all means take it. But do take care of it, Lara.'

'It's odd that she never wanted to go back there.'

'Not odd at all. She'd spent her entire childhood being told how wonderful the West is, and her whole focus was on coming over here. When she finally made it, why on earth would she want to go back?'

'Didn't you ever want to go there?'

'It just wasn't on the cards. A week in Wales once a year was all she ever wanted. And I've never been a great one for travelling myself, as you know.'

Lying awake on her lumpy bed now, listening to the traffic and still keeping to her own side, even though Joe hadn't occupied the other side for several months, her mind filled with the images of Malaysia and Singapore that had popped up as she searched for the convent. Adverts for tours and accommodation, showing white beaches and clear seas, jungle-covered mountains and picturesque villages of houses built of rough wood and bamboo. For the first time in her life it occurred to her that maybe she could go there and see the place for herself. Perhaps if she went to the places her mother had known as a child, she might come to some understanding of what had driven Nell all those years. It might help her to find some connection with her mother and overcome that feeling of emptiness and loss that haunted her.

The money she had saved to put down on a flat with Joe was still in her savings account. It had taken her two years to save up that money and it represented two years of sacrifices: hardly ever going out, making do with clothes from the charity shop, walking instead of taking the bus to work. It would be frivolous to blow it on a trip, and she could almost sense Nell's disapproval coursing through her own veins, but had she ever done anything seriously frivolous in her life before? Her only two acts of rebellion had hardly been frivolous.

Giving up the job in the law firm in the city had been necessary to save her sanity. She'd felt stifled by studying law, even though getting into London University had been hailed as the pinnacle of achievement by her mother. But for her mother's sake she'd stuck at it, even gaining a respectable degree at the end of three miserable years. But when it came to practising it, she'd felt as though she was drowning, her life slipping away beyond her control. And the final straw, after drifting through temporary jobs and flat-shares with various groups of friends for a couple of years, had been moving in with Joe. No, that hadn't been a frivolous move either as it turned out; it had been an act of emotional suicide. Maybe visiting her mother's past wouldn't be frivolous at all.

Lara felt a shiver of excitement as she turned the thought over in her mind. She'd have to wait a few months, of course. It wouldn't be fair to leave Dad at the moment, but there was nothing to stop her planning for when he was coping better.

She'd have to give her notice at the shop, but she'd always hated the job. "Andaman Dreams" on Upper Street in Islington, owned by Letitia Pennington, who described herself as an artist and sculptress, sold bijou gifts and soft furnishings of Eastern provenance at exorbitant prices. Lara knew she had only got the job because of her vaguely Asian looks.

'You'll fit perfectly, darling,' Letitia had exclaimed on first seeing Lara, as if she were a carved box or a wall-hanging. But after a flurry of interest on the back of a couple of articles that Letitia had managed to get into the glossy magazines through her contacts, takings had tailed off and been slim for several months now. Letitia had grown bored of the place and begun to neglect it for a new venture – a gallery selling conceptual art in a converted church in Clerkenwell. No, Letitia would be only too glad to be released from the burden of paying Lara, meagre though her salary was.

The next morning, as Lara got off the bus outside the town hall and walked towards the shop, she sensed that something was not quite right. She realised as she drew closer that the sign that normally hung outside above the door – the golden Buddha's face – was no longer there, and the metal frame rattled in the wind.

The shop was empty and the door locked. She peered through the window and in front of the door was a pile of letters and junk mail, while inside all that remained were empty shelves, and some hooks on the marked walls.

"Andaman Dreams – Closed until further notice" a notice scrawled in Letitia's flowing writing proclaimed.

Lara turned away. 'The rotten cow! She could have let me know,' she muttered, and began to retrace her steps to the bus stop.

CHARLES

Singapore, 1941

From his desk in Army HQ, Charles Simmonds had a perfect view of the acres of lawn in front of the building. He stared out at the team of Indian gardeners who were mowing the grass with two bullocks harnessed to a lawnmower. He'd been watching them on and off all afternoon, and now that the sun was loosening its grip on the day, and the shadows were lengthening, they were almost done. The lawn was perfect. Sweeping strips of dark green alternating with pale. Beyond, purple bougainvillea spilled over the walls of the botanic gardens.

Charles envied the gardeners their simple physical task. So different from his own stultifying duties here in this airless office, pushing papers as chief assistant to the General. He cursed the day he had volunteered to join India III Corps and leave his base in Peshawar to join the forces massing in Singapore to defend the Island from the threat of Japanese invasion. He'd thought he'd be seeing some action. Little had he known he was letting himself in for a desk job.

He felt thwarted. Life was easy, luxurious even, but false, and dare he say it, boring. The days were spent decoding telegrams and processing dispatches for the Regiment at his desk here in HQ, and evenings accompanying Louise to an endless round of bridge parties, dinner parties, swimming parties, interspersed with visits to Raffles Hotel to drink champagne and dance the night away under the chandeliers. Louise never seemed to tire of these superficial pleasures, but to him it was already hollow. He thought about what she would be doing now: soaking in an early evening bath after an afternoon with the other officers' wives at the club. Didn't she ever look further than laughter and malicious gossip? She was the daughter of an army officer herself and had grown up in India. She was used to cantonment life and its petty snobberies. The life of a spoilt memsahib was the only one she had ever known.

He glanced at the clock above the door. His eyes had been drawn to it on and off all day, just as they were every day. It was approaching five thirty. Not that there was much to look forward to, except a sharpener in the mess on the floor below the office, before wandering across the base to the married quarters: to what counted as home.

As he looked at the clock, David Smythe appeared in the doorway. Charles loathed Smythe, with his over-groomed looks and smarmy ways.

'General H needs someone to go into town and collect something from the tailor.'

Charles feigned interest in the document on his desk and then looked up slowly. The man was surely not suggesting that he should run the General's errands for him.

'Why doesn't he use the army tailor?'

'That's beside the point, Simmonds. Ours is not to

wonder why. If you must know, it's something for his wife. A birthday present.'

'Why don't you get one of the bearers to go? That's what they're for. Or his batman?'

'He doesn't trust any of them enough, Simmonds. You should be honoured, old man.'

'Why the devil don't you go, Smythe, if it's such an honour?'

'No can do, old man. I've got a tennis match at six. With General Percival no less. Can't let the old boy down. It'd be more than my career was worth.'

Charles got up from his desk. A trip into town would be a bit of a diversion after all. 'OK, give me the address. I'll go now.'

'The General said you can take the car,' said Smythe, handing him a tailor's receipt. 'The address is on there.'

Charles raised his eyebrows. 'How very generous of him,' he said, pushing past Smythe.

Louise would have to wait. What was it she had planned this evening? God knows. Probably some godawful dinner party where the food was indifferent and the company worse.

The General's black Austin was waiting in front of the steps. The driver already had the engine running. It was gratifying to slide onto the red leather seat and sit back as the car swept through the base and out onto the road to Singapore town. Patches of untamed, verdant jungle gave way to plantations where rubber trees stood in silent lines like a ghostly army. He thought wistfully of the barren beauty of the landscape on the North-West frontier: snow-dusted peaks, mountains of black rock reaching into the clouds, a barren wasteland where only the hardiest creatures could live. He missed it now. The overblown greenery that surrounded him here filled him with torpor.

They passed native villages built of wood and bamboo, and were soon speeding through the outskirts of the town, passing crowded ramshackle neighbourhoods of the Indian and Chinese workers and then on through the European quarter where mock Tudor mansions stood shaded by trees.

The car travelled slowly along Beach Road, past the great white edifice of Raffles and the doric columns of the General Post office and came to a halt. The driver turned round.

'Tailor shop up there,' he pointed towards an alley. Charles looked at the receipt Smythe had given him.

A few steps away from the car and Charles was engulfed in the chaos of the Chinese quarter. Stalls heaving with snakes and eels, others piled high with exotic fruits and vegetables. He was used to the bazaars in India, and breathing in the all-pervading smell of fish-paste mingled with spices excited his imagination. He enjoyed the feeling of being transported by the surroundings, swallowed up by the old town.

He turned the corner and there was the shop. A sign outside announced: "Mr K Hong's Tailor. Fine Ladies' clothes to order".

He stooped through the low entrance. It was gloomy inside and Charles had to pause to let his eyes adjust. By the light of oil lamps, two boys sat cross-legged on the floor sewing and a young woman was turning the handle of a machine in the corner. Mr Hong stepped forward, bowing. He was short, but almost as broad as he was tall.

'Good evening to you, sir,' he said with an ingratiating smile.

'General Heath sent me.' Charles gave the receipt to the Chinese man.

Mr Hong read it and consternation spread over his face.

'I'm sorry, sir. Not quite ready, sir.'

'The General is expecting it straight away. I understand it is a present for his wife. He needs it this evening.'

'It not ready until tomorrow. I'm sorry, sir. You have to wait.'

'Look man. This isn't good enough. The General is an important customer you know. He's not going to be happy about being kept waiting.'

The man turned to the woman at the sewing machine and started to yell at her in Chinese. He leaned towards her, gabbling in her face, wagging an angry finger at her. Charles saw her flinch.

'Wait a minute,' he said, stepping forward. 'There's no need for that.'

'She very lazy. It all her fault. She not work fast.' His eyes were narrowed in anger, flecks of spit flew from his mouth. He turned back towards the girl and slammed his fists on the sewing machine table.

'Look,' said Charles, raising his voice. 'It doesn't matter. I'm sure the General will understand.'

But the man was settling into his tirade now and did not hear Charles' protests. Charles stepped forward and put a hand on the man's shoulder. The man turned back to him.

'I sorry, sir. I tell her to go. She no good. She not work hard. I will finish Lady Heath gown myself. You come back in two hours OK?'

'Look there's really no need to ask her to go.'

'That my business, sir. With respect. She no good anyway. Many problem.'

Charles felt helpless. The girl had risen from her seat

behind the machine and was silently folding the piece she'd been working on, gathering her belongings. Her head was bowed and he couldn't see her face.

'You come back in two hour, sir. All will be ready.'

Charles shrugged and turned away, ducking back out of the shop and into the darkening alley. A rickshaw belting past almost knocked him over. He walked slowly away from the shop, unsettled by what he'd witnessed. It would have happened anyway, wouldn't it? It wasn't just because of him. He wandered back in the direction of the car oblivious to the cacophony around him. He'd have to tell the driver to park up somewhere until the dress was ready. But then something made him stop. He couldn't leave that poor girl like that. She'd probably be destitute. He knew how workers lived from hand to mouth in Singapore so they could send money back to their villages. Something about the accepting way she'd got up from her work and packed up her things had affected him. He didn't have a clear picture of what he should do, but he knew he must do something. He turned round to retrace his steps to the shop but before he had gone more than a few paces, he caught sight of her walking down the alley towards him.

She was petite and moved gracefully, even in the simple black cotton tunic that all sweat shop workers wore. As she got closer, he got a good look at her face. To his surprise she wasn't Chinese. From the colour of her skin and shape of her face he saw that she was a native Malay. Her jaw was set in defiance and her head held high. She caught sight of him and made to move to the other side of the alley to pass him, but he moved in front of her. She tried to sidestep to move past him, but bumped into him and had to stop.

'Look. I'm dreadfully sorry about what happened there,' he said. 'Do you speak English?'

She nodded, but wouldn't meet his eye.

'Could you let me pass please,' was all she said, her eyes on the ground.

'Could I help you? Would you let me give you some money? I wouldn't like to think you lost your job because of what I said.'

She lifted her eyes to his and there was an unmistakable look of disdain in them. Charles was taken aback. He wasn't used to seeing this in the eyes of the natives.

'I don't want your money,' she said. 'Please let me pass.'

With the customary politeness of the English army officer that he was, he stepped aside and let her walk on down the alley. He stared after her, watching as her slim form blended with the crowd and melted into the darkness.

Fascinated by that glimpse of strength and pride, perhaps unconsciously challenged by the look of disdain, he began to move after her. He had to walk quickly to ensure she didn't disappear. He saw her turn left down a side street. He followed at a safe distance. He didn't want her to know what he was doing. He told himself he wanted to find out where she lived so he could help her, but even then in the back of his mind he knew there was more to it than that.

She moved through the now dark quarter quickly and silently. After ten minutes or so she ran up some steps and disappeared into a building near the docks. Charles waited a few moments and then walked up to the entrance. He stood at the bottom of the steps, contemplating the door, wondering whether to follow her. The door opened and a couple of Chinese dock workers came out, dressed in rough clothes. As they passed, they glanced at him with curiosity. He recognised the building as one of the many such hostels where native workers lodged after sweating long hours unloading boats on Keppel Harbour or working in the go-downs shifting produce. He hoped the girl had someone to look after her. She must be living on the breadline already if this was her home.

He turned back and retraced his steps, eventually emerging in the wider streets where the lights were bright amid the comfort of the shops and stalls and bustle of the Singapore evening.

4

CHARLES

Singapore, 1941

Charles hardly noticed the journey back to the base. He sat back as the car travelled down Beach Road and past the towering Cathay building, now floodlit for the evening. Beside him on the seat was Lady Heath's royal blue ball gown wrapped in tissue paper. His exchange with Mr Hong had been brief when he'd returned to the shop. The old man was obsequious again, overly courteous with much smiling and bowing. Charles tried bringing up the subject of the girl, but Mr Hong simply closed his eyes, bowed very slowly and refused to answer. In the end Charles just took the gown and left.

Now he couldn't stop thinking about the look on the girl's face when they met in the alley. She was not particularly beautiful – no more so than thousands of other women in this city – but there was something about the lift of her chin, the spirit behind her gaze that he could not let go.

After leaving the gown with General Heath's batman at HQ, he asked the driver to drop him back at the married quarters. The bungalow was quiet as he let himself in, and stifling hot. Annoyed, he flicked the switch to start the fans. It was past eight o'clock and Louise had gone out. She'd probably turned them off to punish him for being late. The voices of the Chinese cook and amah came from the kitchen at the back of the house. He took off his jacket, undid his top buttons and went through to the poky dining room. A supper of pink ham and congealed coleslaw had been laid out on the table. A squat bluebottle sat on the side of the plate waving its front legs. He glanced with disgust at the sweating meat and poured himself a whisky from the decanter on the sideboard.

He wandered through to the bedroom, taking a gulp of the drink. It coursed through his veins, enveloping him in a welcome fuzzy glow. Louise's clothes were strewn about the room. He pictured her pulling on dress after dress, pouting as she tried different poses in the wardrobe mirror checking which one suited her best, before flinging them aside for the amah to put away. Open jars of cosmetics spilled over on the dressing table, and the room reeked of her heady perfume.

Charles sat down on the bed, his head in his hands. She would already be at the dinner party, relieved probably that he hadn't come along. She'd be chatting away in that attention-seeking manner that made him shrink with shame, lowering her lashes conspiratorially at whoever sat next to her, trivialising every topic of conversation. He had to admit that she was not alone. Most of the wives were the same, their main focus on flirting and gossiping, with a keen eye on their husband's next promotion.

What a fool he'd been. When he'd arrived in Peshawar from Sandhurst three years ago, every young officer on the cantonment had been pursuing Louise, attracted by her bright blue eyes, curvaceous figure and the fact that she was the daughter of the General. He'd been different because he didn't enter the fray, assuming she would never be interested in him. Ironically, his very aloofness had attracted her attention, and very soon she had been actively seeking him out, sniffing out a challenge, determined to conquer his indifference and entice him into her circle of admirers.

And he was taken in just like the rest. He fell for those flashing blue eyes, full red lips, the glimpses of breast swelling under cotton dresses. He'd been flattered that the most sought-after young woman in the camp had singled him out for special attention. The romance had been swift. They spent a couple of months in the dizzy bliss of infatuation; seeing each other every evening and on every one of his days off.

Louise had been born in India and the ex-pat life came naturally to her. She'd not been sent back to boarding school in England like many of her contemporaries but had been taught badly and intermittently by a series of private tutors. Because of this there were huge gaps in her knowledge, but her upbringing had given her a feel for the country that was unusual for an Englishwoman. She took him to places that astonished him. Crumbling temples covered in greenery inhabited only by snakes and monkeys; colourful alleyways deep in the Indian quarter where other Europeans were afraid to venture, abandoned palaces on the shores of mountain lakes, their reflections glittering in the mirror-like waters. At those moments he felt true kinship with her; here was an adventurous free-spirited girl who turned to him with shining eyes to share the beauty.

Back at the cantonment she was different, but in the fog of infatuation, he hardly noticed her high-handed manner with the servants, her taste for gossip and trivia and her dedication to the tedious social circuit. He asked her to marry him as they returned from a blissful day riding in the Kush, and she accepted straight away. The wedding was lavish, befitting the daughter of a general, and accompanied by full military honours. After a week's honeymoon on a houseboat in Kashmir they returned to a small bungalow in the next block to her parents, and Charles had resumed his duties with the Regiment. This meant long weeks away from her. Going to the North West frontier meant leaving family behind, but his leave every few weeks had been like taking up where they left off: afternoons making love under the mosquito net, evenings riding out into the sunset.

When the chance of a move to Singapore came up, Louise encouraged Charles to take up the offer, keen to escape from the radar of her overbearing mother and the confinement of the place where she had spent her life.

'We'll be able to be together more,' she'd said, stroking his chest as they laid in bed. 'You won't be off on that hateful frontier anymore. You'll be all mine.'

On the liner from Bombay, Charles had begun to see a different side to her. It had started out like a second honeymoon, starlit strolls on the deck after dinner, dancing to the ship's band in the ballroom, sunbathing in deck chairs during the afternoons while uniformed flunkeys brought them cocktails. But Louise's ceaseless chatter and gossip about the other passengers had begun to wear thin after a couple of days, and when she latched onto another two couples, and insisted on sitting with them at dinner and flirting with the men, Charles had started to seriously doubt his choice. In Singapore, away from her childhood home, she embraced the life of the base completely. Charles found himself spending more and more time in the mess after work, to avoid the crushing socialising that she thrived upon.

Sighing, he ran a bath in the tiny bathroom, and slid in gratefully, his drink balanced on the shelf beside him. The Malay seamstress kept returning to his thoughts. He wondered where she was now. Eating plain rice on a bunk in the go-down probably, wondering where her next cent was coming from. Did she have a husband to keep her, or children perhaps who might go hungry? He resolved to go back the next evening and wait outside the go-down with some money. He could slip it into her hand, even if she refused to speak to him. She would surely not be too proud to take it, and it might somehow make up for the fact that he was unwittingly instrumental in her losing her job.

He wondered how to spend the rest of the evening and toyed with the idea of going over to the mess bar. But it would just be the same old faces and conversations that had been recycled dozens of times. Would the Japs invade? And if they did, where and how? There were always the doubters who scoffed at those who thought an invasion a possibility. 'Look at the squinty little yellow bastards. They've not got the balls to fight us,' and then the opposing camp, including Charles himself, who were less sure, but whose warnings were shouted down. No, he couldn't face an evening of that again. And that oaf Smythe would probably be there, bragging about his tennis match and his sexual conquests. It might have been Charles' imagination, but he thought that Smythe had been making vile insinuations about Louise the other evening. There'd been the glint of a knowing look when her name came up. No, he just couldn't face any unpleasantness this evening. He dried himself and pulled on his dressing gown. Pouring another whisky, he took down a book of short stories from the shelf and settled himself in the chair in the bedroom to read.

He'd been in bed for an hour or so when he heard the

taxi draw up outside. It must have been after one o' clock. He could tell by the way Louise slammed the door and crashed into the hat stand when she kicked her high heels off in the hall that she was drunk. When she came through to the bedroom, she almost toppled over as she unzipped her sequinned dress, swearing under her breath. He heard her take the pins out of her hair and pull on her nightdress. The bed dipped and creaked as she slipped under the sheet beside him. Her breathing was close and he could smell the alcohol. Only a few months ago, the presence of her warm skin a few inches from his would have been irresistible, but now he remained rigidly still, hoping she wouldn't realise he was awake.

But as she turned over to face him she said under her breath, 'Charles, are you awake?'

He hesitated. Did he really want to talk to her? She put her hand on his shoulder and gave him a gentle shake. He pretended to yawn and stretch.

'Hello, Louise. I didn't realise you were back. How was your evening?'

'Oh, really jolly. Why didn't you come along? I waited for you until half past seven, but it would have been rude to be late.'

'I had to go on an errand into town for General Heath. I'm sorry. I thought I'd be back in time but I had to wait.'

'It was really embarrassing that you weren't there. I don't know what people must think. Betty Alford gave me a hell of a look when I turned up on my own. I could see all the wives whispering about me.'

'I'm sure you managed. You have half the men on the base eating out of your hand. In fact, you probably had a much better time without me.'

'Don't talk like that.'

'Well it's true, darling. I loathe those bloody dinner parties anyway. You know that.'

There was a silence. He thought she had dropped off to sleep and was just preparing to turn over and go to sleep himself, when she said, 'I had a letter from Mummy today. She asked if we were going back to Peshawar for a visit.'

'I can't, Louise. I'd never get leave. Things are hotting up with the Japs. We've got another two regiments arriving from India in December.'

'That's rotten. Especially when everyone knows the Japs are never going to invade.'

'Does everyone know that though?'

'Captain Jamieson was adamant this evening. They're just a bunch of incompetent Asians, who all need thick glasses, and can't organise themselves to fight.'

'That's the accepted view, yes... but I'm not so sure.'

'Oh don't be an old doom and gloom merchant, Charles. Everyone knows Singapore is impregnable.'

'That's what they say...'

There was a pause, and her breathing became even for a while.

'You don't mind if I go home by myself, do you?' she said suddenly. 'Josephine Firgrove is going and she said she and I could share a cabin.'

'So it's all fixed then? You didn't need to ask if I could go at all, did you?' But even as he said this, he knew he wasn't voicing his true feelings. He was already experiencing a sense of relief that he could spend some time alone without being dragged to charity events and bridge parties by the dozen.

5

LARA

Kuala Lumpur, 2000

Lara blinked awake and stared up at the ceiling where a fan whizzed round, wobbling dangerously on its moorings. It took her a few seconds to remember. She groped for her watch. It was six in the evening, and through the slats of the shutters the sky was growing dark. She must have been asleep since she'd flopped down on the bed when she'd arrived just after dawn.

The Number 1 Cathay Hotel had seen better days. Its once grand frontage veranda and portico were scabbed and crumbling. Like the other former shophouses on the street, it was decaying gently, forsaken by most tourists for the modern hotels in skyscrapers in the commercial district.

Lara had stared around her, enchanted, as she stepped inside the hotel that morning. She'd never been anywhere like it before. The airy lobby with its scuffed marble floor, whirring ceiling fans and wide, sweeping staircase, gave it a wonderful olde-worlde atmosphere. She'd stared at the old man on reception when he told her the price of a room. Less than five pounds for a room with a spacious en-suite bathroom!

A porter took her rucksack to her room. She followed up the winding stairs to the first floor. The room he showed her was spacious with a high ceiling and gloomy, antique furniture. There were shutters at the window, and when Lara opened them she saw that the room overlooked a pedestrianised street lined with bars and restaurants. People sat outside eating and drinking, crowds of tourists and locals wandered along the road. It looked relaxed and inviting, and she wanted to go straight out and explore, but exhaustion threatened to overwhelm her. As soon as the porter had left, she laid down gratefully and closed her eyes. The narrow bed seemed to rock and sway beneath her, her mind and body still responding to the motion of the twelve-hour flight.

Now that all the tension and excitement of the journey was over and she was finally here, she felt strangely deflated. All those preparations just for this: a shabby room in a run-down hotel, surrounded by a teeming city going about its business. She thought; no one closer than 10,000 miles cares a damn about me or even knows of my existence. It was a strange feeling, this anonymity, and the knowledge that she was completely alone. A feeling of panic overtook her. Had she been mad to do this? Until now, the furthest she had been was the Greek islands for a holiday with some girl-friends the summer before she met Joe. Had it been an idiotic move to withdraw a substantial portion of her savings and jet halfway across the world on a tenuous mission to get closer to her mother's past? Listening to the honk of the horns and the cries of street hawkers, these thoughts slid over and over each other in her mind until she drifted off to sleep.

Awakening now in the early evening, she felt even more alone. Her stomach was grumbling and she knew she must venture out into the sweltering heat and find something to eat. All she had to sustain her was a packet of airline biscuits and a dubious looking bottle of mineral water that stood on the marble table in the bathroom. The thought of eating alone in a foreign city provoked a shiver of apprehension, but determined not to be defeated before she'd begun, she tucked a few ringgits into her money belt, and a map of the city in her pocket and left the room.

The porter beamed at her, revealing a row of blackened teeth as she descended into the lobby. He took her arm and propelled her towards the front door. As if reading her mind, he said, 'Many, Many restaurants along this very road. Very safe. You not worry. You eat nasi lemak. Nasi lemak very good.'

She left the sanctuary of the hotel porch, stepped into the crowd and, shouldering her way through the throngs of people, she made her way along the street bathed in light from the shops and restaurants. The old man was right. Almost every building was a restaurant, with tables set out on the wide pavement under trees, and boards on the pavement that announced the speciality of each one. She sat down at one towards the end of the road, where the waitress was particularly welcoming and spoke good English.

Lara ordered nasi lemak, discovering from the menu that it was rice cooked in coconut milk and pandan leaf, and gratefully accepted the chilled beer that was quickly brought out. The street was buzzing with movement and sound, groups of people, both locals and westerners wandering along, assessing the restaurants while waiters rushed out and tried to tempt them in, gabbling the praises of the establishment, thrusting menus before their eyes. There were buskers, setting up pitch in front of diners and playing a jarring mixture of Malay folk music and Western rock. Disabled beggars too, holding placards on their laps with details of their plight chalked in huge letters, pushed along by dedicated relatives, the loud music blasting from a box on their wheelchair mingling discordantly with the music of the buskers.

Lara sipped the local beer appreciatively while waiting for her food. Her body was sheened in perspiration. She glanced around at the nearby tables. At the next one was a large Malay family, all chatting at once, tucking into communal dishes. On the next table sat a western couple. The girl was enviably skinny with brown legs, and long blonde hair. The man was tanned too with brown eyes, and fair hair. Lara watched them with envy. They both looked cool despite the intense heat. They were engrossed in one another's company, at times clasping hands together on the table, at others leaning back and laughing at a shared joke, barely aware of their surroundings. Their eyes shone with happiness. With a stab of jealousy, Lara guessed they were on honeymoon.

Her thoughts turned to Joe, and how they'd been just the same when they first met. When they'd gone out to restaurants so caught up with one another, they had barely tasted the food or noticed the surroundings. Going out to eat had just been an interlude in their long dreamy sessions of lovemaking, like coming up for air. But now he would be sitting across the table from someone else, staring into her eyes, making promises about the future, about his love and commitment. Jealousy and loss overwhelmed her and she realised she must look like a woman scorned.

'Madam, here's your food. You OK?' the waitress was asking, placing a plate on the table, a look of concern in her eyes.

Later, as Lara returned along the dark corridor of the hotel to her room, she noticed the same young couple walking a few paces ahead. They were laughing, and the man put his arm round the girl's waist and pulled her close. They kissed briefly before disappearing into the room next to Lara's and closing the door. Lara's sense of isolation almost overwhelmed her again. She went inside and sat on the saggy bed. Her whole body ached for Joe's touch. She felt an almost palpable desire to be taken into his arms once again.

The next morning she forced herself up and out of the hotel and having taken a taxi to KL Sentral station to book a sleeper train the next day to Singapore, she wandered across a main road and found herself engulfed in a maze of narrow streets. They were filled with stalls selling goods of every possible description, from every type of fresh food imaginable, piles of exotic fruit and vegetables, tanks of fish, clothes, toys, birdcages, plumbing parts. Stacks of produce were piled high, overhanging the alleys, shutting out the light from the sun. There was an overpowering stench of drains mingled with the smell of rotting fruit and gutted fish. She held her breath until she emerged onto a wider street, covered at roof level with blue glass. This street was lined with stalls aimed at tourists, selling fake designer clothes, shoes and gifts.

Behind the stalls were shops and cafes. She lingered in front of one, looking to see if it was a good place to stop for a drink, when she noticed with surprise the blonde girl from the hotel paying the waiter and getting up from the table. As she turned towards the door, Lara could see that she was frowning. She looked quite plain in the light of day.

Before Lara could move away, the girl spotted her. She was coming towards her. Lara swallowed. Did it look as though she'd been following her? She felt a moment of panic, but before she could turn and walk away, the girl was next to her and grabbing her arm.

'You're from the hotel, aren't you?' Lara recognised an Australian accent. 'I saw you at breakfast.'

Lara nodded. She hoped she hadn't been staring at them.

'Do you think you could help me? My bag got nicked. I need to get back to the hotel.'

'Of course,' Lara recovered her composure. 'How awful! Have you reported it?'

'Yeah. There's a tourist police office at the metro station. They took the details and gave me a ticket for the insurance and embassy. They weren't very interested. It happens all the time apparently. I'm so annoyed with myself! I was so busy looking at those bikinis over there, I forgot to hold on tight to my bag.'

Lara instinctively checked her own small backpack.

'Shall we get a taxi back? I've got enough money,' she said.

'If that's OK with you? I can wait if you need to do anything,' they began walking. 'I would have got a taxi back myself, but I'm not sure if Alex will be there to pay for it. I can't raise him on his mobile. He's probably gone to some museum...' she trailed off. They were at the end of the covered street now and Lara spotted a taxi in the traffic crawling along the main road. She hailed it and they slid in.

'I'm Chloe by the way.'

'I'm Lara.'

'I'm from Sydney. You sound like a pom.'

Lara laughed. 'I guess I am.'

'You're brave. Here all by yourself.'

'Mad, you might say.'

As the taxi inched forward along Petalang Street, and on through Little India, Chloe told Lara that she and Alex had been travelling in Asia for six months. They'd seen India, Nepal, Thailand, Vietnam, Cambodia. Now they were having a few days' rest in KL before heading off to Indonesia.

'How fantastic,' said Lara wistfully.

'It's been great. We've had our moments of course, but mostly we've got along pretty well.'

Lara remembered the way they'd looked at each other at the cafe the evening before. Pretty well sounded like an understatement.

'I guess we'll have to stay here for a bit now to sort out a new passport. That's not going to go down well with Alex. He's desperate to get down to Singapore... and I need to get back to Oz.'

'Really? You're going back on your own?'

'Oh, I'm only going for a few days. There's something I have to do...' she trailed off and turned to look out the window. For the rest of the journey she was silent.

Back at the hotel, the tanned young man approached them as they came into the lobby.

'Where have you been, Chlo? I've been worried about you.' He caught Chloe in his arms and held her close, burying his face in her neck. Lara stood by awkwardly, wondering if she should just go upstairs quietly. Chloe extracted herself and turned to her.

'This is Lara, Alex. She's been great. She got me home.

I'd still be out there wandering about in the market if she hadn't been there.'

Alex turned his brown eyes to look at her. He held out a hand. 'Good to meet you, Lara. Thank you so much for getting her home. Can we treat you to supper later?'

Lara hesitated. Surely they didn't want her tagging along, spoiling their intimacy?

'Come on,' urged Chloe. 'It's good to have someone else to talk to.'

So Lara agreed, feeling at least that she wasn't quite alone any longer.

They met up in the lobby at the agreed time and headed out.

'We've been here for three days and we've tried a different restaurant on this street each time. They're all fantastic,' said Alex.

They chose one which specialised in seafood. Once they'd ordered, and each had a bottle of beer, Chloe said, 'So what brings you here all on your own?'

Lara wasn't sure she wanted to go into any detail and tell them all about Nell and the orphanage and the certificate. Not yet, anyway.

'I'm researching some family history. My mother was born in Singapore during the war. She died a few months ago.'

There was an awkward silence. Then Alex said, 'I'm so sorry. That must be tough.'

'Yeah. A bit. The worst part is we hadn't spoken in over two years.'

'You're joking!' Chloe looked shocked.

'It's a long story.'

'We've got time,' said Alex. They were both watching her, waiting.

'No... no really,' she said, flustered.

She saw them exchange glances and then Chloe said, 'But how come you're in Malaysia? I mean, if your mum was from Singapore?'

'Oh, that's simple. I got the cheapest flight to South East Asia, which happened to be here. I'm taking the train to Singapore tomorrow. Mum was brought up there in an orphanage and trained as a nurse there, before coming to England. I thought I'd see if I could find her hospital.'

'Alex is into family history too, Aren't you A?'

'Yeah. My great aunt was in Singapore during the war. She was a nurse too. She was killed in 1942 during the Japanese invasion. We'll be going there in a few days too. I've been to various museums here to see if I can find anything out about the war. But there isn't much here in KL. I suppose they're not keen on remembering. The Malays had a hard time of it.'

He stopped as he noticed Chloe was lighting a cigarette, concentrating hard as she held the flickering lighter to it. Alex glanced at her. 'You said you were giving up.'

She shrugged. 'What the hell. I'm an addict,' and blew smoke in his face, smiling.

After the meal they wandered back to the hotel and said their goodnights in the lobby.

Lara went back to her room and called her father. Telling Chloe and Alex about Nell had made her feel down, and she wanted to check that her father was coping alright. He hadn't been overjoyed at the prospect of her going to South East Asia to look into Nell's past, but he hadn't tried to stop her. She'd sensed that he had a grudging admiration for her courage, setting off alone to go halfway across the world. It was something he'd never have done himself, even in his youth.

He sounded surprised to hear from her.

'Lara! Where are you?'

'Kuala Lumpur, Dad, I arrived yesterday.'

He asked her about the journey and about her accommodation. She minimised the shabbiness of the Cathay Number One Hotel and talked up its olde world charm.

She told him about meeting Alex and Chloe and he sounded relieved that she wasn't completely alone.

The line was bad and they couldn't speak for long. His voice sounded a little tremulous and downbeat, and a very long way away. The conversation made Lara even more determined to try to make sure her journey was worthwhile, that she would do everything she could to find out about Nell's childhood.

Lara was tired and got into bed straight away. But sleep would not come immediately and she lay awake, listening to the drone of traffic behind the hotel. There was another sound though, raised voices through the wall. She sat up, straining to hear. At one point she thought she could hear sobbing. She sat still, listening, wondering what to do. But then she hardly knew them. It was none of her business. She lay down again and put her head under the pillow. How strange, after all that affection she had witnessed, that there should be tension between them. She would probably never see them again, though. Tomorrow afternoon she would be boarding the train to Singapore. How odd, to become close to people in an evening and then move on. Perhaps that's the way it would be? Perhaps that was what travelling was all about.

6

SURIA

Singapore, 1941

Suria yawned as she rolled up her sleeping mat and stacked it against the wall beside her neat pile of clothes. It was six o'clock in the morning and the fierce Singapore sun was already slanting through the open spaces high up in the wall that served as windows. The building was a former warehouse, or go-down, and didn't contain many creature comforts. All around her the floor was coming alive. Women were chatting and laughing as they put away their bedding and struggled into their clothes, rubbing their bleary eyes, some returning from their ablutions in the communal washroom at the end of the corridor. Some wound saris round their bodies, others dressed in simple work tunics as she did, yet others pulled on the uniforms of kitchens, restaurants or hotels.

She turned to her friend, Amina, who was brushing her hair in a small mirror that rested on a brick jutting from the wall above where they slept.

'I'll fetch the breakfast,' she said in Malay.

Amina quickly dipped in her pocket and slipped a dollar note into Suria's hand.

'I'll pay this morning. You can owe me,' she said.

Suria flashed a smile of thanks and picked her way through the lines of sleeping spaces to the door at the far end. Next to the washroom, which overflowed into the passage with filthy water, was a concrete kitchen, where two Chinese cooks sweated over open gas rings, frying rice and noodles in flaming woks. They doled out portions of this basic but nourishing fare twice a day for a few cents a dish. Suria held out the two cracked china bowls and received the food. I must make this last, she thought. I can't keep letting Amina pay.

She carried the bowls carefully back to their sleeping place. The two of them sat cross-legged on their rolled-up bedding to eat. Amina did this swiftly and deftly, concentrating so hard on the food that she did not speak until she had finished.

'Not hungry?' she asked Suria. 'You're eating slowly.'

'I might save some for later.'

'I don't mind buying food until you've found another job, if that's what's worrying you,' said Amina. 'You'd do the same for me, wouldn't you?'

'Of course,' whispered Suria. 'But I feel so bad. You need to send the money home.'

'It won't make much difference. It's only a few cents...'

'But it's the second time it's happened. And we've been in Singapore for less than a year.'

'It was hardly your fault that you got caught up in the strike. If I hadn't been ill that day the same thing would have happened to me.'

Suria shivered, as the discomfort and hunger of the two-day sit-in in the sweltering factory returned vividly to her.

She was gripped once again by the sheer terror she'd felt when the police had stormed the building, beating down the leaders of the strike with batons. The shouts and screams, the bloodied faces. Then the long hours in the dark police cell without food or water, until she was finally released. When she'd returned to the factory she'd been told she was dismissed from her job.

'I must be going now,' said Amina, with a note of apology, getting to her feet. 'I don't want to miss the bus.'

Suria smiled weakly. 'There's no need to worry about me. I'll get another job soon.'

Amina turned and looked at her, concern in her gentle brown eyes. 'Tak apalah,' she said holding her hands together in a gesture of farewell. Tears instantly sprang to Suria's eyes. It was what they had always said to each other as children back in the village, when things got tough. It meant "never mind". She hid her tears from her friend though, and forced a laugh instead. 'See you tonight.'

Suddenly, watching Amina's neat frame striding purposefully across the floor towards the stairs, Suria was transported back ten years, to the school yard, sitting in the shade of the frangipani trees to read and watching out of the corner of her eye as the others played hopscotch or tag on the patch of bare earth playground. Amina had always been in the thick of whatever game had been popular, organising the others, making up the rules.

Suria could not remember a day when they hadn't been together. Their families' stilted wooden houses were next door to each other in the little fishing village of Kuala Lapah. Their fathers were friends, and worked the same boat, setting off each evening to trawl for prawns and lobster and returning as the dawn broke. The two girls had played together since they were tiny – first with pots and pans on the bare earth under their houses, where the chickens pecked, a few yards from where their mothers prepared food and chatted. When they could walk, they would wander further afield, to run on the smooth white sand of the palm-fringed beach in front of their houses, or play games on the jungle paths that led away from the village. They took care though, not to stray too far into the thick undergrowth, terrified of tigers and snakes. When they were seven they had both started at the little school in the nearby town, walking the two miles to reach it each morning, on the earth track that led through the jungle, barefoot and hand in hand, returning again the same way together every afternoon.

A few months ago, Suria would have been walking to the bus stop on Orchard road with Amina. They had both got jobs in Firestone Rubber factory in Bukit Timah when they first came to Singapore almost a year ago. The work had been tedious, exhausting and poorly paid, but both girls had been prepared to put up with the long hours and relentless work. They needed to send money back to their families in the village. That's why they had come here.

But there was a poisonous atmosphere on the shop floor, and relations between the native and Chinese workers and the European management were strained. Some of the workers were militant, unwilling to put up with the atro-cious pay and dangerous conditions, whispering to the women on the production line, breathing words of discon-tent, garnering support. One morning, Amina had been ill with fever and had stayed behind at the go-down. Suria began work on the production line as usual, but shortly before the lunch break, the leader of the impromptu union, Chow Fat, had got up on one of the tables and with a mega-phone declared a strike. He told everyone that for the rest of the day they were to do no more work. They were to down tools and sit on the floor, just where they were. They would remain there until the managers had agreed to increase their wages.

The sit-in lasted for two days. They sat down cross-legged where they worked and refused to move. Small groups of strikers went out to fetch food for the others, and an excited carnival atmosphere developed in the stifling cavernous building. That night they slept on the floor, using rubber from the production line for comfort. On the second day towards evening, there was a furious beating on the double doors and a crowd of police burst in, armed with batons. Suria struggled to her feet and rushed to the opposite wall, screaming with terror, with the rest of the women, while some of the male strikers tried to fight with the police.

Suria was lucky that the only consequence for her was dismissal; many of the workers, including Chow Fat, were deported from Singapore. But the experience had shaken her and made her fearful of the colonial authorities.

She had paced the streets and alleys of Singapore town for days after that, looking for another job, asking in shops, market stalls, cafes. Eventually the skills she had learned in the tailor's workshop in the little town a few miles from their home village when she'd first left school had come to her aid. She had been able to demonstrate fast and skilful sewing to Mr Hong when she had seen a sign outside his shop seeking a tailor. At first he was hostile towards her because he would have preferred a man for the job, and a Chinese one at that, but he quickly developed a grudging admiration for her work, holding each piece up to the light of the shop window and examining it for flaws, but finding none. The job was better paid than the factory, and the conditions more pleasant.

There was a catch, though. After a few weeks, Mr Hong began to make it plain with his simpering smiles and over-bearing compliments, that he was attracted to Suria, and that as her employer he expected her to comply with his wishes. He began to sidle up to her when she was cutting cloth at the table, or deliberately squeeze past her when she was walking along the narrow passage between the shop and the back kitchen. After a few months of this, he had asked her to work late one day, and when the boys had gone home, he had asked her into the little back kitchen and served green tea in his best china cups. As she sipped it, feeling very uncomfortable, but not knowing how to refuse, he gradually hitched his chair closer to hers, until his thighs, which overflowed the seat of the chair, touched her own and she could smell the garlic from his lunch on his breath. It was then he placed a fat hand on her own thigh and squeezed it hard, at the same time bearing down with his thick lips towards her own. She let out an involuntary shriek and jumped up, upsetting the teacup and the chair. She backed out of the kitchen, stumbled through the dark shop and out onto the street.

The next morning he didn't mention the incident, but scowled at her as she entered the shop. From then on he found constant fault with her work, yelling at her and accusing her of laziness. That was over two months ago, and she had only stayed because she needed the money (although he had docked her pay each week since, saying that she did not work fast enough), and because she knew that he would have told all the tailors in Chinatown that she was a lazy and unreliable worker.

Nothing had happened to change that, and thanks to the arrogant English officer complaining about the blue silk dress not being ready, she had lost her job. She burned with indignation remembering the way he had tried to stop her in the street afterwards. What right had he to speak to her? These Europeans were all the same. They expected people to jump to their orders, but didn't want to bear the guilt of the consequences. She sighed as she tidied her hair in the little mirror. The go-down was almost empty now, but for two Indian sweepers who squatted with brushes and pans, working silently round the sleeping places, sweeping up the food scraps spilled at breakfast.

She would begin with the street in Chinatown furthest from Mr Hong's shop and ask at every shop along the way whether there was any work. If she started now, she might have a job by lunchtime.

As she stepped out of the front door of the go-down into the alley, he was there waiting. She could not help giving a little start as she recognised him, but she recovered her composure in a second, turned her head away from him and began to walk briskly towards Chinatown.

The alley was not busy at this time of the morning. The shops were just opening up – staff pulling up the shutters, setting out their wares on tables in the street. A bare-chested Indian man in a turban swept the kerbside. As Suria walked she was sure she could hear footsteps behind her. Without glancing behind she quickened her pace. Despite the fact she was young and fit, in this heat she was already breathing heavily; her whole body was bathed in sweat.

'Hello!' he was calling to her now. She ignored his voice and walked even faster.

But a few yards on, she was forced to stop. A bullock cart carrying sacks of flour to a baker's shop was blocking the way. Two Indian coolies were unloading giant sacks and stooping with them on their backs into the building. She glanced either side of her in the hope that there might be a side alley to escape into, but there was nothing. Within a few seconds he was beside her.

'Excuse me,' he was saying. 'I just want to have a quick word with you. Could you give me five minutes?'

He was tall and dark and well built. His face was tanned and had an earnestness about it that was unusual in a European man. He was looking at her with genuine concern.

'I'm in a hurry,' she said coldly.

'You know who I am, don't you? It was me who came into the shop the other day...the day that Mr Hong asked you to leave.'

'Yes. I remember. If it wasn't for you, I would still have a job.'

'I know that, and I'm deeply sorry. I've been trying to speak to you for days, but each time I've waited outside your place, I've been unlucky.'

The coolies had finished unloading the bullock cart now, and were whipping the animals forward. Suria pressed herself against the opposite wall to let them pass. The Englishman did the same.

'Would you allow me to buy you a drink?' he was saying, 'A cup of tea perhaps? It will only take a few minutes.'

She looked up at him again, her eyes wide. Was he mad? British Army officers didn't buy native workers tea. It just didn't happen.

'Please. It would be an honour,' he said.

'I have to get on. I need to get to the shops and look for work. Why don't you just leave me alone?'

'But that's what I wanted to speak to you about. I might be able to help you. Look, let's go in here and sit down.'

They were passing a little canteen where Chinese office workers would crowd in to eat noodle soup at lunchtime.

Now it was empty. She allowed him to take her elbow and guide her through the door. She could not believe she was letting this happen, but perhaps it was the dread of the endless trek from shop to shop, from café to café, that drew her in, the knowledge that the day ahead would be another dispiriting round of rejections and failures. They sat down at a simple wooden table. The owner fixed them with a curious stare as he took the order for a pot of tea.

The Englishman appeared nervous now. He leant forward towards her as he spoke.

'Look. It's been playing on my mind, how you lost your job because of me. I've been thinking. I could ask around for you. I could see if there is anything for you at the places I go to. In the meantime, I'd be happy to advance you some money.'

She sipped the green tea.

'I can't accept that,' she said, looking him straight in the eye.

'I understand how you feel,' he said, 'But really, it would be no problem for me. I wouldn't expect it back. It's the least I could do.'

It was tempting. She thought of her mother, sick at home in the wooden house, of all the medicines she needed, and of her brother who couldn't make a proper living as a fisherman, forced to work on a rubber plantation to make ends meet. But this was charity. She couldn't accept that. She remembered her father, the last time she had seen him, leaping on the back of the transport lorry, heading off for the tin mine in the mountains near Kroh, prepared to sacrifice the life he knew and risk his safety in order to earn his family a living.

She must leave before this went any further. She put her cup down and got to her feet.

'It is kind of you, but I can't take it. I need to earn my own money. Thank you for the tea. I must go now. Please do not follow me again.'

As she left the shop, she caught a glimpse of the expression in his eyes. Was it pain she saw there, mixed with panic? She felt his eyes on her back, following her as she turned and walked towards Chinatown.

7

LARA

Malaysia, 2000

Lara gazed through the train window at the ubiquitous coconut palms flashing past in hypnotic rhythm. Occasionally there would be a break in the bright greenery and a village of painted wooden houses with tin roofs would fly by, replaced quickly again by the relentless wall of trees. As she stared out vacantly, her mind wandered back to the encounter with Alex and Chloe. She wondered again about the raised voices in the night and the undercurrents of tension that had been present in a relationship that appeared perfect on the surface.

Meeting them had been unsettling. It had brought back painful memories of Joe, especially their first few months together. She thought back to that first meeting – a chance encounter in a café in Islington, one damp Saturday morning in March. She'd been to the flea market in Camden Passage and bought some coloured china pots. They were hand decorated with pink and blue tulips in brush strokes, and, she thought, must be antique. They were cheap because they were chipped and one had lost a handle. She thought she might brighten up her dingy room in the shared house in Finsbury Park with them. They were on the table in front of her, and she sipped her mug of coffee in the packed steamy cafe and read a book. Every so often her eyes would alight on the pots, and a little thrill would go through her.

She hardly noticed the young man in a dark great-coat brush past, a guitar swinging from a strap round his neck. The guitar swung back as he moved past and with one sweep the entire collection of pots flew off the table and crashed to the floor, smashing into tiny pieces.

'Oh shit, I'm so sorry,' he said, concern in his dark eyes. 'Look, I'll pay. I'll buy you another...whatever it was.'

Lara was aware that everyone in the crowded café had stopped talking and turned to stare. In the silence, a waitress bustled up with a dustpan and brush and knelt down to clear up the scattered china.

'Don't worry about it,' Lara said to the young man. 'Really, it doesn't matter. It wasn't expensive anyway.'

He shrugged, but still lingered by the table. 'Well, I've got to do something... How about I buy you a coffee?'

He was not like any of the boys she had known at school or university, or the young men she'd met at work. They were familiar types, predictable in everything they said and did. There was nothing familiar about this boy with his messy dark hair falling about his face and his shabby clothes. He was indefinably different. Looking at him, Lara realised how mind-numbingly bored she was with her life. With the job that she loathed and had only taken to please her mother, with her ambitious contemporaries who seemed so sure of their direction, even with the predictable socialising – parties, pub crawls, and with the bickering over the contents of the fridge and the domestic chores with her house mates.

She sensed as she looked at him that he didn't inhabit the world she came from, that the path that had led him to this point in his life had been very different from her own. His accent was unmistakably London, with a pleasing rasp, as if he smoked too much. She could tell he was indigenous North London, not like her, an imposter here. She was filled with a desire to know him, to find out all about his world.

'OK,' she said involuntarily. 'That would be nice.'

He brought her the coffee and sat down opposite her. He took out some rolling baccy and rolled a cigarette. He offered to roll her one, and though she only normally smoked at parties, she accepted. He smiled, and in that smile she saw escape and the chance of a new direction.

As they sipped their coffee and smoked, he told her that he was a musician, struggling to make a living. He lived in a bedsit just round the corner and was in a band that played any gigs they could get – in pubs and clubs. He also earned money by busking in tube stations and on street corners. It was hard, but he was determined to make it. 'And what about you?'

'Oh me?' Lara coloured. Her life seemed so dull in comparison. 'I work in the city.'

'At what?'

'Law,' she muttered, looking down at the stained black and yellow Formica. 'I'm training to be a solicitor.'

'Funny. You don't look like a lawyer.'

'What do you mean?'

'You don't look boring enough.'

She laughed. 'Well what do I look like?'

'I dunno. Like something a bit more exotic. Creative. An artist maybe?'

She was silent. How had he guessed that that was what she had always yearned to be as a child, but that it had been suppressed by Nell's vicarious ambitions. Her mother's brittle voice rang in her ears.

'Art? Waste of time. You should do something proper, my girl. Something professional.'

She shrugged. She didn't want to spoil the moment by introducing her mother to the conversation. 'I...I'm not sure why I chose it. I'm not that keen really. In fact, I actually hate it.'

There. She'd said it. The words that she had not admitted even to herself until that moment, she had uttered to a stranger.

'Then why don't you quit?' He leaned back on his chair and blew a smoke ring at the ceiling.

She hesitated. 'It's not that easy...'

'Sounds easier than struggling on with something you hate. That sounds like hell to me. Why would anyone do that?'

'Look. You don't know me,' she said, her voice rising.

'No, no. You're right. It's none of my business. I'll shut up.'

But his words had sown a seed of rebellion in her mind. He made it sound so simple. Why would anyone carry on with something they had no aptitude for and no interest in? He was right. It was madness. As she sat on the top of the Number 19 bus after saying goodbye to him in Upper Street, she felt a new thrill. The encounter had pointed her in a new direction. She felt liberated, full of hope, and actually happy for the first time in months. As well as that, in her pocket her hand closed round the scrap of paper he had scribbled his number on.

'Give me a call. Let's go for a drink sometime,' he'd said as she leapt onto the platform at the back of the bus. And so it had begun. On the Monday after that she'd handed in her notice at work, and by the end of the month she'd moved in with Joe.

She forced her mind back to the present. It was no use dwelling on the past. She could almost hear Nell's voice inside her head. Joe had let her down. She must put him and all those memories behind her.

At Singapore station she took a cab to Chinatown where she had read there were some reasonably priced hostels. As the taxi crawled through the streets, she stared out at the opulence of the city: high-tech skyscrapers, designer shops, bustling crowds of office workers, sleek cars. She had expected some shabby traces of its colonial past, but there appeared to be none. It must have been a very different city that Nell had left in the 1960s. She wondered if Nell would even recognise it now. The taxi entered Chinatown. There was more colour and history here; gaudily painted shop-houses, hawkers' stalls on the pavement. She got out of the taxi at the end of Temple Street and made her way along the pavement with her backpack, between food stalls and low-key restaurants. The street was lined with shophouses and there were several guesthouses amongst them. She alighted next to one halfway down that looked clean and cheap. She went inside and checked in at the front desk. Even though it was a cheap guesthouse, it was still expensive compared to the hotel in Kuala Lumpur.

～

THE ALEXANDRA HOSPITAL was an immaculate white building standing on a hill in a quiet part of town, amongst luxuriant greenery. As Lara walked up the drive the day after arriving in Singapore, an ambulance passed her with flashing lights. At the reception desk a nurse directed her to the records office on the third floor. She took the stairs, and as she walked up the marble staircase, remembered that when she had been researching her trip, she had read that a massacre had taken place here at the beginning of the war, when Japanese soldiers on their advance into the city, had burst through the building and bayoneted people in their beds. A shudder went through her. It was hardly imaginable in this bright, sunny, efficient place. She wondered if Nell had known about it when she'd come here as a young woman to train.

In the records office, she was told that there were no records kept of individual nurses from the 1960s, but that she was welcome to walk round the grounds and see the accommodation block where all the nurses who trained here, including her mother, would have lodged. Feeling disappointed she walked back through the tropical gardens towards a white painted three-storey block with balconies at the front. Here Nell must have lived for three years while she studied for her nursing certificate. Lara stood back and stared at the block and felt disappointment once again. It was just a building. How could she have realistically expected to have discovered anything here? She began to regret coming to Singapore. There could well be nothing in this giant modern metropolis that could tell her anything at all about her mother.

She spent the next two days searching in vain for some connection with old Singapore. Some of the old buildings were still standing, but it seemed as though they had only been allowed to remain as a concession to the city's colonial past. She walked past Raffles Hotel, not daring to go in, intimidated by the sleek limousines lining up at the entrance, the wealthy looking guests and liveried door staff.

The only time she felt some sense of the island's past was down on the quayside, where for a few dollars she took a ride in a small motor launch, which chugged out to the edge of the harbour where giant cargo ships were moored. The boat plied between the ships, dropping off and collecting crew who wanted to go ashore. Crewmen from all over the region scrambled aboard from ships' ladders and squeezed onto the bench beside Lara. As the boat turned round and headed back to the harbour, she tried to picture what the city might have looked like in Nell's day. She half closed her eyes and tried to imagine what it would have been like without the forest of skyscrapers rearing from behind the low shophouses of Clarke Quay, shimmering and flashing in the sunlight.

As she disembarked from the boat, she walked back past the queue of people waiting to get on. Her eyes flicked along the faces. Her heart gave a somersault. There was one she recognised. She stopped.

'Alex!' she said.

'Oh, hi, Lara. How are you?'

'I'd forgotten that you were coming to Singapore,' she said, realising how comforted she was to see a familiar face.

'Oh yes. I've come to see what I can unearth about my great-aunt at the museums.'

'Well, it's nice to see you,' she said, aware that she was blocking the footway. 'I'd better get on.'

'How about a drink at some point?' he asked.

'Alright. Yes. That would be great.'

He fished in his pocket and handed her a card.

'I'm staying at this hotel if you need to get in touch, but why don't we meet in the bar in Raffles at seven tomorrow evening?'

She examined the card as she walked away, raising her eyebrows in surprise to see that Alex was staying at the Novotel in Clarke Quay. She'd thought he and Chloe were on a budget. How odd that he could afford four-star luxury in Singapore, when he'd stayed in the Cathay Hotel in Kuala Lumpur. But her surprise was soon overtaken with wondering what clothes she might have in her rucksack that wouldn't shame her when she walked into the bar in Raffles.

8

SURIA

Singapore, 1941

Suria and Amina were sitting at a table at their favourite open-air canteen on the waterfront, sipping jasmine tea and watching the boats being unloaded on the quayside. It was a hive of activity. Dozens of Chinese workers, barefoot and in conical hats stooping under huge sacks of supplies, heaving them from the bumboats onto the dockside. The smell of drying fish was all pervasive from the lines of catch laid out on matting on the quay. But the girls were used to that. Along with open drains and spices, it was the smell of Chinatown and of old Singapore.

It was Amina's day off from the factory. The two of them had been walking in the Botanical gardens for the afternoon, and now they were watching the sun go down over a drink on the quayside. Between them on the table lay an envelope with Suria's name written on the front in flowing black script.

'Aren't you going to open it?' asked Amina.

Suria picked it up. She'd been surprised when one of the kitchen boys had handed it to her as they'd left the go-down. She could guess who it was from and was reluctant to look inside.

'All right. I suppose I'll have to,' she said at last. She ripped the envelope open and pulled out a single white sheet. Her eyes skated over the contents.

'Well? What does it say?' she could feel Amina's eager eyes on her face as she read. 'Is it from that Englishman?'

'Yes. It's from him. It says he's heard about a job at Raffles Hotel. A hat-check girl. He's told them about me and they say I can go along for an interview.'

Amina clapped her hands together in excitement.

'That's fantastic! Let me look.' She snatched the letter out of Suria's hands.

'You can take it. I'm not going anyway,' said Suria.

Amina's eyes quickly ran over the letter. She looked up and smiled at Suria, her eyes shining with pleasure.

'You'd be mad not to go. From what he's written here the interview looks to be a formality. What's stopping you?'

'I don't want to take something from an arrogant Englishman, for one thing. He's only doing it because he has a guilty conscience.'

'What does it matter? It's a job, isn't it? Think about your mother, lying there sick, back in your house in the village. What would she say if she knew you'd passed up this opportunity?'

'You don't have to remind me, Amina,' answered Suria frostily. 'I think about her all the time.'

'But at the moment, you're not sending any money back home. This would give you the chance to do that, surely?' said Amina, leaning forward, her eyes serious now.

'It would. Of course. But that doesn't mean I should take scraps from the Englishman's table like a beggar, does it?'

'Oh, Suria, you're far too proud! What does it matter how you come by the job? It looks like a great chance. After all, you might well have gone along to Raffles yourself and got it that way.'

'I know! Don't you think I know that? I don't want to be in his debt, that's all.'

'You wouldn't be in his debt. He would be making up for an injury he's done you. So, everything would be even, wouldn't it?'

'There's something about him that makes me uneasy...' said Suria, thinking about Charles' earnest expression, the way his eyes had lingered on her face.

'What's that?'

'I can't explain.'

'So? Are you going to take it then? It would mean you wouldn't have to scrimp and save.'

Suria had been irritated by Amina's comments before but now she felt her anger rising. She clenched her fists to try to control it.

'Do you mean by that comment that I wouldn't have to rely on you?' she said, turning on her friend. 'I thought you didn't mind paying for things for the time being.'

'I don't mind. You know that. And I didn't mean that at all.'

'Well, why don't you stop cross examining me then?' Suria said getting to her feet.

'Where are you going?' asked Amina, alarm in her voice.

'I just want to be alone for a bit. I've had enough of this discussion.'

With that, she snatched the letter back and left the table, pushing her way along the quayside, dodging coolies carrying sacks from poles on their shoulders, some with barrows loaded with goods, others with packages on their heads. She didn't look back as she turned into a side-street and was soon lost in the maze of alleyways already lit up for the evening, lined with stalls selling eels and snakes, live insects and birds, or piled with exotic fruit, others selling spices or rice. The alleyways were filled with the sound of stallholders shouting about their wares, the laughter and chatter of shoppers and the clack-clack of mahjong tiles from inside the shophouses. At that moment, Suria was pleased to be swallowed up in the crowd, to be anonymous.

She felt tears smarting her eyes as she walked. She hated arguing with Amina, whom she loved dearly, but Amina had pressed all her buttons. Why *was* she being so proud about this? Why wouldn't she just accept the offer and take the job? What was it about the Englishman that was stopping her receiving his help with gratitude? As she walked, shouldering her way through shoppers and workers, ducking under produce, tools hanging from awnings, and washing strung across the alleyway from low windows, she realised that there was something about the Englishman that was drawing her to him despite her antipathy. Against her better judgment she found him intriguing, his kindness appealing. Pride and obstinacy were her only defences against those feelings.

Again, she thought of her mother, coughing and wheezing in the sweltering hut, of her brother struggling each day to make ends meet with the meagre catch from his fishing boat, of her father, miles from home, living and working like a slave in the tin mine. Tears of pity pricked her eyes as she thought of them all, striving as they were to survive. What right did she have, in the face of all their struggles, to turn down a perfectly good job to satisfy her own delicate feelings?

She walked for a long time through the noisy alleys of Chinatown, examining her thoughts and her motives, until eventually she found herself back in her own street. By the time she'd entered the go-down building she'd made up her mind what to do.

Upstairs, Amina was already back in their corner, laying out her sleeping mat for the night, tidying away her clothes. She looked up and smiled as Suria approached.

'OK now?' she asked.

Suria went over to her friend, knelt down in front of her and hugged her tight.

'I'm so sorry, Amina. I was being selfish. Of course I'll go for the job. Like you say, I'm being silly not wanting to accept the Englishman's help. I'll go down to Raffles tomorrow morning with the letter and if it's still available, I'll say I can start as soon as they need me.'

One of the women in the row opposite must have heard what she said, because she instantly wheeled around and stared at Suria, frowning. Suria recognised the woman as Choi, someone from their own village. Choi was known to be difficult and she'd often picked arguments with Suria and Amina. She'd come to look for work in Singapore around the same time as them, and like them had got a job at the Ford Factory. She'd not been involved in the protests and had kept her job when so many had been laid off after the strike.

'What's that you said, Suria?' she asked in a loud, aggressive voice. 'You've been offered a job by an Englishman?'

Suria was taken aback by Choi's tone.

'I haven't been offered a job by him,' she answered, trying to keep her voice calm. 'He told me about an opening and has recommended me. That's all. What's it to you anyway?'

'You shouldn't curry favours from the British. Don't you know, they're finished. When the Japanese invade, they're not going to tolerate people who've been too close to the British.'

'I don't know why you think you're any different,' retorted Suria. 'We're all here because of them. They built this town. Even you, with your precious attitude. You might work at the Ford Factory, but who do you think owns it? Tell me that? British and Americans! They pay your wages and they set your hours. They control your life. Don't forget it.'

Choi stared at her, her eyes narrowing.

'Don't you get above yourself, Suria. You've always thought you were better than the rest of us. But don't ever forget where you come from. I'm watching you and will make sure they know about this back in the village.'

'What do you mean?' asked Suria, but Choi had already turned away.

She felt Amina's hand on her arm. 'Don't worry about her. She's only jealous. She'd give her right arm for the chance of a job at Raffles.'

The exchange unsettled Suria, though. Choi's words seemed to confirm her own misgivings, but as she laid down to sleep that night, she tried her best to put it out of her mind.

IN THE MORNING, after Amina had left for the factory, Suria got dressed in her best silk kebaya and headscarf. Then she set off to walk to Raffles Hotel. She realised after she'd been going some time and was sweating under her scarf, that she should have got a rickshaw, but she would have had to borrow the fare from Amina, and her pride had prevented her from doing that.

It took her half an hour or so to walk through the cramped alleys and backstreets of Chinatown to the banks of the Singapore river. It was still early and the place was waking up for the day. Stallholders were setting out their wares, sweepers were sluicing the alleys with buckets of water, and already the sun was high in the sky and burning her skin. At last she emerged onto a wooden footbridge to cross the Singapore River. She stopped for a moment on the bridge to watch the activity on Boat Quay, where dozens of bumboats were moored and were being unloaded by swarms of coolies, just as they had been the previous evening. The frenetic energy of the city was brought home to her watching that scene; Singapore hardly slept.

On the other side of the bridge, she stepped into the British quarter. There couldn't have been a greater contrast. It was calm and peaceful here; the streets were elegantly laid out with immaculate green spaces and imposing white buildings. She realised that she and Amina had never ventured this side of the river before and it felt a little odd to be here. It was almost as if she was trespassing. She walked alongside the great expanse of lawn, the Padang, where groups of English men and women were strolling around in their solar topees, admiring the columns of the great city hall and the delicate spire of St Andrew's cathedral.

Raffles was a grand white building on Beach Road at the far end of the Padang. In front of it was a line of gently swaying coconut palms. When she finally reached the hotel, Suria stood opposite it, besieged by nerves. The letter hadn't said which entrance she should use. She watched nervously as luxury limousines drew up on the front drive, disgorging elegant-looking English women. How could she go in through that entrance? She'd surely be turned away by the liveried doorman whom she could see scraping and bowing to all the guests as they entered.

She walked to the end of the building, crossed the road and made her way along the side street beside the hotel. At last, she came to an entrance marked "Staff Only". Again she stopped, unsure of herself. Did that mean she shouldn't use that one either? There was a boy standing beside the entrance. He couldn't have been more than thirteen or four-teen, but he was dressed in uniform and it appeared to be his job to mind this entrance to the hotel. Suria approached him.

'I have an interview with the housekeeper,' she said. 'Can I come in this way?'

He grinned broadly at her. 'For someone as pretty as you? Of course.' And he drew the door open wide with a bow and a flourish.

'Go to the end of that passage,' he said. 'Housekeeper's office is on the left.'

She did as she was told, walking tentatively along the tiled corridor, taking in the delicious cooking smells, the banging of pots and pans and voices of the chefs from the nearby kitchens. She knocked on the door marked, "Housekeeper".

A severe looking Indian woman opened it. She was wearing a black dress with a starched white collar and apron. Suria explained that she was here for an interview. The woman frowned.

'Who sent you?' she said.

'Major Charles Simmonds,' Suria muttered, casting her eyes downwards, hoping the woman wouldn't read too much into the recommendation.

'Oh! Major Simmonds!' the woman's tone brightened immediately. 'Come inside and take a seat. Yes, Major Simmonds came and asked me if we had any vacancies a few days ago. He is one of our very favourite customers. He and his wife dine here on a regular basis. Mrs Simmonds is such a beautiful lady. So elegant and stylish. She's a real favourite with the staff here.'

Suria couldn't meet the other woman's eyes. She couldn't understand why, but those words cut her to the quick. And the fact that the housekeeper had made so much of it. Was it intended to put her down?

'Now, we're looking for help in a variety of roles,' the woman went on. 'We need someone to work in the cloak-room, but that isn't often busy, so that person would need to be flexible. Prepared to wait at tables, and clean and make up the bedrooms on occasions. Would that sort of work suit you?'

'Oh yes. It sounds perfect,' said Suria, finding her voice at last and meeting the woman's severe gaze.

SURIA STARTED work at the hotel straight after her interview that morning. The housekeeper gave her a uniform just like her own; a black dress with starched white collar and a lacy cap to pin on her hair. She got changed in a stifling locker-room next to the housekeeper's office. Then she was put in charge of the cloakroom for the rest of the day, taking in hats and umbrellas and the occasional jacket, writing out numbered slips for the customers. She stayed until eleven-thirty at night when the last diners had left the restaurant. It was a boring job, but it was undemanding and it gave her a chance to sit unobtrusively in a corner of the main lobby and watch the guests coming and going across the elegant entrance hall. She'd never been in a position to observe the British at such close quarters before and she found it fascinating.

She noticed that when they came to deposit their things in the cloakroom, they rarely looked her in the eye, and were often brusque or even positively rude to her, especially the women. If they were talking to each other, they wouldn't interrupt their conversation to speak to her, instead they would attract her attention with a click of the fingers. After a few encounters like that she realised that this was the way they were used to treating those around them who were here to serve them and cater to their every need.

It made her think of Charles and how unusual he must be to have taken the time to seek her out and to help her get another job. It seemed to go against the grain of how the British behaved here in Singapore. Even though he was the cause of her dismissal from the tailor's shop, most men in his position would have shrugged and walked away from the situation. She realised that it must have taken strength and character to have done what he'd done. She thought about how he'd taken her for a drink and offered his help, how he'd sought her out and gone out of his way to find a position for her. He must be a truly unique individual to have done that, she concluded.

Suria soon got into a regular routine of working in the hotel. She would walk there from Boat Quay each morning and report to the housekeeper at eight o'clock alongside a queue of other staff. The housekeeper would issue her orders for the day. Sometimes Suria's job was to take care of the cloakroom, sometimes she would accompany one of the housemaids on her rounds of the guestrooms, sweeping floors, cleaning bathrooms, making beds, replenishing fruit bowls and toiletries. She was fascinated by the beauty and luxury of the hotel. She'd never been anywhere like it before. The rooms were cavernous and graceful with tall windows hung with patterned curtains and furnished with antiques, the floors and bathrooms were made of marble.

As she made beds, cleaned bathrooms and dusted ornaments, she couldn't help but compare her surroundings with her home in the village, where her mother cooked on a tiny stove on the veranda of their wooden hut, with pigs and chickens rooting around underneath, and where the family slept together in one room. Conditions in the workers' go-down in Singapore where she was lodging were even worse. She and Amina rolled out their mats on the bare wooden floor and slept alongside dozens of other workers each night; it was often difficult to rest because of the noise. They kept their clothes in a cardboard box, and the place was filled with steam and cooking smells during the evenings.

She didn't mind the work or even the stark comparisons with her own situation; the work was more varied and less strenuous than the work at the factory, and there was no Mr Hong to harass her. At the end of the first week she was handed her pay packet which included not only her hourly rate, but tips on top of that. She was able to repay Amina for the weeks she had supported her and even had enough left to last her for the coming week.

At the start of the second week, the housekeeper told her that she was needed in the restaurant for the evening shift.

'Don't worry, the head waiter will tell you what to do,' said the woman, seeing the hesitation in her eyes. 'You're on housekeeping during the day but report to the restaurant at six o'clock.'

'Of course,' said Suria, feeling a little daunted at the prospect.

The day passed slowly. Suria worked with one of the chamber maids, cleaning rooms for most of it.

'They must like you if they're letting you work in the restaurant,' the other girl said with a touch of envy in her tone.

'Oh, I don't know about that. I think they're short-staffed,' Suria replied.

'Not at all. They only ask the best people. You're on show there, you see.'

When six o'clock came she went down to the kitchens and reported to the head waiter, Mr Antonio, a flamboyant Italian man with a twirling moustache.

'All you need to do, this first evening, is to take food to the tables and collect the dirty plates. No need to take orders today,' he said. 'Watch what the others do. It isn't difficult.'

He showed her the counter, known as the "pass" in the kitchen, where the chefs would place the plates of food for waiters to take to the tables, and the hatch where they would return the dirty dishes. From there she could see into the kitchen, the rows of ovens and hobs, and many chefs in tall white hats busily chopping or frying.

'It's Friday evening so we're going to be busy,' Mr Antonio said. 'Just wait quietly in the corner. I will tell you what to do.'

So, she stood and watched, fascinated once again as the guests arrived in twos and threes, some of them in bigger parties. Many had come from the bar and were carrying cocktails or glasses of champagne in one hand and a cigarette in another. The women wore low cocktail dresses, displaying cleavage and bare shoulders and dripped with expensive jewellery. The men were dressed in dinner jackets, their hair gelled back with pomade. The ceiling fans worked overtime, spreading the smell of expensive cologne around the room. Soon, all the tables were full and the noise under the echoing ceiling was deafening.

Suria watched the waiters approach the tables, take orders on their tiny notepads and rush with them to the kitchen. She kept glancing at Mr Antonio, but for the time being there was nothing for her to do. It wasn't long though before one of the tables called for more water. Mr Antonio clicked his fingers and told Suria to take them a jug from the sideboard. The jug was heavy and full to the brim. As she walked across the marble floor towards the table she was terrified of slipping over or spilling some of the water. Her hands were shaking as she placed the jug on the table.

'Pour it out, could you, girl?' came a languid woman's voice. With her eyes cast down, Suria complied, her hands still shaking. There were four glasses to fill and conversation at the table stopped as the occupants watched her move between them. She was terrified of dropping the jug or splashing water on one of the guests, but she completed the task and returned to her corner.

'Well done,' said Mr Antonio under his breath and she smiled, relieved that her first encounter with the guests hadn't ended in mishap.

Soon, plates of food started appearing on the pass and Mr Antonio told her where to take them. Once again she trembled as she placed each plate before the diners, terrified that she might have mistaken who it was intended for. But soon, she fell into the swing of things and stopped feeling quite so nervous.

The fourth table she approached was a table for two in the corner of the room. She lifted her eyes as she neared it; Antonio had told her the steak was for the gentleman and the salmon for the lady. Her heart did a somersault when she saw who it was; it was Charles Simmonds and his wife. She must have missed them coming into the restaurant. She felt her face go hot and flood with colour. Mrs Simmonds was indeed beautiful and elegant, with elaborate blonde curls and lots of lipstick. She was wearing a revealing black dress and a string of pearls. As Suria approached the table she noticed that Mrs Simmonds was not actually speaking to her husband, she was leaning back and holding an animated conversation with a man at the next table. Suria placed the plate of salmon in front of the lady and turned towards Charles. He was looking at her intently, smiling his gentle smile. She dropped her gaze, not being able to meet his, put the plate down quickly, turned and hurried away from the table, her heart hammering against her ribs.

9

CHARLES

Singapore, 1941

As Charles caught sight of Suria making her way towards their table, carrying two plates so carefully, as if they were precious cargo, her face a study of concentration, his heart twisted with an emotion that took him by surprise. She looked so delicate and vulnerable walking cautiously across the slippery marble tiles of the restaurant, as if the slightest thing could blow her off course. Her forehead was puckered in a frown and her eyes looked nervous; all her previous pride and defiance seemed to have deserted her, and he wondered for a second if he'd done the right thing recommending her for the job. Her eyes widened in surprise when she recognised him. She set the plate of salmon in front of Louise, who didn't acknowledge it or even stop talking for a moment to Gerry Hynes, who was seated at the next table. He would have liked to say something reassuring to her but didn't want to attract Louise's attention. He wanted to avoid having to explain to Louise that he knew this young woman or the reasons why.

Instead of speaking to her, he tried to give Suria a reassuring smile, but she appeared flustered, turned without acknowledging him and hurried away from the table. Louise swung back to the table.

'Thank God for that. The food's arrived at last. The service in this place just gets worse and worse,' she said, stubbing out her cigarette and tucking into the fish. 'Honestly, Charles, Gerry Hynes is such a card. I *will* miss the people here. Such a fun crowd.'

She'd been flirting with Gerry Hynes since they'd bumped into him in the Long Bar an hour or so earlier. Gerry was a bachelor in his early thirties who owned a rubber plantation in Kelantan and was down in Singapore on business. Charles had long given up caring about or reacting to Louise's shameless flirting. It was blatant and predictable and Charles' lack of interest acted like a green flag to the men she targeted.

'You don't have to go back to India, you know,' said Charles, probably because it was expected rather than because he meant it. If she'd turned round then and said she'd stay, his spirits would have plummeted.

'Oh, I know I don't, but Daddy was so insistent,' Louise replied. 'And I haven't seen him or Mummy for months. They miss me so much. And besides, it's getting dangerous to stay in Singapore, or so Daddy says, but I can't see that myself. He's such an old worrier.'

'He's got a point,' said Charles. 'After all, that's the reason we're here in the first place. And more troops are arriving all the time, both here in Singapore and on the mainland.'

He took a mouthful of his rare steak. The texture was

perfect; soft and melting, and mixed with the delicate flavour of the bearnaise sauce it tasted exquisite.

'What time does your boat leave tomorrow?' he asked, trying to sound casual. Out of the corner of his eye he caught sight of Suria again, removing plates from the next table. He tried not to stare. She kept her eyes on her task and didn't look at him once.

'I've told you *so* many times, Charles. You don't listen. I have to be there at ten o'clock.'

'Quite early then.'

'Yes, so I'll need to get back at a reasonable time tonight. I've still got a bit of packing to do.'

'I'll come down to the docks with you in the morning if you like.'

'No need. I know how busy you are at Army HQ. Josephine will be with me so I won't be alone.'

'Don't you want me to come and say goodbye?' he asked.

She shrugged. 'It's not as if we'll be apart for long,' she said, but he noticed she kept her eyes on her food as she said this. Neither of them had given voice to the fact that if the Japanese threat got worse, it would be difficult for her to return, and if the Japs actually invaded, it would become virtually impossible.

Charles thought back to discussions at HQ that morning. A telegram had finally come from Whitehall informing them that only 366 aircraft would be sent to help defend Singapore. This fell far short of the 566 requested and the tone of the response had surprised him. It indicated that RAF pilots were far superior to their Japanese counterparts, that Singapore would have the capacity to defend itself for many months, enabling British warships to be sent over to relieve it from a Japanese invasion. The telegram had enraged the Generals and the General Officer in Command.

They'd gone into a meeting for hours to discuss the situation, but had finally accepted Whitehall's offer without much griping.

'They've got no backbone,' Smythe had said to him as he read the telegram that went back to the War Ministry in London. 'They're living in cloud-cuckoo land in Whitehall.'

For once, Charles was inclined to agree with him. The Japanese threat couldn't be dismissed that easily and the island was ill-equipped to withstand a siege. Everyone on the ground was well aware of that especially those working in Army HQ. But it was also well known that the General Officer in Command, Brooke-Popham would always toe the Whitehall line and not seek to make waves with his masters in London who took the view that the war in Europe was priority and the Japanese were a distant threat.

Charles had suggested that he and Louise should dine at Raffles on her last evening. It was her favourite place in the whole of Singapore. She loved to sit in the Long Bar watching the comings and goings of the ex-pat set, catching up on the latest gossip with the women, flirting with any man who happened her way. Later, after the meal, they would go to the ballroom and dance to the resident band, but Charles was dreading that part of the evening. He'd lost count of the number of occasions he'd sat watching her dance with other men, leaning in close to them, lowering her eyes provocatively, while he smoked and drank himself to oblivion. He sighed, looking at her now. Between mouthfuls, she kept leaning round and chatting to Gerry, in complete disregard of Charles' feelings. Not that he cared anymore. He'd learned to shut himself off from it, but he couldn't help thinking that it would be better to be alone than subjected to Louise's behaviour. He was looking forward to the next morning when they would say goodbye.

He was constantly aware of Suria moving about the restaurant in the periphery of his vision. It was all he could do to stop himself from staring at her. What was it about her that drew him to her? He knew it was more than just a natural desire to help someone he'd unwittingly harmed. Occasionally he permitted himself a glance in her direction, but she never looked back, in fact it seemed to him that she was purposely not looking in his direction. But he was pleased to see that as the evening drew on, she was gaining in confidence. She'd stopped creeping about as if she was terrified of putting a foot wrong and was now moving between tables with ease, smiling at guests, looking more relaxed.

When the meal was over and he was preparing to pay the bill, to his surprise, Louise didn't want to go to the ballroom or the bar.

'I've got to get back home, Charles. As I said, I've still got packing to do. Why don't you go to the bar for a nightcap and I'll get a taxi. I wouldn't want to cut your evening short.'

'I'm happy to come back with you. I could help.'

Louise laughed. 'Don't be silly. You don't want to get involved in packing dresses and making sure I've got the right toiletries. That's what the amah is there for. No, you toddle along to the bar for a nightcap and a cigar. Take your time. I really don't mind at all.'

She gave him a peck on the cheek and swept away. People were finishing their meals and leaving their tables now. He followed the crowd along to the bar and ordered himself a brandy and a cigar and found a table in the corner. There was a loud, jocular crowd in that night, laughing and joking about the shortcomings of the Japanese. It made him uncomfortable to hear it, but he didn't want to intervene for fear of unwittingly letting slip something he'd heard at work, so he looked around for someone else to speak to. There was no one he knew, or at least no one he would welcome having a drink with. Even Gerry seemed to have deserted the place.

He downed his brandy quickly and wandered out of the bar, across the lobby and out of the front door. The evening was balmy and the inky sky studded with stars; a slight breeze stirred the coconut palms that stood sentinel along the boundary of the hotel. He even thought he could hear the ripple of the waves from the seafront on the other side of the Padang, but perhaps that was his imagination. Staring up at the starlit sky, he found it hard to imagine that the peace and beauty of this magical island would soon be disrupted by bombs and machinegun fire. But he knew it would happen.

His thoughts wandered to Suria again. She would have finished work by now, surely. He glanced back at the hotel entrance, wondering if she would emerge from there, but he quickly realised there was probably a staff entrance at the back of the building somewhere.

Without really thinking about what he was doing, he wandered around the edge of the building, and down the little street that ran alongside it. Soon he came across a door marked "Staff Only". That was it. She would surely come out of there.

He sat on a wall opposite and smoked his cigar, watching the door. Before long it opened, and a group of women emerged, chatting and giggling. He couldn't see Suria amongst them. Staff continued to leave in dribs and drabs over the next twenty minutes. He was about to give up and look for a taxi when the door opened and Suria emerged alone. She was unmistakeable. The way she walked, so neat and self-contained, that characteristic way she carried her head, her chin slightly lifted.

His heart beating fast, he stubbed out his cigar and approached her.

'Suria,' he said. She stopped and looked at him. For the second time that evening, her eyes registered surprise.

'Major Simmonds! What are you doing here?'

He smiled. It was difficult to answer.

'I was hoping to see you. I just wanted to say... well, to congratulate you on how well you were doing this evening. And to thank you for taking the job.'

'It's for me to thank *you*,' she said. 'But I must go home. I've a long way to walk and it is very late.'

'No need to walk,' he said immediately. 'I'm getting a taxi. I can drop you home.'

He saw her hesitate momentarily, her shoulders stiffen in resistance and he thought she was going to decline the offer, but he could see from her eyes that she was tired and that she was tempted to accept.

'Alright,' she said at last. 'It's very kind of you. If you really don't mind.'

'Of course not,' and they started to walk to the front of the hotel where a line of taxis waited.

'Wait here,' he said instinctively, leaving her on the pavement while he went to the front of the queue. Something told him that she wouldn't want the doorman or other staff to see her getting into a taxi with him. Equally, he himself didn't want any of the guests wandering about in the lobby to see them together and to get curious.

He got into the first taxi and asked the driver to pick up Suria.

'It's very kind of you,' she said again as she got in, rewarding him with a smile.

'It's no problem. Take us to Boat Quay please,' he said to the driver.

'Where is Mrs Simmonds?' asked Suria as the taxi set off along Beach Road, moving briskly alongside the darkened Padang.

'She's gone home to pack. She's off to India tomorrow to see her parents.'

Suria was silent then, looking out at city hall, resplendent in the floodlights.

'How is the job going?' he asked, keen to change the subject.

She turned back towards him then and he could see her smiling in the light from the streetlamps.

'It's really very good. I'm happy there. Thank you again for helping me.'

'It's the least I could do, given the circumstances. I'm so sorry about what happened,' he said.

'Don't apologise. I would have left anyway at some point. I didn't like it at the tailor's shop.'

'Oh really?' Charles asked, his conscience easing for the first time since the day of the incident. 'Why was that?'

'Oh, various things...' she said evasively, then clammed up again, turning her face towards the window.

The taxi sped on, past the tall colonial buildings on the seafront, over the bridge into Chinatown. Then it was forced to slow down, the pavements here were still alive with people shopping at food stalls, coolies carrying goods on poles across their shoulders, rickshaws making their way along the potholed street. There was light here and colour too. Lanterns lit up the entrances to shophouses, people cooked on woks by the light of Tilley lamps, and the smell of garlic and spices filled the taxi.

It wouldn't be long before they reached Boat Quay and

Suria would get out, thank him with a smile and disappear into the shabby building she called home. Charles began to worry that he might never see her again. He realised that he must do something quickly to make sure that didn't happen.

'I was wondering...' he began and she turned and looked at him, her eyes gleaming in the light from the street stalls.

'I was wondering... if you'd like to meet me for tea one afternoon.'

She didn't respond immediately and he began to worry that she hadn't heard him, or that she was offended by his request. Eventually, though, she said,

'I work long hours. I don't have much free time.'

'Well of course, if it's difficult for you...' he began, but she cut in.

'No, I'd like to,' she said softly. 'I am free on Wednesday. That is my day off.'

He couldn't think immediately of anywhere to take her. He couldn't suggest Raffles, or the Tanglin club, as a Malay she wouldn't be admitted. In the end he said,

'Shall I meet you outside your building at five o'clock? We can walk somewhere from there, if that would suit you?'

'Yes. That would be fine,' she replied.

The taxi swung into Boat Quay and pulled up outside Suria's building. Coolies in filthy work clothes were coming and going through the entrance.

The taxi driver came round and opened the door for her. Charles took her hand and looked into her eyes.

'Thank you,' she said, dropping her gaze.

'No need to thank me. I'll see you on Wednesday.'

He watched her walk up the steps to the entrance to the go-down. She walked proudly, with square shoulders and a straight back. She wasn't ashamed of her humble home. Her pride impressed Charles, and as the taxi turned in the cobbled street and headed out of Chinatown, he found himself longing for Wednesday to come around quickly.

Half an hour later, the taxi drew up outside his bungalow on the base. He paid the driver and walked up the front path. It was odd that there were no lights on inside. Perhaps Louise had finished her packing and gone to bed already. He glanced at his watch. It was only eleven thirty.

He opened the front door and the place was indeed in darkness. The servants had already retired to their quarters. He took his shoes off in the hall and tiptoed through to the bedroom. Not switching on the light for fear of disturbing Louise, he undressed in the dark and slid into bed. There was no sound from her side of the bed, so he felt the sheets to check she was there. Her side of the bed was cold and empty.

'Louise?' He switched on the light. She wasn't there.

Suddenly he needed to get out of there. He pulled on his clothes and went out into the front garden. He sat on a bench and lit a cigarette. There was no way he would be able to sleep until she returned. He tried not to speculate as to where she was. The ruse she'd used to get him to stay in the bar hadn't worked. She'd fully expected him to stay there until the small hours, which is what he would have done on a normal night.

It was past one o'clock when he heard the sound of a taxi on the road. It drew up outside the house and he heard Louise paying the driver. As it drew away, she began to walk up the path. It was clear from the way she staggered and turned her ankle in her high heels that she was very drunk.

'Where have you been?' he asked quietly.

She stopped, stock still.

'Charles?'

'Yes, it's me. I came back early. I thought you were coming home to pack. Where were you?'

'Oh... change of plan. I ended up at the club for a couple of drinks.'

'The club? Isn't that where Gerry's staying?'

'Oh, Charles. Stop being jealous. It doesn't become you.' She carried on walking towards the house.

'Do I have a reason to be jealous?' he asked.

She didn't answer. Instead she fumbled with the door handle and staggered into the house. He heard her kick off her shoes and go into the bedroom. The lamp went on, flooding the front garden with pale light. He could see her shadow on the lawn as she undressed, pulling her dress over her head, throwing it aside, taking the pins out of her hair.

He put his head in his hands and sighed. Was it worth a scene? She would be gone tomorrow, and all this hurt and pain would go with her. And was he so different after all? Arranging to meet a young Malay woman for tea whom he was already half in love with?

He got up from the bench, stubbed out his cigarette and went inside the house. Instead of going into the bedroom, he went to the spare room in the back of the house and turned on the fan to cool the room down. Then he lay down on the narrow, single bed, and without taking off his clothes, drifted into a restless sleep.

10

LARA

Singapore, 2000

Lara got down from the air-conditioned bus and the steamy heat of the Singapore morning enveloped her. She drew a deep breath; she was still not used to the climate here. She wondered how the locals managed to look cool and fresh, battling with the stifling atmosphere and the heavy tropical downpours that burst from the sky at regular intervals.

The bus driver had assured her that this was Bukit Timah but looking at the faceless row of shops in front of her, there was nothing to distinguish it from any of the other suburbs the bus had passed through on the way from the city centre. She glanced at the map she'd picked up at the hostel, on which she'd marked the location of Our Lady's Orphanage with a cross. It looked to be about a kilometre's walk through some side-streets from where she stood. She took a swig from her water container and set off.

The walk took her along quiet, modern roads, lined with tropical trees and luxuriant foliage. Newly built houses stood within lush gardens behind high gates and walls. It seemed to be a prosperous suburb, but there was so little of the past about the area that she wondered whether she'd come to the wrong place. After walking for ten minutes or so, she noticed a small wrought iron gate at the end of a road that led into some overgrown public gardens. Tentatively, she pushed the gate open and stepped inside. The gardens were nestled into a rocky bank, which on closer examination she realised was actually a stone wall covered in moss and undergrowth. It looked as though a fairly large building had once stood here. Perhaps these crumbling stones had once been the convent wall? The path ran the length of the wall, but then stopped abruptly. At the end, mounted into the stones, was a metal plaque.

"This is the site of The Convent of Our Lady, on which stood an orphanage as well as a convent. It was established in 1855 and closed in April 1943."

Lara stared at the words. She knew from her research that the convent wasn't open any more, but she hadn't been prepared for the news that it had closed in April 1943. Her mother's certificate stated that Nell had been taken to the orphanage as a baby in December 1942, so she would only have been there for a few months when the place closed down. Where had she gone after that? Perhaps the children had been rehoused in another convent or orphanage somewhere in Singapore, but if that was the case, however would she find out where?

She thought back to the few crumbs of information her mother had let slip during her lifetime.

'Sister Xavier used to take us down to the market to buy ripe mangoes.'

'Sometimes, after mass, they would take us down to the seafront near the Padang to get some fresh air.'

That must have meant that she was definitely brought up by nuns somewhere on Singapore island. Lara wondered how she could find a list of orphanages here. She hadn't brought her laptop to Bukit Timah, but that was the obvious place to start searching.

Disappointed, she took a snapshot of the plaque with her phone and retraced her steps to the bus stop. Her search into her mother's roots seemed to be fraught with difficulties and leading nowhere. It was so frustrating, but she reminded herself that she'd never expected it to be straight-forward. As she waited for the bus back to the city, she thought of Alex and meeting with him that evening. Perhaps he would be able to help her track down her mother's roots? Alex had said that he was into history and would be doing some research into his great-aunt who'd been a nurse in Singapore when the Japanese invaded. Perhaps he knew where public records were kept in the city?

The bus arrived and she glanced at her watch as she took a seat. There was still plenty of time before she'd arranged to meet Alex at Raffles, but she wanted to make sure she looked presentable and that she didn't arrive late and flustered. She'd read so much about the legendary Raffles Hotel, and guessed there would be a dress code there, but a little part of her wanted to look good for another reason. She stared out at the modern cityscape and let her mind wander back to Alex.

Don't even think about it, she told herself, remembering how Alex and Chloe had held hands and looked into each other's eyes when she'd seen them in the restaurant and how he'd buried his face in Chloe's hair when he'd been worried that she was lost. But despite those outward demonstrations of affection, there was something odd about their relationship, Lara was sure of it; why else would they have been arguing into the night, and why else would Chloe have taken herself off to Australia. It was all very mystifying.

The bus rumbled back through the dense traffic and into Chinatown. She got off on New Bridge Road and walked down Temple Street, past the brightly coloured terraced shophouses that lined the road with their louvred shutters, past the traditional restaurants and dim-sum shops on the ground floors.

When she reached her hostel, she went up to her tiny room and lay down on the bed, putting the fan on full blast to recover from the heat of the city.

Later, she showered, washed her hair and rummaged in her backpack for her two items of reasonable clothing: a flowered skirt and linen blouse. She held them up to the light. They were very creased, so she took them down to reception and asked for them to be ironed. She knew it would be expensive but there was no alternative.

She decided to walk to Raffles instead of taking a taxi; she set off with her tourist map through the narrow streets and alleyways of Chinatown, enjoying the early evening bustle of the crowded quarter; the cooking smells, the music blaring from loudspeakers, the brightly coloured street stalls overflowing with all manner of wares: nuts, pulses, spices, fish, exotic fruit, jewellery and flowers. She walked down narrow alleyways that led past Hindu temples, food-halls and cafes where men sat hunched over games of mahjong, until finally she emerged on the banks of the Singapore river. The glass skyscrapers of the commercial district reared up ahead of her, a stark contrast to the old-fashioned, low-rise streets of Chinatown.

As she crossed the river on the bridge, she glanced across at the expanse of empty water, criss-crossed only by tourist boats. She wondered what it would have looked like when her mother was a child. Stopping on the bridge, she narrowed her eyes and imagined a scene thronging with sampans and bumboats being unloaded by teams of Chinese labourers.

It took another fifteen minutes or so to walk to Raffles through the carefully manicured gardens on either side of Connaught Drive. Finally, she was standing in front of the gleaming white hotel, looking up at its imposing gables, feeling a little daunted at stepping through the doors of such a prestigious establishment. But she didn't want to be late, so she ignored the butterflies dancing in her stomach, crossed the road and went in through the front entrance where a liveried doorman greeted her as he opened the door for her to pass through.

She followed signs to the Long Bar and found herself in a crowded room with a tiled floor and dark-beamed ceiling. It was already busy; tables full of people chatting and drinking. The bar itself occupied the length of one wall and was of polished mahogany with fitted shelves and mirrors behind. Barmen rushed to and fro mixing cocktails and serving customers. Feeling a little self-conscious, Lara wandered between the tables, looking for Alex. She couldn't find him at first and began to panic, worried that he wouldn't be there. Then, relief flooded through her as she spotted him sitting at a table by the bar. When he saw her approaching, he got up and waved and as she arrived at the table, he kissed her on both cheeks.

'It's so lovely to see you,' he said, smiling broadly. 'I've already got two Singapore Slings. I guessed that was what you'd want to drink – here of all places.'

'Oh, thank you,' she said, sitting down opposite him. 'How thoughtful. Yes. I would have ordered one of those.'

'It's great to see a familiar face,' he said. 'To tell you the truth, I've been a bit lonely since Chloe went home.'

'Oh, when did she go?'

'She flew out from Kuala Lumpur yesterday and I got the train straight down here.'

She sipped her Singapore Sling, the perfect balance of gin, angostura bitters and fruit juice, and asked him how he was getting on with his research.

'I haven't done much so far. Today I went to the National Museum of Singapore. They have an exhibition there that tells the story of Singapore, from when Sir Stamford Raffles established a trading port here in the early 19th century, right up to the present day.'

'Sounds interesting, but presumably you didn't find anything out about your aunt?'

'No, but I just wanted to get my bearings here, that's all. Tomorrow I'm going to Changi Museum. That's the site of the old army base which became a prison camp during the war. The museum focuses on the fall of Singapore in 1942 and the Japanese occupation.'

'That sounds interesting,' she replied.

'Why don't you come along? If you're interested in the war it's the place to start.'

'Well, if you're sure you don't mind me gate-crashing?'

'Not at all, it would be a pleasure to go together,' and he flashed her another broad smile, displaying his even white teeth. Lara smiled back, resting her eyes on his perfect features. Then berated herself, reminding herself as she had on the bus that morning, that he was with Chloe, and that they were a devoted couple.

'Have you made any progress with your own research?' he asked.

'Not really, no,' she said, and she told him about her

visits to the Alexandra hospital and to the site of the old orphanage.

'I had no idea that it had closed down in 1943. My mother would have been a baby then. I haven't a clue how to find out where she was taken from there, but I'm sure she was brought up by nuns and I don't think she left Singapore, so I'm virtually certain it would have been a Catholic orphanage on Singapore island somewhere.'

Alex rubbed his chin, deep in thought. Eventually he said,

'Why don't you get a list of Catholic orphanages from the internet and get in touch with each one in turn, asking them if the children from Our Lady orphanage were taken there in 1943.'

'I suppose I could try that. I've tried searching for "Our Lady Orphanage" and drawn a blank. There doesn't seem to be much about it online.'

'Do you have access to the internet? I have a laptop if you haven't. I could look for you.'

'That's so kind of you, Alex,' Lara said, looking into his eyes. 'But I have a laptop myself. I'll look when I get back to the hotel.'

He drained his drink and signalled to the waiter for two more Singapore Slings.

'It's very brave of you coming out here on your own,' said Alex. 'I don't think I'd have had the courage to do that.'

'Not really,' Lara replied. 'I don't think any of my friends would have wanted to come on a quest to find out about my mother's past.'

'Do you have a boyfriend?' he asked and she felt colour creeping into her cheeks at the directness of the question.

'I did, but we've recently split up. So, I'm on my own. When Mum died it seemed a good opportunity to come on this trip. I had a bit of money saved up – we were going to buy a flat together – so it didn't take long to arrange.'

'Oh, poor you! A double whammy, breaking up and losing your mother all at once. It must have been really tough.'

He was looking at her with genuine sympathy. She couldn't hold his gaze for fear of bursting into tears, so she focused on the tabletop.

'Why don't you tell me about it?' he asked gently.

When she'd set off from London she'd told herself to move on, that she wasn't going to dwell on what had happened with Joe, but Alex's concern seemed so genuine and sympathetic, and it felt so good sitting there with him, his deep brown eyes focused on her. She realised that it was the first proper conversation she'd had with anyone since she'd left home. So she broke her resolve and told him everything; about how she and Joe had met, how she'd given up her career and started working in a shop, much to her mother's disgust, how she and Joe had moved in together, how they'd grown apart and started arguing, and then the final straw.

'He'd been growing distant for a few months. Then one day, by chance, I went home early. The shop had had to close because there was an electrical fault. When I went in the flat, there he was, in bed with someone else. In my bed!'

She still found herself burning with anger at the humiliating, painful memory.

'I had no idea that he was unfaithful. It was such a shock.'

'How awful for you,' said Alex, his dark eyes full of sympathy.

'So that was the end. I threw him out that evening. He went to live with the girl in some squat somewhere. She was a struggling musician, just like him. I suppose they had a lot in common.'

'So, how long ago was that?' Alex asked.

'A few months ago. Just before my mum died. It's been a bad year,' she said with a rueful look.

'It must have been so difficult,' Alex said and they were both silent for a time. The bar was even more crowded now, filling up with people drinking cocktails before moving on to the restaurant.

'Hey, would you like to go down to Boat Quay and get a meal from one of the restaurants beside the river?' he asked suddenly. 'I've heard it's great down there in the evenings. It's getting too busy here by far.'

'I'd love that,' Lara said. 'If you're quite sure?'

'Of course. I'll just get the bill first.'

He got up from the table and Lara watched him move easily towards the bar. As she turned back, she noticed a man sitting alone a couple of tables away. His eyes were also following Alex, but when he saw that she'd noticed him, he glanced down at some papers on his table. There was something unsettling about it. Should she mention it to Alex? She quickly decided against that. She didn't want to alarm him or do anything to spoil the evening that had got off to such a good start. Besides, it was probably nothing. She could well have imagined it.

They took a taxi down to Boat Quay and wandered along the cobbled street that ran between the converted shophouses on one side and their seating areas beside the river, the tables spilling out onto the quayside. The place was thronging with people. They found a free table at a Chinese restaurant and sat looking out over the water which danced and sparkled with the reflected lights of the city.

The conversation flowed easily during the meal,

although Lara noticed that Alex hardly mentioned Chloe. Was there something wrong between them, she wondered. And why had Chloe gone back to Australia so suddenly? Neither of them had told her, and she knew it was nothing to do with her, but she couldn't help being curious.

It was late by the time they'd finished their meal and were thinking about leaving. Most of the tables were empty by then, stalls were packing up, waiters stacking the chairs and tables away for the night. Lara felt happy and light-headed as they got up to leave. She'd had two or three beers on top of the two Singapore Slings at Raffles. But as Alex moved away from the table, and she followed him, she noticed a man seated alone at a table in the corner of the next restaurant. He was just paying his bill and preparing to leave too. A chill went through her. He looked just like the man in Raffles she'd noticed watching Alex. She stared at him for a couple of seconds, but didn't want to draw attention to herself, so she looked away and followed Alex out of the restaurant. Had it been the same man? She was almost sure that it was. And if it was, was he following them, or had she been mistaken about him watching Alex in the bar?

Alex took her arm as they walked away and she felt a ripple of pleasure at his touch. But it was tinged with concern about the strange man. If it was the same man and he was following them, what on earth did he want?

11

LARA

Singapore, 2000

Lara spent the next morning sitting on her bed in the guesthouse with her laptop, scouring the internet for convents and Catholic orphanages in Singapore. After a couple of hours she'd compiled a list of ten establishments that were still open and that had been functioning since at least 1942. Some of them had contact details, others only listed addresses. It felt awkward to be telephoning complete strangers with her request for information, and she was feeling a little self-conscious as she dialled the first number.

She explained that she was looking into her family history, that her mother had been a baby at Our Lady Convent and Orphanage in Bukit Timah which had closed down in 1943, and that she was trying to find out where her mother had been taken. Some of the people she spoke to were sympathetic and tried to be helpful, but had no knowledge of Our Lady, others were brusque, dismissing her quickly and ringing off. It was on around the seventh call that the woman who answered said,

'Oh, yes. I know that Our Lady Convent was one of the religious places that the Japanese closed down during the occupation.'

Lara paused, startled at this new information.

'The Japanese closed it down? So, do you know what happened to the orphans?'

'Well, many of them were sent to an internment camp on the mainland. Some died. But those that survived were brought back to Singapore in 1945, after the occupation.'

Had this happened to Nell? Would she have remembered anything about it? She would only have been three or four years old at the end of the war, but she might have recalled something, surely?

'So, do you know which orphanage they might have been taken to after the war?' Lara asked, after a pause.

'I'm not sure, but I believe that some of the orphans from Our Lady were taken to the St Theresa's Orphanage in 1945. That's in Katong. Perhaps you could give them a call?'

Lara thanked the woman profusely and checked her list. The St. Theresa Orphanage was one she'd already called but had been given the brush off. The woman who'd answered the phone had said that they didn't answer enquiries from the public and that she had no knowledge of Our Lady orphanage.

Lara contemplated what to do. Checking her watch, she realised that she'd agreed to meet Alex in an hour's time, so there would be no opportunity for further research until later, but checking the map, she saw that the district of Katong was on the eastern side of the city, in the direction of Changi. Perhaps she'd be able to go there on her way back from the museum.

She and Alex had arranged to meet at the MRT station in Chinatown. Lara arrived a little early. Standing outside the entrance, at the top of the escalator, she scanned the crowds for signs of Alex. She'd been too preoccupied with her research during the morning to allow herself to dwell on the previous evening, but now she thought again about how he'd taken her arm as they left the restaurant at Boat Quay and how they'd walked together like that all the way back to her hotel. It had filled her with warmth and pleasure to feel so close to him, but she was wary of reading too much into it. She didn't want to misinterpret the signs and find herself rejected and hurt again. She kept reminding herself about Chloe. On the pavement outside the hotel, Alex had kissed her on the lips as they'd said goodbye. It wasn't a passionate kiss, but she couldn't help thinking that it meant more than just a peck on the cheek.

The entrance to the MRT station was on a street lined with beautifully restored shophouses, covered with a high glass roof spanning the whole street. There were gift shops and restaurants on either side and Lara watched the tourists come and go, enjoying the buzz and atmosphere of the place. Then, through the crowd she saw Alex approaching and her heart did a little twist at the sight of him striding towards her, looking tanned and relaxed in shorts and a white T shirt.

'Hi!' she said as he kissed her on both cheeks. 'I haven't yet had a look at a map, so not quite sure how to get to Changi on the MRT.'

'Oh, it's easy,' Alex said. 'It's the same line all the way through to Changi. The blue one on the map.'

Lara was impressed, thinking how well he knew the city, having only been here a couple of nights.

They went down onto the platform and boarded the

next train. Alex seemed a little preoccupied this morning, certainly not as chatty as he had been the day before.

'Is everything OK with you?' she asked.

'I've had a bit of a shock actually. I called my family in Sydney yesterday when I got back to the hotel. Mum's not too well. She's had a few health problems lately, but she's had some quite severe chest pains recently. She's going to the doctor today to get it checked out.'

'Oh, that's dreadful, Alex,' said Lara, concerned. 'Do you think you should go home and see her?'

He shrugged. 'Maybe. It's not as easy as all that, though. I can't really change my flight without paying a huge penalty. And that's not really within my budget.'

'Oh no, how awful for you!' she said, thinking of how she'd rushed to her own mother's bedside and been there throughout Nell's last days. It had gone some way towards repairing the rift between them before Nell had died. Lara couldn't imagine not having been able to go to her.

Alex fell silent for a while, but Lara could see from his face that he was struggling with his emotions.

'Would you prefer to go back?' she asked after a few minutes. 'We don't have to go to Changi today.'

He shook his head. 'It's good to be distracted. And I've been looking forward to seeing the museum at Changi,' he said.

She told him about the phone calls she'd made that morning, what she'd discovered about the orphans from Our Lady and how many of them ended up at St Theresa's in Katong.

'I was thinking of stopping off there on the way back,' she finished. 'But I'm happy to go on my own if you don't feel like it.'

'No, I'd like to come along. If you don't mind, that is,' he replied.

They got off the train at Tampines MRT station and went out through a bus station and found a taxi rank. The taxi took them a few kilometres along a dual carriageway, past modern blocks of flats towards Changi. The route took them past the walls of Changi Prison. Lara stared out at it, fascinated. She had read about it in accounts of the war in Singapore and was imagining a forbidding brick-built building. The tall, white, modern complex they were driving past bore little resemblance to the ugly fortress of her imagination.

Just past the jail, the taxi dropped them in front of some gates behind which was a low white building surrounded by trees.

'This must be it,' said Alex. 'Come on, let's go inside.'

The museum consisted of a few rooms displaying sketches and photographs made by the prisoners of war held in Changi jail between 1942 and '45. Lara followed Alex past the displays and information boards, reading of the hideous conditions that men and interned civilians had suffered there; the starvation, cramped conditions, disease and torture. Some of the photographs of bone thin men, their ribs clearly visible beneath their skin, brought tears to her eyes. The gallery of sketches drawn by prison artists was particularly poignant. The risks they had taken to record their experience showed amazing bravery. Alex hardly spoke as they made their way through the museum. Lara watched him anxiously. He was clearly distracted, thinking about his mother. She wished there were something she could do to help him.

They wandered through the museum and out to the open-air chapel where they sat side-by-side on benches in front of the altar, silently contemplating what they'd just observed. Lara thought about all the men who had suffered and died there, many of them very young, and of the civilians who'd also been incarcerated in Changi and suffered starvation, disease and hardships throughout the war.

Afterwards they went outside and found a taxi to take them to St Theresa's Orphanage in Katong. The route took them through the modern suburbs and along a long stretch of seafront, fringed by palm trees and a white sand beach, from which they could see dozens of ships moored up outside Singapore harbour. They were mainly huge cargo ships, lying low in the water, stretching out in a long line along the horizon.

St Theresa's was a modern building next to a school. As they got out of the taxi, Lara noticed that the playground was full of children of all ages, smartly dressed in blue and white uniforms, playing ball games or running about in groups.

They went into the reception area and Lara approached the desk. A young nun, dressed in white habit and wimple looked up and smiled. Lara explained that she'd telephoned that morning to ask whether the orphans from Our Lady had been brought there after it closed in 1943.

'My mother was taken to the Our Lady Orphanage as a baby. She died recently and I'm trying to find out about what happened to her during the war.'

'I'm so sorry for your loss. But we don't have records going that far back, I'm afraid.'

Lara was relieved that the woman was not the same person she'd spoken to earlier.

'I heard this morning that some of the orphans from Our Lady were brought here after the war. Would you happen to know anything about that?'

'Yes. I understand that to be the case,' said the nun. 'Although, I don't know much about it, and as I said, I don't think we have records going back that far.'

'Oh,' said Lara, feeling crestfallen, wondering what to do.

The nun, seeing her disappointment said, 'I'm so sorry. I'm just trying to think how we could help you. Wait a minute... please take a seat and I'll go and ask a colleague if they have any ideas.'

Lara sat down with Alex on some hard, wooden chairs and waited. Alex was silent, staring into the distance, and Lara could tell that his mind was elsewhere.

'If you want to go back without me, I don't mind at all. I'd understand,' she said after a while.

'It's fine, Lara. Don't worry about me. Let's wait and see what this lady says.'

They continued to sit in silence. Lara wished she could find the right words to get Alex to speak about his fears. She knew exactly what he was going through but getting him to open up about it wasn't going to be easy.

At last there was the sound of footsteps in the tiled passage and the nun returned smiling.

'One of my colleagues suggested you should get in touch with Sister Xavier. She's retired now. She's in her mid-eighties, but she was a young nun during the war. She is the only one left who came with the orphans from Our Lady. She might be able to help you. She lives a few streets away from here in an apartment. I'll write down her address for you.'

Lara stared at her, a broad smile on her lips. She could hardly believe what she'd just been told. Sister Xavier! It was the only name from the convent that she remembered her mother ever mentioning. As the woman bent down to scribble on a card, Lara said,

'Do you think I should phone her before I go and knock on her door?'

'Well, she loves visitors, but... I tell you what, I'll go pop into the office and give her a call myself. Tell her you're on your way. That is, if you want to go there straight away?'

'Oh yes! Yes please.'

'Who should I tell her you're inquiring about?'

'Nell. Nell Joseph. They called her Cornelia in the orphanage, I think. I'm Lara Adams, her daughter.'

The nun disappeared through a door and Lara turned to Alex, smiling.

'Isn't that amazing. Mum used to speak about Sister Xavier. I can hardly believe it!'

'That's great news, Lara. I'm so happy for you. But I think I'll go back to my hotel now. I need to try to speak to Mum. She's been to the doctor's today, so she might have some news.'

'Of course. I understand.'

The nun returned smiling. 'Sister Xavier says she remembers Cornelia Joseph very well and she'd be delighted if you'd like to pay her a visit.'

She handed Lara the card with an address written on it.

'It's probably about a fifteen-minute walk from here. Do you have a map?'

Lara nodded. She thanked the young woman warmly and she and Alex went out onto the road.

They walked together along the main road that bordered the seafront for a little way, but after a few minutes, Alex was able to flag down a taxi.

'I'll give you a call later,' he said as he got in. Lara noticed the anxious look in his eyes, how his forehead was puckered up in a frown.

'I hope you get some good news,' she said, her heart going out to him. 'Try not to worry.'

'Thanks. Good luck with your visit.'

She closed the door and watched the taxi pull out into the traffic and disappear in the direction of the city centre. She sighed, feeling so sorry for Alex and wishing she could do more to help him. She wondered briefly if she should have gone back to the hotel with him, rather than go to visit Sister Xavier. After all, she'd waited a lifetime to find out about her mother's past. She could have waited another day or so. But the visit had been arranged now. There was no changing that.

Lara consulted the map and plotted her route to the apartment block off Still Road. As the young nun had said, it only took her ten or fifteen minutes to walk. Even so, she was bathed in sweat when she arrived in front of the tall apartment block. She had wondered how she would get inside; she felt a bit awkward about pressing a buzzer and announcing herself to a stranger, but there was a caretaker sitting behind a desk in the entrance hall who telephoned Sister Xavier.

'Take the lift to the fourth floor,' said the man. 'Sister Xavier will meet you in the hallway.'

Lara emerged from the lift on the fourth floor. A diminutive old woman stood opposite the doors. She stepped forward, stooping slightly.

'Miss Adams?' she said, holding out her hand.

Lara shook it, noticing how cold and leathery the old lady's hand was, but her smile was warm and open. Her face was tanned and wreathed in wrinkles, but her blue eyes were sharp and she smiled at Lara with an amused twinkle.

'Sister Xavier?'

The old lady inclined her head. She was dressed, like

the nun at St Theresa's, in a long habit, with a wimple covering her hair. Hers was navy blue rather than white. Lara wondered why she still dressed like that, when she was so obviously past retirement age. Perhaps nuns never retire though, she thought.

'You look a lot like your mother,' the old lady said, beckoning her towards one of the doors. 'Do come inside.'

'You remember her?' Lara asked, thrilled at the old woman's words.

'Of course. She was one of the first babies I looked after when I arrived at Our Lady as a young novice. Please do sit down. Would you like something to drink? Some water? Tea?'

'Oh, water would be nice. It's very hot outside.'

Lara sat down in an old-fashioned upright armchair. The picture window that dominated the room looked out over the roofs of the neighbourhood. In the distance, across the tree-tops, Lara could see the misty blue of the sea, and that same line of ships she'd seen earlier which formed a thin grey smudge on the horizon. The small living room was full of religious artefacts and memorabilia. On one wall was a huge painting of Christ on the cross, there were several models of the Virgin Mary on the mantlepiece, and on a bookcase stood a tall statue of Jesus in long flowing robes, holding out both hands. The bookcase was filled with Bibles and prayer books. This didn't surprise or unnerve Lara; her mother had been very devout and had loved Catholic artefacts. A small statue of the Virgin Mary had always stood on their mantlepiece at home.

Sister Xavier came back with two glasses and handed Lara one. She took a seat opposite Lara.

'So, tell me. What would you like to know about young Cornelia?' she asked, smiling.

Lara sat forward, looking into the old lady's eyes.

'Everything really. Whatever you know about her. Whatever you can remember.'

'Well, she came to Our Lady Orphanage as a baby of a few months old. A local woman brought her. She'd found her in a storm drain in Chinatown.'

'Why would a baby have been left in a storm drain? Why would anyone have done that?' Lara asked, shocked at such cruelty. 'Would her mother have done that?'

Sister Xavier shook her head.

'The woman who brought the baby in said that she'd seen a Chinese woman putting the baby in the storm drain as she was marched out of a go-down by Japanese soldiers with a lot of other Chinese people. She must have been looking after the baby for its mother, because the baby wasn't Chinese.'

'Why did the Japanese do that?'

The old lady lowered her eyes. There was a pained expression on her face.

'It was called the Sook Ching massacre. The Japanese wanted to get rid of all sympathisers of the Kuomintang regime in China. If people didn't come forward to report to them, they simply rounded them up, marched them out to one of the beaches and executed them by firing squad.'

'How awful,' Lara breathed, feeling the colour draining from her face. Sister Xavier nodded.

'It was dreadful. It happened quite early in the occupation. After that everyone was terrified of what the Japanese might do.'

'It was lucky my mother wasn't taken too,' said Lara.

'Yes. The woman looking after her must have been so strong... Someone had tucked an amulet into the baby's clothes. It was a beautiful amber stone set in silver.'

'Was this it?' Lara asked and fished in her pocket for the amber jewel on the silver chain.

Sister Xavier held out her hands for the amulet and examined it closely. She nodded.

'Yes... This was it,' she said. 'It's beautiful. We locked it away in the safe and when Cornelia came to leave the orphanage, we gave it back to her.'

'Do you think that was her mother, then, Suria? That name's engraved on the back.'

The old nun nodded.

'It was. That was her name. She came to the orphanage once. At the end of the war.'

Chills went through Lara at this revelation.

'I thought she must have died,' she said in surprise. 'If she came to the orphanage, why didn't she take my mother home with her?'

The old lady bowed her head, not meeting Lara's eyes.

'Now, it's difficult to explain about that. She came at the end of the war because she wanted to take the little girl away with her. But the holy Mothers wouldn't allow it.'

'Why? Why would they have done that?'

'They said she wasn't the right sort of person to bring up a child. That she would have been a bad influence on the girl.'

'Why?' asked Lara, puzzled. 'Whatever had she done to deserve that?'

'I cannot think. I've always wondered that myself. It's a good thing that Cornelia herself never found out about it. It could have had a very damaging effect upon her if she had.'

'She died a few months ago,' said Lara. 'That's why I've come here. To try to find out more about her childhood. I feel guilty really, that I didn't do it during her lifetime.'

Sister Xavier's eyes widened with shock and she held out her hand.

'Oh, I'm so sorry, my dear. I had no idea. She died very young.'

Lara took the old nun's hand and nodded. 'She was in her late fifties. I always thought she was as strong as an ox, that she would go on forever.'

'She suffered terribly when she was a baby. It probably weakened her for life,' said Sister Xavier, squeezing Lara's hand and letting it go again.

'Can you tell me about it?' asked Lara.

'We were taken to an internment camp, you see, over on the mainland. One day, the Japanese came to the orphanage. That was when we were at Our Lady in Bukit Timah, of course. They ordered us all out. I remember it clearly. It was early in the morning and the children were only just waking up. We only had time to snatch up a few belongings. They loaded us onto the backs of trucks, drove us over the causeway to the mainland and to a camp deep in the jungle. We had to live in bamboo shelters and survive on meagre diet of rice and vegetables. There were no medicines at all. Over time, some of the babies got sick and died. There was nothing we could do to help them. It was a dreadful ordeal.'

'How awful for you. Did my mother get sick?'

The old lady nodded. 'She had a chest infection for a long time. It was touch and go. She was less than a year old. She pulled through, but she was always sickly as a child. If she got a cough it would last for weeks and leave her weak and depleted. May I ask what she died of?'

'Pneumonia. She had a chest infection for months. It just got worse. When they admitted her to hospital, they said it was pneumonia.'

'It is not a surprise,' said Sister Xavier gently, 'but hard to take all the same.'

'Can you tell me what she was like as a child, Sister?'

The old lady smiled, her gaze faraway as she remembered.

'She was a disciplined little girl. She worked hard and she was hard on herself in other ways too. She didn't find it easy to make friends.'

Lara nodded. 'That sounds like Mum,' she said. 'But I'm intrigued about her mother, Suria. Why did they send her away?'

'As I said, I tried to work it out myself but wasn't able able to come up with an answer. I know Suria came here directly after Singapore was liberated. I saw her myself coming through the gates and I spoke to her as she waited in the front hall to see the Mother Superior. She was very pale and thin and dressed in rags. She looked utterly beaten and exhausted. I know she told Mother Superior about the amulet and from that they knew Cornelia was her child. But Mother Superior wouldn't let her take the child away. She wouldn't even let her see the little one.'

Lara tried to imagine the scene, a desperate woman, perhaps recently released from captivity, tracking down the baby she'd lost during the war, only to be told that she couldn't take her baby away with her. That she couldn't even see the child. How devastating would that be to someone who already appeared weak and defeated?

'Did you try to find out why?'

Sister Xavier looked a little ashamed and dropped her gaze.

'I did, there were so many rumours going around about it amongst the younger nuns. Some said the mother was a criminal, others that she was a prostitute, others that she was a Japanese sympathiser. But Mother Superior never told anyone her reasons. And we novices were all terrified of her. She wasn't someone you could challenge easily... so no one ever really knew. And no one told Cornelia about the incident. As I said, it would have been too upsetting.'

'Where did the mother, Suria, go after that? Did she ever come back?'

Sister Xavier shook her head. 'No. I was there in the front hall when she arrived though. She told me that she wanted to take Cornelia back to her village on the mainland. I expect she went back there. Someone who saw her leave said that she'd said she would come back, but she never did.'

Lara leaned forward. 'Did she say where her village was?'

Sister Xavier shook her head again. 'She said it was a fishing village. Not far from Desaru on the east coast. She said she was looking forward to seeing her family again. She said she hadn't seen them since before the war.'

Lara said her goodbyes to Sister Xavier and left the apartment. She walked down the busy road towards the seafront, thinking she might pick up a taxi there. As she walked, she hardly noticed her surroundings. She couldn't stop thinking of a desperate mother, surviving the Japanese occupation and returning to claim her baby, only to be turned away and never to see the child again. She couldn't get the cruelty and sadness of that situation out of her mind.

12

CHARLES

Singapore, 1941

The weeks flew by and Charles quickly got used to life on the base without Louise. He no longer found himself looking over his shoulder, wondering what new ways she was devising to manipulate or humiliate him. He felt a delicious sense of freedom he'd not experienced since he and Louise had been married. Even though war was fast approaching, and he knew that Singapore and the whole of Malaya were in danger, on a personal level he felt more relaxed than he had in a long time.

On the morning Louise left, he'd woken in the spare room to the sound of her rushing about, opening and shutting cupboards, shouting at the servants to find this or clean that. He'd got up to say goodbye, the memory of her lies the previous evening fresh in his mind. They sat stiffly over breakfast, hardly speaking. Neither of them mentioned what had happened the night before or the fact that he'd spent the night in the spare room. Louise looked pale that morning, her skin dull and her hair yellow and lifeless. Because it was just the two of them, she wasn't bothering to smile or even to look at him. He hoped she felt guilty about the way she'd tried to deceive him, but he suspected that guilt wasn't in her makeup.

She hardly touched her food, spooning her coffee in her cup without drinking it. When the taxi arrived and tooted its horn, she jumped up from the table and rushed to the bedroom to gather her hand luggage. The servants were already taking her suitcases out. Charles dabbed his face with his napkin and strolled outside. Josephine waved to him from the taxi and he went over to speak to her.

'Good morning, Josephine,' he said, noticing how heavily made up she was.

'Is Louise ready? I don't want to be late.'

'Yes. She's coming right away.'

'Oh good. I expect you're going to be so sad and lonely without her, Charles. She's always the life and soul of the party, isn't she?'

He nodded. 'It will certainly feel very different around here without her,' he said carefully.

'But wonderful for me that she's coming to India! She'll certainly be a fun travel companion. It was lovely of her to suggest the trip.'

'Did *she* suggest it?' he asked, half to himself. Hadn't Louise told him that Josephine was already going and wanted someone to share a cabin with? He shook his head. The way Louise operated never ceased to mystify him.

He heard her heels on the path and she appeared behind him.

'Goodbye, darling,' she said, pecking him on the cheek.

'You'll write, won't you?' he asked automatically, opening the car door for her.

'Of course. As soon as I get there.'

'Well, safe journey then,' he said, closing the door. The taxi pulled away hooting its horn, Louise and Josephine waving out of the window with handkerchiefs. As it rounded the corner and disappeared from view, Charles heaved a huge sigh of relief, went back inside and finished his breakfast, reading the newspaper from cover to cover without interruption or disturbance of any kind.

Life at work was getting busier, with the Japanese threat looming ever larger. His team had recently moved into "The Battlebox" at Fort Canning, a series of fortified underground rooms, where intelligence was gathered and strategy developed ahead of any invasion, for the army, the navy and the air-force. The passages were narrow and the rooms claustrophobic and although it was air-conditioned, the place always felt stuffy and cramped. However, the atmosphere was full of tension and excitement and at last Charles felt as though he was at the heart of something meaningful.

He'd been working on "Operation Matador", a plan for assembling troops in southern Thailand so they could be ready to intercept any Japanese troops landing there or on the east coast of Malaya. Equipment, numbers, logistics, sites of camps, troop movements, and all the back-up an army might need, had to be worked out painstakingly, with charts, plans and statistics. It had taken months, and Charles had worked long hours since Louise had left for India. A few days ago the plan had been submitted to London for approval, which meant his workload had dramatically reduced.

The days dragged now, with little to do but wait for the report to be approved so he and others could start putting it into motion. He tried to occupy himself by helping colleagues, discussing tactics and timings, the latest decoded telegrams from military intelligence, rumours of what the Japanese were planning. Three new airfields were being built on Singapore island, but Charles couldn't help thinking that the RAF was hopelessly unprepared and ill-equipped, with only the 300 or so old-fashioned aircraft to defend the region, rather than the 560 plus they had requested from London. He knew that the army too wasn't sufficiently equipped; they had no tanks, the northern shore of Singapore island was woefully under-defended, and many of the new troops arriving were raw recruits with virtually no training.

He became more and more discontented with his role, even though to work in the Battlebox was a sought-after position and was at the heart of the planning operations. Many would have jumped at the chance to be part of that. But Charles felt restless; he would have far preferred to be out in the field with his men. Now the Operation Matador report had been filed, he wondered if there might be an opportunity for him to move on.

One day, he spoke to Colonel Cotton, his immediate superior, and asked him about the possibility of going back into the field. Colonel Cotton looked at him over his glasses.

'I thought you were enjoying the work, Simmonds. You've certainly made a very good job of the Matador report. Why this change of heart?'

'Well, sir, I was very surprised to be placed in the role when I came out to Singapore. To be perfectly honest, I volunteered so I could see some action. I didn't expect a desk job.'

'Really, Simmonds? That's very odd. The order for you to be assigned to a desk job in Far East Command came from your former general on the North West Frontier. General Daniels to be precise.'

A bolt of shock went through Charles at his words. General Daniels was Louise's father, his own father-in-law. It was clear to him immediately that this was Louise's doing. She didn't want him to be away with his men, possibly stationed in the jungle or in far-off locations. She wanted him home every evening, so she could parade him at drinks parties, dinner parties and dances.

'I rather assumed you had requested the role yourself and that General Daniels was merely backing you up by putting in a word for you.'

'No!' Charles blurted out, realising that he was shaking and that his fists were clenched.

'Are you quite alright, Simmonds? Has something I've said upset you?'

'I'm sorry, sir, but I never asked General Daniels to put me forward for a desk job. I believe my wife may have asked him to do it. I'm quite annoyed about it, frankly.'

'Your wife?' the colonel's moustache twitched in amusement.

'She's the general's daughter. I can't believe he would have asked otherwise.'

'How interesting. I rather assumed that you'd seen enough action on the frontier to last a lifetime and that you wanted a rest from all that.'

'Not at all. It's why I joined the army, and it's why I volunteered to come out to Singapore.'

'All right. What an unusual situation. But I quite under-stand your position. I'll discuss with my superiors and see what I can do.'

One evening he arrived home from work early, the empty hours stretching ahead of him. The house was silent as he went into his bedroom, showered and changed, wondering how to spend the time before bed. There was always the officers' mess, but he wasn't sure if he could face an evening of army talk, after having just come away from a full day of it.

In the dining room, the bearer brought him supper. Overcooked fish and plain boiled potato. It was tasteless and didn't dispel his hunger. At least Louise had made sure they ate proper food every evening, he thought grudgingly. Now, without her presence, standards seemed to be slipping.

Charles felt a wave of loneliness, but he realised that he wasn't pining for Louise. It was Suria who he was thinking of. They had met for tea, as arranged, the Wednesday after Louise left. He'd waited outside Suria's building at five o' clock and she'd emerged looking fresh, her eyes sparkling. She was wearing a simple white blouse and a pleated skirt. He thought how amazing it was that she had emerged from that squalid building looking like that when he knew that she probably slept on a roll on the floor and that the bathrooms in that building left a lot to be desired.

'Where would you like to go?' he asked. 'The café we went to before?'

She laughed. 'I don't think so. How about the quayside? My friend and I often go there on her day off.'

The two of them walked side-by-side through the busy Chinese quarter towards Boat Quay. As ever, the narrow streets were thronging with people; stalls were set up on the pavement selling everything from plumbing parts to caged birds; stallholders were cooking over woks on makeshift food stalls, and the air was filled with the smell of cooking spices and the cries of hawkers. It felt wonderful to walk through Chinatown with Suria beside him; their elbows sometimes touching briefly as they were jostled by the crowd. When that happened, a tiny shock went through him, as if an electric current had passed between them, invisible but powerful.

They found a hawker stall down on the quayside and sat at a simple wooden table sipping green tea from chipped china cups. Feeling a deep contentment come over him, he smiled at Suria and she smiled back at him, the skin at the corners of her tip-tilted eyes wrinkling with pleasure. Behind her, he could see the frenetic activity down on the water, where boats were being unloaded and loaded at breakneck speed by multitudes of Chinese workers. He realised that sitting here opposite Suria in this unpretentious place in the poorest but most colourful quarter of Singapore was infinitely preferable to an evening in the luxury of Raffles with more prestigious company.

He asked her about her job and she told him how happy she was working at the hotel; she'd been serving in the restaurant every day since he'd been there and each time she grew in confidence.

'I'm even taking orders myself now,' she said proudly. 'Mr Antonio, the head waiter, said how well I was doing yesterday.'

'That's wonderful.'

Suria was talkative that day; more talkative than he'd known her to be before. She was obviously beginning to trust him and to relax in his company. She told him how happy she was to have a well-paid job because it meant that she could send money home to her mother who was sick and bedridden in their fishing village on the mainland. It was the reason she'd come to Singapore.

'I came here with my best friend, Amina,' she said, 'It's wonderful to be together. It makes it fun. I think I'd be unhappy and homesick if she wasn't with me.

'But what about you?' she went on. 'Don't you miss your home?'

'Oh, it's a long time since I was at home,' he said. 'I grew up in London, but I signed up for the Indian Army in '32. I've only been back on leave a couple of times since then. All my friends had moved on, I didn't really enjoy it. I think of India as my home now.'

'What about your parents?' she asked, her face serious. 'Don't they miss you?'

'My father died when I was a child. My mother remarried and had another family. I don't think they miss me at all, to tell you the truth.'

'How very sad,' she said.

The time had flown by. They'd drunk several cups of tea and enjoyed a snack of fried noodles. Gradually, the sky darkened, and the sun went down behind the go-downs on the quayside. Charles would have sat there for hours with her. He loved watching her eyes sparkle as she spoke and how her expression could change from amused to sad to serious in the blink of an eye.

Finally, she got up to leave. 'It's almost eight o'clock. I need to go. Things settle down early in our lodgings. Amina has to get up at dawn, so she'll need to go to sleep. She'll be expecting me.'

Charles got up too, paid the hawker for their tea and walked with her back to the door of her building.

'Can we do this again?' he asked, feeling a sudden panic at the thought of letting her go without arranging another meeting.

'Yes, that would be nice,' she said simply, flashing him a smile. 'But I work every day except Wednesdays, as I said.'

'Next Wednesday at the same time?' he asked.

'Alright,' she said and with a wave she darted up the steps and disappeared into the go-down.

He would have dearly loved to meet her before Wednesday came around again, but knew it wasn't possible.

So, for the next three Wednesday afternoons, at the same time, he waited outside the go-down for her and they went for tea together at the same hawker stall on Boat Quay. They spoke of inconsequential things, the trivia of their lives and of their pasts, but for Charles those meetings were the most meaningful thing he'd done since arriving in Singapore and he looked forward to them all week.

But his work had interfered and three weeks passed without him being able to meet her. He'd been so pressed to get the report out on time that he'd had to send a messenger with a note to say he was sorry but he couldn't make their appointment. It was the last thing he wanted to do, but he had no choice. He pictured her puzzled face as she read the note. Would she think he'd lost interest in her?

He felt a powerful need to see her again; to watch her face as she spoke, see the light in her eyes, the proud lift of her chin. Now the report was done, he scribbled a note to her apologising for not having been in touch for so long, and inviting her to tea the coming Wednesday.

Now, as he finished his tasteless supper and poured himself a brandy, he pictured her working in the restaurant in Raffles before walking home and settling down for the night on the floor of the go-down. He wished he could do something to take her away from that situation. But he knew she was proud and that she wouldn't accept charity.

Loneliness threatened to overcome him. Again he thought of the mess bar, but couldn't face that. He asked Ali, the bearer, to call him a taxi to take him to Singapore town. He'd heard that the bars were lively now, with the recent increase of troops from Britain and Australia. It would be a good opportunity to experience it for himself.

The taxi dropped him on Orchard Road and he wandered down a side street and soon found himself amongst narrow streets filled with girlie bars. He picked one indiscriminately, shouldered his way through the raucous crowd to the bar and ordered himself a beer. Looking around him, he realised that the place was heaving with British and Australian troops. Most were in uniform and he picked out the uniforms of the Argyll and Southern Highlanders and the Manchester Regiment, who he understood had arrived by ship that day. The atmosphere was rowdy, most of the men around him being drunk. He downed his drink quickly, fearing that things would end up in a fight, and went out onto the street. As he moved along the road, he could sense the tense atmosphere amongst the crowds of boisterous men. Perhaps it was the heat, or maybe the newly found freedom, having been confined to an uncomfortable troop ship for weeks on end.

Skirmishes were breaking out all around him, and not only that, some of the troops were throwing things at the windows of some of the bars. In front of him the Black Cat bar was being pelted with stones and bottles, and the Lucky Lady bar a few doors on had its door broken down. As he reached the end of the road, three vans pulled up and military police spilled out, wielding truncheons.

His mind flew to Suria. She would surely be leaving work in the next hour or two. If the brawling was going on all over the city centre, as he guessed it was, she wouldn't be safe walking home through Chinatown alone. Leaving the busy streets behind, he took a footbridge over the Singapore river and entered the quieter British quarter. He hurried along beside the Padang and emerged outside Raffles, where he sat on the low wall opposite the staff entrance, as he had done the last time.

This time there was a young doorman stationed on the door, opening it for staff as they emerged in dribs and drabs. Eventually, Suria came out alone and the doorman made a joke to her. Charles heard her laughing in response. She waved and set off down the side street. He slipped off the wall and walked after her.

'Suria?' She jumped as he approached, but her eyes lit up when she saw who it was.

'Charles! What are you doing here? Did you eat in the restaurant again?'

'No. I came to warn you that there's a lot of trouble in the old town. I don't think you should walk there alone.'

She frowned. 'Trouble? What trouble?'

'British troops fighting, smashing up buildings.'

A shudder went through her, but she turned to him with her defiant look.

'I'll be alright,' she said. 'You don't need to worry about me.'

'I know that you don't normally need to be looked after. I just came to warn you, that's all. I'm happy to take you home. I think we should get a taxi. It's far too dangerous to walk.'

In the light of the streetlamp he saw her face soften.

'There's really no need, but I would enjoy travelling with you,' she said. He smiled inwardly and took her arm. They walked around to the front entrance of the hotel and got into one of the taxis waiting to ferry guests home.

The taxi travelled along the Padang towards the Singapore river. The lights from the seafront threw huge shadows across the grass at the far edge of the Padang. The place was quiet and empty, in complete contrast to the noise of China-town and the red light district.

'Did you get my note?' he asked. 'I was so sorry not to be able to see you for the past few weeks. I had so much work on it was impossible to get away.'

'I knew it would be something like that,' she said, smiling up at him. 'I wasn't worried and I did get your note.' Not for the first time he found himself admiring her self-possession and strength.

He remembered the last time they had met and walked together through Chinatown. Their arms had brushed together but he'd stopped short of taking her arm. He realised that they were getting to know one another better and she trusted him and was more relaxed in his company. Now their arms touched occasionally as the driver took bends a little too quickly.

The taxi driver skirted round the southern edge of Chinatown, trying to avoid the worst of the rioting, but as it turned into the narrow streets of the quarter, they could see smashed windows, and mobs of soldiers, arms linked, walking around looking for trouble.

'I'm glad we're not walking,' he said as another group pushed past.

'I am too,' Suria admitted.

At last the taxi arrived outside her building. The crowds had thinned out here. They both got out.

'Thank you for bringing me home,' she said.

'It was nothing. If it happens again tomorrow, I'll come again,' he said.

'Oh, I'm sure the military police will have sorted it out by then, don't you think.'

'I hope so,' he said. 'But I'll check to make sure.'

'You're so kind, Charles,' she said. 'But I must go inside now. It is very late.'

He wanted to pull her towards him and kiss her, but he didn't want to upset the fragile trust that had grown between them. It was too soon, he told himself. Then he reminded himself that he was a married man. Even though Louise had treated him so cruelly, he didn't think it justified him doing the same to her.

'See you on Wednesday,' Suria said, heading up the steps. She turned at the top and waved to him. He waved back, then, once she was inside the go-down, got back in the taxi and asked the driver to take him back to the base.

BACK AT HOME he poured himself another brandy and went to take it outside to the veranda at the back of the bungalow so he could drink it watching the stars. As he went through the front hall, he noticed a letter propped up on the table which he hadn't seen when he came home from work.

He took it up, noting the Indian stamp and Louise's writing on the envelope. She'd written a few times before, telling him the gossip from the station at Peshawar. Reading between the lines, he'd been sure that she'd been out dancing or drinking every evening since she'd arrived. She didn't tell him who she'd been with though, and Charles noticed that omission. He ripped the letter open, expecting more of the same. He took it outside to sit in one of the basket chairs to read it.

Dear Charles,

I hope this letter finds you well.

I've been doing a lot of thinking since I left Singapore. I know that what I'm going to tell you will cause you pain and I'm sorry for that. I never meant to hurt you, Charles, but I won't be coming back to Singapore and think we should separate formally.

I know I haven't made you happy, but in turn I felt that you've always tried to crush my spirits. I can't help my upbringing and the fact that I love to go out and enjoy myself. I know you disapprove of the way I am, but I think you should have tried harder to understand me and what I need to make me happy.

I've met someone back in Peshawar who adores me and wants to marry me if you'll set me free. He loves me for what I am and doesn't want to dampen my spirits.

I'm sorry if this saddens you, but I really believe that it will make both of us happier in the long run. Daddy knows a good family lawyer in Singapore and will send you his details. I hope you won't try to make this difficult.

Yours

Louise

Charles read the letter through several times and, as he did so, he tried to gauge his reaction. He realised that he felt none of the pain and sadness that Louise expected. All he felt at her words was relief and a sense of freedom; a huge weight lifting from his shoulders.

13

LARA

Singapore, 2000

Lara asked the taxi driver to drop her at the top of Temple Street. She needed to walk for a while to allow herself to process everything that Sister Xavier had told her. The description of her mother's personality and temperament rang true and she was sure that the old nun was genuinely trying to help and was telling her the truth. But why had the Mother Superior sent Suria away at the end of the war and refused to let her even see her own child? It was an act of cruelty that surely no caring person would have done in good conscience, without having a very good reason. The thought of Suria, weak and thin from her wartime ordeal, walking away from the orphanage empty-handed, when she'd gone there expecting to leave with her baby, tore at Lara's heart. She was determined to find out more about what had happened back then, but at that moment she had no clear idea how to go about that.

She walked on past her own guesthouse and plunged into the busy streets and alleyways of Chinatown, in the direction of the river. It was good to walk; to stride out and stretch her legs. Sitting in Sister Xavier's stuffy apartment and in the taxi that had crawled through the traffic afterwards had made her feel confined and restless. It was mid-afternoon now and the place was busy with locals and tourists milling in the streets shopping at stalls, eating at open-air restaurants. She walked down a pedestrianised street where Chinese lanterns of all colours of the rainbow were strung above the walkway. The air was alive with traditional Oriental music and spicy cooking smells. Lara realised she was getting used to this now, appreciating it and beginning to find it familiar and comforting.

As she reached the Singapore river, her phone rang.

'Lara? It's Alex.' He sounded distraught.

'Hi, Alex, did you speak to your mother? How is she?'

'She's been admitted to hospital. It's touch and go I think.' She caught a note of panic in his voice.

'I'm so sorry. Do you want me to come over to your hotel? Is there anything I can do?'

'No, it's fine. I just need to get back to Australia as quickly as I can. I'm looking into flights now.'

'Of course. I understand.'

'I'm having a bit of a problem with funds though. I can't get access to my savings quickly enough, so I might not be able to go until I've sorted that out.'

'Oh no. That's awful,' she said, wondering how she would have coped if she hadn't been able to rush straight to Nell's bedside when she'd heard of her illness.

'I can lend you the money if you like,' she said on an impulse. Was that a rash move? Would he be offended by this? She knew Alex well enough now, she figured, to make the offer in good faith. She trusted him and was aware that she was growing more fond of him than she should. She hoped he would take it as a gesture of friendship.

'Oh,' he said, surprise in his voice. 'I didn't mean...'

'It's no trouble. I insist. If it means you can get back to Australia quickly. I'd hate to think you couldn't get to see your mother when she's as ill as that. You need to go as quickly as you can. I can transfer the funds, or get them out of the bank for you. Whatever's easiest.'

'You're so kind, Lara. I didn't expect this. The trouble is, tickets at short notice like this are really expensive. I've found an outfit that's got the best offers on, but they only take cash.'

'That's no trouble. Why don't we meet at the bank and I'll get the cash out for you? How much might it be.'

'Around $3000 US for a return ticket I'm afraid,' he said, 'Although I could make do with a single. It's a bit cheaper.'

'That shouldn't be a problem. Where shall we meet? I just need to go back to the guesthouse and get my cards and passport.'

'There are banks in Raffles Place. We could meet there in, say, an hour? Could you do that?'

'Yes – I'll be there. Which bank?'

'HSBC. Let's meet inside just in case one of us is late. It's cooler in there.'

'Alright. I'll see you in an hour.'

She rushed back through the busy streets, bumping into people in her haste. Where it had felt good to mingle in the crowds before, now the press of people blocking her way was an annoyance. She tried to run, but it wasn't easy. At one point she tripped on a kerbstone and nearly went flying. It was further to her hostel than she'd estimated and going so quickly made her hot and sweaty.

Finally, she reached her hostel in Temple Street. She'd

left her passport and bank cards in the safe, so she stopped
at reception to retrieve them. The woman was maddeningly
slow, insisting on Lara filling out forms in duplicate and
signing them before she was prepared to release her belongings. Once Lara had them, she asked the woman to call her
a taxi to take her to Raffles Place, then she rushed upstairs to
change her T shirt and splash water on her face.

When she came back down, the woman was shrugging
helplessly, a pained expression on her face.

'Taxi not come yet. Quicker to walk. Not far.'

Sighing, and consulting her map, Lara decided she was
right. She set off back down Temple Street and turned into
Pagoda Road, one of the pedestrianised walking streets that
she'd just rushed back through, the one with the Chinese
lanterns overhead. The stalls were just as busy as they'd
been a few minutes earlier. The end of the street was baking
hot and covered with a Perspex awning, reminding her of
Petaling Street in Kuala Lumpur. She emerged through a
bright red archway beside a Hindu temple, a tower above its
gateway covered in layers of decorated statues of Hindu
gods. She hurried along the pavement of South Bridge
Road, past converted shophouses, relics of old Singapore,
while up ahead loomed the glittering skyscrapers of the
commercial district. The walk seemed to take forever, but
with each step the tall buildings got closer and eventually
she found herself on a pedestrianised walkway that ran
between tall glass buildings on one side and the river on the
other. She realised that this was another part of Boat Quay,
but very different from the place where she and Alex had
eaten a couple of nights ago.

Eventually she arrived in front of the HSBC building,
another glass-fronted one in a dense forest of glass buildings. She walked around its base to find an entrance. At last

she found some double doors and pushed one to enter, but it was only possible to do so by speaking through an intercom and being admitted through a security pod. She pushed the buzzer and to her surprise, a woman's voice said;

'Miss Adams?'

'Yes?' perhaps Alex had already told them she was coming.

'Wait there one moment please. A colleague is coming to speak to you.'

'What?' she asked, exasperated, then a man stepped forward. He was tall and dark, with a fashionably stubbly beard, and dressed in jeans and a T shirt. She realised that he'd been waiting in the porch of the building. It struck her that he didn't look like a bank employee.

'Miss Adams?' he asked. 'Lara Adams?'

'Yes. What is this please?' she stared at him. His face was familiar, but she couldn't place it immediately. But after a few seconds it clicked. It was the man she'd seen watching them that evening she and Alex had met in Raffles and later when they'd dined at Boat Quay. She gasped at the revelation.

'Who are you?' she asked, waves of panic washing over her. He took her arm.

'Step this way please. I'm from the Australian High Commission. I just need to ask you a few questions.'

She had no choice but to allow him to take her elbow and usher her through a side entrance and into a conference room. The air conditioning was glacial and the contrast with the steamy air outside, mixed with the shock of what was happening, left her shivering and covered in goose-bumps.

'Sit down please. Would you like some water? I'm sorry to alarm you,' his voice was calm, gentle even.

'Yes. Yes please.' She took a sip of the water he offered her and realised her hand was shaking.

The man sat down opposite her.

'As I said, I'm from the Australian High Commission. I've been working with the Singapore police and Interpol because we've been watching a young Australian couple who we believe are engaged in criminal activities.'

Her mouth dropped open. 'Alex?' she muttered.

The man smiled. 'Is that what he's calling himself? His real name is Peter Woodruff. He's from Sydney, Australia, and a known fraudster. He and his girlfriend Stacey Johnson have been perpetrating scams on young backpackers for months now. They've just left Thailand where the Bangkok police were onto them.'

Lara couldn't stop staring at him. 'I can't believe it,' she kept saying. 'This can't be true. I know him. He's quite genuine,' but all the time her mind was spinning. Could this be right? Could Alex and Chloe have taken her for a ride? Anger rose up inside her. She'd trusted them.

'You might think you know him. He's probably done a very good job of gaining your trust. He's probably even made you think he's interested in you romantically.'

Lara felt her face go hot and took her eyes away from the man's face.

'But everything he said was true,' she said, staring down at the polished table, although she was beginning to wonder now. 'I met him and his girlfriend, Chloe, in Kuala Lumpur a few days ago.'

'And I bet they told you she had to go back to Australia, did they? Pretended to be arguing, so you thought you might have a chance with him?'

She nodded. He pulled out a photo and pushed it across the table towards her.

'Here's a picture of the two of them at the Novotel yesterday evening.'

Lara stared at it. Alex and Chloe were sitting at a table in a bar, drinking.

'But how do I know this was taken yesterday?'

'Trust me. I've been following them both since they left Bangkok a fortnight ago. They've been doing this sort of thing for months. They gain your trust, make up a story about having to go back to Australia urgently and not having enough funds... does that sound familiar?'

She nodded, shamefaced. How could she have been so gullible?

'Don't blame yourself. Many girls have fallen for this before you. Young men too. Sometimes they've worked the other way around. Normally they invent a story about themselves – something very close to their victim's own experience, so the victim feels they have something in common.'

She thought quickly, but shook her head again. It was such a shock, such a turnaround from her previous mindset that she couldn't quite believe it. What shocked her most though, was how she herself had been taken in by everything Alex and Chloe had said and done. Victim? Is that what I am, she wondered.

'They said that Alex was looking into family history. He had an aunt who was killed in the fall of Singapore, apparently. A nurse.'

'And were you here to look into your own family history?'

She nodded, feeling very foolish. 'My mother was brought up in an orphanage here in Singapore. I've come here to find out what I can about her childhood.'

'And I bet they didn't tell you about Alex's aunt until

they knew what you were here for,' the man said, leaning forward, looking into her eyes.

'I suppose not,' she agreed, trying to pin down the sequence of events.

'There would have been something else too. Something aligned to your own life that would have made you want to part with your money. Could you tell me what it was?'

She nodded slowly and dropped her head, afraid that tears might come.

'He told me that his mother was very ill. That she'd been taken into hospital and he had to go back to Australia urgently.'

'And does that chime with something in your own life?'

'My mother died recently,' she admitted in a low voice. 'I was able to go to her beforehand though. Spend the last days with her. It was very important to me.'

'Of course. I'm so sorry to hear about your mother,' the man said gently. 'But that just goes to show how ruthless they are. Their tactics are to find someone's weak spot and prey on it. In the past they've gone for similar things. A sick relative, a fire, a company insolvency, a burglary at home, all things that their victim has experienced.'

Lara shook her head again, still finding it hard to take in. 'It's unbelievable,' she said.

'Some of their victims haven't just lost one lot of money. There's been the airfare, then a call to say further expenses are needed at home – hospital bills, something like that. I could go on. Several people have lost more than $10,000 to their scams.'

'I wondered how he could afford to stay in the Novotel,' Lara murmured.

The man laughed. 'Well, that's one of their weaknesses. They like luxury and because of that they get careless sometimes. The Novotel doesn't fit with their profile but they couldn't resist it. I expect Stacey wanted somewhere nice to chill while Alex took you out and worked on you.'

'What's happening to him now?' asked Lara with a shiver, imagining the two of them discussing her, planning how to manipulate her, laughing about her.

'He's been arrested and has been taken to the police station to be questioned by Singapore police. She's also been picked up from the hotel. The police will want you to make a statement in the next couple of days, once you've had a chance to think about it and have recovered from today.'

'OK,' Lara suddenly felt a wave of loneliness pass through her. She'd thought of Alex as a friend, someone she could count on so far from home. Suddenly, that had been swept away from her and she felt vulnerable as well as foolish.

'Are you OK?' the man asked.

'I just feel a complete idiot,' Lara said.

'It was understandable to want to put your trust in someone if your mother has just died. Don't be hard on yourself,' he said. 'Look, I'm going off duty now. How about a drink in Raffles? You probably need something pretty stiff after the shock you've had.'

'OK,' she said, brightening a little. 'Why not?'

'Just wait here for a couple of minutes – I just have to check in with the bank manager quickly, then let's get a taxi over there.'

Lara waited in the bare conference room, analysing her feelings. The man was quite right. She had been all too ready to put her trust in someone, and Alex had ticked all the boxes. Good looking, charming, it had felt as if they had a lot in common, although now she knew how contrived that had been. At least she hadn't parted with any money, she reflected. She could have been in the position of having been duped by Alex, but also have parted with 3000 dollars. She shook her head again, wondering how she'd let it happen. Then, remembering the kiss he'd given her after the meal at Boat Quay, and how she'd hoped it meant something to him, she wiped the back of her hand over her lips.

'How stupid I am,' she muttered.

The man returned and held the door open for her. 'The taxi's waiting,' he said.

As they were driven across the bridge and along beside the wide-open Padang towards the hotel, he said,

'I'm Christian Henderson by the way.' He held out his hand. Lara shook it.

'You know my name,' she said, smiling back. 'I saw you a couple of times when I was with Alex. You were following us after all.'

He nodded. 'Yep. We've been tailing the two of them since they left Bangkok. I followed you up to Changi this morning too.'

'Really?' she said, surprised. 'Well I certainly didn't see you.'

'No, well, I try to be careful, but sometimes more successfully than others. We knew he'd get you to meet him at a bank at some point – that's how he operates – so when he turned up at HSBC, we were ready to swoop.'

The taxi arrived at Raffles Hotel, entered the sweeping front drive and stopped in front of the entrance. A doorman bowed and opened the front door for Lara.

They walked together through the lobby to the Long Bar. Lara looked around her. It was much quieter now than it had been when she'd been here with Alex; it was late afternoon and the early evening rush hadn't yet started.

How much had happened in those few short hours since she'd last been here, she thought.

'What would you like? A Singapore Sling, or something a bit stronger?' Christian asked.

'A Sling would be lovely,' she said, finding a table by the window while Christian went to the bar. She looked out over the tropical gardens, her mind still running over and over what had happened to her. How could she have been so gullible? Especially after the way Joe had treated her; used her and deceived her over a period of months. She should have learned from her mistakes to be less trusting of people, especially men. She glanced over at Christian, wondering about *him* now. Was she right to have accepted his offer to come here for a drink? Especially after what had happened with Alex. Christian certainly appeared trustworthy; didn't he work for the High Commission? Hadn't he been helping her? Even so, she reminded herself that she needed to be extra careful now.

He returned with the drinks shortly and Lara stiffened slightly.

'You OK?' he asked. 'You've had a dreadful shock and I'm sorry for that. It's just that we had the opportunity to pounce and we had to make a decision.'

'Well, I'm glad you did, otherwise I might have lost 3000 dollars,' she said taking a large sip of the drink, letting the alcohol seep through her veins, calm her shattered nerves.

'So,' he said, leaning back in his chair, sipping his drink. 'Cheers! Here's to a good result today.'

They clinked glasses and drank again. Then Christian asked Lara about her family research.

'Have you discovered anything? Was the trip to Changi museum useful?'

'Not really, but afterwards I went to the orphanage

where my mother ended up. I spoke to an old nun who had known her as a child. She told me some interesting things about my grandmother.'

'Oh really? Tell me about it.'

So, slowly at first, then, gaining confidence as she spoke, she told him about Nell. First, she told him about her own trip to the Alexandra hospital where her mother had worked, and how she'd discovered nothing from that visit. Then she described her trip to Bukit Timah, about how the orphanage at Bukit Timah had closed down and how the orphans and nuns were interned by the Japanese on the mainland. Finally, she told him about St Theresa's, and the strange story of Suria being turned away empty handed when she'd arrived there after the war. All the time he listened earnestly.

'That's a fascinating story,' he said when she'd finished.

'I need to find out more about why Suria was sent away from the orphanage. I think the key might be to go to her village in Malaysia, but I'm not sure how to find out where it is.'

Christian rubbed his chin. 'Tricky one. Do you know anything at all about it?'

'I know it's near Desaru,' she said. 'That's all I know.'

'I'd like to be able to help you, but it's difficult to advise what to do.'

'Well, at least I've got somewhere with my search. I could have come all the way out here and found out nothing at all.'

They fell silent and sipped their drinks for a while.

'But what about you? What brought you to Singapore?' Lara asked after a pause.

He told her that he was a diplomat and that he'd worked in the Department for Foreign Affairs in Australia. He'd been posted here to the High Commission in Singapore two years ago. He'd been appointed police liaison officer, charged with helping the Singapore police with any of their cases involving Australian citizens.

'It's fascinating work, but a lot of it pretty routine; lost and stolen passports, petty drug smuggling. This case has been the most interesting thing I've been involved in so far.'

The conversation flowed easily, and before long the bar had filled up around them and was as crowded as on the previous time Lara had been there. The sky grew dark outside. They drank two more Singapore Slings each, then Lara said,

'Look, it's been really kind of you to bring me here, but I really should be getting back to my hostel. I think I need an early night.'

'Of course. But I'll come and collect you tomorrow morning to take you to the police station so you can give your statement, if that's OK with you?'

She nodded and got up to leave.

'Look, I can easily drop you off home in a taxi if you like. I live over that way,' said Christian, getting up too.

She agreed gratefully and wandered towards the exit. On the wall beside the door, her eyes were drawn to a set of black and white photographs depicting Raffles in former times. There were a couple of pictures of the gracious building, with vintage vehicles standing outside the front entrance, and one or two of the interior; the ballroom filled with people in evening dress sweeping round the dance floor; the lobby with its chandeliers lit up. Then there were some photographs of the staff from that era. A uniformed doorman, bowing and smiling broadly, the manager, looking important in a three-piece suit and finally a group of restaurant staff, standing stiffly in a line. Lara's eyes were drawn to one of the women in that group. Petite and neat, her face was serious and her chin held high, she reminded Lara powerfully of Nell. She peered closely at it, chills of recognition going through her. Around the woman's neck she could distinctly make out an amulet. She looked at it for a long time unable to believe what she was seeing. It was the exact shape and size as the one Lara carried in her purse.

14

CHARLES

Singapore, 1941

The day after Louise's letter arrived, Charles awoke with a new sense of freedom. It felt as though he'd suddenly been relieved of a great burden. He showered, dressed for work, and strode through to the dining room with a new sense of purpose, only to be greeted by a bowl of lumpy porridge and cold toast in the toast rack.

He called Ali, the bearer, and told him that from that day on he wanted egg and bacon for breakfast and whatever fruit was available. Ali shook his head solemnly.

'Memsahib won't allow fried breakfast, sahib. She says it unhealthy and makes the house smell of grease.'

'Well, memsahib isn't here now, Ali. It's just us. So, we don't have to worry about what she thinks anymore.'

Ali bowed his head. 'But she will come back soon, sahib.'

'No. That's where you're wrong, Ali,' Charles couldn't disguise the triumph in his voice. 'Memsahib won't be coming back at all. So, we can have whatever food we want. And I do like a cooked breakfast.'

Ali brightened visibly. He was clearly curious about why Louise wouldn't be returning, but, discreet as ever, he didn't ask any questions.

'I will bring you egg and bacon right away, sahib,' he said with a broad smile. Then he retreated into the kitchen with a spring in his step. Charles heard a lot of excited conversation amongst the servants, accompanied by the banging of pots and pans and soon the smell of frying bacon wafted into the dining room.

Charles decided not to write back to Louise straight away. She was obviously keen to tie the knot with her new love interest (whoever that might be). It had all happened so quickly on her return to India, that Charles wondered if it had been going on since before they left the station in Peshawar to come out to Singapore. It was quite possible. He decided to let her wait a while, especially in the light of his discovery that she'd tried to thwart his career.

When he arrived at the Battlebox that morning, he asked to see Colonel Cotton.

'Did you consider my request, sir?' he asked, coming straight to the point.

'Request?' the colonel looked up vacantly. He was surrounded by papers, clearly distracted.

'To go back into active service, sir. We spoke about it the other day.'

'Ah yes,' he said evasively, 'I *have* been thinking about that, Simmonds. One slight snag though. I wouldn't want to go against General Daniels' orders.'

'Surely they weren't actually *orders*, sir?' protested Charles.

'No, no, I accept that. But I wouldn't want to displease the man. He's a very influential and senior ranking officer in the Indian Army.'

'Sir, I was going to keep this news to myself. But General Daniels will no longer have any interest in my career. My wife wrote to me only yesterday, telling me she wants a divorce. I intend to comply with that request.'

The colonel looked up, his face colouring. He was clearly disconcerted. 'Good God, Simmonds,' he blurted. 'What dashed bad luck. Not good for an officer's reputation. Not good at all.'

'I'm not too bothered about my reputation. It's my wife who's instigated this. She wants to marry someone else. I think I can live with it. And now that I don't have my wife's feelings, or her father's, to consider, there's even more reason to go back into the field and see some action as soon as possible.'

'I can see what you're saying there, Simmonds. Yes, I suppose if you're shortly to be a single man again, there's less of a reason to keep you out of harm's way. I'll tell you what. I'll have a word with General Heath this afternoon. See what he thinks. I'll revert to you as soon as I can.'

Charles left the office satisfied with the discussion and went back to his desk to pore over some Japanese telegrams that had been intercepted and translated. He felt the thrill of anticipation about the possibility, that was more of a probability now, of going back to join his unit. On a personal level, he was completely free to do so; no Louise and no General Daniels to worry about. But then his mind turned to Suria, to their chaste meetings and their growing friendship that meant more to him every time they met. How would she react to this news? It would probably mean they couldn't meet up as regularly, and once the invasion began, as it surely would soon, he would be directly in harm's way.

But then he told himself not to think that way, that it was arrogant of him in the extreme to assume that she shared his feelings or that she would worry about him. He needed to put it out of his mind.

Two days later, on the Wednesday afternoon, he left the Battlebox promptly after finishing work and took a taxi down to Chinatown. He'd been thinking about it all day with a warm glow of anticipation. He remembered how he'd almost kissed Suria the other evening when he'd brought her home during the drunken brawls, but had held back because of Louise. Now he didn't need to hold back, but maybe he should anyway. He didn't want to frighten Suria or to put her off. He knew she was devout and innocent and that she might not feel about him the way he felt about her.

The traffic in central Singapore was unusually light that afternoon and the taxi dropped him off in Chinatown early. He had half an hour or so to kill and didn't want to stand outside the go-down drawing attention to himself for that length of time. Instead, he wandered through the noisy, colourful streets, browsing the exotic wares displayed on the stalls and in shop windows, half thinking he might buy Suria something as a keepsake. He found a narrow alleyway off one of the main thoroughfares that was filled with gold dealers and jewellers shops. He peered in the windows, looking at the trinkets on display: earrings, rings, lockets. In one, his eyes alighted on a beautiful amber stone set in silver on a silver chain. He knew straight away that this was the one. He could picture it around Suria's delicate neck, looking beautiful against her creamy skin and dark features.

He went inside the shop and asked the man how quickly he could do an engraving.

'Five minutes, sir,' said the owner, smiling with black-ened teeth. 'What would you like?'

Charles scribbled the words "For Suria" on a piece of paper and waited inside the cramped, gloomy interior of the shop while the old man fixed magnifying glasses to his spectacles and took the amulet into his workshop at the back. A loud, grating sound ensued and after a few minutes the man returned, holding up the amulet with a triumphant smile.

The detour to the jewellers had made Charles a little late and Suria was already standing outside the go-down when Charles arrived, peering into the crowds looking for him.

'I'm so sorry I'm late,' he said rushing up to her. The anxiety in her eyes evaporated as she caught sight of him and she turned to him with a sweet smile.

'It doesn't matter. I have only been waiting for a few minutes.'

He slipped his arm through hers. 'Shall we go to Boat Quay as usual?' he asked.

'Yes, let's,' she said, but as they moved forward into the crowd a woman approached them. Her face was thunderous, her mouth scowling, her eyes narrowed. She barged in front of Suria and pushed her backwards.

'Hey!' Charles tried to get between them.

'I have warned you about getting friendly with Englishmen before!' the woman spat, prodding Suria's chest with a finger. 'No good can come of it. You will see!'

And then she was off, vanishing back into the crowd as quickly as she'd come.

'What was that about?' Charles asked, shaken at the venom behind the words. Suria was trembling, her face white. He put his arm around her shoulder.

'Are you alright? What was she talking about?'

But Suria didn't answer, just ducked her head and walked on. He could feel her shoulders shaking as they walked.

When they arrived at Boat Quay, they sat down at their

usual table with a view of the busy harbour. Charles called the waiter and asked for jasmine tea. He leaned forward to speak to Suria, still anxious that she looked pale and shocked.

'Perhaps we should go to a bar where they sell something stronger?' he suggested. 'It might help to calm you down.'

'No. I don't drink. I'll be alright.'

When the tea came he asked her again what it was all about.

'She's from our village on the mainland,' said Suria quietly. 'She's jealous of me and Amina. She always has been. We were all at school together. Her parents were very poor, but her father was a drinker, and her mother... well, her mother...' Suria paused, her eyes averted from his, struggling for the right words. 'She went with men for money. Choi is full of hatred and jealousy. She was very angry that you helped me get a job at Raffles.'

'Does she live in your go-down?'

Suria nodded. 'She's made our lives difficult since we arrived here. But accommodation is hard to come by in Singapore and when I was out of work there was no chance of finding anywhere else to live.'

'And now? You could surely find somewhere else now you have work?'

'Perhaps. But Amina is talking about going back to the village. She is worried about the Japanese invasion. She wants to be with her family if it happens.'

'She's right to worry. Have you thought about going home yourself?' He watched her face, waiting for her reply. Going back to her village, in a remote part of Malaya, would probably be far better for Suria than staying in the city, if war was coming, but at the same time he was terrified of losing her.

She shook her head. 'I need to work. There is no work in the village. My mother is ill, so I need to send money back to her each week. She needs to buy medicines.'

Of course, he knew that. 'But if Amina goes home, please tell me you will think about moving from the go-down. I hate to think of you there alone at the mercy of that spiteful woman.'

'Perhaps,' she said, and then fell silent. They watched the buzz of activity down on the boats in silence. Charles thought he should try to take her mind off the incident.

He asked how work had gone that week and she began to tell him of various things that had happened in the restaurant and kitchen, and gradually the colour returned to her cheeks and the sparkle to her eyes and after a while it was as if everything was back to normal. She asked him about his week and although he racked his brains, there was little of interest he could tell her about work since everything he was working on was classified.

'Have you heard from Mrs Simmonds?' Suria asked with a sideways look.

Charles took a deep breath. 'As a matter of fact, she wrote to me this week.'

'Is she coming back soon?' Suria's eyes were steady, but he could tell that she was curious about the answer.

He shook his head. 'Actually, she won't be coming back at all. She's asked for a divorce. She's met someone else in India who she wants to marry.'

Suria's eyes widened. 'I'm so sorry for you,' she said. 'You must be very sad.'

'Don't be sorry for me. Things weren't right between us

for a long time. It's probably best for both of us in the long run.'

She was silent for a time, digesting the news. He watched her face, wondering what she was thinking.

'I'm probably going to change jobs now,' he told her and she looked at him with interest.

'I'm hoping to go back to my unit soon, so that I can fight if there's an invasion.'

'But you might get hurt,' she said.

'Perhaps. But I'm well trained, and it's why I joined the army. I don't want to be stuck in an office.'

'I understand,' she said, but he could see that she looked troubled.

'Would you still come to see me?' she asked after a time.

'If I was stationed in Singapore, I'm sure I could. If they send me onto the mainland though, it might be difficult.'

'Oh,' she said, disappointment in her tone, but she didn't protest or attempt to dissuade him. All she said was, 'I would miss our meetings.'

She looked straight into his eyes as she said that, and in them he saw the strength of her feeling. It made his heart beat faster as he hadn't been sure before, but now he could see that her feelings matched his own. He slid his hand over hers on the table and she didn't draw hers away.

The conversation moved on and she spoke of the village again and how her mother had been sick for years now. It was clear that she felt a strong love and loyalty for her family and that her mother's illness had affected her deeply.

'That's why I came here and that's why I need to stay, whatever happens,' she said.

'But it might not be safe if the Japanese invade,' he said. 'You would be better off in your village.'

'Do you think it will happen?' she asked, anxiety in her voice.

'Almost certainly, but I'm not sure when. It could be in several months, it could be next week.'

He suddenly felt anxious for her, living in that squalid go-down, working in a place that was one of the landmarks of British rule and would surely be a target for bombers or an invading army. How selfish he'd been to even contemplate his own feelings in this context. Of course she would be better off in her village, away from the main targets of Japanese aggression. He wondered if there was a way he could ensure her safety.

'Would you go home to your village if you could be sure your mother had enough medicine?'

She smiled. 'I would think about it, but that's not going to happen. We are poor. My father works in a mine and sends very little money home. My brother is a fisherman and doesn't earn much money.'

Charles hesitated for a moment, wondering how to broach the idea that had just come to him. He cleared his throat.

'How would you feel if I offered to send money to your mother for her medicines? Would you be prepared to go home then?'

Her eyes widened with surprise and instantly she frowned and slid her hand away from his.

'I can't accept charity. I need to earn my own money,' she said, drawing herself up to sit stiffly, her voice cold.

'I'm sorry,' he said quickly, regretting having mentioned it, but at the same time wondering what he could do to help her and her family.

Conversation was difficult for the next few minutes. Charles found himself introducing subject after subject, but meeting a wall of resistance. He thought about returning to the issue of her mother's illness and apologising again for being insensitive, but realised that could make things worse. But gradually, as he persisted, and asked her to tell him about her friend, Amina, she began to relax. She clearly loved her friend and told Charles some anecdotes from their schooldays and how close they'd been.

'It was Amina's idea to come to Singapore. I would never have dared to do it on my own, or even thought of it. She is so outgoing. It was her who found us both jobs in the Ford Factory, her who found us accommodation.'

'You must be very close,' said Charles and Suria nodded.

'I would really miss her if she does decide to go home. But I wouldn't blame her at all.'

Charles judged that the moment was right and he produced the amulet from his pocket.

'I bought this for you,' he said, handing it to her. 'I hope you don't mind. I'd like you to keep it. As a token of our friendship. So, if in the future I have to go away to fight, it will be a keepsake from these meetings of ours.'

Suria took the delicate amulet from him and held it up to look at it.

'It's beautiful,' she said. 'Really beautiful. No one has ever given me anything like this before. Thank you. I'll treasure it, always.'

She unclipped the clasp and put it round her neck, fastening it into place.

'How does it look?'

'It looks... beautiful,' he said, admiring the way the colour picked up the tone of her skin, her deep brown eyes and black hair. It looked almost as he'd imagined it would, only more stunning.

Later, they walked back to her building arm in arm and

she put her head on his shoulder affectionately as she'd never done before. As they said goodbye, he decided to take the plunge. He kissed her on the lips and to his surprise and pleasure she returned the kiss briefly and shyly, before breaking away and running up the steps into the go-down.

15

CHARLES

Singapore, 1941

Colonel Cotton eventually confirmed to Charles that he would be able to re-join his regiment, India III Corps, but that he would need to travel to Kuala Lumpur to lead the unit assigned him. He would also be required to serve a fortnight further in the Battlebox while they found someone to replace him. Charles had mixed feelings about this news. He had anticipated being placed in one of the Indian Army units that were stationed on Singapore Island, so it was a surprise that he had to go to Kuala Lumpur. His immediate thought was that it would be difficult for him to see Suria, but he reminded himself that if he'd managed to persuade her to go back to her village, that would have been impossible anyway. His heart sank though, as he contemplated a further two weeks atrophying behind a desk; he couldn't wait for the final order to come. In those last couple of weeks, decoded Japanese telegrams crossed his desk that showed Japanese troops were massing on Hainan Island off Indochina. This made him even more certain that the invasion would happen in a matter of weeks, or even days.

The knowledge made him increasingly anxious for Suria's safety, especially as he was aware that he would have to leave Singapore soon with no idea as to when he might be able to return. They met as usual each Wednesday and it was becoming clear now to him that she shared and reciprocated his growing feelings. She would take his hand as they walked through Chinatown together, look longingly into his eyes and hold his hand over the table as they talked in the café. Now, she always returned his kisses passionately at the end of each evening.

He was gratified to see that she wore the amulet each time they met.

'It looks beautiful on you,' he said admiringly during one of their meetings.

'I wear it all the time, Charles.'

'Even at work? I thought they were strict about the uniform at Raffles?'

'Well, they are. I wore it for a few days last week, but yesterday the housekeeper noticed it and asked me to take it off. But the funny thing was, we had a staff photo taken last week and I was wearing it then. When she sees that when the photograph is developed she won't be pleased.'

Suria laughed, her eyes lighting up with mischief. Her laugh was infectious and Charles couldn't help joining in.

But as his feelings deepened, he became more and more worried for Suria's safety. He tried to tell her of his fears, but each time he began to speak to her about it, he was met with a brick wall of resistance. She would set her jaw in its defiant line and repeat what she always said;

'I've told you, Charles, I can't afford to go back to my village. My mother needs the money I earn here. There are no jobs for me back in the village. And anyway, Singapore is meant to be a fortress, isn't it? Surely all those British troops here aren't going to let the Japanese just walk in here and take over, are they?'

'They will do their best, but the Japanese are formidable opponents. Nothing can be guaranteed. You'd be far safer hidden away on the mainland in your village with your family. Your friend knows it's true, doesn't she?'

Suria looked down at the table and then admitted that Amina had left for the mainland only the previous afternoon.

'Why didn't you tell me?' Charles asked, his anxiety mounting.

'I did tell you that she was thinking of going.'

'Yes, but not that she had a date fixed. You could have gone with her. Did she try to persuade you?'

'She knew I wouldn't go, so she didn't try very hard. And you're not listening to me, Charles. I can't just leave here,' she said leaning forward and looking into his eyes. 'I need to work. My family depends upon me. Why can't you respect that?'

'I do respect that. Of course I do. But I'm worried for you. And now Amina has gone home, you will be on your own, at the mercy of that crazy woman in your go-down.'

'I can deal with her. She's just a bully. Please. Don't waste your time worrying about me.'

Reluctantly, he dropped the subject and they talked of other things, but all evening it preoccupied him. He was wondering if there was any way of persuading her to leave. He couldn't let it go, and as he sensed the evening was drawing to a close, he returned to the issue of Suria going back to her village.

She rolled her eyes with impatience at his words.

'I only say it because I'm worried for you,' he protested. 'Especially as I will have to leave here myself in less than a fortnight.'

She looked at him with surprise and pain in her eyes then.

'Leave here? Where are you going?'

'To KL. That's where my regiment is stationed. I told you I wanted to go back into active service. I didn't realise they would post me away, but I can't refuse to go. I'm not sure if I'll be able to get back to Singapore that easily.'

'Oh, Charles. I *will* miss our meetings,' she said.

'I will too. It's meant everything to me these past few months. Look, whenever I can get back, I will. And whatever happens, if there *is* a war, I will come back to Singapore and find you afterwards.'

She felt for his hand on the table and he could see tears standing in her eyes.

'Why don't we go out somewhere different next Wednesday?' he asked, thinking that it would be fitting to mark the occasion. 'It will be our last outing. Have you ever been to the Great World Amusement Park? It's not far from Chinatown.'

She shook her head. 'Amina and I always wanted to go, but it is a little expensive. We made do with the Botanical Gardens instead.'

'Well, I will treat you. I haven't been either, but people say it is well worth a visit. There are apparently some fantastic sights there; magicians, ghost trains, shooting galleries and fairground rides, even Chinese opera, and lots of food stalls and places to eat and drink.'

'I would love that,' she said, her eyes shining.

'Shall we meet outside it then? Next Wednesday at five

o'clock? I could go there straight from work so we have more time.'

'Yes, let's. It's not far from where I live.'

At the end of the evening, after kissing her goodbye outside the go-down, Charles watched Suria walk up the steps and turn and wave to him from the entrance. She was smiling, but his heart twisted with pity, imagining what might be in store for her when she got upstairs, at the mercy of the aggressive woman, Choi.

As he strolled back through Chinatown, amongst the thronging evening crowds, he wondered if there might in fact be some way of relieving Suria's financial burden. Perhaps, he wondered, if he were to send her mother some money anonymously, she would accept it and Suria would have no further need to work in Singapore. He walked on, deep in thought, dodging rickshaws and men wheeling sack-barrows laden with goods. But he had no idea of the name of Suria's village, let alone where her mother might live, or even what the mother's name was. He didn't even know Suria's own full name. But then, strolling past a fruit stall, an idea came to him and he was so struck with it that he stopped in the middle of the road, narrowly missing colliding with a boy carrying a basket of oranges on his head.

In the morning, he told Smythe he had an errand to run and called a taxi to take him from the Battlebox at Fort Canning into town. It was a short journey, but it was a hot day with the sun high in the sky and he didn't want to be away from his desk for too long. As the taxi sped through the colonial district, he looked out at the tree-lined roads, the beautifully proportioned buildings, the manicured grass of the Padang, and he couldn't help feeling a twinge of sadness that all this peace and beauty might soon be swept away by a violent conflict. As the taxi swung onto Beach Road with its line of majestic palm trees bordering the front of the great hotel, he found it almost impossible to believe.

He was dropped outside the entrance to Raffles, and as the doorman opened the front door for him, he glanced over at the cloakroom counter, making sure that Suria wasn't on duty there today. He was almost sure that if he avoided the restaurant, he wouldn't bump into her.

The receptionists greeted him by name and with welcoming smiles.

'What can we do for you? Would you like to book a table, Major Simmonds?'

'Not today. If possible, I'd like to speak to the housekeeper.'

A bellboy guided him through the maze of service corridors at the back of the hotel, where the ceilings were lower and the paintwork not as pristine as in the guest areas. The boy stopped at a door marked "Housekeeper" and gestured for him to knock and enter.

The housekeeper was pleased to see him, ingratiating even. She stood up and held out her hand.

'Major Simmonds, what a very nice surprise! Do take a seat. What can I do for you today? You are aware, aren't you, that we employed the young lady you recommended? She has proved an excellent and trustworthy employee in the short time she has been here.'

'Oh yes. And I understand she is very grateful for the opportunity you have afforded her, as am I.'

The housekeeper beamed and looked at him enquiringly.

'As a matter of fact, it is about the same young lady that I'm here today. I understand that her mother is ill. I would like to send a gift to her village, but I'm afraid I'm unaware of her address. Would you happen to have it?'

'Of course, Major Simmonds,' the woman said smoothly. 'We always ask for addresses of family when people are engaged. I have it right here.'

She thumbed through an index box on her desk and pulled out a card.

'Here it is,' she said. 'I will write it down for you.'

She scribbled something on a piece of paper which she handed to him. He glanced down at the address which was in Kuala Lapah, near Desaru.

'And her mother's name?' he asked and the woman hesitated and frowned slightly. He realised that asking such a question sounded strange, and that the woman would be thinking that he should already know the mother's name if he was a family friend, as he'd told her when he enquired about a job for Suria. It was odd enough that he didn't know the family's address. But he brazened it out by looking straight at the woman, not taking his eyes away from hers. She looked down at the card.

'Fatima,' she said. 'Fatima Ismail.'

He thanked her and got up to leave. 'Oh, and by the way,' he said as he left, 'I'd be grateful if you kept this to yourself. I intend the gift to be anonymous.'

'Of course,' the woman murmured, getting up to shake his hand, with a puzzled frown on her face.

Charles rushed back through corridors to the entrance of the hotel, again hoping Suria hadn't spotted him. A taxi was waiting on the drive and he asked to be taken to the Fullerton Building on the banks of the Singapore river. The post office was housed at one end of that imposing, pillared building, and Charles slipped inside under its grand portico and bought a postal order for seventy-five dollars. He was aware that Suria probably earned less than a third of that sum each month and he wanted to be sure that the amount would last her mother for several months. He then bought an envelope and a stamp and mailed the order there and then to Puan Fatima Ismail in Kuala Lapah.

The next day he received orders to join his unit in Kuala Lumpur along with details of the transport that would take him there in ten days' time. He realised that it would give him time to say goodbye to Suria properly and to see her at least twice. Work was getting busier, with more intelligence flooding into the Battlebox, revealing manoeuvres taking place on Hainan Island, and the Japanese warships arriving there. He found himself busy over the next few days; drawn into meetings analysing the latest intelligence and discussing tactics. Despite his previous aversion to desk work, he found himself enjoying the pressure and excitement during those last days.

He spent the evenings packing up his belongings in the bungalow on the base. Some of Louise's clothes still hung in the wardrobe, so he asked her amah to pack them up and send them on to Peshawar. Even as he did so, he wondered if they would ever arrive at their destination, but there was no real alternative. She had written to him twice since that first letter, asking for his response to her request for a divorce. He knew he should write back, but every time he sat down to do so, his bitterness surfaced and he found himself writing things that he knew he would regret. He would screw the letter into a ball and throw it in the bin. He just wanted to put it all behind him and move on with his life. He was glad to be leaving this bungalow, with its echoes of Louise and their mutual unhappiness.

The next Wednesday came around quickly and he left work early and walked along River Valley Road towards the

Great World Amusement Park. He was glad he hadn't taken a taxi, it was good to stretch his legs and relax. He was looking forward to seeing Suria's face light up when they met, then tucking his arm in hers and striding into the park. He wondered if her mother would have told Suria about the postal order. If so, he hoped to be able to persuade her that she should now think about leaving the island.

The road was busy, so full of people pressing towards the park that the traffic was choked and crawled along at walking pace. He pushed his way through the crowd until he saw the white gates up ahead with Chinese lettering on the archway and the words Great World Amusement Park in English above them.

Keeping an eye out for Suria, he queued in front of the ticket booth and bought entrance tickets for two. By the time he'd done that it was ten past five. He resumed his place beside the pillar, scanning the crowds for her face. She was normally very punctual. Perhaps she was late because of the crowds, or perhaps she'd got lost or underestimated the distance.

The place was thronging; families, couples, groups of young people barged past him. The steamy air was thick with the smell of candy floss and ice cream. From inside the park he heard the loudspeaker announcement, 'Roll up, roll up. See the world's fattest man,' and later, 'See the daredevil tightrope walker,' and 'watch a lady being sliced in half...'

Charles grew more and more anxious. Wherever could she be? Had that woman, Choi, done something to prevent her from coming? He went over and over their last conversation, wondering whether he'd misunderstood their agreement to meet here. Had she expected him to turn up at the go-down after all? No, he was sure that they'd agreed to meet here.

He paced up and down in front of the entrance, dodging the crowds moving in and out of the park, all the time growing hotter and more anxious. He realised after a time that he'd been waiting there an hour. The sun was going down now, the golden strip of sky growing bigger and brighter as it dropped towards the horizon, the sky turning dusty pink with grey clouds dotted around. Finally the golden strip burned fiercely for a few moments before vanishing below the horizon. Within a few minutes it was dark, but the area around the gate was brightly lit with fairy lights and street lamps.

With one last look around him, Charles left the gateway behind and set off down River Valley Road in the direction he'd come from. His thoughts were spinning all over the place, imagining all sorts of reasons why Suria hadn't come. He'd made up his mind to head to the go-down to see if she was still there, but as he walked, pushing his way back through the still advancing crowds, a dreadful thought occurred to him. Perhaps she hadn't got held up, got lost or been delayed by Choi; perhaps it was deliberate and she had taken a conscious decision not to meet him that evening.

16

LARA

Singapore, 2000

L ara was transfixed, staring at the old staff photograph on the wall in the Long Bar in Raffles Hotel. She was dimly aware of the hubbub of the evening carrying on all around her; the jazz music in the background, the chatter of the guests, but she felt as though she'd gone into a time-warp. The photograph, in fading black and white, with those long-gone faces peering at the camera, transported her back to the 1940s. She lost track of time, drawn into the scene, completely captivated by it, when she felt someone touch her shoulder. Startled, she turned to see Christian Henderson standing behind her, a concerned expression on his face.

'Everything OK?' he asked.

'Sorry,' she said. 'I was just looking at these old photos.'

'You look pale,' he said. 'You've had a hell of a shock today. Would you like me to walk you home, or can I call a taxi?'

'It's not the thing with Alex,' she said. 'It's this photo.'

Christian's eyes followed her gaze to the photograph of the group.

'I think this woman here might be my grandmother.'

She pointed to the woman in the photograph. He peered at it closely.

'Do you really? How's that?' he asked.

'She's wearing the amulet that I found with my mother's papers. Sister Xavier told me that the amulet was found with my mother when she was left in the storm drain as a baby.'

Lara reached in her bag and drew the amulet out for Christian to look at. He took it from her and held it up to the light, examining it closely.

'Wow. It does look remarkably similar to the one in the photograph,' Christian said. 'But do you think it would have been an unusual piece of jewellery at that time?'

'I'm not sure,' said Lara. 'But it's not just that, it's the woman's face. She looks exactly like my mother. Look,' she said, pulling out the photograph of Nell that she always carried in her purse. It was a portrait, taken when Nell was in her twenties. She sat stiffly, in her starched nurse's uniform, her face set and serious. Christian nodded as he peered at it; the high cheekbones, the shape of the face, the full lips and the almond-shaped eyes.

'You're right. They could be the same woman,' he said.

'I'm wondering if someone at the hotel might be able to tell me something about the photograph. Perhaps they've got a list of the people in it somewhere?'

'We could go to reception and ask. But it's doubtful, isn't it? It's such a long time ago. Before the Japanese invasion even.'

'It's a longshot, I know, but I need to find out what I can.'

They wandered through to the front of the hotel and

into the reception area with its galleries reaching up to the roof of the building. The man on the desk was polite and tried to be helpful but knew nothing about the old photographs in the bar. Disappointed, they were just about to leave, when an older man came out from an office behind the desk. The receptionist signalled to Lara to wait a moment.

'If you bear with me,' he said, 'I will just speak to the concierge. He has been here many years and might know something about the photographs.'

When the two men had finished conferring, the concierge came out from behind the desk and approached Lara and Christian.

'I understand you are interested in the photograph in the bar of some of our restaurant staff from the 1940s,' he said.

'I think my grandmother might be in it,' Lara replied. 'I know she was in Singapore during the war and it certainly looks like her.'

The man nodded, 'I started working here in the 1970s, he said, and there are a few of the staff who worked here during the war years who are still alive. In particular, there's old Aziz, who worked as a bellboy here in the hotel. He started working here as a teenager in the early forties and carried on until he was in his late sixties. He is in excellent health and still comes to visit us. He sometimes pops in when it's quiet in the afternoons. Sometimes on a Monday or a Tuesday. Would you like me to give him your details? I'm sure he'd be only too happy to help you.'

'That would be great,' Lara said, smiling broadly. She wrote her name and the address of her guest house on a notepad on the desk, together with her mobile phone number.

As they walked towards the exit she said to Christian, 'It's a bit of a longshot. And who knows when the old man might turn up. It could be weeks. I'm not sure I can stay in Singapore that long.'

'Well, let's see, shall we? Today is Friday, so with luck, you'll only have a couple of days to wait.'

Lara suddenly felt the weariness of the day descend on her. So much had happened since she'd got up that morning, she could scarcely take it all in. Was it only a few hours before that she'd awoken in her room in the hostel and started phoning round the orphanages in search of news of what had happened to Nell when Our Lady orphanage had closed? She'd discovered St Theresa's and Sister Xavier and all the new information the old lady had been able to tell her about Nell and Suria; then there had been the shock of the news about Alex and Chloe, and finally, the surprise of seeing the picture in the bar. Her mind was reeling with everything that had happened and exhaustion was threatening to overcome her.

She felt Christian's eyes on her face.

'You look bush-wacked,' he said with a sympathetic smile. 'I'll find a taxi,' and he went out onto the forecourt ahead of her. Lara followed, glad that he was taking charge of the situation, that he'd been there to keep her company that evening and that he would be there to help her when she had to give her statement to the Singapore police about Alex and Chloe.

She followed him outside and slid gratefully onto the back seat of a taxi beside him. She fell asleep on his shoulder as the taxi swung out of Raffles and headed down Beach Road.

∾

THE NEXT MORNING Lara awoke late and all the memories of the day before came crowding back. She remembered that Christian had said he would collect her at eleven to take her to the police station. It was almost ten now. She couldn't believe how long she'd slept. She showered quickly and dressed carefully in her skirt and blouse, wanting to look as smart as she could for a visit to the police station, even applying lipstick and mascara. Then she went down to the little café on the ground floor and ordered coffee and toast. She thought about her father; it was a couple of days since she'd called him. He didn't have a mobile phone, so she had to pick times when he would be at home. Calls were expensive, so she tried to limit them to two or three times a week, but she worried about him, all alone in the cottage, grieving for her mother and missing her. She made a mental note to call him later. She needed to tell him about her discoveries about Nell and Suria. She already knew she wouldn't be telling him anything about Alex and Chloe; she didn't want to worry him.

At eleven, she was waiting in reception when Christian arrived. He had a taxi waiting outside, and she slid into the back seat, just as on the previous evening. She remembered how she'd fallen asleep on his shoulder, and felt her face going hot at the memory; he seemed to be very kind and thoughtful, but after all, she hardly knew him. This morning, she took care to sit well apart from him.

Once out of Chinatown, the route took them along fast-moving dual carriageways between modern apartment blocks and shopping centres. Lara stared out at the modern city. Even though it was built up, everywhere she looked there was evidence of tropical greenery; trees in the middle of the carriageway, greenery in the lush gardens of the apartment blocks. She was struck how new everywhere was.

It must have been very different in her grandmother's day, and even in Nell's youth, as she grew up in the fifties and early sixties. The area that she was travelling through now, might well have still been jungle in the 1940s. Suria probably wouldn't recognise the place if she were to come here now.

The taxi turned off the main road, drove up through some parkland and up a steep, tree-lined hill and stopped in front of a long, imposing khaki and cream-coloured building that could have been mistaken for a warehouse.

'This is Pearl's Hill Police HQ,' said Christian.

She felt her stomach tighten with nerves as Christian ushered her inside through double doors. She knew she'd done nothing wrong herself, but any contact with authority, especially so far from home, felt threatening somehow. She took some deep breaths and tried to calm herself as she walked beside Christian along the never-ending tiled corridors. She couldn't help bringing to mind the television programmes she'd seen about backpackers getting into trouble abroad.

'There's nothing to worry about,' Christian said, as if he sensed what she was feeling. 'All they want is a statement from you. No one's going to interview you or cross-examine you. We'll be out of here in an hour at the most.'

They went into an interview room and a police officer in a smart navy uniform with lapels and silver buttons took a statement from her. He asked her to describe every detail from her first meeting with Alex and Chloe, down to the very last phone call when he'd asked her to get cash out to buy him a flight to Australia. He wrote it all down painstakingly slowly and a couple of times he looked up at her when she told him something particular, that made her think he didn't believe her. It seemed to take an age, but when she and Christian finally returned along the corridor she realised they had been in the station less than an hour.

There was another taxi waiting for them and Christian asked the driver to take them back to Chinatown.

'I was wondering,' he said, as the taxi sped back along the freeway, 'what you're doing for the next couple of days?'

'I haven't thought really,' she said. 'I'm at a bit of a loss now. It seems odd to say this, but I was beginning to rely on Alex for company. Until yesterday that is. And there'll definitely be no contact from the old man from Raffles until at least Monday, if at all.'

'Would you like to come on a road trip? I have a motorbike. It might be fun.'

She turned to look at him and for the first time he appeared a little unsure of himself. Was this wise? She hardly knew this man, and yet she felt she was already growing to like and trust him. But she'd trusted Alex and that had ended badly. Could she rely on her own instincts anymore?

'Don't you have work to do?' she asked.

'It's Saturday. What do you think?' He looked so eager, his smile so open and friendly.

She smiled back as she relented. 'I'd love to. I hope you're safe on a motorbike though, I'm sure I'll be a nervous passenger.'

'Is there anywhere you'd like to go in particular?' he asked.

She shrugged. 'I'm not sure. I don't really know what there is to see. All I've seen is city so far. Is there any countryside anywhere in Singapore?'

Christian thought for a moment, then said. 'I think we should go to Pulau Ubin. It's a separate island, to the east of Singapore. But it's like stepping back in time. There are still traditional villages there built of wood, houses on stilts. The whole place is unspoilt – a nature reserve with untamed jungle.'

'That sounds great,' she said.

An hour later Lara found herself sitting on the back of a powerful motorbike, her arms wrapped tightly around Christian, clinging to him for dear life as they sped along the freeway to Changi Ferrypoint. She hadn't realised how terrifying this would be, or how exhilarating in equal measure. She told herself to relax; that he was an experienced rider, that he wouldn't let her come to any harm, but she couldn't help her nerves swooping and diving as they rounded bends at an angle, or sped through a gap between two speeding cars.

At Changi point, a quiet jetty overlooking an expanse of sea, there were several old blue and white painted ferries lined up, waiting to take passengers. Christian secured the motorbike, they bought tickets from a booth and boarded one of the boats that looked almost full. Christian explained that ferries to Pulau Ubin departed once they had twelve people on board, so there was no set timetable.

'We could be waiting a long time, then,' said Lara, but after about five minutes a bus drew up and several people came on board from it and sat down on the rough wooden benches. The skipper powered up the throaty engines and they were off.

The journey over to the island across Serangoon Harbour only took ten minutes or so. They passed fishing boats and pleasure craft moored up in the harbour. Ferries going in the other direction crossed with them, belching out black smoke. At one point their boat had to slow down to allow a huge, lumbering cargo ship to pass in front of it as it headed out to sea. Lara smiled at Christian. It was good to be out on the water, away from the city with its busy roads and gleaming skyscrapers, to feel the wind in her hair, heading to a place where the pace of life was slower and gentler.

The boat docked at a wooden pier in a small village. To one side of the pier was a rocky beach fringed with palm trees, and behind the beach, a row of simple wooden houses on stilts. Locals sat on their porches watching the world go by, or fished from the dilapidated pier. On the other side of the pier was a mangrove swamp, where the remains of former jetties lay rotting in the mud. Chickens pecked around in the dirt and dogs lazed in the afternoon sun.

They hired mountain bikes from a shop at the end of the pier and set off to explore the island. They were soon out of the village, riding along a dirt track through dense jungle and abandoned rubber plantations. Soon they came to a lake surrounded by coconut palms and tropical undergrowth, its surface dotted with pink flowering waterlilies. They stopped to admire the beauty, and as they did so, a flock of white birds lifted from the surface.

'It's an old quarry,' Christian explained. 'They took granite from here to build the causeway from Singapore to Johor in the nineteenth century. There are a few of them on the island.'

'It's beautiful,' said Lara. 'This whole island is beautiful. Thanks so much for bringing me here.'

'I suppose it's a taste of what life might have been like in parts of Singapore fifty or so years ago,' Christian replied.

Lara thought of Suria then. Had she lived somewhere like this during her childhood?

'My grandmother came from a fishing village,' she said.

'Where was that?' Christian asked.

'Somewhere near Desaru on the east coast of Malaysia.

At least that's what Sister Xavier told me yesterday. I don't know for sure, and I've no idea of the name of the village.'

'Desaru?' said Christian. 'That's not too far at all. I could take you there if you like. We could go tomorrow if you don't have other plans.'

'Oh, that's very kind of you, but I couldn't trouble you to do that.'

She noticed the way his skin wrinkled at the side of his eyes when he smiled and couldn't help but smile back. She gave herself a shake. This was moving too quickly by far. Hadn't she learned her lesson with Alex?

'Look, I'm not sure why you're being so generous to me,' she said. 'I don't really deserve your kindness.'

'Why do you say that?' he asked. 'And I'm not being kind. I'm enjoying your company.'

'But you don't have to look after me, Christian. I've been an idiot, trusting Alex. There's no need for you to take pity on me.'

'Look, you weren't the only one who got taken in by him, by the pair of them, in fact. Don't blame yourself. He's a professional fraudster, why would you have seen that coming? I did feel sorry for you, of course. Especially when they targeted you in KL. They actually followed you from the airport. Did you know that? But I don't feel sorry for you anymore. I can see how strong you are. Anyone would have got taken in by them.'

'So you were watching even then?' She thought back to the ride on the airport bus into Kuala Lumpur and a chill went through her to think that Chloe and Alex had targeted her at the airport and followed her into town. That's obviously why they were staying at the same hotel. She'd been captivated by the scenery on that bus ride, the mile upon mile of oil palms lining the route, the startling blue of the sky and the bright green of the trees had fascinated her. She hadn't paid any attention to her fellow passengers.

'Yep. I followed them since they left Thailand. I felt sorry for you in KL. You looked so alone, and you just walked straight into their trap... but there was something else, too.'

She looked at him, frowning. 'Something else?'

'Yes. I found myself being drawn to you. There was something about you. Some sort of determination shining through, inner strength perhaps. I can't describe it. Seeing how they were deceiving you, it made my resolve to nail them even stronger.'

Lara felt the colour creeping into her cheeks and looked down at her handlebars.

'I'm sorry. I've embarrassed you now,' he said. 'I didn't mean to. Shall we ride on? There's lots to see and the last boat goes back to Changi at six.'

They carried on pedalling through the jungle, glimpsing blue sea and sky through gaps in the trees, sometimes passing stilt houses grouped beside the water, sometimes patches of white, sandy beaches. At one point they found a wooden observation tower and climbed to the top, above the jungle canopy and gazed out over the trees towards the glittering sea to the mainland beyond. Later they found a wooden walkway that took them out over the sea so they could walk along beside the beach, watching the waves lapping at the rocks and the wind swaying the palm trees at the edge of the sand.

They rode on and came to a café, housed in a wooden hut adjacent to someone's home. A woman brought them fried fish and rice and Coca-Cola.

'I'm sorry I embarrassed you back there,' Christian said as they ate.

'Don't worry about it. I just feel a little wary at the

moment,' she said. 'Not in the mood to trust someone new, if you know what I mean.'

'The thing is,' he said leaning forward and looking into her eyes; she noticed that his were brown and flecked with hazel. 'I feel as though I already know you. I know it sounds stupid, but all those days following you and watching out for you, seeing how those parasites tricked you, I felt as though you were someone I knew. Someone I had to look out for. Does that sound ridiculous to you?'

She shook her head. 'Not ridiculous at all. It's just an odd situation, I suppose. You have known me longer than I've known you. I've got some catching up to do.'

He laughed. 'That is true. And I understand that the whole thing with Alex will have knocked your confidence sideways.'

'It's not just that,' she said, staring down at the table. 'Something happened at home too. My last boyfriend...'

Then it all came out in a rush; how she'd met Joe, thrown up everything and moved in with him. How her mother had refused to speak to her for the last two years of her life, and how Joe had used her and betrayed her, shortly before her mother's death. How it had all left her bruised and reeling.

'I'm so sorry to hear that. How awful for you. No wonder you are wary. Especially after what happened with Alex.'

They cycled back to the ferry pier and took the last boat back to Changi. The sun was going down as the old ferry chugged across the harbour and the light took on a brilliant quality, where everything around seemed to be illuminated in sharper focus. Lara felt a sense of peace overcoming her, looking round at the magical scenery. She felt calm for the first time since she'd come here.

As he dropped her off outside her guest house, Christian said,

'Would you like to go to Desaru tomorrow?'

'I'm not sure,' she said. 'Maybe that could wait for a bit. I think I'll probably just have a quiet day.'

She could tell from his expression that he was disappointed, but he simply said,

'OK. I could maybe take a day off next week. I've built up a lot of leave.'

'Yes, perhaps,' she said. 'Thank you so much for today. It's been great.'

'No problem. I'll be in touch.'

She watched him speed off down Temple Street, feeling a little guilty about not accepting his offer for the following day. But her inner caution had got the better of her. If he was serious and genuine, he would understand her reticence and ask again.

With a sigh she went inside and asked at the desk for her key.

'There is a message for you, Miss Adams,' the receptionist said and handed her a note.

Frowning, she opened it.

Dear Miss Adams,

I called at Raffles today. The concierge gave me a message that you'd like to speak about your grandmother who worked in the hotel in the 1940s. I can tell you what I remember, if that will help. Please meet me in the hotel reception tomorrow morning at 11am.

Yours,

Aziz Soma

17

CHARLES

Singapore, December 1941

Charles paced away from the Great World Amusement Park, pushing through the advancing crowds, his spirits at rock bottom. His mind was spinning with possibilities as to why Suria hadn't come to meet him as arranged. It was so unlike her to be even a minute late, that he was convinced something must have happened to stop her from coming. Had she had to go into work on her day off? Had she mistaken the day or the time of their meeting? Had the crazy woman in the go-down finally got to her, perhaps even attacked Suria physically? Or had Suria set off to meet him, but had had an accident on the way? There was also a further possibility; that it had been a deliberate decision of hers not to come and that she'd decided not to see him again. But what could have prompted her to make such a decision? He thought back to the passionate way she'd returned his kisses the last time they'd said goodbye, one short week ago, and the way she'd looked into his eyes as they sat at their familiar table in the café on Boat Quay that evening.

When he was clear of the crowds, he waved down a taxi and asked to be taken to Suria's go-down near Chinatown. The crowds of shoppers and pedestrians were thick as the taxi nosed its way through the narrow streets. Charles noticed many uniformed British and Australian soldiers milling about on the walkways, spilling out of bars and restaurants. At least they looked relatively peaceful that evening, in contrast to the night of the riots.

At the go-down he walked up the steps to the entrance, thinking he would ask around amongst the occupants to find out if Suria was upstairs. There was a Chinese man sitting on a stool by the door. He looked up at Charles inquiringly.

'I've come to see one of the residents. Suria. Suria Ismail,' he said.

'She not here,' said the man, bringing the betel nut he was chewing to the front of his mouth and releasing a string of red spittle on the steps beside Charles' feet.

'You know her then?'

The man nodded.

'I know her. But she not here.'

'Do you know where she's gone?' Charles asked.

The man shrugged.

'She not live here any more,' he said in a flat voice.

Charles stared at him. The noise and clamour of the quarter crowded in on him; the honking of horns, the ringing of bicycle bells, the cries of hawkers, the discordant music blaring from loudspeakers outside a nearby shop.

'Do you know where she's gone? When did she leave?' he asked finally finding his tongue again.

The man shrugged and spat another stream of betel juice on the steps.

'A few day ago.'

'And do you know where she went?'

The man turned and looked straight at him now. In his eyes was a look of loathing for Charles coupled with extreme disinterest in his questions.

'I not know.'

Charles was about to leave when someone emerged from the door of the go-down. He recognised that stomping walk and wild-eyed look in an instant. It was Choi. When she noticed him standing there, she lunged towards him.

'If you're after your fancy woman, she isn't here,' she shouted. 'You should be ashamed of yourself carrying on with a Malay girl. You should leave us alone. You British are finished here.'

Charles tried to ignore the aggression in her tone.

'Do you know where she's gone?'

'How would I know? I used to tell her what I thought and she couldn't take it. One evening she upped and left.'

Charles retreated down the steps and walked back through Chinatown until he reached a main road where he flagged down a taxi and asked the driver to take him back to the army base. He didn't want to stay out alone feeling as he did. He knew he would have headed to a bar and drunk himself senseless.

Back at the bungalow, he took the whisky decanter and a glass out onto the veranda. He sat in the flickering light of a Tilley lamp being dive-bombed by fireflies and mosquitoes and drowned his sorrows. He'd been expecting to eat at a food stall at the Great World and hadn't eaten anything since lunchtime, so the alcohol went straight to his head. As he sat there miserable and alone, he thought about Suria and about what Choi had said. Perhaps there was some truth in her words? Perhaps he shouldn't be pursuing a young Malay woman, so far apart from him in status and wealth. It was an unequal relationship from the start and he knew that but had tried to ignore it.

Despite those nagging doubts, he wondered where she'd gone. Perhaps she'd relented and gone back to the village after all, as he'd been encouraging her to do, but if so, why hadn't she let him know, why hadn't she said goodbye? He thought back over all the times they'd spent together. There was nothing in what she'd ever said that would lead him to suspect she would leave without saying goodbye. After she'd forgiven him for getting her dismissed and accepted that his offers of help were motivated by kindness, she'd been nothing but sweet and friendly towards him and, in more recent weeks, she'd been quite loving. He couldn't reconcile the way she'd been with him recently with the way she'd left without saying goodbye. It didn't stack up.

It was after midnight when he staggered inside to bed. Ali was waiting respectfully in the drawing room, his hands behind his back, his brow furrowed into an anxious frown. Charles did his best to walk steadily past the old man and to say 'Goodnight' without slurring. Once inside his bedroom he collapsed into bed and went straight into a deep sleep.

In the morning, his head was pounding and, despite the ceiling fan whirring above him, his body was running with sweat. He put it down to the alcohol the night before, forced himself up and into the shower. He wasn't sure he could face the fried breakfast which the servants now provided unfailingly each morning, but didn't want to offend them, so he went through to the dining room and ate as much as he could, drowning it with copious amounts of black coffee and orange juice.

He was in no mood for work, but when he entered the Battlebox, Colonel Cotton's secretary asked him to report to the colonel straightaway.

'Your orders have come through early, Simmonds,' said the colonel. 'You are to report to your unit in KL the day after tomorrow. That means you will finish off here today, then travel up there tomorrow by train in time to report there the following morning.'

'Thank you, sir.'

'We shall miss you here, Simmonds. You've done a fine job. Especially on the Matador report.'

'Thank you, sir. Any news on that from London?'

'Yes, I believe so. It's got the green light from Whitehall, but the generals here are stalling on it. Who knows if it will ever get the go-ahead from them. But that doesn't detract from the fact that it was a fine piece of work.'

'Well, thank you, but it was a team effort, sir.'

He returned to his desk and began to finish off his last pieces of work, but his head was still pounding and he found he had no energy to tackle even the simplest of tasks. His mind kept straying back to Suria, wondering where she was, if he would ever see her again. Her failure to show up at the Great World had had an almost physical effect on Charles. He could feel it in his chest, a heavy, pressing sensation that weighed him down. It was as he imagined grief might feel. He did his best to put her out of his mind and to get on with his work.

He'd finished before the end of the afternoon and decided to go home early to pack. Smythe looked disappointed as Charles said goodbye,

'I was rather counting on giving you a send-off at the mess tonight.'

'Sorry, old man, don't think I could face it. Had a bit too

much last night,' he said, thinking there could be nothing less appealing at that moment than getting drunk in the mess with Smythe for company.

Back at the house, he asked Ali to help him pack his belongings into his trunk. The furniture belonged to the army, so there was little that he owned in the house. It didn't take them long to pack. Charles hadn't accumulated much during his stay in Singapore. There were a few clothes, books, toiletries, but most of the space was taken up with various items of his uniform.

After that, he went through to the kitchen and spoke to each of the servants in turn. He gave them each their final wages together with a substantial tip. They'd all been so helpful and hardworking and he knew they'd had a lot to put up with whilst Louise was in residence.

His final act was to sit down at the bureau and write a letter to Louise to agree to the divorce that she'd requested. Now that he was leaving their marital home for good, he felt ready to take that step. He sealed the letter and asked Ali to take it to the post office the next morning.

By this time it was growing late.

'You not want supper, sahib?' Ali asked.

Charles asked for something quick and light and was brought mulligatawny soup and bread rolls. As he ate he thought of Suria again. Now he was leaving Singapore it seemed even more pressing to find out where she was. How could he leave the city without saying goodbye and finding out why she'd not turned up the previous evening? It was late now, but he knew he wouldn't rest until he'd done his best to find her.

There was one obvious place to go. Raffles Hotel. If she wasn't working this evening, one of the staff he knew would be sure to give her a message from him. They might even be able to tell him where she was staying now, although the housekeeper was unlikely to be on duty during the evening.

He asked Ali to call him a taxi and was soon being driven along the road that led from the base near Changi barracks to the city centre. It went through simple villages where chickens and pigs rooted around on the road, scattering at the approach of the car, then on through patches of untamed jungle, where, through the open window, Charles could hear the night-time sounds of the jungle; the whoop of monkeys and the buzzing and whirring of insects. For once it jarred on his nerves. It seemed to be taking forever to get there.

As they drove in through the eastern suburbs of the city, past the villas of Europeans with their colonnaded verandas and extensive gardens, the roads became busier; clogged with slow-moving traffic. When they reached the suburb of Geylang, they hit a traffic jam. Cars and buses sat stationary, belting out fumes and smoke, in a narrow street lined with shophouses. There was an accident up ahead; a bullock cart and rickshaw had collided and a commotion was going on drawing a large crowd of angry people.

'This is bloody ridiculous,' Charles said.

The taxi driver turned round and shrugged.

'Take long time, sir,' he said. 'No go.'

'It's alright. I'll walk the rest of the way,' he said.

'Long way to Raffles, sir,' said the driver.

'It's fine. I need some fresh air,' he said, and gave the man the fare.

He was glad to be out of the taxi and striding freely along the pavement beside the motionless traffic. Despite the fact that it was very late, it was still stiflingly hot and the area was bustling with life. Gas lamps lit up the pavements and all the shops were open and doing a thriving trade.

Charles loved this aspect of Singapore, the sheer pulsating energy and its people of all different races. He realised he'd grown to appreciate the place and felt a little nostalgic to be leaving it all behind. It was fitting that he should be walking through the city on his last evening, he might not get another chance to see the place like this, so convinced he was that invasion was imminent. But glancing down the side streets, he saw a less appealing side to the area; the many brothels of the district lit up by fairy lights, as was the tradition, customers hanging around on the pavement outside.

He walked as quickly as he could; conscious that it was late and that the restaurant in Raffles could well be closing up. He didn't want to miss this last chance to see Suria. Panic began to set in at the thought that she might have left before he could get there. He strode over the road bridge that crossed the Kallang river and the smell of exotic spices wafted up on the night air from the estuary – another thing that Charles would miss.

Soon he was striding through the lanes and alleyways of Little India. Here, as in Geylang, the place was buzzing with life. Traditional Indian music was being played at high volume from several different shops, the different harmonies clashing and vying for attention. The air smelled heavily of incense and spices. Charles breathed it deep and savoured it as he passed shops selling garlands, jewellery, colourful sarees, brightly coloured powders, and hole in the wall curry kitchens vying for space with fortune tellers' establishments. He pushed his way through the crowds, marvelling as he always did at the sights and sounds, taking them in for what could be the last time before he eventually emerged from a side street onto Beach Road.

Now the crowds thinned out and he was able to make quicker progress. As he walked along the edge of a wide grass verge, under the trees that lined the road, he noticed how bright the moon was that night; how it lit his way even in places where there were no street lights. He quickened his pace, knowing that it wasn't far now to the hotel.

As the hotel came into view, its white façade gleaming in the moonlight, framed by gently swaying coconut palms, an unfamiliar droning sound came from the sky, from the north of the city. He stopped and stared; it was the sound of aircraft. His heart began to pound; was this the RAF practising? Highly unlikely at night. Could it possibly be enemy aircraft? He thought back to the discussions at work; at the frantically decoded messages that had revealed weeks ago that the Japanese were massing on Hainan Island. Could this be the night they finally made their strike?

The low buzz in the sky got louder and closer. It was then that Charles realised that the streetlights were still on, blazing out in the night, giving the enemy the perfect view of every street and landmark in downtown Singapore. And no air-raid signal was sounding either. The drone of the aircraft got louder and louder and then, he saw them, bursting into his vision from the direction of Changi in the north east; a squadron of silver fighter planes, gleaming in the moonlight. These planes seemed to Charles to be flying far too high to drop bombs. They continued on course, flying straight over the city and within seconds the beams from searchlights lit up the sky, followed by the ack-ack sound of anti-aircraft fire accompanied by the wail of sirens.

Charles set off running, his only thought was to get to Suria, and as he ran a second formation of planes flew over, this one much lower, so low that the vibrations from their engines seemed to shake the ground beneath his feet. He could see them up ahead as they flew over Raffles Place, endless sticks of black bombs dropping from their undercarriage. Then came a series of blinding flashes, illuminating the sky above the rooftops, the sickening noise of bombs exploding and the crash and rumble of buildings falling. Charles carried on running towards Raffles Hotel, praying it hadn't been hit. As he ran, he watched the sky ahead. The planes banked, circled back, flew over and struck again. Again the flash and boom of the explosion followed by further crashes of falling masonry. This time, judging from the distance, he guessed it was Chinatown, with its tightly packed streets and crowded tenement blocks.

Sweat was pouring off him now and he was panting; life in an office for months on end had done nothing to prepare him for running in this heat. The hotel loomed ahead of him. Thank God, he breathed, it looked to be intact. As he ran, others were running beside him towards the hotel and he caught the intense panic in the air. At last he was on the front drive and at the door. It stood open and inside the entrance hall people were dashing about, eyes wide with fear. At the desk, the receptionists were trying to calm a growing crowd of people all clamouring for attention. Charles walked on to the restaurant. The tables were deserted. Waiters scurried round with trays, clearing tables despite the chaos that ensued elsewhere. The head waiter stood in the middle of the room. Charles approached him.

'I need to see one of your staff,' he said. The man wasn't concentrating on his words. He seemed rooted to the spot, his eyes staring into space. 'Suria Ismail,' Charles went on. 'Is she working tonight?'

Still the man didn't answer him. Charles left him standing there and spoke instead to one of the waiters.

'Do you know Suria?' he asked. The man's face broke into a smile.

'Oh yes, sir. Yes, I know her. She has just finished work for the evening.'

'Do you know where she is? It's important that I see her tonight.'

'She has a room upstairs now. Staff quarters. Back stairs. I not know the room number, sir.'

'Never mind. Thank you. Thank you so much.'

He left the restaurant and turned into the passage that led to the kitchen. He had no idea where the staircase would be, but he knew it must be in this direction. The passage led him past numerous closed doors. Soon he passed the housekeeper's room and was heading towards the rear entrance, but before he reached it, a passage led off to the left and at the end of that was a set of narrow stairs. He followed them upwards. They were poorly lit and stiflingly hot. They led straight to the top floor and a passageway just under the roof. He followed it. There were many numbered doors along the passage but there was no one about. He knocked on one and it was opened after a few seconds by a short Chinese man in pyjamas. The man blinked at him in surprise and looked taken aback when he asked if he knew where Suria's room was, but Charles drew himself up and told him it was of vital importance that he spoke to her.

'Number 40. Women's end,' the man muttered pointing along the passage. Charles thanked him and hurried on. There was a swing door that presumably separated the men's from the women's quarters and number 40 was a few doors beyond that. He stood in front of it, taking deep breaths to calm himself, and then he knocked firmly on the door.

Silence. Perhaps she wasn't in after all? God forbid she had walked out towards Chinatown for something after her shift. He knocked again and then the door opened. First a crack, then a little more. Suria's face appeared in the gap. She was still wearing her waitress' uniform. A black dress and white apron.

'Charles!' she said, 'What are you doing here?'

'Are you alright?' he asked, relief flooding through him that she was here, safe and well. 'You heard the bombings?'

'I'm alright,' she said, but her face was white and her voice trembled. She pulled back the door.

'I was worried about you,' she said, and he noticed that her face was wet with tears. 'I'm glad you came.'

He took her in his arms and held her tight while she clung to him. He felt the sobs rack her body, but he held her until they had stopped.

'What happened to you yesterday evening?' he asked. 'I waited for you at the Great World. I've been so worried. Why didn't you come?'

She wiped her face with the back of her hand. 'I'm sorry. I'm so sorry. Just now, when I heard the bombs, the whole building shook and I thought I might die. But I thought of you, and I realised what you meant to me. I felt so sorry that I treated you like that.'

'It doesn't matter,' he said, kissing her hair and holding her again.

'I was angry with you. My mother wrote to me and told me about the postal order. I knew it was you. It had to be. I was furious that you could have done that against my wishes.'

'I'm sorry. I'm so sorry. I just wanted you to be safe, to go away from here. It was the only way I could think of. But it was wrong. I see that now.'

'It doesn't matter now,' she said, looking up into his eyes. 'I realise you were being kind, that you wanted the best for me. I was being too proud. I've done that before and I realise now that I shouldn't have done.'

'Let's forget about it shall we?' he said, and kissed her then, full on the lips and she returned his kiss, moving close, her arms around his neck, pulling him towards her. But then, suddenly she broke away from him.

'People are dying out there,' she said, 'We shouldn't be in here. We should go out and see if we can help in any way.'

'You're right,' he said, seeing the determination and compassion in her eyes. It hit him then how much he loved her and how the last twenty four hours had been hell on earth not knowing where she was or what was going on in her mind.

18

SURIA

Singapore, 1941

Suria followed Charles along the passage on the top floor of Raffles Hotel and down the narrow staff staircase. Over his shoulder he was carrying the cloth bag into which she'd stuffed old clothes and towels she thought might do for bandages. Suria's emotions were in turmoil. She was still reeling from the rush of relief she'd felt when she'd opened the door and Charles had been standing there. A feeling of warmth and peace had enveloped her as she looked up into his eyes, and she realised then something she'd known for a while now; she was in love with him and there was nothing she could do to stop that.

The past few days since she'd taken the decision to cut off communications with Charles had been the most miserable time she'd endured since arriving in Singapore. Even through the dark days of unemployment after being dismissed from the Ford Factory she'd not felt so wretched. She'd quickly regretted her hasty action in not going to meet him at the Great World Amusement Park, and the thought of him standing at the entrance looking out for her and expecting her to arrive had torn at her heart.

But her pride wouldn't let her back down, and the reason she'd cut off communications with Charles was never far from her mind. Throughout those days she kept thinking back to the letter her mother, Fatima, had sent her; Fatima hadn't written it herself, of course, she had asked the local schoolteacher to write it for her. He often helped out the villagers that way for a small fee. Suria had recognised his flowing writing and elaborate phrases straight away. The letter had told her that an anonymous postal order for a large sum of money had arrived out of the blue. As soon as Suria read that she thought of Charles. It had to be him. There was no one else she knew with such funds at their disposal; particularly no one who would have sent them to her mother anonymously like that.

The arrogance of the gesture was what angered Suria most of all. It reminded her of how Charles had acted in Mr Hong's shop and how he'd pursued her afterwards, trying to make amends, assuming that she would accept his offer of help and that he could automatically fix things for her. It was typical of the general arrogance of the British in Singapore and as such it got to her. There was no getting away from the fact that he was a member of the ruling class and she was one of the ruled. Not only that, she was one of the poorest of those subjects too, at completely the opposite end of the social and economic ladders from him. It was only when she'd got to know the man personally that she'd realised there was a lot more to him than arrogance and wealth. He was a genuinely kind and caring human being, whom she warmed to more and more each time they met. And before she knew it she was falling under his spell, counting the days until they met, her pulse racing on Wednesday evenings as she put on her best clothes, checked her face in the mirror and ran down the steps in the go-down, knowing he was waiting outside to take her to tea.

But when he'd gone behind her back like that to send her mother money, anger and humiliation displaced all other emotions. She felt manipulated. She knew he'd done it to try to get her to leave Singapore and go home to her village. He'd mentioned it so many times. She put aside the special bond that was growing between them, she forgot how her heart pounded when he looked into her eyes as they sat together at Boat Quay, how she could speak to him about any subject under the sun and she knew he would understand.

He turned to look at her now, as he descended the three flights of stairs down to the ground floor, solicitous as ever, checking that she was alright. She smiled back at him, reassuring him that she was fine. She'd forgiven him for his blunder after a couple of days. She'd realised that he'd been motivated by fear for her own safety, and it was partly her own stubborn pride that had stopped her taking his money when he'd offered it, so she could give up her job and return to the village. But it was that same pride that wouldn't let her contact him, even though she understood why he'd sent the money, or to backtrack from the position she'd dug herself into.

Then she'd taken the decision to move away from the go-down and she realised he wouldn't know where she was. She'd moved into the hotel because life in the go-down had become untenable since Amina left. Choi took every opportunity to harangue her about anything and everything. She was particularly vicious about Suria's relationship with Charles, taking any chance to taunt her about it, calling

Suria a 'white man's whore'. When Suria told her as calmly as she could that although it was no business of Choi's, in fact she was no longer seeing Charles, Choi had jeered at her, 'So the white man got tired of using you as his plaything and tossed you aside?'

Now, they reached the bottom of the stairs and left the hotel by the back entrance. As soon as they stepped outside and turned to walk in the direction of Raffles Place and Chinatown, they saw that the sky ahead of them was red, lit by fires that were burning in the bombed buildings. They set off quickly along St Andrew's Road, past the darkened cathedral towards the burning buildings. Others were rushing with them, towards the site of the bombings; a horse-drawn fire truck passed them, its bell clanging, the firemen running behind, pulling on their uniforms, adjusting their helmets.

They crossed the Singapore river on Cavenagh Bridge and hurried on towards Raffles Place. As soon as they turned the corner into the square Suria gasped with shock at what she saw. A tall building had collapsed into the middle of the square, leaving a gaping hole in the façade, and fire was raging inside it. The explosion had caused masonry to spray out over the whole area. Cars were flattened under it, rickshaws lay battered and buckled by the force of the blast. And everywhere she looked lay injured people. A woman squatted beside the motionless form of her baby, next to an upturned rickshaw. She was rocking back and forth, wailing in her grief. The fire truck was already stationed in front of the devastated building, four men directing the great hose at the most intense part of the fire. Even from here Suria could see that although the water pressure was high, it was hardly making any impression on the raging flames.

It tore her heart not to be able to help the grieving mother, but beyond her she could see people writhing about on the road in pain. Some were pinned under sections of brickwork, others simply lay there, stunned by the force of the blast. She knelt down beside the first person she came to. It was an old Chinese man – a rickshaw-wallah by the look of his clothes. He lay on the ground, groaning in pain, cradling one of his arms that was broken and bleeding. He'd managed to pull himself free from the pile of bricks that lay beside him, but he was bleeding profusely from the shoulder. Charles knelt beside her and they both leaned over the old man. Charles spoke to him, trying to calm him down and keep him still, while Suria tried to clean his wound and stem the flow of blood by bandaging his arm. As she worked, the old man's face was still contorted in pain, but he stopped moving about and yelling. Finally, the bandage was secure.

Sikh ambulance workers were already bringing bamboo stretchers into the square. Charles beckoned a group over and they laid the stretcher down beside the old man and eased him onto it. Then, they picked the stretcher up and took it out of the square to waiting ambulances that were lined up in the next street. Suria watched them go, hoping against hope that he would make it to the hospital. Then she turned to the next victim; a British man pinned under some fallen beams. A group of workers were trying to pull the beams off him and he was crying out in pain, his face pale and sweaty. Charles approached him, knelt down beside him and spoke to him gently as the beam was finally eased off the man's chest. Charles and two other men moved the man out from under it, then Suria knelt down and did what she could to clean and bandage his chest until the stretcher bearers arrived. It was clear that he had broken several ribs and was in great pain.

She went on, moving from victim to victim, Charles helped them to move so she could get to them and to calm them down. Other people were bringing water to the victims and yet others digging in the rubble of the collapsed building to look for survivors. Some of the people she approached lay there motionless, clearly killed outright by the blast. Suria checked their heartbeats to make sure, then left them to tend to people who had some chance of survival. All the time the fire raged on. The firefighters were doing their best to put it out, but it was simply too fierce. Other fire trucks arrived after a time and joined in the fight. Gradually, over the hours, its ferocity reduced and finally, the flames had been tamed and were under control.

By that time, the first light of dawn was creeping into the sky. Suria had used up all the old pieces of clothing in her bag. She was dropping from exhaustion. She looked at Charles in the half-light and saw that his face was grey with tiredness, streaked with soot and blood.

'You look dead beat,' he said to her. 'Shall we go back?'

'There are more people who need our help,' she said looking around. There were still prone people dotted about the square with serious injuries who they hadn't had a chance to get to. 'We can't just leave them.'

'The ambulance crews are here now. Lots of them. We've done what we can.'

He was right. There were a lot of rescue workers in the square now, tending to the injured, as well as those trying to clear the wreckage. Reluctantly Suria got to her feet. As she did so she noticed the sky in the direction of Chinatown was black with smoke. There were fires there too. She thought of the go-down and all the hardworking Chinese labourers and their families she'd got to know there. And all the others who lived in tiny cubicles in tenement blocks and worked on the docks for a pittance.

'Look, Charles,' she said, pointing. 'That's Chinatown.'

'It's dreadful. Unbelievable,' he said, shaking his head. 'I can't believe they dropped their bombs there in a residential area.'

'Should we go there and help?' she asked.

He shook his head. 'We're exhausted and it's a long walk. There will be rescue workers down there too. You've done enough, Suria. You need to rest.'

She realised that she was crying, with helplessness and exhaustion. He took her arm and reluctantly she allowed him to guide her in the direction of the hotel and home. They walked in silence, each with their own thoughts of the horrors they'd witnessed over the past few hours. They were beyond words, but they'd been there together, worked side by side, and she knew that he understood how she was feeling. There was no need to speak.

When they arrived at the staff entrance of the hotel, Charles stopped by the door.

'I need to go back home now. I haven't had a chance to tell you before, but I am leaving tomorrow. I came to say goodbye.'

The words hit her like a hammer blow. She looked up at his dear face, tears gathering in her eyes and spilling down her cheeks.

'Going? Where to?'

'I told you the other day. Don't you remember?' his voice was gentle. 'I have to go to Kuala Lumpur, to join my regiment.'

A sob rose in her throat. How could she have wasted these last hours with her anger and her pride? She might never see him again. They could have been together. She could have taken time off to spend with him.

'Don't go,' she said automatically.

'I have to go, Suria. I'm a soldier. It's what I'm trained for and it's why I came to Singapore.'

'No. I know you have to go to Kuala Lumpur. I meant don't go now. Come up with me. We can talk. Say goodbye properly,' she wasn't clear what she was asking, but she knew she couldn't let him go like this, in the street, not after what they'd been through together.

'If you're sure?' he said, looking into her eyes intensely.

'Quite sure,' she said, taking him by the hand and pulling him through the door.

It was Suria who led the way along the passage and up the narrow staircase; his hand was still in hers and she could feel the strength and warmth in his touch.

She unlocked her room and pulled him inside. She switched on a lamp.

'Please, sit down,' she said, suddenly shy in the light. There was only one chair; a hard wooden one. Suria had put a cushion on it she'd bought in Chinatown to try to brighten the room and make it more comfortable. He sat down and she poured them both a glass of water from a pitcher on the chest. She handed him one and sat down on the bed to drink hers.

'I will miss you, Charles,' she said. 'I'm so sorry now that we've spent this time apart. I was being too proud. Like before.'

He leaned forward and took her hand and a thrill went through her at his touch.

'Please don't waste time saying sorry,' he said, again looking into her eyes with intensity. 'I'm so glad I came to say goodbye. I couldn't bear leaving Singapore without seeing you.'

Then he leaned forward and kissed her on the lips and despite the fact that they were both grimy and their bodies covered in sweat, she found herself kissing him back passionately, sliding her arms around his neck, pulling him towards her. As she did so, she thought of her mother and how she would disapprove; how the whole community would disapprove, but she knew in her heart that this felt right, that she loved and trusted Charles. It was what she wanted. Still kissing her, he moved on top of her and she felt him unbuttoning her blouse as they sank together onto the mattress, his lips on her neck and moving down to her breasts. She put her arms around his back, pulling him towards her until they were moving together in unison.

Afterwards they slept together on the narrow bed, their bodies entwined, but as the sun rose in the sky and its blinding rays lit up the dusty room, Charles stirred beside her. He kissed her eyelids and she opened her eyes to see him looking straight into them.

'I'm so sorry, my love, but I have to go. The train leaves at eleven and I need to get my belongings from home.'

She propped herself up on one elbow. She knew he had to leave but she was dreading the final parting. She stroked his hair. There was a painful lump in her throat and she knew that tears were gathering in her eyes.

'Whatever happens, I will come back and find you,' he said. 'You should go back to your village, but I can't make you go, I know that now.'

'Will you write to me?' she asked, her voice faltering.

'Of course. I'll write as often as I can. I just hope the letters get to you. The Japanese have probably invaded somewhere in northern Malaya by now. Their ships must be close for the planes to have been able to fly to Singapore.'

He kissed her one more time, then got out of bed and put on his bloodstained clothes. Suria got out of bed too and wrapped her kimono around herself. He pulled her towards him for one last, lingering kiss and then he was moving towards the door, his hand on the doorknob.

'I love you, Suria,' he said, opening the door. 'Don't ever forget that.'

Then he was gone. She sank back down on the bed, buried her face in her hands and wept.

19

LARA

Singapore, 2000

L ara waited anxiously near the reception desk in the lobby of Raffles Hotel. It was eleven o'clock on Sunday morning, and since she'd received the letter from the old man, Aziz, the previous evening when she'd returned from Pulao Ubin, she'd counted down the hours to this moment. She'd hardly slept that night, there had been so much to think about. The information she'd discovered so far about her grandmother, Suria, had gone round and round in her mind. An image of Suria, pale and thin and dressed in rags, arriving at the orphanage to take her baby at the end of the war, kept surfacing in Lara's mind. She couldn't rid herself of the terrible tragedy of that young woman, destitute and defeated as she already was, leaving the place without her child in her arms.

She kept thinking, too, about the photograph in the bar in Raffles; the tell-tale amulet around the young woman's neck, her face peering out at the camera. Her features were so familiar to Lara, she could have actually been Nell. There were subtle differences though. This woman's face was softer somehow, and her eyes had a flash of rebellion, whereas Lara's mother had been rigid and unbending, she was very conventional and didn't seem to have a disobedient bone in her body. Poor Nell! Lara had felt a sudden rush of pity for her mother. What a very narrow life she must have led, always afraid of authority, hidebound by rules and regulations. For the first time Lara felt a glimmer of understanding. If Nell had been brought up in an orphanage by strict nuns, observing rules and conventions must have been the way to survive.

In the small hours Lara had also let her mind stray to Christian. She recalled how much she'd enjoyed the trip to Pulao Ubin, remembering the exhilaration of the motorbike ride; how she'd clung to him and felt his body against hers. He was good-looking, she acknowledged that, tall, well-built with dark hair, melting brown eyes and finely chiselled cheekbones. And it was flattering that he wanted to spend so much time with her. But, as she'd already acknowledged, it was all proceeding far too quickly. She didn't want to be burned again the way she'd been burned by both Joe and Alex, although in very different ways. She knew that she needed to be cautious, to take time to get to know him, to not rush into something without proper thought. She was looking forward to seeing him again next week, but she was also looking forward to spending Sunday alone, strolling beside the river or the sea, relaxing and letting her thoughts settle.

Now, she looked around her in awe at her elegant surroundings; the grand lobby with its marble floor and elegant furniture, the galleried balconies and vaulted ceiling in the roof, which let in natural sunlight. She sat as inconspicuously as she could, perched on the edge of one of the upholstered chairs, not wanting to draw attention to herself. She was acutely aware that she wasn't a guest, and although she'd put on her only decent clothes for the occasion, she still felt scruffy and underdressed in comparison to the well-heeled guests who swept in and out in their fashionable clothes. But the concierge had told her to sit down and wait here so it was unlikely that anyone would object to her presence. She glanced at her watch. Would Aziz actually come after all? His letter had been short and to the point and had given her confidence that he would be there to meet her. But, he was very old, she reminded herself. Perhaps he had forgotten, had a sudden change of heart or had been too unwell to make the trip.

It was eleven fifteen and she'd almost given up hope, when she spotted an old man coming in through the entrance and she knew straight away that it was Aziz. He was a little bent and wizened, but he was dressed smartly, walking with a cane, which he raised respectfully to guests as he passed them. The concierge came out to greet him, holding the old man's hands in his own, then both men approached her.

The concierge introduced them.

'I'll leave you to it, then,' he said, returning to the desk.

Aziz shook Lara's hand and greeted her with a broad smile, then he took a seat opposite her.

'I hear you want to know about someone who worked here in the hotel during the war,' he said. 'The concierge told me when I came in yesterday. I don't normally come in at weekends, but tomorrow I have to go into hospital, so I won't be able to come on my usual day.'

'Oh dear,' said Lara, feeling a sudden rush of concern. 'Nothing serious, I hope.'

'Not really, no. A minor operation. But at my age, who

knows...' He said it cheerfully with a toothy grin. Lara smiled at his carefree attitude and wondered if he was hiding his true feelings.

'When they told me you wanted to talk to me, I came straight to your hostel in Chinatown, but you were out,' he said.

'I'm sorry. It was very kind of you to come. I didn't mean to put you to any trouble,' Lara replied.

'No trouble. I enjoy talking about the old days, truth be told. I'm always ready to help people who ask about it. So, how can I help you?'

Lara explained that she thought she might have seen her grandmother in the photograph of restaurant staff from the 1940s hanging in the bar.

'The young woman looks exactly like my mother and she was wearing an amulet, you see. Exactly like this one.'

She fished in her bag and drew out the amber amulet on its silver chain. 'I know she was in Singapore at the outbreak of war, but I don't know much else about her. My mother grew up in an orphanage you see and didn't know anything about her parents.'

Aziz was staring at the amulet, his face had drained of colour and his eyes were wide with astonishment.

'Suria,' he murmured. 'I remember her wearing this to work once or twice. But jewellery was not allowed and the housekeeper forbade it.' Lara's heart began to beat faster and her scalp tingled at the thought that Aziz had known her grandmother.

'That was my grandmother's name,' she said. 'There's an inscription on the back of the amulet. Look.'

She handed it to the old man and he took it with trembling hands. He peered at the inscription, screwing up his eyes. He looked at it for a long time, he seemed transfixed by it. When he finally handed it back, Lara saw that there were tears in his eyes.

'So you knew her? Suria? My grandmother?' she said as gently as she could. He seemed to be in a reverie, not really noticing his surroundings or even Lara, but finally, his face cleared and he focused back on her.

'Yes. Yes, I knew Suria. She started work here in 1941. I got to know her because I used to work on the staff entrance, letting people in and out. She always took the time to speak to me. Not every member of staff bothered to do that.'

'And do you remember how long she worked at the hotel?'

'Not very long,' he said, almost in a whisper. He dropped his gaze, looking down into his lap, frowning deeply and wringing his hands.

'Are you alright?' she asked. 'I'm so sorry if this is upsetting. Would you like me to get you a drink?'

He rubbed his nose with the back of his hand and looked back at her, his eyes sad, full of pain.

'No, no. It's quite alright. It's just brought back some sad memories, that's all. Suria left sometime in 1942,' he said. 'She'd had her baby by then.'

Lara swallowed. It was extraordinary, getting so close to information about her own mother's birth and early childhood like this.

'The baby was my mother, Nell,' said Lara.

He shook his head.

'Not Nell,' he said. 'That's not what Suria called her baby. She called her Charlotte.'

'Charlotte?' she repeated. It was amazing that her mother had gone through her whole life with the name that had been given to her by the nuns, never knowing the name that her own mother had given her at birth.

The old man nodded. 'Charlotte. I'm quite sure. She told me the baby's name the day she came back to work.'

Lara hesitated. She didn't want to upset the old man further, but there was so much more she needed to know.

'Did you know anything about the baby's father?' she asked tentatively.

He shook his head. 'She never told any of us anything about the father, but it was a British man for sure,' he replied. 'Rumour had it that he was in the British Army, that he'd gone off to war when the Japs invaded. That was just rumour. But I do recall a handsome army type coming to meet her outside the hotel a few times. He would sit on the wall outside the staff entrance, waiting for her to finish work. I never knew his name though.'

Lara digested this fresh information. Nell had suspected that she was probably only half-Malaysian, but she'd had no real proof of that. Now, that was looking more likely.

'Do you know what happened to Suria when she left here?' Lara asked, suspecting that he'd probably already told her everything he knew.

He shook his head and looked down at his hands again. He screwed up his eyes and Lara realised he was fighting back the tears.

'I'm so sorry to upset you,' she said again. 'You don't need to answer if you don't want to.'

'She was taken. That's all I know,' he muttered.

Again, Lara's scalp tingled at this fresh revelation. Taken? Whatever did that mean? Taken by whom? And where to? But the old man looked so distressed, she was afraid of upsetting him more by asking further questions. She watched his face as he gradually composed himself. Perhaps she would try one more time.

'When you say taken, do you know who took her? And where they took her to?'

'It was the Japs. That's all I know.'

'Did they take her to an internment camp?'

He shrugged and shook his head, again, a look of sadness in his eyes.

'I don't know any more than that. All I know is that they took over the hotel. One minute it was full of British people, trying to shelter, or to find a way of leaving Singapore. The next thing we knew they were gone and the place was full of Japanese officers.'

'And they took my grandmother away?'

He nodded then lowered his eyes. 'The Japanese soldiers could be cruel. But I don't know any more,' he said with an air of finality, and Lara realised that he'd said all he was going to say about that. It was pointless asking him further questions.

'Did you ever see her again? After the war I mean?'

He nodded and brightened a little. At least he'd stopped wringing his hands and the sad, haunted look gradually left his eyes.

'She came to see me once after the war. She looked so different – thin and... and beaten, somehow. She was looking for her little girl. Going round all the orphanages in Singapore to make enquiries. She was near to despair.'

'Did you see her again after that?' Lara asked, remembering again what Sister Xavier had told her about Suria being turned away from the convent by the Reverend Mother.

He shook his head. 'She said she wanted go back to her village near Desaru on the mainland. I'm not sure if she ever went back or not. I never saw her again. I looked out for her, but she never came back here.'

'That's a shame,' said Lara, seeing the sadness in the old man's eyes.

He nodded. 'I had a soft spot for Suria. She was a few years older than me and so strong willed. I looked up to her. I was a little in love with her too, I suppose,' he said, smiling wistfully at the memory.

Lara smiled back and tried to imagine this bent old man in his youth. It wasn't that difficult; his eyes were bright and perceptive with a twinkle of mischief. She imagined he would have been chipper, full of fun and humour.

'Did she tell you the name of her village?' Lara asked after a pause.

'Yes. She often mentioned it when we used to talk before the war. Kuala Lapah I think it was called – or something similar. Just north of Desaru it was; a fishing village of just a few houses.'

'Thank you. I might take a trip there and see if anyone remembers her,' said Lara.

'You should do. But I'm afraid I don't know her address, or anything more about her family.'

'It doesn't matter. You've told me so much already. I didn't even know the name of the village before.'

The old man smiled and got to his feet. He held out his hand. 'I'm so glad I could help you. I must go now and have a chat with the concierge, and visit my friends in the kitchen, then I have to return home to rest.'

Lara shook his hand again.

'Oh,' he said, 'if you need to ask me anything else, here's my address.'

He handed her a scrap of paper on which was written an address in Little India.

'Good luck at the hospital tomorrow,' said Lara. 'I hope it goes well.'

He smiled again. 'Thank you. It's nothing serious, but thank you for your good wishes.' Then with a bow of his head he turned and made his way to the desk. The concierge came out from behind the desk and put an arm around the old man's shoulders, then the two men walked away into one of the passages leading off the lobby.

Lara left the hotel, her heart brimming with emotion, her mind full of the things the old man had told her about her grandmother. She just wanted to be alone now, to take a walk somewhere she could think and process what she'd just heard. She could see some gardens beside the river, so she made her way towards them along under the gnarled and wizened rain trees that lined Connaught Road.

What she'd learned from Aziz was incredible. It had been fascinating and astonishing to meet someone who'd actually known her grandmother. She'd warmed to the old man's kindness and sense of fun immediately. He'd told her some useful information about Suria, including the name of her village, but there was so much more to know, she was convinced of that. What had happened to her grandmother at the hands of the Japanese? She recalled now how Sister Xavier had been reluctant to speak about Suria and the reasons for Mother Superior refusing to let her take her own child. She'd caught a similar reluctance from Aziz. What could have happened to her grandmother to have beaten that strength and purpose out of her? Whatever it was, it had to have had a devastating effect upon her, and its effect seemed to have lived on down the years in the minds of those who'd known her.

Lara crossed the stretch of mown grass between Connaught Drive and the waterfront. There was a broad walkway beside the river and she walked along it in the direction of Cavenagh Bridge, admiring the imposing

Fullerton building on the other side, with its gothic columns, and the soaring skyscrapers of the commercial district behind it, imposing too in a very different way. She sat down on one of the stone seats that were raised up from the walkway, giving a better view of the river. A converted bumboat chugged past with eyes painted on its stern. It made her think of what it must have been like to sit here in the 1940s, when the river and Boat Quay would have been filled with working bumboats, their cargoes being unloaded by hand by swarms of Chinese coolies. She wondered if her grandmother had ever sat in this very spot watching the frenetic scene.

Now she'd got this far in her search, she was determined to find out more if she could. There was no reason why she shouldn't make the journey to Suria's village and ask around to see if anyone remembered her. She thought about Christian's offer to take her there on the motorbike. It seemed a long distance to travel that way, but the bike was powerful and Christian was a skilled rider. Would it be taking advantage of him to take him up on the offer, she wondered. She reminded herself that she'd determined to take things slowly with him. But at the same time, he *had* offered after all, and it would be good to have someone with her who was familiar with the country. What harm could it do? Making her decision, she reached in her bag for her mobile phone and dialled his number.

SURIA

Singapore, 1941

C harles had been gone for a month and Suria felt the loss of him every day. Her life had fallen into a predictable routine, although everything that was going on around her was far from predictable. Singapore had become a tense place to be since the bombing raid of the 8th December. After Charles had left that morning, Suria had to get up and serve breakfast to the guests as usual. She was exhausted and drained after the night she'd spent tending to the wounded in Raffles Place, but despite that she was glowing all over with the memory of the passion she'd shared with Charles. For days afterwards she experienced a disconcerting mixture of pain and elation.

Over the shoulders of the guests that morning she read the headlines in the newspapers; *Britain and United States at War with Japan*, they screamed. *Japanese troops land at Kota Bharu and advance on Malay peninsula*. The Straits Times carried several photographs of bombed out buildings, people being removed from wrecked houses on stretchers, and the rescue services hard at work, with the headline; *Singapore Bombing: Japs strike early at the heart of the city*. It was what she'd expected, but it was still a shock to see it there in black and white. As she cleared plates from a table on which one of the guests had left a copy of the Straits Times, her eyes lingered over the article below the headline. It stated that the raid on Singapore had taken place three hours after an attack on Pearl Harbor, during which the US Fleet had been devastated. Shock washed through her at these revelations. It felt as though nothing and nowhere was safe anymore, as if the foundations of her very world had been taken away from her.

Her mind flew to Charles. He would be getting on the train right at that moment, heading across the Johore Causeway, bound for Kuala Lumpur to rejoin his regiment. Kota Bharu up on the north-east coast near the Thai border where the Japanese were advancing, was a long way from Kuala Lumpur, but in her anxious state, Suria couldn't help fearing the worst; that Charles was heading into the path of the enemy. He would probably be on the frontline, in direct combat with the Japanese army very soon. She also thought of her family; of her father in the mine near Kroh, of her mother and brother in the village near Desaru. It was true that the village was tucked away in a quiet corner on the south-east coast, but would they be safe there? She hoped fervently for their safety, but there was no way of knowing for sure.

There was an excited hubbub in the breakfast room that morning. The talk amongst the guests was all of the war and what the coming days and weeks would bring. Suria listened to what they were saying as she brought their food from the kitchen, filled coffee cups and removed dirty plates. Some guests were convinced that the allied forces would sweep the Japanese army away quickly and effort-lessly, but others weren't so sure. Suria glimpsed the fear in their eyes as they realised what this could mean for them-selves and their families. They could end up trapped on Singapore island, where the Japanese were surely headed.

After breakfast was over that first day, during her morning break, she slipped out of the hotel and walked quickly towards the site of the bombings the night before. She needed to see that those who had been injured had all been taken to safety. As she walked along the Padang towards Cavenagh Bridge, she saw that the sky ahead, normally so blue in the mornings, was still black with smoke. The fires were still burning in the buildings of Raffles Place and in Chinatown. She crossed the bridge and walked along the river on the other side, but when she reached the entrance to Raffles Place, the way was barred by police barricades. Army officers were turning people away. Suria walked up to the barricade, dread in her heart. The fire engine was stationed where it had been the night before, still pumping water into the building. The flames had died back but could still be seen licking up the inside of the building. The devastation in the square was all the more apparent in daylight. Piles of bricks, rubble and broken beams were strewn all around, and amongst them the buckled cars and rickshaws she'd seen the previous night. The woman who'd sat wailing in grief beside her dead baby had gone, but there were still many bodies lying motionless on the roadside and on the walkways.

'You can't hang around here, miss,' said one of the soldiers, his face stern. 'Nobody can come in or out of Raffles Place.'

She walked back to the hotel, her head bowed, thinking of all those who'd been wiped out by the senseless bombing.

But there was nothing she could do for them now. The authorities were in charge and people were being cared for.

Two days after the night of the bombing, although there had been no more air raids, Suria was dismayed to see headlines announcing the sinking of the *Repulse* and the *Prince of Wales*; the two great British battleships that had been sent to defend Singapore. She remembered discussing them with Charles as they sat on Boat Quay, and how relieved he'd been that they'd arrived, as Singapore previously had no warships. Now, as the papers were quick to point out, Singapore had no Naval cover and very little air cover either. A few days after that, further bad news came from the battlefield; The Japanese Army was advancing quickly and had inflicted a savage defeat at Jitra on allied forces from Indian, Punjab and Ghurka regiments. Suria's heart stood still when she read that. She knew Charles was with India III Corps. Had he been sent north for this particular battle? If so, had he survived?

Time dragged for Suria, now that Charles had left. She berated herself continually for wasting those last few precious hours with him and for acting so impulsively in cutting off contact with him over the postal order. How trivial that all seemed in retrospect. God forbid that something should happen in the forthcoming battles that could mean she might never see him again. She went hot and cold at the thought of that and tried to put it out of her mind.

After a week or so, a letter arrived from Charles with a Kuala Lumpur stamp on the envelope. Suria recognised his writing straight away and her heart soared in relief. She rushed up to her room to read it, her hands trembling as she ripped the envelope open. The letter was full of loving words, reassuring Suria that Charles would be back to find her as soon as he could and urging her to go to her family in the village. He told her that he and his unit were out training in the jungle outside the city, preparing to halt the Japanese in their advance, but he didn't give an address for her to write back to, and she guessed that it might be difficult for him to receive letters if he was moving from place to place.

The atmosphere in the city became fevered and panicky over the coming days, with daily news of defeats of Allied forces by the Japanese army as they advanced south, ripping down the peninsula and leaving devastation in their wake. The British were finally waking up to the fact that they had woefully underestimated the Imperial Japanese Army and that defeat was now a possibility. Many families were preparing to evacuate by ship to India or Australia. Every time Suria walked down Orchard Road on her days off, she had to push past long, restless queues that spilled out on to the walkway from the headquarters of the shipping firms.

But the night skies remained quiet. People began to hope that the raid on 8th December had been a one off, but they couldn't be sure. Then their hopes were dashed when news came of another night-time air raid in mid-December. This time on the airfield at Tengah, destroying aircraft and the airstrip but without great loss of life.

The staff in the hotel were all on edge and anxious, but the management wanted to give the appearance that everything was continuing as normal. The restaurant continued to function and guests danced in the ballroom to the resident orchestra into the early hours every night. Far from there being a dip in business, Suria noticed that more and more guests were arriving all the time and the restaurant was full to bursting each evening. Families with children were cramming into guestrooms meant for couples. She noticed it out on the streets too. The city was becoming packed with people of all races, especially the British.

Aziz, the young doorman, seemed to have his finger on the pulse.

'Those families are all fleeing from the mainland and Penang Island. Plantation owners, civil servants, managers of mines. They're running from the battle. You know the British just abandoned Penang the other day? They evacuated the British but left all the Asians to the mercy of the Japanese.'

'I saw that Penang had fallen,' she said. 'So that explains why there are so many new guests in the hotel.'

'Some of them are trying to book themselves onto ships so they can evacuate, others still think Singapore is a fortress and that they'll be protected here.'

'What do *you* think?' she asked him.

He shrugged. 'I'm not sure, but whatever happens you and I will be all right, won't we? The Japs want to free us Asians from British rule. They're on our side. I don't think we have too much to worry about either way.'

She doubted that but didn't want to worry him by disagreeing. What did she know about it anyway? She found the situation confusing and terrifying in equal measure. She thought long and hard about going back to the village, as Charles had urged her to do, but something was holding her back. She knew her mother still needed the money. What Charles had sent had been a huge help, but the family had built up debts over the years and Suria didn't feel ready to give up her salary. And besides, if she were to stay in Singapore, Charles might come back here one day. She didn't want to miss the opportunity of seeing him.

Christmas came and went and the celebrations in Raffles were lavish and extravagant. Dozens of turkeys arrived to hang in the cold store, and the chefs spent hours plucking and preparing them for the feast. Suria was surprised to see that the British guests wanted a full roast dinner with stuffing, roast potatoes and all the trimmings followed by Christmas pudding, all served with lashings of alcohol. She wondered how they could eat and drink so much in this hot, steamy climate, and watching them tuck in to the rich food made her feel a little nauseous. At one point she had to rush to the staff bathroom when the nausea got the better of her. Mr Antonio told her to go upstairs to rest.

'You look as white as a sheet,' he said. 'We can manage here. It is almost done.'

She lay in bed, concentrating as hard as she could, taking deep breaths to make the nausea subside. She listened to the sound of music floating upstairs from the ballroom into the small hours. It seemed as though the guests just wanted to forget what was happening around them, at least for one night. She thought of Charles and wondered how he was marking Christmas in his camp. Her heart and body ached to hear his voice and feel his touch.

The next morning she felt a little better, but was shocked to see the headlines in the papers as she served breakfast; *Hong Kong falls to the Japanese. British Civilians Interned.* This was another body blow to the British empire and would surely give the Japanese soldiers fighting in Malaya hope that Singapore was within their grasp. Again, she observed the nervous glances of some of the guests and listened to the bravado of others.

The Christmas celebrations continued unabated, but on New Year's Eve, when there was a full moon, the bombers struck again in the middle of the night. This time it wasn't in the heart of the city; it was Sembawang Airbase to the north of the island. All the hotel staff were talking about it the next morning, shocked and sickened that seventeen Chinese and Indian civilians living near the airfield had been killed by the bombs.

'It seems as if the Japanese aren't worried about the civilian Asian population,' Suria said to Aziz the next day. 'It was Chinatown that suffered most during the first raid, remember.'

'I'm sure they don't want to kill civilians. Especially not Asians,' he said. 'But every war has collateral damage.'

The bad news headlines continued each and every day. There were no more letters from Charles and Suria had no way of knowing whether he'd written. Services were becoming erratic, she was aware of that, but she couldn't help worrying for his safety.

After the bombing raid on New Year's Eve, there were Japanese air raids virtually every night. Suria got used to the sickening drone of Japanese aircraft approaching from the north-east, the wail of the sirens and the frantic hammering of the anti-aircraft fire. People would take cover as best they could, but there were no air raid shelters nearby. Suria was terrified that the hotel, so visible from the air and such a symbol of British colonialism, would be an obvious target. Each morning the devastation from the night before would be plain to see; more and more buildings were razed to the ground, more and more people were made homeless and there were fresh casualties every day. People were nervous and hostile now, the atmosphere tense and desperate.

Suria felt very alone. The other girls who worked in the hotel were friendly and they all got on well when they were working together, but she didn't know any of them well enough to confide in them. She missed Amina so much during those days, remembering how they'd shared every-thing, their hopes and fears and their innermost secrets.

They'd laughed together, struggled together and supported each other through thick and thin. Amina knew all about Charles, and although Suria sensed she didn't approve, she'd always listened when Suria wanted to speak about him and had been ready with advice.

Suria even missed the go-down, during those first days of the war. Although life was hard there, everyone had struggled together and she'd made many friends amongst the Chinese women who had come to be with their husbands, or who themselves worked in the factories, restaurants or shops in the city. She wondered whether the go-down had been hit during the bombing raid. One day she walked over to Chinatown during one of her breaks, enjoying the walk over the Padang with the sea air blowing in from the harbour. When she entered Chinatown she was shocked to see that many shophouses had been destroyed by the bombings. Piles of rubble and debris blocked the streets and she had to find alternative routes many times. When she neared the go-down she was overcome with nerves, holding her breath as she rounded the bend, bracing herself to see it in ruins.

There it was, at the end of the street, looking exactly as it had when she'd left a few weeks before. The Chinese boy who manned the door was sitting on his stool at the top of the steps reading a newspaper, workers in their conical hats and blue overalls were going in and out. She walked to the bottom of the steps and looked up at the door, wondering whether to go in and speak to some of the women she used to know. Instead she turned on her heel and walked away, worried that Choi would be there and have something vicious to say. In her fragile state, Suria wasn't sure that she could take it.

A month had gone by and as well as daily news of Allied

defeats coming in from the mainland, Suria was preoccupied with something else. Something much closer to home. She was already highly anxious about the war, and this new worry compounded her anxiety. Since Christmas Day, when she'd first felt nauseous, she'd experienced the same thing every day, usually in the mornings, sometimes in the evenings. When her monthly period didn't appear during the first week in January, her anxiety mounted. Was it just because she was worrying so much about the situation and missing Charles so badly? She was usually regular, but recalled how she'd missed periods during her months of unemployment when she'd been dismissed from the Ford Factory. It had been anxiety then that had caused it, but also lack of nutritious food. That couldn't be to blame this time. Here in Raffles, she ate in the staff dining room every day and the food was nutritious and plentiful. Finally, she had to admit to herself that there was a strong possibility that she was expecting. She couldn't work out how she felt about it at first. Part of her was overjoyed to be carrying Charles' baby. But another part was full of dread and fear.

One day, during her morning break, she had no energy to go outside and walk. In any case, she didn't want to see the newspaper headlines on the boards in the shopping district and their gloomy pronouncements. There was never any good news and reading about the ceaseless defeats made her even more anxious and fearful. Instead, she lay on her narrow bed in her stuffy attic room and stared at the cracks in the ceiling, wondering what to do about her situation.

One of the things that was troubling her the most was how her family might react to the news. She recalled a young unmarried woman in the next village to her own, who'd left to work on a tea plantation in the Cameron Highlands but had returned to the village several months later clearly heavily pregnant. Her widowed mother would have gladly taken her in, but the village elders had forced the daughter to leave the village so the mother went with her. No one knew where they went, they walked into the jungle with all their belongings and had never been seen since. Suria shuddered thinking about it now. Although life in Singapore was cosmopolitan in comparison, she knew that having slept with Charles she had committed *khalwat*, an illegal act according to Syariah law. It had not felt like an illegal act at the time, it had felt loving and warm and perfectly right.

She shuddered at the thought of what might happen to her if she were to return to the village now. She could easily be expelled just as the poor unfortunate girl had, or punished in some other terrifying way. Life in the village was dominated by the mosque and religious observance had been an integral part of her life growing up. But in Singapore she and Amina had taken advantage of the distance from home and their newly found freedom. They had visited a mosque only a few times since their arrival and after that had gradually let the practice lapse. But that didn't mean that the religion she'd been brought up with wasn't an ingrained part of her. She still believed in God and prayed to him each day. She knew now that whatever happened in Singapore, she wouldn't be going home.

21

SURIA

Singapore, 1942

A few days later came the shocking news that Kuala Lumpur had fallen to the Japanese. Suria read the headlines at breakfast, then, horrified at what she'd read, took one of the leftover newspapers up to her room, her heart thumping. She sat down on the bed and read the article with tears in her eyes. The city had been bombed mercilessly from the air for days. The Allied troops had withdrawn, and the Japanese had entered the city after only a few skirmishes. Law and order had broken down and shops in the city centre had been looted by civilians. Several Allied soldiers had been taken prisoner by the Japanese and thrown into Pudu jail. Suria gasped when she read that. What if Charles had been taken? What if he'd been killed in the bombings or in the battle? She fingered her amulet, trying to keep faith with him and to send him her love. She felt sure he was still alive somewhere out there and that he would come back to her one day. Wouldn't she have known somehow, if he'd perished? Feeling nauseous again, she lay back on the bed. How would she get through these agonising days of not knowing?

She realised that she needed to put her thoughts down on paper, to try to make sense of what was happening. There was no possibility of writing to Charles as she had no idea how to get a letter to him, so she decided to write to Amina instead. She had no one to confide in in Singapore, so the next best thing would be to pour her heart out to her friend in a letter. When her sickness had eased a little, she found her writing paper and a book to lean on and scribbled a letter to Amina. The words poured out of her, she had so much to tell her friend. She wrote ten pages, then folded and slid them into an envelope. There was no knowing whether the letter would get to Amina, or whether she would write back, but the very act of putting her thoughts down on paper had made her feel a little better.

When she felt strong enough she walked out to the General Post Office in the Fullerton Building and mailed the letter. The whole area felt unnaturally crowded and there was a long, slow-moving queue for every counter. It made her a little late back to work and Mr Antonio gave her a sharp look as she pulled on her apron and straightened her hair in the lobby beside the kitchen.

One of the waitresses, a petite Malay girl called Minnie, sidled up to Suria and asked if she was alright.

'I've noticed you haven't looked well lately,' Minnie said with a sympathetic look. 'You were sick the other day, weren't you?'

Suria nodded but didn't want to be drawn. 'It's nothing serious,' she said, trying to muster a smile.

Minnie touched her arm. 'If you are having trouble, my sister is a nurse. She can help you. She works at the Alexandra Hospital.'

Suria stared at her, wondering what she meant. Had Minnie guessed she was pregnant and was alluding to the possibility of a way out? She shuddered, having already dismissed such a thing from her mind.

In the days that followed, Suria read of more inevitable Allied defeats in the papers. The Japanese Army was reported to be making its way down the peninsula on bicycles. Although fewer in number than the Allied forces, the Japanese were well-trained and skilled at jungle warfare. They were also far better equipped, with tanks and air power. It seemed to Suria that the Allies were doomed to failure. It was agony not knowing where Charles was or even whether he was still alive. Her eyes scanned the newspapers hungrily for news of India III Corps. She read of its soldiers retreating after various battles, but that was the most information she could glean about Charles' regiment.

She read about battles at Kampar, Slim River at which two Indian battalions suffered severe losses, Gemas and Maur River after which Allied forces withdrew into the surrounding swamps and plantations. On 31st January they withdrew over the Johore Causeway to Singapore Island, blowing up the causeway behind them to delay the Japanese advance. Singapore was even more crowded now with civilians piling into the city, sleeping rough on walkways and in parks. And now it was full of soldiers too. When Suria read about the withdrawal her heart stood still. If Charles was still alive and hadn't been taken prisoner, he would surely be in Singapore now. That gave her some comfort at least. She didn't dare to hope that she might see him, but perhaps he might find a way of getting a letter to her.

A letter arrived back from Amina, expressing surprise and joy at Suria's news, telling her to be strong and not to give up hope. Amina also told her that Fatima was doing well, and filled her in on gossip from the village; who was sick and who'd got married, who was out of work and who'd left to find work. It made Suria homesick for the slow and simple life of home, where you knew everyone for miles around, could wander on the beach or in the rainforest for hours and not see another soul.

All day, every day, the distant boom of exploding shells could be heard. The Japanese were shelling the minimal defences on the northern shore continually. It was a terrifying sound. They'd also bombed the fuel depots at the naval base and black smoke billowed over the city, blocking out the sun, making everything taste and smell of burning oil. Added to this was the stench of burning rubber. The British were burning rubber supplies in the warehouses near the harbour to stop the Japanese getting their hands on them. Daytime air raids on the city became a daily occurrence and the bombers were bold now, knowing the British had few planes left with which to prevent them; they flew low over the streets, strafing pedestrians with machine gun fire, picking off people randomly as they walked. Whole streets were devastated by the air raids; power cuts were frequent and it was rumoured that the water supply was running low.

The manager of Raffles called the staff together and told them not to go out into the city during daylight hours and to be vigilant if they went out after dark. Suria felt even more trapped after that and her anxiety mounted. She was terrified not only for everyone around her, for herself and for Charles, whom she hoped was out there fighting somewhere, but also for her unborn child. She was acutely aware that if something happened to her, her baby would perish along with her. She also knew that the anxiety she experienced constantly could not be good for her in her condition.

Her sickness didn't abate; in fact, it seemed to be getting worse. One day, when she'd had to rush to the washroom during breakfast and was bending over the sink, Minnie came in.

'Are you still ill, Suria?' she asked, her face full of concern. Suria nodded. There was no hiding it.

'I know what's wrong with you. I can tell. You don't need to worry, I understand. You know I told you my sister is a nurse. She might be able to give you some medication to help with the sickness. She will help you, I'm sure.'

Suria looked into Minnie's eyes, about to say that Minnie was mistaken, but she saw such friendship and compassion in the other girl's eyes that she dropped her gaze and said, 'It's true, Minnie. I can't deny it.'

'If you want me to ask my sister, I will,' said Minnie.

'Thank you, but I'm hoping it will get better in a few weeks. If not, I might do.'

'You know, if you haven't seen a doctor, I'm sure she would be happy to check you over, to make sure everything is alright,' said Minnie.

'That's very kind, Minnie. I might just do that.'

As they returned to the restaurant together, Suria felt her heart swell with gratitude towards Minnie for extending the hand of friendship. She was glad to have someone to confide in at last, even though no one could ever quite replace Amina.

The next day, a messenger came to the back door of the hotel and handed a note to Aziz. It was scribbled in haste, written on a page torn out of a book, but when Suria saw the writing on the folded paper her heart leapt. She rushed up to her room to read it, taking the stairs two at a time.

My darling Suria,

No doubt you'll have read some worrying headlines, so I want to let you know that I'm still safe and well. I'm camped in a rubber plantation with my men in the north of the island, ready to defend the Straits of Johore. Conditions are harsh here, especially when it rains, but the men are in good spirits.

I hope you are well and taking good care of yourself. I want you to know that I love you and that when this is over I will come and find you. I would like to marry you, Suria, if you'll have me?

There is no way of you replying to this note, but I will live with hope in my heart until we meet again.

Your ever loving,

Charles

Suria burst into tears at reading his words. She lay on her bed grasping Charles' note to her, basking in the joy of the knowledge that he was alive and within a few miles of where she was and that he'd asked her to marry him. In all her fevered anxieties about her situation, she hadn't considered marriage. She also hadn't realised quite how much the lack of knowledge about Charles' safety had been playing on her mind.

As soon as her tears subsided, she grabbed her writing paper and scribbled him a note in return.

My dearest Charles,

I got your note this morning. Thank you for writing to reassure me, I've been very worried about you. Words can't describe how relieved I am to hear you're safe.

The answer to your question is YES. I love you Charles and want to be with you forever. I have some news for you which can wait until we are together.

I think of you all the time and my thoughts will be with you in the coming days. Please take care of yourself, my darling.

Your loving,

Suria

She pushed it into an envelope and wrote "Major

Charles Simmonds, India III Corps Singapore" on the front. That was as much as she knew of his whereabouts.

Then, since it was her day off, she took some money, went out onto the street and hailed a taxi on Beach Road. She asked the driver to take her out of the city towards the north coast. He glanced at her, his eyebrows raised.

'It is impossible to go far in that direction, miss. The troops are occupying the land north of the reservoirs.'

'Could you just take me as far as you can?' she asked. He shrugged and started the engine, manoeuvring the old vehicle around a large crater in Beach Road caused by a stray bomb.

He drove her out through the heart of the city where she was shocked to see how much devastation the air raids had caused. Every street seemed to have suffered bomb damage. Whole houses had been wrecked, tenement blocks with gaping holes in their facades, warehouses obliterated. And there were people everywhere, sleeping on the pavements, sometimes in the open air, sometimes under tarpaulin covers anchored to fences or walls.

Gradually the buildings thinned out and soon they were driving through Tanglin, the wealthy suburb that many British officials and businessmen had made their home. It had been a beautiful place and Suria recalled walking around it with Amina on their trips to the Botanical Gardens. They had marvelled at the spacious houses with their wide verandas, set in beautiful grounds, many of them with tennis courts and swimming pools. Now several of those homes had been bombed, reduced to piles of rubble, and the grounds had been neglected with the plants growing rampant and the jungle encroaching. In many places the road was rutted by exploded shells and the driver had to slow down and find a way of getting through.

They drove on, into the rainforest that grew unchecked right up to the edge of the built-up area, through Bukit Timah, a collection of houses and buildings dotted around the Ford factory. Suria felt a wave of sadness as they drove past the gates of the rectangular white building. It brought back disturbing memories of the violence and stress of the sit-in all those months ago.

Beyond Bukit Timah the road became rougher and ran through patches of farmland for a while before the jungle closed in again; palms and bamboo thickets leaning over the road, creepers from tall teak trees dangling down in front of the car.

Once again, the driver glanced round at her, his eyes incredulous.

'Are you sure you want to carry on?' He'd asked several times.

'I want to go as far as possible,' she kept saying.

They drove on through another small settlement, Bukit Panjang, but shortly after that as they rounded a bend in the road they saw a barrier up ahead blocking the road.

'We have to turn round now,' said the driver, slowing down. There were many soldiers standing at the barrier, smoking, guns slung over shoulders. The taxi came to a standstill.

Suria got out of the car and approached them.

'You can't go beyond this point, lady, it's occupied by troops now. India III Corps.'

Suria smiled in relief.

'I have an important letter for Major Charles Simmonds of India III Corps,' she said. 'Please could you see he gets it?'

She held the letter out to him. The man looked a little surprised, but took the letter.

'Major Simmonds? I'll do my best to get it to him.'

'Thank you so much,' said Suria getting back into the taxi.

As it made its way back through the jungle she leaned back on the leather seat and closed her eyes, picturing the letter being handed to Charles in his camp. She imagined his face lighting up when he saw her writing on the envelope, how he would smile, rip it open and read her words. She hoped they would give him hope for the future and strength for the coming battles.

SINGAPORE WAS NOW UNDER SIEGE. Everyone expected the Japanese to attack in a matter of days. Their shelling of the north coast carried on ceaselessly. It could be heard clearly in the city centre making the overcrowded population nervous and jumpy. On the morning of 8th February, the newspapers were reporting that Japanese troops had landed on the north coast and that fierce fighting was taking place. The next day came news of allied defeats. The armies had retreated. They'd been pushed south to Bukit Panjang. Suria stared at the headlines. She'd been driven through there only a couple of days before. It was just a short journey from the city. Her blood ran cold thinking how close the Japanese were now. And where was Charles in all this fighting? Had he survived? Had he been wounded, lying in a field hospital somewhere out there? She yearned to find out but there was no way of knowing.

Suria wrote two more letters to Amina, but none came back in response. She wondered if hers had got there, and if Amina had tried writing but the letters simply hadn't got through. The days wore on with air raids over the city centre continuing and news coming in every day of more allied retreats. Suria's sickness worsened by the day. She suspected that anxiety had a great deal to do with it. She could hardly keep any food down now and was growing thinner every day. She was worried that, malnourished as she was, the baby wouldn't be getting enough nutrition to grow properly.

One day, Mr Antonio sent her to her room to rest. She had fainted in the kitchen whilst serving breakfast. She lay on her bed, trying to take sips of water and to calm her nerves. There was a knock on the door. It was Minnie.

'Are you alright, Suria?' she said, coming inside and kneeling beside the bed. 'I'm so worried about you.'

'I feel so bad about not finishing my shift,' said Suria. 'I'm alright now, though.'

'You mustn't worry about the shift. We managed fine. You are getting thin, though. That's not good. I will ask my sister and we can go and see her at the hospital tomorrow. Alright?'

Suria nodded weakly. She'd been reluctant to admit that there was anything wrong at first, but now she realised that she might need some help. It would be reassuring to speak to someone medically qualified.

The next morning, after breakfast she was feeling a little better, but Minnie insisted they should go to the hospital.

'You might feel better now, but it could come back or get worse. Best to get some advice, don't you think?'

They took a taxi to the hospital. The sun was high in the sky and the air felt steamy. Inside the taxi it was oven hot. The taxi edged through the downtown area, across the river and towards River Valley Road. It was slow going. The traffic crawled through the city, having to take diversions for bomb craters or collapsed buildings many times. Because often one carriageway was closed, it moved at the pace of the slowest vehicle, often a rickshaw or a bullock cart. Suria leaned out of the window, trying to get some air but it hardly made any difference; she thought she would suffocate in the heat.

They made slow, painful progress through the heavy traffic along River Valley Road. Suddenly people on the pavement were running for cover, looking to the skies and pointing, terror in their eyes. Suria leaned out of the taxi window and looked at the sky. A formation of sleek bombers were approaching, diving towards the city. Then she heard the rattle of the anti-aircraft guns and the wail of the air raid siren, but as she opened her mouth to tell Minnie they needed to take cover, the first bomb exploded in a nearby street, masonry and debris spraying into the air, bits landing on the roof of the taxi. The two girls crouched down in the passenger well, holding hands, both trembling. The taxi driver had left the taxi, running for cover in a nearby building.

They heard more bombs exploding in neighbouring streets, but the bombers had passed over now. Suria knew that they wouldn't come back straight away. Taking Minnie by the hand, she crawled out of the taxi and stood on the road, her legs shaking so much she thought they would give way. There was a devastated building right up ahead, dust billowing from it as the wreckage settled. It was blocking the road.

'Let's walk home,' said Suria.

Minnie shook her head. 'The hospital is closer than the hotel. Why don't we go there? We can see my sister after all and rest for a while before walking home.'

'Alright,' said Suria still dubious, but allowing herself to be persuaded.

They picked their way along the road and whenever they came to a pile of rubble, they skirted round it carefully.

Everyone seemed to be on the move on foot. The traffic was stationary now, most people had abandoned their vehicles. The sound of shelling could still be heard up ahead, but it wasn't close enough to trouble them. The sun was still beating down mercilessly. Suria's mouth was dry and filled with dust. She felt faint and nausea rose to her throat, but she carried on, gripping Minnie's hand, praying that the refuge of the hospital was not much further.

They walked for a long time, passing many bombed-out buildings, where rescue workers combed the wreckage for survivors and ambulance workers tended the wounded. It must have taken them almost an hour to get to the hospital gate. The gleaming white building was set well back from the road, amongst spacious grounds of tropical shrubs and immaculate lawns. They turned off the road and began walking up the drive towards the entrance with the constant boom of shells landing all around them. Some of them seemed very close. Suria was trembling. She was looking forward to sitting down in a cool building and drinking some water.

But as they neared the entrance to the building they saw something up ahead that stopped them in their tracks. A dozen or so soldiers, bayonets drawn, were making for the entrance. For a split second Suria assumed they were British soldiers, arriving to defend the hospital, but she quickly realised that the uniforms were unfamiliar. They were khaki and the soldiers wore matching khaki caps. And, looking closer, she could see from their hair and features that they weren't British.

A man appeared in the entrance, wearing a white coat. He was holding a white flag on a pole with one hand, his other hand outstretched, trying to halt the soldiers. The first one lunged at him with the bayonet and the man fell backwards, blood spreading all over his coat. The soldiers stepped over him and went on into the hospital. Suria and Minnie exchanged terrified looks.

'We need to leave,' said Suria.

Minnie appeared rooted to the spot, her eyes wide with fear. The soldiers had disappeared inside the hospital now, and screams could be heard from the open windows.

'Come on,' said Suria, tugging Minnie's hand. 'We need to get away from here. Quickly.'

Still Minnie wouldn't move. She seemed to be unable to process what was happening. But suddenly came the boom of a shell exploding somewhere in the hospital grounds, and the shock of it startled Minnie to her senses.

'Minnie. We need to go,' repeated Suria, tugging at her friend's arm.

'My sister's in there,' said Minnie, her cheeks streaked with tears. 'What are they doing to them?'

Still the screams and yells echoed from within the hospital. Suria shook her head.

'I've no idea. But there's no point going inside. We can't do anything against the soldiers. We need to run now, or they might come outside and see us here.'

'I should go in and help her,' protested Minnie and Suria's heart went out to her. But she knew that there was nothing either of them could do at that moment except save themselves. Suria suddenly felt strongly that she didn't want to die. That she wanted to live to save the child she was carrying.

'Alright. You're right,' said Minnie at last. They ran back down the drive and out onto the road. There they began to retrace the painful steps they'd just taken to get them to that point. Suria no longer cared about the thirst she felt, how her bones were aching and how her whole body was running with sweat. She was just pleased they'd got away from the hospital in one piece.

'I'll go back later,' panted Minnie as they ran. 'I need to know what's happened to her.'

Suria didn't reply. She'd spotted two British soldiers at a barricade at the end of a bombed-out street; they were stopping people from entering. Further down the street a fire engine was pumping water while firemen directed a hose at a burning building.

'We need to tell them what's going on,' she said, walking quickly towards the barricade.

When they told the soldiers what was happening at the hospital, they sprang into action.

'I'll speak to the colonel straight away. He can radio for help,' one of them said, setting off at a run down the bombed-out road, skidding over the rubble and darting around piles of debris. The other soldier turned to the girls.

'You need to get back home and into safety as soon as you can. The Japs have advanced quicker than anyone thought. They're inside the city now, so there'll be fighting on the streets before long. It won't be safe out here.'

22

LARA

Singapore, 2000

Christian offered to take Lara to the village near Desaru after she'd told him about Aziz's visit, and that Aziz had told her where Suria had come from.

'Why don't we go there tomorrow?' he asked. 'As I said, I have the day off work.'

'Are you quite sure? It seems a long way to go on a motorbike.'

'You're joking aren't you?' he asked, laughing. 'I've been all round Malaysia on it. Thailand and Vietnam too. It's a fantastic way to see a country.'

'If you're really sure,' she said, hesitating, her nerves racing at the memory of how she'd felt on the way to Pulao Ubin; terror and exhilaration all at once.

'But this time, you'll need to wear proper clothes,' he said. 'Bike leathers. It's too far to go without them.'

'Funny that,' she said, laughing. 'I forgot to put any in my rucksack when I packed.'

He laughed too. 'I've got some spares that will probably fit you. I'll bring them with me when I pick you up, along with the spare helmet.'

They arranged for him to collect her from the guest-house at nine o'clock in the morning. As she ended the call she wondered who the leathers had belonged to. It must have been a woman. An ex perhaps? A friend or a sister? Far more likely to be an ex she decided.

She spent the rest of the day as she'd intended, exploring on foot, wandering through Chinatown, enjoying the sights and sounds, the bustle and the exotic smells of the district, then on through the commercial area, across Cavenagh Bridge and through the Queen Elizabeth gardens beside the river. It was good to stretch her legs, to think about everything she'd discovered about her grandmother over the past few days. To let it settle in her mind. As she walked alongside the Padang, she spotted the red roof tiles of Raffles Hotel in the distance. On an impulse she walked towards it. There was something she needed to take with her if she was going to Suria's village. She'd forgotten to ask for it earlier, she'd been so bowled over by what Aziz had told her.

As Lara walked up the drive and entered the lobby, she thought about Suria. What had this place looked like in her day? Had it been as luxurious as it was now? Who had stayed here? Would Suria have come in through the front entrance as she was doing herself? Lara guessed not. It frustrated her that there was so much she didn't know about colonial and wartime Singapore. She resolved that she would do as much reading and research as she could about that time, to understand more about her grandmother and about the world her mother had been born into.

She crossed the marbled lobby, approached the desk and asked for the concierge.

When he emerged from his office, he recognised her straight away.

'What can I do for you, Miss Adams?' he asked smiling. Lara felt a little awkward about making what she knew was a slightly strange request.

'The photograph in the bar,' she said. 'The one of the restaurant staff in 1941 with my grandmother in it,' she said. 'I was wondering if I could maybe take a picture of it myself with my camera? You see, I'm going back to her village tomorrow. I want to know if anyone remembers her. It would be so much easier with a photograph.'

'Of course. Come on through. The bar is very quiet at this time of day. I will come with you and explain to the barman.'

'Thank you so much,' she said and followed him through the corridors to the Long Bar. The concierge spoke briefly to the barman then turned back to Lara.

'Go ahead,' he said, nodding towards the picture.

Lara looked at it again for a moment, amazed afresh at the resemblance between her mother and the young woman in the photograph. Then she reached in her bag for her digital camera and took several shots of the group in the photo. Once they were stored on her camera, she was able to enlarge the image so that only Suria's face was visible on the screen. She stared at it, thrilled and amazed at the woman staring back at her. The image was blurred and faded with age, and the light in the photo wasn't good. But even so, it was as if Lara was staring back at the image of a long-lost friend.

THAT EVENING, Lara went out to eat a simple dish of fried noodles at one of the local food stalls. When she returned to her room, she called her father on her mobile phone. As always when she called him, he sounded astonished to hear from her, as if it amazed him that they could be speaking to each other across thousands of miles. She told him that she'd found the orphanage where her mother had grown up. Then she told him about meeting Sister Xavier and what Sister Xavier had said about Suria coming to get Nell at the end of the war, and how she was turned away empty handed. Her father went quiet at hearing that story. In the end he said, his voice shaking with emotion,

'But that's truly dreadful. Inhumane. Why would a nun, of all people, have done that?'

'I've no idea,' Lara replied. 'But I intend to find out as much as I can. I've found out where Suria came from. A village on the coast in the south of Malaysia. I'm going there tomorrow to see if anyone can tell me anything about her.'

'You're very brave,' said her father. She could hear the admiration in his tone, even at this great distance. 'How are you going to get there?'

'I've met someone. He works in the Australian High Commission. He's going to take me there.'

She stopped short of telling him that she was going to travel a hundred and fifty kilometres on the back of a motorbike. There was no need to worry him.

'And how are you doing, Dad?' she asked.

'Oh, not so bad. I've joined the ramblers and have started going on some of their local walks. It's good to get out and about and meet new people.'

'That's great, Dad,' she said, and this time there was

admiration in her tone. He'd never been very outgoing; Nell had always been the sociable one, the face of the family. Lara knew how hard it must have been for him to have taken this step. She guessed it was a measure of how lonely he was, but she was glad that he was now making an effort to move on from the death of her mother.

In the morning, she was waiting in the reception area of her guesthouse at nine o'clock when she heard the roar of Christian's motorbike on Temple Street. A thrill went through her at the sound of the throaty engine, and as before she felt a mixture of fear and excitement at the anticipation of the journey to come.

He came into the hostel and another thrill went through Lara at the sight of him. He seemed to fill the lobby with his presence. He was dressed in black leathers and held his helmet under one arm and a leather bag in the other. He grinned at her.

'Good morning!' he said, his eyes lighting up when he saw her. 'Do you want to try these on?'

He handed her the bag.

'Do you think they'll fit?' she asked tentatively.

'Probably. They belong to my mother,' he said smiling, his eyes on her face. 'She's about your size I reckon. You might be a bit taller...'

'Your mother?' Lara's mouth dropped open and she felt colour flooding her cheeks. So, it wasn't an ex after all. She could tell from the way he was looking at her that he knew exactly what had been going through her mind, and that it was amusing him.

'Yeah. Didn't I tell you? She came with me on a trip round Malaysia earlier in the year when she came over for a visit from Oz.'

'No. You didn't tell me. I think I'd have remembered that!' Lara replied. 'She must have some guts.'

Christian laughed. 'You're right about that.'

'I'll be back in a moment,' said Lara, dashing back to her room. She pulled the leather trousers on over her shorts and slipped the jacket over her T shirt. Christian was right. They fitted perfectly. She returned to the lobby.

'Hey, look at you!' he said, his eyes appraising her. Again she felt colour creeping into her cheeks.

'Come on, we'd best get going,' he said and she followed him out to the bike. She pulled on the helmet he handed her and got on the seat behind him. The sun was beating down, the street hot and steamy, and Lara immediately began to sweat in the heavy leathers.

'Don't worry,' Christian said, turning to her, as if reading her thoughts. 'You'll soon cool down once we're on the road.'

He kicked the engine into life and they took off down Temple Street. Lara clung on tight, her arms wrapped around his waist, as they zigzagged through Chinatown, swooping past stalls, around groups of pedestrians, ducking their heads as they passed under objects hanging from shop awnings. But soon they were out on the open road, speeding through the slow-moving traffic between lines of stationary vehicles, moving quickly towards the outskirts of the city and the north of the island. The traffic had thinned out as they neared the Johor Causeway. Lara stared ahead of her, marvelling at the stretch of sparkling blue water that separated Singapore from Malaysia.

At the Singapore immigration checkpoint at Woodlands, they went through in the motorbike lanes which were moving quite quickly. Then they were speeding across the causeway with bikes all around them moving at the same pace. Again, Lara experienced that feeling of exhilaration at the speed, at the closeness of Christian's body to her own and at the feeling that came from powering across the wide-open sea under the bright blue sky.

On the other side, they showed their passports at the Malaysian immigration checkpoint and once clear of that they were out on the open road once again and the freeway going east towards Desaru. Christian opened up the throttle and moved between the cars and into the fast lane. Lara, unsure whether to be terrified or excited, decided to put her fears aside and to embrace the experience.

The countryside flashed past; it was flat but lushly green for much of the way. Oil palm, banana and tapioca plantations lined the route, interspersed with villages and small towns. It was fascinating to see the countryside unfolding in this way; almost as if she was watching a film that had been speeded up.

They'd been going for about an hour when Christian pulled off the freeway onto a side road.

'Do you fancy a coffee or something?' he called over his shoulder.

He found a coffee shop in a small community a few kilometres from the freeway. Lara was glad to take off her helmet and leather jacket as she got down from the bike. She noticed that the visor was already covered in tiny dead flies and insects.

They sat at a table outside and the owner brought them coffee.

'Thank you for bringing me today, Christian,' Lara said, taking a sip.

'Don't thank me. Please, it's my pleasure,' he said, smiling at her. She noticed how earnestly he looked at her, how the skin around his eyes crinkled as he smiled. 'I love an excuse to get on the bike.'

'It's amazing that you took your mother round Malaysia on it,' she said.

'Yeah. Ma is completely up for anything like that. She was a bit of a hippy in the sixties. Spent a lot of time in India in an ashram. She still loves to travel.'

'She sounds an amazing woman,' Lara smiled, thinking of her own mother who had been the direct opposite in every way. Buttoned up and disciplined, a devout Catholic, who'd never travelled anywhere except to come to England to take up a position as a nurse in London. Lara recalled how she'd disapproved of what she called "hippy culture". Try as Lara might, she simply couldn't imagine Nell on the back of a motorbike.

'I expect you miss your mum don't you?' she asked.

He nodded. 'My dad ran off when I was young, so it was just me and her for a long time. We were very close. She got married again when I was a teenager to a really lovely guy who had two kids of his own. We became a family then. In the holidays we used to travel round Australia in his camper van.'

'It sounds like you had a lot of fun,' said Lara wistfully, thinking about how lonely and pressured her own childhood had been as the only offspring of an ambitious mother.

'I guess so,' he said. Then he went silent and looked down at his hands. Lara sensed he wanted to tell her something, but that he was having difficulty finding the right words. In the end he said,

'She was pretty good to me over my divorce too.'

Lara's scalp tingled at the shock of the revelation.

'Divorce?' she said, her mouth dropping open in surprise for the second time that morning.

He nodded. 'Yep. I thought I should come clean about that at some point. You were very honest with me about what happened with Joe.'

'I appreciate that,' said Lara. 'Do you want to tell me about it?'

'I find it really difficult to talk about,' Christian replied, a little shamefaced. He looked so downcast for a moment that Lara reached over and squeezed his hand.

'You don't have to tell me anything if you don't want to,' she said.

'No, no. I'd like to tell you,' he took a deep breath and flashed her an uneasy smile. 'We met at university and were an item all the way through. When we both left and started our careers, it seemed natural to move in together. Katie's mother was very traditional and so it wasn't long before there was pressure to marry. I felt way too young for that, but went along with it.'

He paused and took a sip of coffee, avoiding Lara's eyes.

'Things went downhill when my job took me to Canberra and she had to stay in Sydney. We couldn't afford to see each other every weekend. But when we did get together I could tell that something was wrong. Katie began to be really cold with me. When I confronted her about it, at first she denied it, but in the end she told me that she was seeing someone else.'

'Oh, poor you!' said Lara. 'A bit like what happened to me.'

He nodded. 'Only she wasn't seeing a stranger. She was seeing my best friend, Andy. We'd all been in the same group of mates at university. We'd all been so close, such good friends. I was stunned that he could have done that to me...'

'How long ago was that?' asked Lara.

'Oh, a couple of years ago now. When I had the chance to come out to Singapore I jumped at it. The divorce came through a few months ago. Katie's living with Andy now. I heard on the grapevine that they're planning to get married.'

'I'm so sorry, Christian. You must have been through hell.'

'I'm over it now, but it has been tough going sometimes. I won't deny it,' he said, lifting his head and looking into her eyes again. 'Thanks for listening, Lara. It's probably the first time I've told someone who didn't already know something about it.'

'Not at all,' she said. 'I'm glad you told me.'

The rest of the journey to Desaru was on quieter roads, through farmland and plantations, dotted with tiny communities. As they sped through the countryside, Lara thought about Christian's revelation. Her heart went out to him, knowing at least something of what he must have been through. She was grateful that he'd felt able to share it with her.

At last they turned onto a road that ran along beside the ocean. Lara stared out at the strip of white sand, fringed with swaying coconut palms, and at the vast expanse of shimmering sea that melted into the misty blue sky at the horizon. It was picture perfect. She hadn't imagined that it would be as stunningly beautiful as this. She thought of Suria, growing up in the midst of all that beauty. Her family must have been very poor for her to want to exchange this for waitressing in Singapore.

After a few kilometres they were coming into the

outskirts of a small town. The road was lined with modern hotels and resorts, cafes and bars.

'Desaru's a holiday resort nowadays,' Christian explained over his shoulder. 'Popular with Malaysians from Johor Bahru.'

He pulled the bike off the road onto a parking area facing the beach. 'I just need to check the map,' he said. 'I think the village is a little way north of here.'

He spread the map on the seat of the bike and Lara pored over it with him, leaning in close, their heads almost touching. Kuala Lapah was just to the north of Desaru, a little way back from the sea. Looking at the name on the map made Lara tingle with anticipation. Within a few minutes they would be there. Would someone there remember Suria? It was unlikely, she had to admit that to herself, but even if they didn't she would be able to see the place where her grandmother had grown up.

They got back on the bike and carried on along the Desaru strip. A couple of kilometres beyond the last hotel, the little community of Kuala Lapah came into view. It was a line of simple, single-storey houses with a small mosque at one end. Some were brick built, but many were made of wood. They were set a little way back from the seafront. Beside the road was a car park from which a small jetty jutted out over the sea. Three or four fishing boats were moored up there. To one side of the car park was a shack that looked like a shop, but as they got closer they could see that there were a couple of tables outside.

Christian parked the bike and they both approached the building. A couple of fishermen were sitting eating at one table, so they took the other one. A middle-aged woman came and took their order. She was very welcoming and full of smiles. Lara guessed that they didn't get many western tourists here. She didn't speak much English, so Christian ordered in Malay.

'Impressive that you know the language,' said Lara after the woman had gone back into the hut. 'Where did you learn?'

He shrugged. 'I learned a bit through work before I came out to Singapore. I'm a bit rusty. Everyone in the city speaks English.'

'What did you order by the way?' she asked.

'Oh – two prawn satays and a pot of jasmine tea. Those guys are eating satays and they look delicious.'

'Sounds great. The bike ride has certainly given me an appetite.'

Christian smiled. 'Me too. But we didn't just come here to eat, did we? Where shall we begin?'

'I think I might need you to help out with your language skills if no one speaks English around here,' she replied. 'I hadn't thought of that. How stupid of me!'

'Not stupid at all. It's easy, spending time in Singapore, to think that everyone speaks English. I'll do my best, but my Malay is a bit limited, I have to tell you.'

'That's so kind of you, Christian. Well, why don't we start here? We could ask the café owner and those two fishermen. What do you think?'

'Alright. No time like the present,' he said. Then he turned and addressed the two men at the other table. They were dressed in rough work clothes. One looked to be middle-aged and the other in his twenties Lara guessed. Too young to remember the war. They listened to Christian's faltering sentences, then conferred together for a few minutes. Lara held her breath, wondering what they were discussing. But the older one turned back to Christian shrugging and shaking his head.

'They don't know anything, I'm afraid,' said Christian.

'Did you tell them her name? That she grew up here before the war?'

'Yes, I told them everything I could about your grand-mother. Look, our food is coming out now. I'll ask the owner.'

The woman put the plates on the table, then Christian began to speak to her. He repeated what he'd said to the fishermen. Lara watched the woman's face for any sign of recognition as Christian was speaking. She was peering at him, a slight frown on her face. It was clear she was having trouble understanding what he was saying.

'Could you show her the photograph, Lara? She might understand then.'

Lara took her camera from her pocket, switched it on and scrolled to the image of Suria. She held it up and showed it to the woman. The woman peered at the screen, but shook her head and said something in Malay to Christian.

'She doesn't know anything,' he said. 'She doesn't recog-nise her.'

'Could you ask her if there's anyone old still living in the village who might remember?' Lara asked, and waited while Christian relayed the request. Her face lit up in a smile and she responded quickly to Christian. Lara could hear the warmth in her voice.

'Her aunt still lives here. She's well into her eighties, but still very independent apparently. Her house is the last one in the village on the right.'

The woman spoke again. 'This lady will take us there once we've finished lunch,' Christian said. 'She's about to close up the café and have a break.'

Lara tucked into the prawn satay. The prawns were

succulent and delicious and she guessed that they'd been caught by one of the boats moored up at the jetty that very morning. She had to hold herself back from wolfing them down in her desire to get through them quickly so that they could visit the old woman.

It was a good thirty minutes before the clattering of pots and pans in the tiny kitchen subsided, and the café owner emerged, taking off her pinafore. The two fishermen had shambled away, with good natured nods goodbye and were by then back on their boat sluicing down the decks with buckets of water.

The woman smiled and nodded for Christian and Lara to follow her. She got onto a battered scooter while they put their helmets back on and got onto the motorbike. They followed her out of the car park and down the village street where a few villagers sitting out on their porches waved at the woman as she passed. Chickens and dogs searched around in the dust under the houses. She pulled up on the road outside the last house on the right and Christian pulled in beside her. Lara's heart was beating quickly now. The house was a modest wooden building, small but well maintained. Would this old lady remember Suria? She must be roughly the same age as her.

They followed the woman down the path between carefully tended lines of vegetables. She went up some wooden steps and knocked on the front door. It was a few minutes before it was opened by an old lady, wrinkled and bent with age, but as she spoke her voice was full of energy and humour.

The café owner said something then motioned them to come inside.

'She says to come in,' Christian translated. 'We can explain who it is we want to find out about. She remembers the war well and knew everyone who lived in the village at the time. She speaks English too.'

'This is my aunt Amina,' said the café owner in faltering English.

Lara went up the steps and the old woman held out her hand. Lara took it and looked straight into her eyes. They were wreathed with wrinkles, but as the old woman looked back at Lara she gasped and pulled Lara towards her, staring straight into her eyes, speaking quickly and urgently in Malay.

'What is she saying?' Lara asked Christian.

'She says she recognises you. That you look like her friend from long ago.'

The old woman asked them to sit down on a low settee. She sat down opposite, not taking her eyes off Lara's face for a moment. The niece brought them jasmine tea and sat down herself. Lara looked around at the old lady's home. It was a single room; small and sparsely furnished, with one corner obviously serving as a kitchen, but it was neat and well kept. The front window looked out over the palm trees towards the sparkling sea.

Christian began speaking. Lara heard him say the name Suria and the old woman gave a start.

'Suria!' she said. Then, with trembling hands, Lara brought out the camera and showed her the photograph of her grandmother. The old lady drew it towards her and stared at it for a long moment. Tears gathered in her eyes and ran down her wrinkled cheeks.

'Are you her granddaughter?' she asked, staring at Lara. 'So her daughter survived the war?'

Lara nodded. 'She trained as a nurse and came to work in England. That's where she met my father. Sadly, she died a few months ago.'

The old lady reached out a bony hand and took Lara's and squeezed it. Her hand felt cold and leathery to the touch.

'I'm so sorry to hear that, my dear,' she said.

'That's why I came here. I wanted to find out more about my mother's childhood and something about my grandmother.'

Amina took a great, shuddering breath and sat still for a few moments, her head bowed. Then she began to speak hesitantly in English.

'Suria and I were best friends as children,' she said. 'We went to school together. When we were old enough, we both went to Singapore and got jobs to send money back to our families. That was a year or so before the war. We were very poor, but we worked hard and enjoyed ourselves when we weren't working. We lived in a go-down with lots of poor Chinese workers. But things became difficult and dangerous in Singapore when the Japanese invaded Malaya. I decided to come back to the village. But Suria refused to return. She wanted to keep earning money for her family because her mother was sick. But there was another reason she wanted to stay; she had met an English officer and she wanted to be with him.'

'Do you know his name?' Lara asked, holding her breath for the answer.

Amina nodded. 'Charles. His name was Charles. I don't remember his last name. Suria met him in an unusual way. She was working in a tailor's shop and he came in to collect something and complained because it wasn't ready. Suria was dismissed because of his complaint, but he got in touch with her afterwards and helped her to get another job. It was through him that she got the job in Raffles.'

'That's where I saw this photograph,' murmured Lara. The old lady nodded.

'She enjoyed working there. She stayed in Singapore through all the bombings and the invasion. She wouldn't leave. She wrote me a couple of letters at the beginning, but once the Japanese had invaded, the letters stopped coming.'

'What did she say in her letters?'

Amina dropped her gaze and drew another deep breath. Then she looked up.

'She said she was pregnant with Charles' child. I must admit that I was shocked at the time. We were brought up as devout Muslims, and in the village she would have been an outcast. But Singapore wasn't so strict. She seemed happy that it had happened.'

'You know that her child – my mother – ended up in an orphanage?' asked Lara.

The old lady nodded and closed her eyes.

'Suria came back here after the war. She told me she'd managed to track her child down. The little girl was in a Catholic orphanage but the nuns wouldn't let Suria take her away. But Suria was only here in the village a day or so. Her mother and father were dead by then. Her brother had sold their house and moved away...'

Amina stopped and once again closed her eyes. She took a few more deep breaths and was clearly struggling with difficult memories.

'Why was she only here for such a short time?' asked Lara gently. She didn't want the old lady to clam up.

The old lady dabbed her nose and eyes with a handkerchief and cleared her throat.

'She was hounded out. Someone... I think it was a very difficult woman called Choi, told everyone what had happened to Suria during the war. They found out she was here and they came to my home and surrounded it. They were banging on the doors and walls. Someone even threw a stone which broke a window. She had to leave, for her own safety.' Amina shuddered at the memory, her face grave.

'Why?' asked Lara, puzzled. 'Why would they do that? What happened to her during the war?'

Amina looked up then and turned to look at Lara, a tortured look in her eyes.

'You mean you don't know?'

Lara shook her head, chills of dread going through her.

'Could you tell me about it?' she asked in a small voice. The old lady nodded.

'I've always wondered what happened to her child and whether she had survived the war. I felt guilty that I didn't go to Singapore myself and remove her from the orphanage. But she wouldn't have been safe here, and I had nowhere else to take her. I've never had much money. But now I know she survived and went on to have a family, I owe it to you and to Suria to tell you what happened.'

'Thank you,' breathed Lara, a lump forming in her throat.

'It will be hard for me to tell and even harder for you to hear,' said Amina. 'I don't know all the details of what happened to her, and the truth is probably far more horrific than I know, but I will do my best to tell you what I can.'

23

SURIA

Singapore, 1942

When Suria and Minnie finally got back to the hotel from the hospital that day, physically exhausted, their emotions shattered from what they'd seen, Aziz opened the staff door for them.

'Take a look in the lobby,' he said as they greeted him. 'I've never seen anything like it.'

They walked through to the end of the passage that led to the lobby. The place was packed out with British people with their luggage. They were mainly women and children, some sitting on the floor, others perched on crates and suitcases. Most of them looked hot and grubby, their clothes crumpled. Exhaustion and fear was etched on their faces. Suria guessed that they were fleeing the fighting, and that they had nowhere else to go. A crowd had gathered at the desk, people were waving their arms, clamouring for attention, haranguing the receptionists. When the girls passed the restaurant on their way to their rooms, Suria saw that it was overflowing with guests, the waiters rushing around with trays and plates, looking harassed. The noise of raised voices was deafening.

'Perhaps we should ask Mr Antonio if he wants help,' Suria said to Minnie, but Minnie shook her head.

'I need to go back to my parents' place to see if my sister is there. I'm so worried about her,' she said through tears.

'Of course, you go on,' said Suria, squeezing Minnie's hands. 'I hope she's there and that she's safe.'

Suria turned back to the restaurant, found Mr Antonio and offered her services for the evening.

'Thank you, Suria. I know it's your day off, but you can see what we're dealing with here,' he said, wiping sweat from his brow.

'Why are there suddenly so many people in the hotel?' she asked. He shrugged.

'The Japs have advanced into the city now. I heard that there are no more ships leaving from Keppel harbour. These people probably came to Singapore thinking they could get onto a ship to Australia, but now they're trapped in the city. They have nowhere else to go.'

Suria looked around at the noisy restaurant. Like the lobby, it was crammed with British families, many with babies and small children. What would happen to them if this place was overrun by Japanese troops like the hospital had been? Chills went through Suria at the memory of what she'd witnessed there only a couple of hours before.

That evening came the devastating news that the British had surrendered to the Imperial Japanese Army and that all of the eighty thousand Allied troops on the island of Singapore had been taken prisoner. They'd been marched out to Changi, through the city streets, which were full of jeering crowds. When she heard the news, Suria immediately thought of Charles. Had he been taken prisoner too? Had he had to suffer the hardship and humiliation of that march to prison? Or had he died in the final battle for the city? She couldn't bear to think of either of those consequences. If he had been taken prisoner, what would happen to him? She'd heard many horror stories of how the Japanese treated their prisoners of war. They had no mercy, there were many tales of torture and of massacres of troops they'd taken prisoner in Malaya. Suria went hot and cold with fear for Charles' safety.

She noticed that the guests in the hotel became even more restless and fearful now that the city had fallen to the Japanese. The atmosphere was one of chaos and panic amongst the British people crowded into the rooms and into every public space in the hotel. Food stocks were running low and there was little to offer them at mealtimes. On the next day, just after dawn, what everyone had been dreading actually happened. The hotel was stormed by Japanese soldiers. They burst through the main entrance, leaping over the walls, rampaging across the gardens and in through the garden doors, and, pushing Aziz aside, some burst in through the staff entrance. Suria happened to be upstairs at the time, preparing to come down to help out at breakfast, when she heard shots and screams coming from the lobby. She rushed to the bannisters on the first-floor landing and leaned over to see what was happening, with dread in her heart.

The British guests were panicking, trying to run away from the soldiers, making for any exit, but there was no escape. One of the Japanese officers was screaming at them in English, his face red and full of fury.

'You have to line up!' he barked. 'Do not try to run! This hotel belong to Imperial Japanese Army now. All you British are going to Changi prison. Line up! Line up!'

Soldiers prodded the British into line with their bayonets. People were screaming, crying, mothers were grabbing their children, clutching them in their terror. But gradually, a ragged line began to form in the lobby, families bunched together, clinging to each other, mothers sobbing, children with tears running down their cheeks. Suria's heart went out to these people who, as individuals, had done nothing wrong. They were just part of the bigger machine of the empire, in the wrong place at the wrong time.

'Those poor children!' Suria heard Minnie's voice at her shoulder. 'What will happen to them in prison?'

Suria shook her head, wondering herself. It was too awful to contemplate.

'Did you find your sister?' she asked. It was the first time she'd seen Minnie since they'd parted after the ill-fated hospital visit.

'Yes! She hadn't gone to work that day. She had an upset stomach. Thank God for that – it saved her life.'

Suria embraced her friend. 'You must be so relieved,' she said and Minnie hugged her back, but their attention was soon drawn back to what was happening below them in the lobby.

A Japanese officer had commandeered a table and chair and the queue was being directed towards him. He was writing down names, slowly and carefully. Once people were registered, they were sent outside to wait on the Padang.

'How are they going to get to Changi do you think?' Minnie asked.

'I'm not sure,' Suria said. 'The soldiers had to march there yesterday. Perhaps they will too?'

'How will they cope? It's over twelve miles from here to Changi. They'd have to walk in the heat of the sun.'

Suria shook her head, wondering herself.

'Do you think we should go down and speak to Mr Antonio?' she asked Minnie. Minnie shook her head.

'I'm sure no one will be serving breakfast today,' she said. 'It would be best to keep out of the way until we know what's happening.'

So, they did that. For hours they watched, petrified, but mesmerised too as the queue moved forwards slowly and painfully. Details of every guest were written down in the book, then people were dispatched outside to assemble for the onward journey. No one was speaking anymore. Fear had stunned them into silence. There was just the occasional sound of a baby or small child whimpering. Japanese soldiers stood over the queue with guns and bayonets, making sure people stayed in line. When finally, the last guest had been registered and sent outside, one of the officers barked some orders at the troops and they immediately dispersed in different directions.

Suddenly, from outside came the unexpected sound of singing. First it was a few straggly voices, gradually joined by others, until it sounded like a choir in full voice. Chills went down Suria's spine at the sound. The girls looked at each other as they heard the familiar words of a song that they knew to be a British favourite: *There'll always be an England.* They rushed across the landing to a window which gave a view over the front drive. The column of dishevelled civilians guarded on both sides by Japanese soldiers with drawn bayonets, marched away from the hotel carrying their suitcases and boxes, singing at the tops of their voices, punching the air defiantly as they went.

But then came the sound of the soldiers running through the rooms inside the hotel, banging doors, shouting out in their guttural, unfamiliar tongue.

'It sounds as though they're searching the building,' said Suria. Her instinct was right and it wasn't long before they heard boots crashing up the stairs towards them. The two girls stood with their backs to the window, petrified. Suria found that her legs trembled so much she thought they might give way. The soldiers emerged from the top of the staircase, bayonets drawn, their faces full of hate and fury. Ignoring the two girls standing there, they went from room to room, kicking the doors open, slamming around inside the rooms, opening cupboards, kicking their way into the bathrooms. All the time they carried on yelling in Japanese. The violence in their voices froze the blood in Suria's veins.

Once they'd finished searching all the rooms on the first floor, they carried on their deadly progress up the stairs. Suria grasped Minnie's hand as terrified squeals came from one of the rooms. A woman appeared at the top of the stairs, her arms behind her back. She was being held by two soldiers. One of them also dragged a little girl by her arm. Tears were streaming down her face. Suria watched in horror as mother and child were forced down the stairs, all the time sobbing and crying out in terror. More screams came from the top floor where a further three people were brought out from their hiding places. One a young woman who was kicking and screaming so much that the solider was dragging her by her long blonde hair.

Suria's mouth went dry and she found she couldn't swallow. She was so petrified she just wanted to melt away. What would happen to her and Minnie? She wondered if they would be safer up in their rooms, although perhaps the soldiers would search up there too? What would they do to the staff? Surely they wouldn't take Asians prisoners as well? Hadn't they promised that they were on their side, that they would treat the native population well?

When the noise had died down, and they were sure the soldiers had finished their search of the hotel, Suria and Minnie crept upstairs to Suria's room, where they huddled together on the narrow bed, still terrified, wondering what the coming days would bring, hardly daring to speak.

Later that morning, the hotel manager called all the staff together in the dining room. They all trooped in, speaking to each other in hushed tones, the corridors guarded by Japanese soldiers. Everyone stood in a circle to listen to the manager who climbed up to stand on a table to address them. Suria looked around at the faces of her colleagues. On each she could see fear and confusion in equal measure. Even Aziz, who had expressed such optimism for the Japanese invasion looked bewildered and frightened having witnessed the way the British women and children had been treated.

The manager cleared his throat and a hush fell over the assembled company.

'Ladies and gentlemen,' he began. He was Italian, like Mr Antonio, and Suria recognised the accent. 'I've called you together on this unusual day to let you know, as best I can, what will happen to the hotel now.'

Suria watched the man's face. He was portly and middle-aged. His face was flushed, his black hair was plastered to his head as if he'd been sweating profusely, and she could see from his eyes that he was afraid. They kept flicking to the back of the room where the Japanese soldiers stood along the walls, their weapons drawn.

'As you know, Singapore has fallen to the Japanese and is now under their control. The same applies to this hotel. It will be given a Japanese name and become quarters for high-ranking Japanese officials. As staff here, I hope you will continue to serve those who stay here with the same professional pride you have always shown. In fact, it will be a privilege to serve these officers.'

A murmur of surprise went through the room and people looked at one another, frowning.

'You will be paid properly for your work and I expect you to rise to this new challenge as you have to everything that's happened here over the past few months. Now, I am going to get down from here and I'm going straight to the kitchens to help the chefs prepare lunch for those officers who are already here.'

He clambered down from the table, and moved towards the kitchen, the crowd parting to let him through. Mr Antonio bustled over.

'Suria, Minnie. Please stay and help prepare the tables for luncheon. We are expecting a full house today.'

It took the entire waiting staff a full hour to clean the room and lay the tables. Many of the families had used it as a place to sit and wait for news over the past twenty-four hours and the place was filthy and full of litter. When the room was finally ready, the Japanese officers started to arrive and take their places at the tables. Just looking at them sent Suria's nerves into overdrive. As she went to the tables to take orders, she dropped her gaze, not wanting to look any of them in the eye. She didn't believe Aziz's stories of how the Japanese wanted to free the local population from British rule. She was more inclined to believe the tales of atrocities, especially having witnessed the brutal way the women and children had been treated that morning.

She took orders and brought food obediently throughout that first lunchtime. She tried to remain as invisible and neutral as she could, not wanting to draw attention to herself, but each time she happened to look up, she noticed that one or other of the officers was looking at her with lust in their eyes. If they weren't leering at her, they were looking at one of the other girls. When she went to collect plates from a table where a fat, lascivious looking officer was sitting, he grabbed her thigh between his thick fingers and pinched it hard. Suria couldn't help letting out a little squeal of shock. Everyone in the restaurant turned and stared and several of the Japanese laughed at her. She felt her cheeks flaming with embarrassment as she hurried back across the floor towards the kitchen.

'I'm so sorry, Suria,' said Mr Antonio, shaking his head. 'Most uncouth behaviour.'

But that wouldn't be the last time she was humiliated while she was serving the officers. As the days and weeks wore on, it became a regular occurrence. Her thighs would be squeezed, her bottom slapped, her cheeks pinched, amid raucous laughter and clapping from the officers. It happened to all the young waitresses who served in the dining room. There was clearly a lot of bawdy talk too, and Suria was grateful that she didn't understand their language. The girls learned to grit their teeth and accept the humiliation as part of the situation they were facing. Suria tried to complain to Mr Antonio, but he just shook his head.

'There is nothing I can do, Suria. They are our rulers now.'

'But can't we do other work? Men could serve them instead.'

Again, he shook his head. 'I threatened them with that, but they said I would be punished if I take the waitresses away. They insist on things staying as they are. I'm sorry, but I can't do anything about it.'

The hotel was renamed – *Syonan Ryokan* – and the Japanese flag was hoisted above the roof in place of the Union Jack.

Suria survived by keeping a low profile. She took care to keep her appearance neat and low-key. She didn't want to appear attractive to the officers, but nothing seemed to deter them. Everyone around her was subdued and frightened. They stayed in their rooms, aware that if they met one of the officers in the corridors they would have to bow, a low bow from the waist. If they failed to do it properly, they would be slapped or kicked.

The news from the city was terrifying. During the first few weeks, every Chinese man between the ages of 18 and 50 and some women too had to report to screening centres where their details were taken and they were interrogated to see if they were sympathisers of the Chiang Kai-shek movement in China. Many who were found to have links to the movement were massacred on the beaches of Singapore. It was called "Sook Ching"; purification by elimination. Rumour had it that the British prisoners of war from Changi jail were sent in work parties to bury the dead.

This horrified Suria and she couldn't think about it without trembling with fear. She remembered all the Chinese people who had shown her such kindness in the go-down, had shared their food with her and kept her spirits up during many difficult days she'd spent there. She knew that some of them at least were political and likely to be supporters of Chiang Kai-shek. She couldn't bear the thought of those kindly people being taken away and shot. She thought about going there to see her old friends, but it was too terrifying to contemplate. Hardly anyone went out on the streets except on strictly necessary errands. There were soldiers everywhere and checkpoints on all the bridges and junctions.

She heard that food was starting to get scarce for the local population, but the hotel had no difficulty in securing plentiful supplies for the officers. The chefs had to learn their preferences. They wanted sushi and sashimi and Japanese noodles of different descriptions, but they also had a taste for English food. Mealtimes became an ordeal for Suria and all the girls who served. The behaviour got worse over time, with Japanese officers getting drunk most evenings, and when they got drunk they became even more predatory. Suria worried for her baby. Her belly was beginning to swell and she was terrified that one of the Japanese would discover that she was pregnant. She wasn't sure why, but she had a feeling that it could put her in danger, so she did her best to hide her expanding girth.

Sometimes the officers brought young women to dine with them in the hotel. This was a respite for Suria and the other waitresses, but it made them fear for the safety of these young girls. Most of them didn't look Japanese; they were either Korean or Chinese. Some were even Malay. Underneath their makeup they appeared dead-eyed and subdued, and it was clear that they weren't accompanying the officers to eat at Raffles out of choice. After they'd eaten, the officers would take them up to the bedrooms, but by the morning the girls were usually gone. Suria wondered about where they came from and where they were staying. She felt desperately sorry for these beaten, exhausted looking young women, forced to be with the Japanese officers against their will. She would have liked to speak to them, to understand more about their plight, but none of them ever looked into her eyes, or left the tables unescorted.

To make matters worse, there was a particular officer who took a fancy to Suria and would always insist on her serving his table. He was taller than most Japanese and was running to fat. His stomach bulged over the top of his trousers.

'Beautiful girl!' he would call when he spotted her, beckoning her over, trying to hug her to him. Suria always resisted, which angered him.

'One day you will regret this, girl,' he said to her on one occasion when she pulled away from his touch. He narrowed his eyes as he spoke. The way he looked at her sent shivers down her spine.

A few days later the housekeeper called Suria into her office. She fixed her with a stern look.

'It has become obvious to me that you are expecting a baby,' she said.

Suria hung her head. She couldn't deny it, but she knew that the housekeeper would be scandalised by the fact that she wasn't married.

'I'm afraid this means that I have to dismiss you from our service,' the woman continued. 'It is no longer appropriate for you to go on working here in your condition. Especially with the clientele we are dealing with now.'

Suria nodded. 'I understand,' she said. There was no point in trying to argue with the housekeeper. She'd seen other women dismissed for the same reason and in a way it was a blessing in disguise. It would mean that she would no longer have to put up with the pinches, bawdy comments and general harassment in the dining room. She had saved a little money while she'd been working and knew that she could live very cheaply somewhere in Chinatown.

She packed up her room, cramming her belongings into the two flimsy bags she had arrived with all those months before. She looked around at the room with regret. It held such fond memories; it was where she and Charles had made love that one and only time.

The time came for her to say goodbye to Minnie. The girls clung to one another.

'I'm not going far,' Suria said through tears. 'I'll let you know where I am and we can meet.'

She left the hotel with a heavy heart and headed towards Chinatown. As she walked, she noticed how the grass on the Padang had been neglected and left to grow. The bomb craters that pockmarked the road had not been repaired and weeds were sprouting from them. There was barbed wire strung along the riverside walk, and as she approached Cavenagh Bridge she could see the checkpoint manned with soldiers at the entrance to the bridge. Fear seeped through her as she approached. She had done nothing wrong, but just the sight of them standing there, smoking, with their guns and bayonets slung over their shoulders, made her tremble. But they nodded her through once they had scrutinised the identity card that had been issued to her by the hotel.

She walked on into Chinatown. It had changed little since she'd last been there during the siege a few months before. So many buildings had been destroyed, piles of rubble in the street, in some places covered in lush greenery already. Little paths wound over these mounds where people had found a way through. Suria was shocked by how many gaps there were in the terraces of shophouses. They looked like missing teeth. She wondered how many people had lost their homes, not to mention their lives, during the bombings.

The atmosphere on the streets of Chinatown was subdued. There were only a few thin voices hawking wares, hardly anyone cooking on woks on the pavement and the street stalls she passed were practically bare. Gone was the usual bustle and clamour of the district. People went about with their heads bowed, looking dishevelled, hardly looking each other in the eye.

Suria had told herself that she wouldn't go to her old go-down, fearing that Choi would be there, but she found herself at the top of the street and suddenly felt drawn to it. She wanted to check that the Chinese people she'd got to know when she and Amina had lived there had survived the Sook Ching. So, taking a deep breath, she walked up to the building and was relieved to see the same boy sitting on a stool outside the entrance, flicking through a magazine.

'Hey, Li Wei,' she called, remembering his name. He shaded his eyes against the sun and peered down at her. Then, recognising her, he beckoned her forward. She mounted the steps.

'How are things in the go-down?' she asked him. 'Is everyone safe?'

'Most,' he said, a flicker of sadness passing his eyes. 'Some were taken during the Sook Ching.'

'Oh! How dreadful. Who was that?' she asked, shock flooding through her.

He reeled off seven or eight names, people she didn't know. Suria imagined them being marched away at gunpoint by unsmiling Japanese soldiers. Chills went through her at the thought.

'Is Choi still living here?' she asked. He shook his head.

'She had a big argument with someone and moved out. I don't know where she went,' he said and Suria's spirits lifted.

'Are there any free spaces upstairs? I need a place to stay,' she asked tentatively. He told her there were plenty of free spaces, and that she should speak to the manager. So she went inside the go-down, up the familiar steps and into the dormitory, making her way between the sleeping mats to the corner where she and Amina used to sleep. The women, squatting on their haunches chatting, sewing or peeling vegetables, looked up as she passed and greeted her with friendly smiles. The place was just the same. Familiar smells of cooking and drains, familiar sounds and familiar faces. Strangely, although it was one of the roughest and cheapest places to stay in the whole of Singapore, there was something comforting about being back there.

24

SURIA

Singapore, 1942

Suria settled back into the life of the go-down quickly and soon it was as if she'd never left. Two young Chinese women, Mae and Suki, who slept opposite her, noticed her pregnancy and began to take a great interest in her welfare. They brought her herbs and ointments to ease her aches and pains, cooked her special meals, and insisted on washing her clothes alongside their own after they'd finished their day's work.

She felt guilty accepting all this kindness from these women who were so desperately poor themselves; Mae was a street sweeper and Suki transported fruit from the harbour to market stalls in baskets hung from a pole across her shoulders. But they insisted that they were glad to help her. They told her that they'd both left children behind in Hokkien Province in the care of relatives and that helping Suria reminded them of the happiest times of their lives.

'When your time comes, we will help you deliver,' said Mae. 'We know what to do.'

'Thank you,' she breathed, relieved.

She'd not contemplated the reality of what would happen when the baby arrived, but it had been in the back of her mind constantly. Sometimes though, she feared for her new friends. There were still men in the go-down who were in the Kuomintang; Chiang Kai-shek sympathisers who had somehow been missed by the Japanese during the recent purge. Sometimes these men organised hushed and secretive meetings at the far end of the go-down. Mae and Suki would attend the meetings and it terrified Suria to see them sitting on the edge of the circle of people listening with rapt expressions to one of the men giving an impassioned speech.

She tried to warn them about the dangers, but they wouldn't listen.

'These men are our friends,' they insisted. 'They work in the resistance against the Japanese in China and they try to protect us here too.'

'But you know you could be taken away and shot for supporting them, don't you?' she asked. In response they shook their heads, frowning, not wanting to discuss it. Nothing she said would persuade the two women to stop attending the meetings. So, they all skirted around the subject and Suria tried to put it to the back of her mind.

Conditions in Singapore became harsher and food scarcer as the occupation continued. Stories were rife of Japanese brutality; people being beaten up for not bowing correctly at checkpoints or executed for minor transgressions of the rules. Once or twice when she was out walking or buying food, Suria caught sight of work parties of British POWs, either on the backs of covered trucks, clearing bomb-sites, or doing some sort of construction work. They had begun to look pitifully thin and weak, their uniforms in rags, some of them were barefoot.

Each time she saw any prisoners, she would search for a glimpse of Charles, but always without success. She thought of him constantly as the baby grew inside her, regretting that she hadn't told him about her condition in the one letter that she'd written to him since they'd parted. She began to think about writing another letter and trying to get it to him in Changi. The more she thought about it, the more she wanted to try, especially as the birth became imminent.

Eventually, as her time approached, she put pen to paper, breaking the news to Charles about the baby, telling him how much she loved him and was missing him, how she feared for his safety. Then she sealed it and wrote his name and rank on the envelope. Without telling anyone in the go-down, she took some money and went down to speak to Li Wei, the boy on the door. She knew he had many contacts in Chinatown, and that he might be able to help her.

He looked up from his newspaper when she approached.

'I need to go to Changi,' she said. 'Do you know anyone who might take me there for payment?'

He peered at her. 'Changi is very dangerous. So many Japanese there. Many checkpoints on the way, too. Why do you need to go?'

'I want to deliver a letter,' she said.

'Why don't you just pay someone to take it? That way you wouldn't have to go yourself.'

She considered this briefly, but dismissed it and shook her head. 'I need to make sure it is given to someone trust-worthy,' she said.

'Should you really be going out there in your condition?' Li Wei said, eyeing her bulging stomach. 'Wouldn't you be better off here where you're safe?'

She shrugged. 'I'm not due for another three weeks. So, do you know anyone who might help?'

'Wait here.' She watched him amble down the steps, cross the road and disappear down one of the alleys opposite. She sat down on his chair to wait, picking up his newspaper. Scanning the pages, she was shocked to see that it was full of Japanese propaganda; how the Imperial Japanese Army had freed the population of Singapore from the oppression of British rule; how they were improving and rebuilding the city after the British had destroyed so many installations before the surrender including the docks and the oil depots.

When Li Wei returned, a bandy-legged old Chinese man walked beside him.

'This is Mr Ho,' Li Wei said. 'He will take you to Changi in his van. You will have to sit in the back under some empty sacks to avoid suspicion. He doesn't speak English, or Malay. I've explained where he is to take you.'

Mr Ho looked at Suria gravely and jerked his head sideways, motioning her to follow him. She walked behind him down the stuffy alleyway, to a street corner where a battered vehicle stood. It looked very old; the sort of vehicle that was used for food deliveries. The old man opened the back door and she clambered in, immediately overwhelmed by the extreme heat of the van and the smell of rotting fish. There was no doubt about the sort of food that was normally transported in the van.

There were a few empty hessian sacks on the floor. The old man pointed to them and motioned for Suria to cover herself with them. She sat back against the side of the vehicle, struggling to find a comfortable position and did her best to cover herself with the sacks which scratched and irritated her skin. As soon as the van started bumping along the cobbled streets of Chinatown, she knew that it would be an uncomfortable journey. She was thrown up and down and slipped around, trying to get a grip on the floor with her feet but failing each time.

Once they were out of Chinatown and on a wider road, things became a little smoother, but it was still painfully bumpy. The road continued like that for some miles until Suria sensed that they were out of the city and travelling through the jungle. Leaning forward and peering through the windscreen, she could see lush green fronds and undergrowth encroaching onto the road. It had been raining and the smell of fresh rain on the dusty surface rose from the road. It felt good to be out of the city. It was the first time she'd been out since she'd travelled to the north of the island to take the first letter to Charles. It seemed so long ago and so much had happened since that day.

They passed through villages and hamlets, with wooden houses raised on stilts, where people sat out on their porches, goats and chickens rooted around in the dirt and dogs ran alongside the van barking. It made Suria smile to travel through these sleepy old places, seemingly untouched by the occupation. As they emerged from the jungle onto a wider road, the van came to an abrupt halt and Suria heard voices; the guttural accents of Japanese soldiers. It was a checkpoint. She shrunk under the sacks, aware that the top of her head was probably showing, but there was nothing she could do about it. Her pulse raced as she heard the rustle of paperwork. The old man was showing his ID card and permits. There was a pause, then further questions. The soldiers were having trouble getting Mr Ho to understand.

In the end one of them banged on the side of the van, the engine started up again and the vehicle moved forward. Suria breathed again, pushing the stinking sacks off her face.

At last they were driving through a settlement of brick-built buildings and Suria guessed they had arrived in Changi. The old man pulled the van up on the kerb and turned to Suria.

'Changi,' he said, 'POW camp,' and he nodded in the direction of a group of forbidding looking low grey buildings grouped around a square. He came round to the back of the van and opened the doors. Suria clambered out and stretched her aching limbs, taking deep breaths, trying to dampen the nausea caused by the smell of fish. She looked over at the building. It was surrounded by barbed wire fences. She shaded her eyes and watched for a minute or two. She could see a few skinny looking prisoners moving about in the courtyard, another group digging a patch of ground a short distance from the fence. Two Japanese soldiers appeared at one corner of the compound bearing rifles, and began to patrol the length of the nearest fence. Suria watched them, holding her breath. If she was to go anywhere near the fence it would have to be between their patrols. She turned to Mr Ho.

'Wait here, please,' she said, trying to indicate with her hands what she meant. He sighed, nodded briefly and got back into the van.

She waited until the soldiers had completed their patrol of that side of the building, turned the corner and were moving away. Then, half crouching, she started to advance across the scrubland towards the barbed wire fence, trying to stay within the cover of bushes. But to move between bushes she had to cross open ground, and running in a stooping position wasn't easy in her condition. The sun beat down mercilessly, her heart was pounding and sweat was pouring down her face. It seemed to take an age to get there, but finally she was nearing the fence.

The group of prisoners digging earth were only a few yards away. Looking around for signs of Japanese, she crept up to the fence and in a hoarse whisper called to the group of men. None of them noticed, so she tried again, this time a little louder. On the third attempt one of them looked up, saw her standing there and automatically checked around him. Then he approached the fence. As he came towards her, Suria could see how thin he was. His cheeks were sunken and his legs, beneath his ragged shorts, were skin and bone.

As he came closer she could see the fear in his eyes. She felt a twinge of guilt that he was risking his safety to speak to her.

'What's the matter, lady?' he asked in a low voice, coming up close. His face was dirty and his eyes bloodshot and weary looking.

'Could you take a letter to a prisoner for me?'

'I could try. Who is it?'

She handed him the letter, pushing it through the mesh of the fence. The envelope tore a little as she did so and rust smeared the writing. The prisoner took it and stared at it, narrowing his eyes.

'Major Simmonds. I don't know him.'

'He's in the India III Corps. Could you try to get it to him?'

She pushed some dollars through the fence. 'Take these,' she said. The man's eyes brightened and he took the money quickly, secreting it in his shorts.

'I'll do my best. The Nips are coming. I need to get back,' he said and hurried back to where he'd been working.

Suria tried to thank him but he was already too far away and she didn't want to shout. She saw him exchange a few words with the other men before picking up his shovel again and resuming the digging, his head down. Out of the corner of her eye she became aware of the Japanese guards approaching and she knew she needed to get back to the van. She scurried over to the nearest clump of bushes and crouched down behind them. At that moment, the guards appeared at the corner of the camp and started to make their way along the fence she'd just left. She was less than fifty yards away and prayed that they wouldn't turn and spot her. She waited there, holding her breath until they'd moved on, then resumed her half crouching, half running progress back to the van. When she was close enough to see it properly she noticed something unusual and crouched down again, watching keenly, her heart in her mouth.

Two guards were approaching the van. Both had rifles slung over their shoulder. She watched, terrified, as they banged on the side of the vehicle, then they went round to the driver's door and wrenched it open. They were shouting at the driver, pointing, gesturing for him to move on. After a few moments, the engine started up and the van drove off, skidding on the dusty road, taking a bend in the road too fast. It disappeared into the jungle and was gone. The guards, laughing together, walked back towards the camp and were soon out of earshot.

A sob rose in Suria's throat. Here she was alone, in a place riddled with Japanese guards, heavily pregnant without any means of getting back to the go-down which was over twelve miles away. She had no food or water with her although she did have some money. How would she make it that far on foot? How would she get past the check-points? And was it all worth it anyway? Would Charles receive her letter? There was no way of finding out for sure. She wished with all her heart that she hadn't made this journey on a foolish impulse.

There was no option but to start back towards the city on foot. She was terrified of being spotted by the Japanese, so wherever she could she walked beside the road rather than on it. This was difficult on the jungle stretches, where the undergrowth was too thick to pass through. It was baking hot, the sky overcast and gloomy, threatening a downpour. She hurried on, keeping an ear out for approaching vehicles. A couple of times she had to dive into the undergrowth as lorries rattled past carrying prisoners to and from Changi.

She'd been walking for half an hour or so when she came across one of the villages they'd passed through on the way there. The village dogs surrounded her, barking and baring their teeth. Her heart was pounding, but she was used to village dogs from home, so she spoke to them calmly and they let her pass, following her with wagging tails. An old woman waved to her from the porch of one of the houses.

'Sister, come up and have a drink,' she shouted. Suria turned back and went towards the house gratefully. The old woman told her to sit down on the porch and brought her some water. Suria gulped it down gratefully.

'Where are you going?' she asked. 'We don't get many people walking out this way. Not with the soldiers everywhere.'

Suria explained that she'd been to Changi to deliver a letter, but that her transport had left without her. The old lady shook her head, tutting.

'You really shouldn't be walking in your condition. With it being so hot, it is a long way.'

'I know, but I don't have a choice,' said Suria.

'My husband can take you. He has a motorbike. I will call him now.'

'That's kind of you, but what about the checkpoints? I don't have any ID,' Suria said miserably.

'Oh don't worry about those. My husband knows his way around the backstreets. He can avoid the checkpoints. Does it all the time.'

She went inside the house and emerged with a stout old man, stretching and yawning. He smiled at Suria.

'Come with me,' he said.

The motorbike, stored behind the house, was nothing but an old moped, rusty and battered, the seat losing its stuffing. Suria's heart sank when she saw it, but it would be better than walking and she was grateful for the kindness of the old couple.

The man pulled it off its stand and, straddling it, started the engine. Suria climbed on board, and they set off from the hamlet, the old woman waving from her porch. They put-putted through the countryside until the checkpoint loomed ahead. Then the old man veered off the road and onto a dirt track which led through farmland, over potholes, across tiny bridges over ditches. In places it narrowed and became a footpath. Occasionally they came across people working on the fields, who stood aside to let them pass, greeting the old man with smiles and waves. Suria clung to him, gritting her teeth when they went over the bumps, grateful for his help but willing the ride to be over.

Soon they were back on the road, beyond the checkpoint and the way became less bumpy, but as they got closer to the city and began to travel through the outskirts, Suria felt cramps in her lower abdomen and she began to fear that her ordeal that day might have damaged the baby. But she gritted her teeth and tried to ignore the pain as they rode on through Geylang and Katong, over the Kallang river and towards the downtown area.

The rest of the journey was a blur. The pain came in waves over her abdomen and spread to her back. They started mildly, but rose to a crescendo. It was all she could do to hang on to the old man and to stop herself from crying out. When they finally reached the go-down, another pain ripped through her as she was getting down from the motorbike and she collapsed to her knees in the gutter, groaning.

Li Wei came rushing down the steps and with the help of the old man, managed to get her up to her place in the dormitory. As she eased herself onto the mattress, the old man stood there staring down at her, scratching his head. She had the presence of mind to fumble in her pocket and hand him some of her remaining dollars. He took them and backed away, his hands pressed together in gratitude, giving her a huge smile, displaying broken and blackened teeth.

'I will find Mae or Suki quickly,' said Li Wei. 'Your baby is coming.'

'No!' she said appalled as she watched him run to the top of the stairs. 'It's not due yet,' but at that moment, she felt a gush of water between her legs and a new, even more intense pain gripping her abdomen. Perhaps Li Wei was right. She propped herself up on her elbows and breathed through the pain of that contraction, but no sooner was that over than another one began, low in her belly, getting higher and stronger until she couldn't help crying out with the intensity of the pain. It went on like that for a long time. Each contraction felt stronger and more painful than the previous one. It seemed an age before Li Wei returned with Mae. Suria was terrified that the baby would come and she wouldn't know what to do. She'd already felt the urge to push, but had held back, closing her eyes and panting to stop herself.

Mae immediately took control, helping Suria with soothing words and firm directions. She sat behind Suria and massaged her back and shoulders, telling her when it was time to bear down and guiding her through each shuddering, agonising, straining push. At last, with one final heave, Suria felt the head move and the baby sliding out between her legs. Mae immediately collected it up, cleaned the blood away with a towel and handed the baby to Suria. She was smiling broadly.

'Well done, Suria. You've been so brave!' she said. 'It's a little girl.'

Suria took the baby in her arms and held her to her breast, marvelling at her tiny fingers and toes, her perfect features, her slick dark hair. And looking at her, she was sure she could see Charles in her face.

She'd already thought of a name; Charles if it had been a boy.

'Charlotte,' she said to Mae. 'This is Charlotte.'

'That's such a beautiful name,' said Mae, sitting down beside Suria and putting her arms around her. Just then Suki arrived. She'd been running, her face was streaming with sweat.

'You've missed all the fun!' said Mae and they all laughed.

～

A FORTNIGHT after little Charlotte was born, Suria asked Mae to look after the baby one morning. She put on her best clothes and walked through Chinatown, across the river, through the checkpoint on the bridge and on across the Padang towards Raffles Hotel. Chills went through her as she approached the building and saw the flag with the blood red sun emblazoned on it, flying high above the roof. She remembered the odious behaviour of the Japanese officers in the dining room; the pinches and the squeezes, the terrified looks on the faces of their young "comfort women". Did she really want to do this? But she drew herself up, steeling herself. She knew that this was the only place she would earn enough money to pay either Mae or Suki to look after Charlotte and have enough left over to live on. If she lived frugally, she might even be able to start sending money back home again.

She went straight to the staff entrance. Aziz was on the door. He looked just the same as he always had and his eyes lit up when he saw her.

'You're back, Suria! We've all missed you. How is your baby? Girl or boy?'

'A little girl: Charlotte. She's very well thank you, Aziz. I've come to see the housekeeper. Is she in?'

'Of course,' he said waving her through.

The housekeeper welcomed her with a warm smile and immediately gave her back her old job.

'You know what it's like serving in the dining room nowadays,' the woman said a little awkwardly. 'We've had several girls leave because they can't cope with what goes on there. I know you're made of sterner stuff than that, though.'

'Is Minnie still here?' Suria asked.

'Yes. Minnie is one of the strong ones.'

So, the next morning, Suria kissed Charlotte goodbye

and left her in the care of Mae. Mae had volunteered to give up her job sweeping the streets to look after Charlotte while Suria worked. Over the past couple of days, Suria had weaned the baby onto a bottle so she could leave her to the care of others, and her own milk was gradually drying up.

Suria thanked Mae many times for her kindness, but Mae just said;

'It's me who should be thanking you! Who wouldn't rather look after a beautiful little baby than sweep the filth and rubbish off the streets of Singapore?'

'Well I'm still very grateful anyway,' said Suria, suddenly remembering that she was wearing her amulet and that restaurant staff weren't allowed to wear jewellery. She unclipped it and slipped it into Charlotte's basket, underneath the fleece that served as a mattress. Then she left. She was a little late, so she didn't linger or look back to wave as she made for the go-down steps.

As she walked through the bomb-damaged streets towards the Singapore River, she thought of Mae and Suki and how fortunate she was to have made such warm, loving and caring friends. Her only source of disagreement with them had been their membership of the Kuomintang, but they'd all learned to accept the others' position and not to speak of it.

Mr Antonio was delighted to have Suria back and when Minnie saw her, she rushed to her and they embraced. Minnie wanted to know all about the baby's progress. She'd visited Suria and Charlotte in the go-down two days after the birth.

'You must come and see her again when we both have a day off,' Suria said.

They served lunch to a half-empty dining room and Suria was pleasantly surprised that the officers who came to

eat were busy talking to each other. They paid little attention to any of the waitresses. She also noticed that the fat
officer who'd made her life so difficult before was not
present. She mentioned this to Minnie as they stood
together waiting for orders in the kitchen.

Minnie's face clouded over.

'Oh, you mean Colonel Kimura,' she said. 'He isn't here
now, but he often visits and he may come later. He hasn't
changed. I've got a bruise on my thigh where he pinched me
the other day.'

Suria's heart sank at those words and she began to dread
what the evening might bring. She wondered whether to try to
leave early and rush back to Charlotte and the go-down, but
she soon realised that if she was going to do this job, she would
have to face Colonel Kimura sometime, so it might as well be
that evening. She knew Charlotte was in safe hands and that
Mae and Suki weren't expecting her back until after midnight.

During their break that day, Suria and Minnie walked
together on the Padang, breathing in the sea air and
catching up on each other's news. Suria asked about the
hospital. Minnie fell silent for a few moments and dropped
her gaze.

'So many people were killed that day,' she said quietly
after a pause. 'Massacred in their beds. Some patients were
even bayoneted on the operating table. Many doctors and
nurses were killed. My sister was so lucky, but my heart
bleeds for all those others who were there and who weren't
lucky.'

Suria was besieged by nerves in the build up to dinner
time, but tried to put her fears aside and to focus on her
work. She concentrated on laying the tables in her area,
making sure the silver was polished, the candles were lit,

there were fresh flowers, and that everything was ready for the evening.

Officers began to arrive. Some had already been drinking in the bar, others ordered drinks as soon as they sat down. Soon all the tables were full and the dining room was filled with male voices. Suria rushed around taking orders, bringing drinks and nibbles to the tables.

When Colonel Kimura walked in she was just emerging from the kitchen with a tray of plates. Her hands began to shake when she saw him and she almost dropped the tray. She stood still and watched him walk to a corner table that wasn't one of hers. Praying that he wouldn't notice her, she took the tray over to her table and handed out the food, but as she turned to go back to the kitchen she heard the colonel's booming voice.

'Beautiful girl!' he shouted. Suria kept her eyes to the floor and carried on walking. 'Beautiful girl!' he called again.

'I've missed you. Come to me. Come to me now!' Suria stopped walking and froze to the spot.

She felt the eyes of everyone in the restaurant turning to look at her.

'Come to me!' he ordered again. She had no choice. She turned back and walked towards his table, not lifting her eyes from the floor, a sick feeling in her stomach, her heart hammering.

She arrived at the table where Kimura sat with a group of other senior officers. They were all looking at her, some with lust, others with derision.

Kimura pulled her to him, circling his great arms around her waist. He looked up at her. She refused to look him in the eye.

'Tonight, you will come to my room,' he said. 'I have waited for you to come back. The time has come.'

Panic swept through Suria and she shook her head furiously.

'Don't refuse me,' he said, 'No one refuses the great Kimura. You will come to my room and you will be mine.'

Suria tried to back away, but his arms were locked around her waist. She could smell cigar smoke and alcohol on his breath. She looked at his face, pudgy and sweating. The thought of his lewd suggestions made nausea rise in her throat.

He pinched her chin and turned her face towards him. She closed her eyes, refusing to look at him, but he pulled her face down close to his.

'If you won't consent, you will regret it. There is another way.'

She wondered fleetingly what he meant. He released her from his grip and as she backed away he said, 'So, I ask you again. Will you come to my room?'

A sob rose in her throat which threatened to silence her, but she took a deep breath and found her voice. 'No!' she said vehemently. 'No, never!'

She turned and hurried back to the kitchen, tears streaming down her face, trembling from head to toe. She felt Minnie's arms around her and Minnie's voice in her ear.

'Are you alright, Suria? Take no notice of him. He is a brute.'

Suria went to the washroom and splashed cold water on her face. She wondered what to do. Should she just run home? Abandon the shift? She thought of the money she was earning and how others now depended on her. So she took a deep breath, went back into the restaurant and carried on serving.

The evening wore on and some tables were finishing their meals, diners began drifting away. Suria was clearing up her tables, putting knives and forks on her tray. She glanced across at Colonel Kimura. He was finishing his dessert, ladling trifle greedily into his mouth. Perhaps he'd forgotten about their earlier encounter. She began to relax, looking forward to getting home to Charlotte, chatting with Mae and Suki, lying down to sleep beside the baby. She took the tray to the kitchen, then went through to the locker room to change. Minnie was there too, taking off her uniform, putting on a red shalwar kameez.

'Are you alright now?' Minnie asked.

'I suppose so. It was a shock, that's all,' Suria said. 'I suppose I'll get used to it again.'

'I'll walk with you a little way,' said Minnie, linking arms as they left the building. Aziz saluted them as he opened the door for them to leave.

'Aren't you living at the hotel anymore?' Suria asked.

'I am, but tonight I'm going to see my parents. My mother hasn't been well.'

They crossed Beach Road together and started walking across the Padang. Suddenly Suria was aware of a Japanese army truck drawing up on the road beside them. Four soldiers jumped out of the back and within seconds had surrounded them. They were all bearing guns.

'What is this?' she asked.

'You come with us. Colonel Kimura orders,' one of them answered in broken English.

'No!' she said, trying to push past them, but she felt something sharp digging between her shoulder blades. Two soldiers seized her, one on each side and began to drag her towards the lorry. She screamed to be released and tried to wriggle out of their grasp, but they were too strong for her.

Out of the corner of her eyes she saw that Minnie was also being dragged towards the lorry. She was also screaming and sobbing as she went. They reached the back of the lorry and were forced up the steps and over the tailgate. Suria found herself sprawling on the floor. She sat up to see the soldiers leaping in behind her. One of them picked her up and sat her down on the bench. Minnie was pushed down beside her. The lorry started up and began moving.

'Where are we going?' she asked, but no one answered her. They met her question with stern looks, their eyes full of derision. She could feel Minnie trembling beside her as the lorry plunged on into the darkness of the Singapore night.

25

SURIA

Singapore, 1942

S uria peered out of the back of the truck as it bumped through the streets of Singapore, trying to gauge from the light of the streetlamps where they were headed, but it was impossible to tell; many lights had been damaged in the bombings. There was hardly anyone on the pavements now. It was after midnight and there was little in the way of nightlife for the locals under Japanese rule.

Suria couldn't stop fretting about baby Charlotte. Would she be crying for her mother now, unable to settle to sleep without her there? Suria had never been away from her for so many hours before and it was tearing her heart out to be separated from her baby. She thought about Mae and Suki. They would be looking out for her now, anxious for her return, but she knew that between them they would take care of Charlotte as best they could until she could get home. How long would she be away, though? Where were she and Minnie being taken? She fumbled for Minnie's hand on the bench beside her and gripped it hard. Minnie gripped hers back and Suria felt a little comforted by her touch. At least they were together and could face whatever the Japanese had in store for them side by side.

It wasn't a long journey. Twenty or thirty minutes at the most. They were still within the city, passing through an unfamiliar residential area, when the lorry slowed and juddered to a stop. The engine was turned off and there was a sudden silence. It filled Suria with dread. She tried to exchange glances with Minnie, but all she could see was the whites of her eyes. The driver was speaking to another man in Japanese. Then the engine rumbled into life again and the truck moved slowly forwards and turned off the road. Looking out, Suria could just make out that they were moving through some open metal gates with coils of barbed wire along the top.

Her heart was pounding now. Was this an internment camp? If so, why were she and Minnie being taken there? They were native Malays and should have been safe. But as the lorry moved forward, it was clear that this couldn't be an internment camp in the normal sense. It was a residential street lined with two-storey terraced houses, with balconies on the first floor. There were lights on in some of them. Suria noticed women leaning on the balcony railings in a couple of the houses, smoking. The women were dressed all in white. Were they nurses? Was this a hospital? Her mind was racing, filled with questions.

The lorry came to a halt again outside one of the houses. A soldier leapt down from the back and opened the tailgate. He motioned for the two girls to climb down. Suria hesitated, but another soldier prodded her in the chest with his bayonet, so she had no choice but to comply.

It was an ordinary terraced house like the others in the street. The front door opened and a tiny Japanese woman emerged. She came down the front path, tottering on high heels, and said something sharply to the soldiers. She looked to be in her fifties or sixties; her face was lined, but she wore thick white makeup and bright red lipstick. One of the soldiers pushed Suria into line so she was standing next to Minnie. The woman stepped forward, took Suria's chin in one hand and peered into her eyes. Then she felt her hair, put her fingers into her mouth to inspect her teeth, felt both her ears. Then she lifted Suria's dress and looked at her legs. She was muttering to herself all the time in Japanese. Then she did the same to Minnie.

'What is this about?' asked Suria, finding her voice. 'Why are we here?'

The woman turned back to her and smiled unpleasantly, displaying yellowing teeth. The smile didn't reach her eyes.

'This is a comfort station,' she said. 'You are here to work. Only officers come here. Not regular soldier.'

Chills of horror went through Suria. Minnie started sobbing quietly beside her.

'No!' she said. 'This is a mistake. We work at the hotel. We have families. We cannot stay here.'

'You are here to work,' repeated the woman, raising her voice this time. 'You have no choice. Don't give me trouble or you will be punished. Now follow me. I will show you inside.'

Suria glanced up the road, quickly assessing the chances of running away, but even from here she could see that the whole area was enclosed with high fences topped with rolls of barbed wire and there were guards on the gate carrying guns. She felt a prod in her back from a bayonet pushing her forward. She stumbled up the path to the front door of the house, following the Japanese woman. Minnie cried out behind her as the guards pushed her forward too.

Once inside, they were taken up a narrow wooden staircase and along a narrow passage lined with doors. Grunting sounds came from inside some of the rooms, sobbing, panting or shouting from others. At the end of the passage, the woman pushed two doors open, showing two tiny rooms; no more than cubicles really. They were side by side. There was a bed in each, a tiny chest with a jug and bowl and a rail for hanging clothes. On each rail hung a white uniform, like the ones Suria had noticed on the other women.

'You change into these,' snapped the woman. 'Be quick. Officers will be here soon.'

She left them, and they heard her high heels clatter down the stairs.

'What is this?' Minnie asked Suria. 'What's going on?'

Suria sat down on her bed feeling sick to the core. She was shaking all over. She knew what this meant, what the grunts and shouts from the other rooms signified, why the two of them had been abducted off the street. She thought of the dull, beaten look in the eyes of the comfort girls who'd accompanied the Japanese officers to dine at the hotel. How she'd pitied those poor girls, but it was happening to her and Minnie now. She knew she had to explain to Minnie.

'They've brought us here to serve the officers, Minnie. We're comfort girls now, do you understand what that means?'

Minnie looked at her with horror in her eyes. She started crying, sobbing uncontrollably.

'They can't do this to us. This is wrong. How can they do it?'

Suria tried to comfort her, but she had no answers. She wanted to cry too, but she knew she had to stay strong for

Minnie's sake and her own. She needed to focus, to think of a way of getting them both out of this situation. She put her arms around Minnie and pulled her close.

'Be brave, Minnie,' she said. 'We will find a way of getting out of here.'

At that moment there was the sound of boots thumping up the wooden stairs and male voices joking and laughing in the passageway. Suria's terrified eyes locked onto Minnie's and the next second, Colonel Kimura appeared in the doorway with another man behind him. He was smoking a cigar. He looked at the two girls clinging together on the bed, trembling, and roared with laughter.

'I said you'd pay, didn't I?' He pointed at Suria with his cigar. 'And you *are* going to pay. Many, many times over. Pay until you are beaten, like the British you love so much. When we've finished with you, you'll wish you acted differently.'

He lunged forward and grabbed Minnie by the arm. Minnie yelled out and clung to Suria, but Kimura prised them apart. He manhandled Minnie out of the cubicle. She made as if to run along the passage, but the other man caught her by the hair, and dragged her along the floor of the passage. All the time she was kicking and screaming.

'Let her go!' cried Suria, trying to get up from the bed to help her friend, but Kimura was blocking the doorway. The door to the next cubicle slammed, shaking the walls and Minnie's screams continued from inside.

'I hope you won't fight like your friend,' said Kimura, coming towards Suria. She backed away, but there was so little room she was soon pinned against the back wall. Kimura was coming towards her, blowing smoke in her face, smiling his fat smile.

'You are my prize,' he said getting closer and closer and

she saw the lust in his eyes. 'I will be your first. I've wanted you since I first saw you.'

She tried to dodge sideways, but the bed blocked her way. Her heart was thumping and her thoughts were scrambling. She was trapped. Trapped like a caged animal. A scream escaped from her and mingled with the screams coming from Minnie's room. Kimura's hands were on her shoulders now, he was pushing her down onto the bed.

'Don't fight me, girl,' he said, getting angry now. She let out another yell and tried to push him away. He pinned her down and clamped his hand over her mouth. His hand was dirty, stinking of tobacco. Suria opened her mouth and sunk her teeth into his palm. Kimura roared, his anger clearly mounting. He slapped her across the face and her head fell back onto the pillow, she was stunned by the pain. He was on her then, kneeling over her, pinning her down with one hand and unbuttoning his trousers with the other.

She felt his weight crushing her and, try as she might, she couldn't get out from under him. She could hardly breathe and she could smell his breath and the stale sweat on his clothes. Nausea rose in her throat and she cried out again as he forced her legs open with his hand and then entered her, thrusting so hard that she thought she would be torn apart. It only lasted a minute or so until he let out a shout and collapsed on top of her, panting. She tried again to get out from under him, but he pinned her down with both hands. His face was red with exertion, but he was also angrier than ever.

'You not a virgin!' he roared at her and began slapping her face in a forehand, backhand motion while she cried out and the tears streamed from her eyes. She became aware that Minnie was crying too through the wall, and that she was no longer screaming as she had been. She was sobbing quietly to herself. Suria yearned to go to her, to comfort her.

When Kimura had stopped slapping Suria, he got off the bed and pulled his trousers up over his fat legs, buckling his belt with his pudgy hands. Suria watched him, terrified, unable to move from her prone position on the bed. His face was still clouded with anger. He snatched up the cigar which he'd left smouldering in an ashtray on the chest and dived towards Suria. She tried to move away, but despite his bulk he was quicker than her. He stubbed the burning cigar out on her arm, her flesh screaming out in pain with each stab. She yelled out, trying to move away, trying to shield herself, but still the cigar stabbed into her flesh and the pain kept coming.

'Whore!' he yelled, then he left, slamming out of the tiny room, leaving the walls trembling in his wake.

Suria sat up and slowly moved her legs over the side of the bed. Every inch of her body was trembling, every part of her recoiling in horror at what had just happened. She stood up unsteadily and, pouring water from the jug into the bowl, took a flannel and washed herself as best she could; trying to wash the filth and slime of Kimura from between her legs. Minnie was still sobbing in the next room. Suria quickly dried herself and went to the door, meaning to go to Minnie to comfort her, but her door opened and another Japanese officer stood there, smiling, his eyes narrowing with desire as he caught sight of Suria standing there.

Thinking quickly, she tried to dive under his arm, to get out of the room, but he blocked her way. He was strong, muscular, far stronger than Kimura, and she was no match for his strength. Within seconds he had pinned her down on the bed and was unbuckling himself and although she tried to keep her legs closed, he prised them open and plunged inside her just as Kimura had. She cried out in pain and anguish and she heard Minnie's cries from the next-door cubicle echoing in unison.

When this one had finished, there was another one waiting at the door to take his place. Suria barely managed to get up from the bed between each successive assault. She tried to fight each one off, biting, slapping, wriggling. Once, she managed to crawl under the bed, but the man reached in after her and dragged her out, covered in dust. She lost track of how many men raped her that night; fifteen or sixteen before the grey light of dawn crept in around the edge of the door. All of them were rough with her, slapping her and bruising her body, leaving her shaking and exhausted. When the last one had departed, she forced herself up from the bed and washed herself again with the water left in the bowl. Blood was streaming down her legs and her arms were covered in cigar burns and bruises.

On unsteady legs, she went through to Minnie's room. Minnie lay on her bed, curled up, hugging her knees to her chest. Blood covered the sheets and Minnie's face was swollen on one side, a bruise beginning to bloom below one eye, her lips swollen and bleeding. Her body was convulsing with sobs. Suria sat down beside her and put her arms around her.

'I'm so sorry, Minnie,' she said, but Minnie didn't answer. Guilt racked Suria. It was her fault that this had happened. If she hadn't refused Kimura in the restaurant... although how could she have done anything else? She would never have consented to him voluntarily. A shudder went through her as she thought of his hands on her body, the anger and venom in his face as he stabbed her with his cigar. She held Minnie tight, trying to comfort her, to take away some of the pain of the past few hours. But even as she clung to her friend, she knew that there was nothing she could do to take away what had happened, and all the shame and humiliation that went with it.

Exhaustion suddenly overcame Suria and she lay down beside Minnie, snuggling up against her back, closed her eyes and fell into an uneasy and restless sleep.

Singapore, 1942

When she awoke, Minnie was sitting up beside her and the old Japanese woman was standing in the open doorway.

'Good,' she was saying. 'You are awake now. You must go downstairs to the bath-house. Wash yourselves and go into the day room for breakfast. You will not starve here. You will be given three meals a day. Daytime is free for resting, but after dark you are expected to work, like last night.'

Suria drew herself up. 'We won't do it!' she said. 'You can't do this to us. We are Malay citizens.'

The woman smiled her evil smile again. 'You have no choice. Colonel Kimura has commanded that you work here. We cannot go against his orders.'

'But this is a crime! It is rape!' she said.

The woman shook her head. 'You are ianfu now. Comfort women,' she said slowly, enunciating her words. 'That is your job, to give pleasure to Japanese officers. Some of them reported that you fought against their advances. I don't want to hear that again! You will submit. It is their right to have you.'

'We will not submit. We want to go home. Now, today!' Suria shouted, she could feel Minnie trembling beside her.

Again, the woman shook her head. 'This is your home now, and I am your mamasan. That is what you will call me. You will get used to this and if you are compliant it will be easier for you. Now come. You must put on your uniform, and come down to wash and eat. You can rest later. If you don't come down I will get one of the guards to come up here and make you.'

When she'd gone Suria helped Minnie out of her blood-soaked clothes and to put on the white uniform before returning to her own cubicle and putting on her own uniform. Then they walked along the passage and down the stairs side-by-side.

The staircase descended into a room full of tables at which many girls, all dressed in white uniforms, already sat, eating food. They were waited on by a diminutive Malay man who scuttled between the tables with plates and glasses, keeping his eyes averted from the people he served.

Mamasan was standing at the bottom of the stairs.

'Good. You have come down. Now, before you eat, you must come and bathe.'

She showed them through to the back of the house where there were three or four tiled cubicles with taps and buckets.

'Make sure you are clean. Officers won't tolerate filthy women,' she said.

They went into separate cubicles and Suria took off her uniform and sluiced herself with cold water from the bucket. The water on her damaged skin felt soothing, bringing some relief from the cigar burns and the bruises.

She thought about the go-down and of Charlotte. Mae and Suki must be desperately worried about her by now. Would they go to the hotel and ask after her? Would the hotel be able to free her and Minnie from this dreadful ordeal? She doubted it. Kimura was a powerful man and the Japanese were in command here. They could do what they wanted and subjugated citizens like herself had no rights. Anger and fear rose inside her, but she resisted the urge to cry. If she was to have any chance of getting away from this place, she needed to keep a clear head.

She dried herself and got dressed again. Minnie emerged from her bathroom.

'We must try to get away,' said Minnie. 'There's a back door at the end of the passage. If we creep out we could try to run.'

'Alright,' said Suria, 'we can try,' then, looking round for mamasan or the guards, they crept along the passage to the back door of the house. It was locked of course. Bolted from the outside. They tried to shake it by the handle, thinking the bolt might come loose. But as they did so there were footsteps behind them.

'You can't get out that way!' said mamasan and when they turned to look at her she slapped both their faces. 'There is no point. The compound is enclosed with high fences and barbed wire. The gate is guarded. You will not escape. Now come with me and eat.'

The other girls looked up briefly from their breakfast as Suria and Minnie entered the dining area, but none of them showed any interest in the newcomers and went straight back to their food. Mamasan pointed to a table where they should sit. There were three other girls at the table already, but none spoke as the two of them sat down. The servant brought bowls of porridge with milk and put them in front of Minnie and Suria.

'I can't eat,' said Minnie. 'I feel sick.'

'Try, Minnie, you need to keep up your strength,' whispered Suria but Minnie shook her head. Suria forced a few spoonsful of porridge down, but her stomach, so full of nerves and turmoil, recoiled and she nearly vomited it back.

One of the other girls said something to her neighbour and Suria saw that these girls weren't Malay or Chinese. She vaguely recognised the language as Korean and as she looked around the room, she noticed that all the girls must be Korean because they were all speaking the same language. She wondered how they came to be here. Had they been abducted off the street as she and Minnie had? Brought here in dreadful conditions in ships? The cruelty of the Japanese seemed to know no bounds. Looking round at the other girls she saw the same look in all their eyes. They looked subdued, defeated. None seemed to have any spark of life. All of them were young and must have been pretty before this happened to them. Now they appeared to be just the shells of the girls they must once have been. She shuddered. Would this happen to her and Minnie? Would they lose their fighting spirit and end up beaten and subdued? She knew she would do everything in her power to prevent that from happening.

Mamasan appeared in the doorway.

'If you are finish you may take fresh air in the street or go upstairs to rest. Lunch is at midday.'

Suria was on the point of protesting once again that they shouldn't be here; that the woman must let them go right away, but she decided to remain quiet and see if there was any opportunity for escape when they ventured out.

'Come on, Minnie, let's have a look outside,' she said,

taking Minnie's hand. Other girls were already on their way out. They gave Suria and Minnie shy smiles as they passed. Although Suria didn't feel like smiling, she smiled back and felt a sense of kinship with these poor, beaten young women.

There were a lot of women out on the street already, walking up and down, stretching their legs. The street was lined with terraced houses just like the one she and Minnie had been sent to and every house probably contained ten or twelve girls. All were dressed in white uniforms giving the place the look of some sort of health facility. Suria glanced at their faces trying to assess whether any of them might be Malay, but they all appeared to be Korean. All looked run down, many with bruises on their faces and limbs, all with pale, unhealthy looking skin. And as she'd noticed at breakfast, all these young women looked defeated, accepting of their dreadful situation, devoid of fight or any sort of spark.

Minnie hardly spoke as they walked the length of the road to the far end. The end of the street was bounded by a high wire fence with coils of barbed wire along the top. It was impossible to get behind the houses as the fence went right up to the walls of the last houses. Suria and Minnie stood looking at the fence. Suria's heart sank. There would be no escape in this direction. As if to compound that thought, two guards holding guns appeared on the other side of the fence and paraded along it, staring in at Minnie and Suria with narrowed eyes.

They turned back and walked to the other end of the road where another fence and double gates barred any exit. There were guards here too, but these ones sat on chairs, outside a little hut, their guns on their laps. They were relaxing, chatting together, smoking cheroots.

Suria glanced at Minnie. 'Maybe we could bribe them? I have twenty dollars in my pocket upstairs.'

'Perhaps,' said Minnie, but her eyes were downcast.

'Come on, we should at least try,' said Suria.

Suria approached the guards, Minnie trailing behind her. The two men stopped talking and stared at her as she approached. Trying to control her nerves, and smiling steadily, Suria asked them if they spoke English. One of them nodded and stood up.

'Little bit,' he said.

Suria went up close to him and rubbed her two fingers together to signify money. He raised his eyebrows and smiled. He moved closer to her.

'We need to get out of here,' she said. 'Would you help us for money?'

The guard frowned. 'How much?' he asked.

'Twenty dollars.'

His face fell and he put his hands on his gun, making a shooing motion at Suria with it. Then he turned back to speak to his colleague. Suria's spirits dropped. Every moment she and Minnie remained inside the street they were in danger. How could they get through another night like last night? All the women around her led their lives like that. How could they submit to twenty or so men every night of their lives? What did that do to their bodies and minds? Had something inside them switched off to enable them to get through it? She shuddered thinking about it. She made a vow to herself that she would never submit. That as long as she was there she would fight against what was expected of her, even if this meant that she would be punished.

When darkness came that evening, Suria knew what it meant. She and Minnie had been sitting downstairs, but when the sun had gone down, mamasan came and told them to go up to their rooms. Suria looked at her with loathing.

'What if we refuse?'

'I will call the guards to take you up there. You are in demand. Many officers want you. You should be flattered. Go up and do your duty. If you don't, or if you fight like yesterday, punishment will follow.'

Suria lifted her chin and looked up at mamasan, right into her flint-hard eyes. 'I won't go up,' she said.

Mamasan leaned towards her and yelled something in Japanese, spraying spit at her. Then she lunged forward, slapping Suria in the face, and dashed out of the room calling for the guards. Two guards were there in seconds brandishing guns, filling the hallway with their presence, their faces full of anger and violence. Once of them grabbed Suria's arm and jerked her up out of the chair. His fingers dug into her skin, causing her to cry out. The other one grabbed Minnie. They dragged the girls into the hallway and pushed them up the stairs. Both girls were screaming, kicking and fighting, but that only angered the guards more.

Suria found herself powerless to resist. She was dragged upstairs, bundled into her cubicle and thrown down onto the bed. Then the guard backed out and slammed the door. She listened for his footsteps walking away but he didn't leave. He was standing outside the door talking to the guard who'd pushed Minnie into her cubicle. Suria turned onto her stomach and sobbed into the pillow, she was careful to cry silently so that no one would hear.

That night, and for virtually every successive night for months, Japanese officers lined up outside her door to take their turn with her. As she'd promised herself at the outset, she didn't submit once without a fight and sustained many beatings as a result. Her face and body were constantly covered in bruises and scratches. Kimura came several times a week and she reserved her strongest resistance for him. He always laughed at her rage, picking her up and throwing her on the bed like a ragdoll, smiling his evil smile as he humiliated her.

Suria grew thin through the stress and terror of her daily existence, the bones on her hips stuck out and her ribs were soon visible beneath the skin. She saw the same decline and change in Minnie's appearance. The two girls went through their days like sleepwalkers, following their enforced routine, constantly dreaming of escape.

Each day was the same. They would get up, go down to eat porridge, wash the shame of the night from their bodies in the washhouse. Then they would walk in the street outside. Although many of the other girls smiled at them, they had no common language so communication was difficult. They would go back inside to have lunch and sleep in the afternoons. Suria's sleep was haunted by nightmares; sometimes they involved the men who abused her, but the more terrifying ones involved Charlotte. Suria thought of Charlotte constantly, hoping fervently that Suki and Mae were still looking after her. She tried not to think about Charles. She couldn't bear to remember what they'd shared; it was such a contrast to what she was going through now.

On Mondays there was no work in their particular house, although other houses had different rest days. First thing on a Monday morning the doctor would arrive. He was a thin, bent Japanese man who never smiled. It seemed to Suria that he was deeply ashamed of his work. Each girl in the house had to line up to be examined by the doctor. This was carried out on a couch in the corner of the dining area with a thin curtain pulled across for privacy. The doctor sometimes took blood or swabs and administered medicines where needed. If one of the girls had missed their period he would give them pills to take care of the situation.

Every day Suria and Minnie would look for ways to escape, even though from the very first day they suspected there were none. They would walk up and down the fence at each end of the street examining it for weak points, trying to find a way of getting behind the houses. They often tried the back door of the house again, but it would never budge. Suria still held out the hope that the guards on the gate would help them, even though they always shooed the two girls away with guns whenever they came close. She'd seen the glint of greed in the eyes of the one she'd spoken to on the first day and she felt sure that he would be tempted by money, although twenty dollars was clearly not enough.

One day, when they'd been in the comfort station for many months, her chance came. Kimura came to her one night. He was her last visitor and he was obviously drunk. After he'd overcome her resistance and violated her, he lay down on her bed, exhausted by his exertions. Within seconds he was asleep, snoring loudly. Suria slipped off the bed carefully and picked up the jacket that he'd thrown on the floor. Keeping an eye on the sleeping Kimura, she went through the jacket and in an inside pocket she found what she was looking for: a leather wallet with several hundred crisp Japanese dollar notes inside. As quietly as she could and with her heart pounding, she took out three hundred and hid them in one of the drawers of her cabinet. Then she sat down at the end of the bed and waited for Kimura to wake up.

When she and Minnie went to the washhouse in the morning, Suria told Minnie what she'd done and that the money was their best chance of escape. Minnie's eyes widened with fear.

'What if it all goes wrong?' she asked.

'It might go wrong, and we'd have to be prepared to face the consequences. But we have to try! We can't stay here being brutalised every day. It's killing us, Minnie.'

'So what are we going to do?'

'I'm going to get the guards to open the gates for us. They will do it for three hundred dollars, I'm almost sure they will. So, will you come with me?'

Minnie nodded reluctantly, but Suria could tell that she was terrified at the prospect.

Later, when the two of them were taking their morning exercise, Suria approached the guards on the front gate. They were the same men she'd spoken to on the first day. Although they shook their heads and tried to wave the girls away, Suria persisted, going right up to the one who she knew spoke some English. Once again, she rubbed her fingers together to indicate money. He stopped frowning and looked at her intently.

'Would you help us for three hundred dollars?' Suria asked when she got close to him. The guard glanced at his companion and jerked his head for the other man to join them.

'You have three hundred dollars?' the first guard asked, his eyes sceptical. Suria nodded.

'It could be yours if you help us get out of here. All you'd have to do is open the gate,' she said. He eyed her carefully.

'Much danger for us if we open gate for you. Severe punishment.'

'I know,' she said. 'But three hundred dollars is a lot of money.'

The two guards conferred in Japanese, their eyes furtively flicking aside every so often as they spoke to check no one in authority was approaching. Suria waited, standing there beside Minnie who stood motionless, staring at the ground. Suria watched the guards, noticing how the one who spoke English was having to persuade the other. For all she knew they would turn her over to their superiors for trying to bribe them, but something told her they would take the bait.

Sure enough, after a few minutes the first man looked up and beckoned to Suria. He put his face close to hers and she almost flinched at the smell of sweat and tobacco on his skin. It reminded her so powerfully of the men who abused her each and every night.

'You come here at four o' clock. Cannot do after dark as officers come to gate. So, four o'clock with money. No deliveries at that time. We will let you out.'

Suria and Minnie looked at each other, fear and excitement running through their veins in equal measure.

'We will be here then,' said Suria.

The day dragged. It was stiflingly hot in the house and there were no fans in the cubicles. Suria lay on her bed as she normally did and tried to catch some sleep. But her nerves were so tense that it was impossible to relax. All she could think of was getting out through that gate, running down the road and putting as much distance between her and this place as she could, finding her way back to the go-down. Would it be safe to go there, though? Kimura would surely find out where she lived from the hotel and track her down. But that would take time, wouldn't it? And how could she bear to be away from Charlotte a moment longer than she had to? She prayed that Charlotte would still be there and being cared for by Suki and Mae. She would be over six months old now. How she would have changed! She would be smiling and taking notice of her surroundings. How

Suria craved to see that smile and hold Charlotte in her arms again.

At ten to four, Suria took the money out of her top drawer and slipped it into the pocket of her uniform. She knocked on Minnie's door. Hand in hand they crept downstairs. All the other girls were asleep, their rhythmic breathing could be heard through the thin walls of their cubicles. Even mamasan was resting in her room at the front of the house at this time. As Suria put her hand on the front door handle she heard mamasan sigh heavily and turn in her sleep. Suria froze, worried that mamasan would get up, but within seconds the snoring started again.

Suria opened the door and they went outside and into the street. It felt odd to be out at this time of day. The street was empty. Instinctively, Suria felt for Minnie's hand. The other girl was trembling just as she was. They walked in silence towards the gate at the end of the road, keeping close to the front gardens of the houses, thinking they would be less visible that way.

The guards came into view. They were sitting on their chairs talking as they always were, their guns leaning beside them. The two girls stepped out of the shelter of the front walls and walked towards the gate. The guards stood up and the taller one nodded for them to approach.

'Where's the money?' he hissed as they got closer.

'Open the gate first,' said Suria, meeting his gaze.

He nodded to his companion who drew the bolt back and opened the gate a foot or so. Suria and Minnie squeezed through the gap.

'Money now!'

She handed him the three hundred dollars.

'Come on, Minnie, run!' she said and they started to run

along the road outside the compound. But suddenly there was a shout from behind them.

'Stop!'

Suria turned in horror. It was Kimura. He must have been waiting in the guards' hut. Terror coursed through her. He was pointing his gun at them.

'Run, Minnie,' she yelled, but they'd only gone a few steps when three shots rang out and with an agonising cry Minnie stumbled and fell face-first on the road.

'Minnie!' Suria turned, horrified. Minnie had been shot in the back and in the head. Blood was rapidly spreading over the collar of her uniform. Suria was overwhelmed, her mind numbed by the shock. Should she go to her friend or try to save herself? She looked back. Kimura was right behind her now. In those few seconds he'd caught her up. He was panting and his face was streaming with sweat. She felt the butt of his gun as he shoved it in her back.

'You won't get away that easily,' he said.

THEY DRAGGED Suria back through the gates and threw her down in the dust. She tried to raise her head, but within seconds the guards were kicking her, beating her with their rifles. She bit her lip and tried not to react to the pain, but when she felt her ribs cracking she couldn't help crying out. It seemed to go on for an age. She tried to shield her head with her arms, but the guards pulled them away roughly and kicked her head too. She was sobbing then, crying out for them to stop. She shouted that she was sorry, that it wouldn't happen again. But worse than the pain was the thought that Minnie was dead. Poor, innocent Minnie, who was only here because of her, who had lived a life of torment and humiliation for over six months and who had been Suria's only comfort throughout her terrible ordeal.

At last the guards had finished their punishment. They dragged Suria to her feet and held her upright. Blood was pouring from her cheek where she'd been kicked and every bone and muscle in her body was screaming out in pain. Kimura was standing in front of her, smoking a cigar casually. He gave her one of his evil smiles, took the cigar out of his mouth then came at her with it. This time it wasn't her arms. The guards held her tight and one of them fisted her hair, keeping her still as Kimura went straight for her face, pressing the burning butt into her forehead and cheeks time after time. She closed her eyes and gritted her teeth but the pain was unendurable and she cried out again and again for him to stop.

He barked an order to the guards and they dragged her along the road and back to the house. Girls were looking out of the windows of the other houses, coming out into the gardens and onto the balconies to see what the commotion was. Suria bowed her head in shame as she was dragged back to her house.

Mamasan was standing in the doorway, her eyes flashing, her face like thunder. She started shouting in Japanese, shaking her fist at Suria, but when she saw the burns on Suria's face she turned her attention to Kimura who was coming up the path. She was yelling at him, pushing him in the chest, beating him with her fists.

The guards pushed Suria up the stairs, dragged her along the passage and shoved her into her cubicle. The door slammed behind her and she sunk onto the bed weeping, wishing she was dead. But in moments Kimura appeared in the doorway, unbuckling his trousers, pulling off his boots.

'No!' she shouted, sitting up, scrambling to the corner of

the bed, trying to get away from him, but the pain in her ribs made her slow.

'You stole from me. You try to escape. You pay now!' he said, grabbing her ankles and pulling her down the bed. He ripped her uniform open, the buttons flying off in all directions, and then he was on her, forcing himself into her as he had so many times before. All she could do was cry out in agony as he brutally raped her, the pain from her beating almost making her pass out.

AFTER THAT DAY, Suria almost gave up hope of surviving her ordeal. Only the thought of her daughter kept her from finding a way of ending it all. And without Minnie's company, she was more down and lonelier than ever before. She was given no time to recover from her beating at the hands of the guards. She was back on duty that very night after Kimura had taken his leave.

'What about Minnie?' she asked him before he left, her eyes full of tears. 'What will happen to her body?'

'She will be buried in a mass grave, like the Chinese from the Sook Ching,' he replied as he buttoned up his jacket. 'We've had another purge. There were still pockets of those Kuomintang traitors out there, especially in China-town, despite the best efforts of the Imperial Japanese Army.'

Waves of horror passed through Suria at those words. What about Suki and Mae and the others in the go-down who still held their meetings and still tried to resist Japanese rule? Had they fallen victim to this latest purge? What about Charlotte? Would the Japanese have assumed she was a Chinese baby and taken her away alongside them. She imagined them all being dragged away in the night, screaming and kicking, taken by lorry to a remote beach, lined up and marched into the sea. She closed her eyes and gritted her teeth to stop the images coming. She couldn't bear to think about what might have happened.

27

SURIA

Singapore, 1943

Suria grieved for Minnie all day, every day. Her grief was new and raw, tinged with guilt, and it didn't diminish over time. She was well aware that if Minnie hadn't been walking across the Padang with her on the night she'd been seized, she would still be working as a waitress in Raffles. She was also aware that the botched escape attempt was entirely her idea. How could she have been so naïve as to trust the guards? Now she realised that because of her desperate need to get away, she'd been blind to the risks. Of course they would betray her! They would have been punished in the worst possible way if it had been discovered that they'd helped her and Minnie escape. Three hundred dollars wouldn't make up for the risks she had asked them to take.

The days wore on as before in the same punishing, humiliating routine. Suria missed Minnie's company so badly that she felt it almost like a physical pain. There was nothing and no one to replace Minnie. She started to try a few words of Korean in order to communicate with the other girls and they appreciated her efforts, smiling and nodding at her first stumbling attempts at their language. But it was difficult and she never managed to get beyond the basics.

A new girl was moved into Minnie's cubicle. She was also Korean and looked as beaten and defeated as all the others. Her skin was sallow and spotty, as if she'd been kept inside for far too long, and her body was covered in bruises, as were the bodies of so many of the girls.

Suria went through her days like a sleepwalker. She thought constantly of Charlotte, wondering how she might have changed, what she might look like now, what she was doing at any given moment. Each night, when darkness came, she went through the motions of resisting each and every officer who came to take their turn with her. It was second nature with her now, but sometimes she wondered why she didn't just try to make life easier for herself by submitting, even just once. But there was a tiny chink in her innermost heart that wouldn't let her do that. She knew it would be the end of her already shredded self-respect if she submitted willingly. Instead, she found a way of switching off while the abuse was happening. With practice, she became able to deaden her mind. Sometimes it felt as if she didn't occupy her body at all, as if she was hovering above it, observing what was happening to her from a vantage point. It helped her to get through each painful night.

The months wore on and Suria lost track of time. The seasons came and went and she barely noticed them passing. What difference did it make to her if it was rainy or if the skies were clear? There were only two extraordinary events that punctuated those months and years. The first of those was that another girl tried to escape by climbing the fence at the far end of the compound. She'd got halfway up when the guards on the gate spotted her and came at her with their rifles, firing shot after shot at her. She fell off the fence and lay on the ground, blood seeping from the many wounds on her body. Instead of picking her up, the guards left her there and forced every comfort girl in the station to file past the body the next morning. The line moved slowly, many of the girls were sobbing, holding hands, saying prayers of respect for their dead friend as they passed. When it was Suria's turn she could hardly bear to look at the body, with its staring, glassy eyes and flies crawling all over the congealed wounds. It reminded her of Minnie and brought back to her powerfully the shame of Minnie's death.

A few months later, one girl succeeded in hanging herself from the beams in one of the washhouses. She'd torn a sheet into strips and plaited them together to make a rope strong enough to hold her body. Two of her friends found her later that morning and rumours began circulating straight away. One of Suria's neighbours, a girl called Sun Jung managed to communicate what had happened by using simple words and hand gestures. It saddened Suria that another young life had been wasted through the brutality of the Japanese, but she knew she could never do anything like that. Not while there was a chance that Charlotte was alive and out there somewhere. She would no longer be a baby though. If she'd survived she would be a toddler by now, walking and talking. With pangs of regret that she wasn't there to see her daughter grow, Suria wondered which language she would be learning.

Suria had been in the comfort station well over two

years when she noticed that the atmosphere had started to change. The mood amongst the Japanese officers was becoming noticeably tense and irritable. Then one night came the drone of low-flying aircraft and the familiar crash of bombs exploding in the city. Suria's heart leapt when she heard it. The skinny Japanese officer who was trying to push her down on the bed at the time, gave a shout of anger and, without bothering to fasten up his trousers, rushed out into the passage. All the other officers in the comfort house were doing the same; doors were banging, feet clattering on the stairs. Suria lay back on her bed relieved, and for the first night since she'd arrived, was able to sleep in peace until dawn.

The bombing raids went on sporadically for months and the mood of the officers got worse by the day. They grew even more violent and rough with the girls and Suria began to fear for her life.

She asked Kimura about the bombings. He laughed but didn't give much away.

'Americans and British think they can beat the Imperial Japanese Army. They are deluded, of course,' he replied. 'If they do take the city back it won't be good for you. It won't be good at all.'

The next day she tried to tell her neighbour, Sun Jung, what he had said. Her Korean was still not good but she managed to communicate the gist of Kimura's words. Sun Jung's face fell when she understood what Suria was saying. She drew her fingers sharply across her throat, then spread her hand wide, pointing to the whole street.

'He means we will all die?' asked Suria, shock rushing through her. Sun Jung nodded gravely.

'They will kill us all if they lose,' she said.

The bombings intensified as the months drew on. Fewer

officers came to the comfort station each night and the girls took it in turns to take nights off. Mamasan was clearly unhappy, moping around with a long face, sometimes not even bothering to get dressed in the mornings. Suria spent those months in a state of terror, expecting a firing squad to appear at any moment to do away with the girls. But when the end came, quite suddenly, in August 1945, it was far less dramatic than that and there were no casualties, except for one.

Kimura had been to visit Suria that last night. He had seemed preoccupied, not giving as much attention to the fight as he normally did. When he left her, she thought she saw tears in his eyes, although she could hardly believe that to be the case. Early the next morning a single shot rang out and shortly afterwards a scream went up from the wash-house. All the girls went running down in various states of undress to see what the noise was. One of the girls was standing in the doorway of the washhouse screaming. Peering between the heads and shoulders of the other girls, Suria could just make out what was inside. It was Kimura, slumped in the corner. He'd shot himself through the mouth and his brains and flakes of his skull were spattered all over the wall.

Feeling faint, nausea rising in her throat, Suria groped her way back to the front of the house. Mamasan was usually in the dining room at that time but she was nowhere to be seen. The front door stood wide open. Suria wandered out, down the front path and into the street. There, she stood blinking for a moment because in front of her was an extraordinary sight. The guards on the front gates were no longer there, the gates stood open and girls were fleeing through them and onto the road outside. Suria followed the crowd, barefoot and dressed in her white uniform. As if in a dream she shuffled out through the gate, her shoulders jostled by a hundred other girls hurrying to freedom.

The girls made their way along the street outside the comfort station. None had any money or any belongings, they all just needed to get away from there and Suria was swept along with the crowd. People who lived in the nearby streets had come out of their houses to watch the tide of young women sweep along the road. Some shouted unkind words, but others threw them money or gifts of fruit.

Suria happened to glance at a group of local women who'd gathered in front of a building to watch. Some of them were jeering and throwing stones. Suria stopped dead and looked at the women again, stunned at what she saw. There in the crowd was a face she recognised, the last person she would have wanted to see at that moment. It was Choi, her face contorted with anger, she was lifting her hand to throw a stone when she her eyes lit upon Suria. Her expression registered surprise and she immediately redirected the stone, aiming it straight at Suria's body.

'Whore!' she shouted with venom, spit flying from her mouth.

28

LARA

Singapore, 2000

Amina paused at this point in Suria's story. She'd stopped several times as she told the tale, sometimes to dab tears from her eyes, at other times to take a sip of the jasmine tea that was now cold in the cup beside her. In the silence, Lara's eyes wandered to the window, to the palm trees swaying gently in the breeze and to the sparkling sea beyond where the waves swelled and receded up and down the white beach leaving flecks of foam in their wake. She'd taken refuge in this view of the sea many times as she'd listened to Amina telling the shocking story of how Suria was abducted by the Japanese and forced to serve as a comfort woman. There was something soothing and hypnotic about the rhythm of the waves that helped Lara to come to terms with what was being said. She realised that unconsciously at some point during the telling of the story, she must have reached out and taken Christian's hand and was now holding it firmly in her lap. His touch had given her strength as Suria's ordeal unfolded, and she'd often felt Christian's eyes on her, communicating sympathy, checking for her reaction, making sure she was alright to carry on.

She was glad she'd finally got to the heart of why Nell had ended up in an orphanage, but Suria's story had shocked her to the core and brought tears to her eyes on many occasions. She'd not known anything about the comfort stations that served Japanese soldiers during the occupation, or about the young women who'd been abducted off the streets or from their homes to work as sex slaves in these brutal establishments. It was hard to take in what Amina was telling her, to understand what had happened to Suria and how her life had been destroyed by the experience. Lara's heart swelled with pity for her grandmother and for her mother too, who'd been brought up as an orphan as a result.

'So, what happened to her when she left the comfort station that day?' she asked gently after a long silence. Amina seemed to have gone into a reverie, her eyes closed, her chin almost on her chest, but at the sound of Lara's voice, she sat up straight. She took a deep breath and started talking again.

'She found her way back to the go-down, of course. It was a long walk and she was very weak, but she finally got there. By then there were British troops on the streets helping people. She looked out for Charles but didn't see him anywhere. She was almost afraid to bump into him in the state she was in. When she got to the go-down, she discovered that what she'd been dreading had actually happened. Mae and Suki and many others in the go-down had been taken away in the second phase of the Sook Ching and never heard of again. Desperate for news of the baby, Suria asked everyone in the go-down and everyone living nearby about what had happened. Eventually someone told her that a stranger had found her baby in the storm drain with the amulet and had taken her to an orphanage, but they had no idea which one.

'So, when she'd borrowed some money from someone in the go-down to buy herself some new clothes and some food, she set off on foot doing the rounds of all the orphanages in Singapore. It took her days and at most establishments she drew a complete blank. Finally, her search took her to St Theresa's orphanage in Katong. The nuns seemed helpful and kind and she was shown in to see the mother superior. She told the mother superior about the amulet and about her baby, but then she made a mistake. Mother superior's face was so kind and trusting that Suria went on to tell her about what had happened to her during the war. She told her all about the comfort station and the conditions there, about how young girls had been abducted to serve as slaves and about the hardships she herself had suffered at the hands of the Japanese.

'The mother superior looked at Suria with tears in her eyes. She laid her hands on her head and said; "My poor dear child, I know you have suffered greatly, but with that experience behind you, I'm afraid you are tainted for life. Your little girl is here, but I cannot let her come home with you. I don't think you are morally suited to bringing up a child".

'Suria pleaded with her but the mother superior wouldn't change her mind. She wouldn't even allow Suria to see the child that day. Finally, Suria left, heartbroken. She felt at rock bottom as she walked back to the go-down. She had nothing left. No money, no child, no man, nothing. Suddenly she wanted to get out of Singapore. She was so ashamed of what she'd become and what had happened to her that she didn't even want to see Charles again. She couldn't face telling him that she'd lost their baby and that she herself had been raped by hundreds of men over the past three years. She just wanted to melt away.'

Amina paused, dabbing her eyes with a handkerchief. She swallowed, took another deep breath and composed herself.

'But she realised that there might be one last hope for her. She thought that if she could only get back to the village, *this* village, she might be able to regain her strength and find a way of getting her child back.

'She had no money for a bus or a train, so she walked here. She set off from the go-down, saying goodbye to those who had helped her there, including Li Wei who still sat on his chair at the top of the steps, flicking through magazines as he guarded the door. It was a long walk. It took her two days. On the first day, she walked all the way to Changi, out through the city, along the main road and through the quieter roads that the taxi had taken her along when she'd delivered her second letter to Charles in 1942. When she reached Changi itself, she saw that the prison gates were open and that many British men were milling around. They all looked desperately thin; skin and bone, dressed in rags, but they also looked relaxed now. Their captors had departed and they were waiting to go home. She hurried on past the prison, pulling her scarf over her face. She didn't want to see Charles or for him to see her.

'That first night she lay down on Changi beach under cover of some shrubs. She slept fitfully, aware of the sound of the sea and the rustle of insects and creatures amongst the leaves around her. The next morning, she took a small ferryboat from Changi point to Tanjung Belungkor on the mainland. She sat amongst locals with their buckets of prawns, chickens and babies, and watched the dark strip of the densely forested North Eastern Islands slide past on the starboard side.

'The journey in the small boat only took an hour or so. At the port of Tanjung Belungkor, Suria ate some noodles at a food stall and bought a can filled with water and set off along the sandy road through the thick, tropical forest towards Desaru. Although it was early morning, the sun was already high in the sky and she quickly found she was tired and sweaty. She'd only been walking for a little while though when a farm truck stopped and the driver asked her if she'd like a lift. She accepted gladly and jumped up into the cab beside the driver. They passed through coconut palm plantations and patches of dense, untamed jungle until they reached a crossroads where their ways parted.

'Suria walked the rest of the way home to the village and night was falling by the time she arrived. First, she went to her old family home, but discovered that her family was no longer there. She was devastated not to have found them there as she'd been longing to see them. But she then came to my house, where I was cooking the evening meal on the fire in front of the porch. At first I didn't recognise her, she'd lost so much weight and looked so tired and beaten; she had tiny scars from burns all over her face and bruises on her arms, but as soon as I saw the expression in her eyes I knew who it was. We embraced for a long time, and when our tears of joy had subsided, we sat down on the porch, ate the evening meal together and Suria began to tell me what had happened to her during the three long years since she'd last been in touch.'

Amina paused again, the mist of distant memories filling her eyes. She took another sip of tea and turned back to Lara.

'So that's it. You know the rest. I told you at the beginning. Choi somehow found out that Suria was here and she quickly poisoned the rest of the villagers against her, saying that Suria had voluntarily slept with many Japanese officers, that she'd become a prostitute for them.'

Lara shook her head, unable to understand such cruelty.

'So, as I said, she was only here for a couple of days. On the second evening, a gang of village men came and surrounded the house, banging on the doors and walls, yelling abuse. It was terrifying. They broke the window. Suria and I clung together, crying. They went away eventually, shouting that they would come back the next day.'

Amina paused again, dabbing her eyes, clearly struggling to carry on. Lara waited patiently until the old lady was ready to speak again.

'After the crowd had finally gone away that night, Suria told me that she was going to leave. She said I wouldn't be safe while she was here. I tried to get her to stay, pleaded with her. I said we could reason with the villagers, go to the headman and tell him the truth. But she wouldn't hear of it.

'So, the next morning I gave her as much food as she could carry and a pack to carry it in. She set off on foot before dawn. She said she would go into the rainforest and find a remote village where she could live safely. But I could see from her eyes that she wasn't going to try very hard. At the first hurdle I knew that she would be ready to lie down and give up the fight. I watched her walk down the road and into the forest. I will never forget watching her walk away. She looked so small and vulnerable, it tore my heart to see her go. I cried for days afterwards. And you know, I've carried that pain deep in my heart to this day. I've never seen or heard from her since that moment.'

Amina fell silent and looked down at her hands which

she was twisting over and over each other in her lap. Lara glanced out at the sea again, the glittering swell of the ocean, the hypnotic rush and pull of the waves on the beach. She thought of Suria walking into the jungle, away from the village where she'd been born and raised, her head down, her shoulders hunched. What had happened to her after that? Where had she ended up? Had she simply been swallowed up by the rainforest never to have emerged?

'Thank you. Thank you for telling me Suria's story. I know how difficult it must have been.'

'I'm so glad you came,' Amina said with a sad smile. Then she turned to her niece; 'Rania, would you bring more tea my dear. I have one more thing to tell these young people.'

'Of course, Auntie,' the woman said, getting up and going over to the kitchenette in the corner.

Lara looked at Amina expectantly. What more could there be for her to say? Could there be yet more dark secrets in her mother's past?

Amina leaned forward and fixed Lara with her beady brown eyes.

'I have her letters, you know. I haven't read them for years, but I'd like you to have them.'

'That's very kind of you, but surely you want to keep them for yourself?'

'No. I have my own memories of Suria. And your need is greater.'

Lara thought for a moment. Then came up with the obvious solution.

'I could take them back to Singapore, have them photocopied and send them back to you.'

Amina's eyes lit up. 'Of course! What a good idea. Why didn't I think of that? I have them right here.'

She got up stiffly and moved slowly to a chest in the corner. She opened one of the drawers and took out a small cardboard box.

'They are in here. Please. Take them. From them you will find out what you can about your grandfather. Perhaps she even mentioned his full name, I don't remember.'

Amina handed Lara the box. Lara opened the lid and looked inside. She saw an envelope on top with Amina's name and address written in beautiful flowing script. With trembling hands she picked up the envelope and pulled the letter out. The ink was faded and the paper brittle with age. She opened it out and read the first few words, but then she looked up, disappointed.

'Of course, it's in Malay,' she said.

Amina frowned, momentarily disconcerted. 'Oh! Oh, I'd forgotten. Of course she wrote in Malay. It was our language, although we both learned to speak English at an early age. I'm sorry, my dear. I could translate some of it for you, but the letters are very long. It would take a long time...'

Lara thought for a moment, then Christian leaned forward and cleared his throat.

'I know some Malay myself. I could translate them for you Lara. I'm not fluent, but I could have a go.'

29

LARA

Singapore, 2000

Later, they left Amina and Rania with warm hugs and thanks, and promises to keep in touch. They got back onto the motorbike and rode back to Singapore without stopping. Lara was glad that it was impossible to hold a conversation on the back of the bike. It gave her an opportunity to think about Suria and let the full impact of the story Amina had told her sink in. The sun was setting as they powered across the Johor causeway, colouring the sky every shade of pink and grey, interspersed with streaks of red and gold. The view was breath-taking and Lara felt a lump in her throat at the astonishing beauty of the evening. It contrasted so starkly with the ugly and shocking truths she'd heard that day.

When they'd cleared the immigration checks in Woodlands, Christian pulled the bike over and turned to Lara.

'Shall we go to eat somewhere quiet? I could start to translate the letters for you this evening.'

Lara agreed straight away, grateful that he understood

her burning desire to read the letters, and that he knew she wanted to do that as soon as possible. They got back on the bike and Christian took her to a quiet café near Bukit Timah, tucked away down a country road, surrounded by tropical gardens which were lit up by fairy lights. They sat on the veranda and ordered beers and food.

When their drinks arrived, Christian began to translate the first letter. It was ten pages long, the writing was scrawling and Lara had to wait while Christian first deciphered the writing, then found the right words to translate it into English. The letter was full of news of the occupation, of bombings, of the deprivations of the siege of Singapore, but it was also suffused with Suria's love for Charles. Suria poured her heart out to Amina. She told her everything that had happened between her and Charles since Amina returned to the village; how their love had grown and blossomed, and how they had finally made love on the night of the first bombings when he was due to leave to join his regiment. There was no doubt that Suria was deeply in love with Charles. Her love for him leapt off the pages. Lara watched Christian's face as he translated, the beautiful smile that lit up his face, his gentle eyes and the crinkly lines around them that appeared when he laughed.

'I can't tell you what he means to me, Amina. I think about him all day, every day,' he read. 'I can't get him out of my mind. He is the kindest, most caring, most loving, and most interesting person I have ever met.'

As Christian translated those words, he looked into Lara's eyes, and it was as if Suria's words echoed down the decades and gave a special meaning to the two of them sitting opposite each other under the stars on that warm Singapore evening.

The letter went on to tell Amina of Suria's pregnancy

and of how she feared for Charles' safety and longed to hear from him but that no word had arrived.

The second letter was slightly shorter. It told of the escalating fighting, of Suria's fear for her own safety, for her unborn child and for that of Charles. Towards the end of the letter, she described how she'd had a letter from Charles asking her to marry him and how she'd taken her response to him on the battle lines near the north coast of Singapore.

'The taxi driver wasn't at all happy at going that far out of the city. The shelling was really loud out there. We got to a barrier across the road manned by soldiers who were stopping people from going through. I got out and went up to them, gave them the letter and asked them to get it to Major Charles Simmonds of India III Corps. I tried to make it sound official and important. I hope it worked!'

As Christian translated those words he looked into Lara's eyes and thrills went right through her body.

'That's it! Christian, that's so brilliant. Charles Simmonds. Major Charles Simmonds. That's my grandfather.'

Christian leaned forward and gripped her hand on the table.

'That's great news,' he said looking into her eyes. 'It should be quite easy to track him down from online records.'

'Yes. I'll do that. I'll start tomorrow,' said Lara.

'There should be a list of those who served in Singapore in India III Corps online somewhere. There are also details of those prisoners forced to work on the Thai-Burma railway. It's quite likely that he would have been taken there if he was at Changi. I can give you a list of websites if you like? We often get Australians at the Commission asking how to research their fathers and grandfathers who were at the fall of Singapore.'

'That would be great. Thank you so much. I'd never have got this far without your help.'

He laughed. 'Oh, I think you would,' he said. 'I'm sure you'd have managed OK. You just wouldn't have got scared witless on the back of a motorbike, that's all.'

After they'd finished eating, he took her back to China-town on the motorbike, zigzagging through the late-night traffic. He parked up on the street outside her guesthouse and they stood on the pavement to say goodbye. Lara suddenly felt awkward and she could tell that he did too.

She was at a loss for words, but she thanked him again. 'Like I said, I'd never have got there without you,' she said. 'And I'm so glad you were there with me to hear my grand-mother's story. It really helped me you know, you being there.'

'I was glad to be there, Lara. It was such a horrific thing to hear about. You were very strong. You *are* very strong.'

He put his arms around her and kissed her then, full on the lips, and she kissed him back as she'd wanted to do many times over the past few days. She'd always held back before but this time it just felt right. She felt his body pressing up against hers and she slid her hands around his back, pulling him closer. But then she became aware of people walking past on the pavement and suddenly felt a little exposed and self-conscious. She pulled away. Half of her wanted to invite him up to her room there and then, the impulsive, passionate side, but the sensible side won. The side that said, *there'll be plenty of time to get to know him better. No need to rush things.*

'Will I see you tomorrow?' he asked and she could see

from his eyes that he understood her dilemma, understood everything.

'I have to work during the day,' he said, 'but shall we meet up at six?'

She nodded. 'I'd love that. It will give me time to do my research.'

'Great. I'll send you a text with the best websites to look on,' he said, backing away, smiling.

He put his helmet on, got back on the bike and kick started the engine. Lara stood on the pavement as he roared away, raising her hand to wave goodbye. She already felt bereft of his company, part of her wishing she'd made a different decision.

Two days later Lara was back on the bike again, her arms clamped around Christian's waist. They were powering through the busy streets of Singapore, heading north on the freeway, speeding through the northern suburbs of the city. The sky was overcast and grey and it was raining gently. Lara couldn't help thinking of her grandmother, making the hazardous journey north of the city to deliver a letter to Charles while Singapore was being shelled from the mainland. How different things would have looked back then. Suria would have been travelling through rough farmland and untamed jungle instead of past the clipped hedges and landscaped verges of today. Once clear of the city, they turned off the freeway onto Turf Club Road, speeding past the wide green expanse of the racecourse. Then Christian took another turning and they travelled along a narrow tree lined road, under a modern white archway and drew up in a car park at the foot of an impressive flight of steps.

'Here we are,' said Christian, pulling up the bike and switching off the engine. They both got off and stowed their helmets on the bike.

'Are you ready?' he asked, concern in his dark eyes, and again Lara felt butterflies in her stomach. She was glad Christian was there to help her through this.

It was raining softly as they walked towards the steps, although it still felt warm and muggy. Lara thought of her father's words when she'd called him on the phone the day before. She'd told him everything she'd discovered about Suria and about how her mother got to the orphanage. From his silences at the other end of the line, she could tell how shocked and moved he was by the story. When she'd finished, he said,

'Nell would have been so proud of you, you know Lara, managing to unearth all of that. It can't have been easy.'

'Would she really?' she asked, thinking of her mother's critical nature, her ruthless self-discipline and high standards.

'Of course. She was always proud of you, whatever you might have thought, she just wasn't that good at showing it.'

He'd asked her when she was coming home and she'd said she wasn't sure. Hesitatingly at first, she began to tell him about Christian, but once she started, she'd found she couldn't stop talking about him.

'So, I think I'll stay on here for a bit, Dad,' she'd finished.

'I'm so happy for you, Lara,' he said. 'Maybe I shouldn't mention this, in view of what you've just said, but I've been wondering if you'd like some extra company for a couple of weeks? I'm getting lonely here. I thought I might fly out to join you.'

'Are you quite sure, Dad?' she asked, incredulous. To her

knowledge he'd never been further than northern France in his whole life.

'Of course! You know, I'm a bit of a history buff myself. I've always been interested in the fall of Singapore. I'd love to come and see where Nell grew up, and Raffles Hotel and all the museums. If you could bear to have me, that is?'

'It would be fabulous, Dad. I can't wait for you to meet Christian,' she replied.

'Right. I'll start looking into flights then.'

Now, smiling, she turned to Christian, tucked her arm through his and they walked up the steps together in silence. She'd spent the previous day on the internet, searching through the sites Christian had recommended. It hadn't taken too long for her to track down Major Charles Simmonds of India III Corps. She'd learned that he'd been captured at the fall of Singapore in 1942 and transported to Thailand to work on the Thai-Burma railway in November that year. At the end of the war he'd been taken back to Changi, but there the trail had gone cold. She read something of the plight of the prisoners on the railway and tried to picture Charles, dressed in rags, labouring in the jungle under the heat of the tropical sun, probably ill, probably beaten and starving. She discovered that many thousands had died in those conditions and wondered how any had managed to survive.

She'd continued her research, hoping against hope to find out what had happened to Charles at the end of the war, but had drawn a complete blank. It wasn't until she tried another tack that she found her answer, an answer that had brought tears to her eyes. Now she had come to visit the place where her research had finally led her.

They reached the top of the flight of steps and walked on through some wrought iron gates. They stopped to stare in awe at the rows of white gravestones that were spread out in front of them looking ghostly in the mist; thousands of them arranged in neat lines covering the neatly mown grassy slope. At the top of the hill, a tall memorial towered above the graves.

'Do you have the location?' asked Christian and Lara nodded, looking down at the paper she'd brought with her which said that he was in row C, plot 71.

When she'd drawn a blank with her research into Charles' army record, she'd looked into where prisoners who'd perished in Changi had been laid to rest and she'd discovered that all their graves had been moved to Kranji War Cemetery after the war. She'd tapped Charles' details into the Commonwealth Graves website and stared at the screen, aghast at what she was seeing. The site had come up with the exact location of his grave. Her search was at an end; Charles hadn't survived the war. He'd died in Changi in early 1945.

Now, they made their way slowly between the rows of graves, reading some of the headstones, shocked at how young so many of the soldiers who'd lost their lives were. Most were between eighteen and their late twenties. Finally, near the top of the hill, they found Charles' plot.

It was a white stone like all the others. There was a cross carved into it as well as an eight-point star with a crown on top. Lara guessed it would be the emblem of his regiment. The inscription was simple; *Major Charles Simmonds; India III Corps. Died in Changi 20th February 1945, aged 35.*

Lara stared at it for a long time and, as she stared, she thought of everything she'd learned about Charles and Suria over the past couple of weeks. She thought about how her mother, and ultimately she herself, were products of their love. She knelt down, took the amulet from her pocket, dug a small hole in the earth at the base of the stone with her fingers and slipped the amulet inside.

'She's with you now,' she whispered covering the amulet up with the earth.

She felt Christian's hand on her shoulder and as she turned to look up at him she realised that it had stopped raining. As he smiled down at her the sky brightened and the sun emerged from behind a cloud, lighting up Christian's face and flooding the cemetery with a brilliant, golden light.

I HOPE you enjoyed reading *The Amulet* as much as I loved writing it.

If you'd like further information about my books, please sign up to my newsletter on my website (www. annbennettauthor.com) for news and updates. When you subscribe you will be offered a free download. You can also follow me on Facebook for information and previews of future books.

You may also enjoy *Bamboo Road: The Homecoming*, another WW2 tale of love and survival, this time set in Thailand. Please turn over to read an excerpt.

EXCERPT FROM BAMBOO ROAD:THE HOMECOMING

CHAPTER 1

First light in Bangkok. Sirinya stands beside a small suitcase on the platform at Thonburi station, a little way apart from the crowd. She is waiting for the early train. The city is already awake. She can feel its heartbeat, sense its raw energy. The air is filled with the shrill blasts of horns and the hum of a million engines. In the distance, through the shimmering pollution haze, she sees the glow of lights from traffic crawling along a flyover.

She shifts in the heat. Despite the hour, sweat is already running down the inside of her blouse. Twenty-five years in a cold country and she has almost forgotten the sultry climate of her homeland. But now, as the hot air wraps itself around her in a clammy embrace, she remembers, and it feels as natural as breathing. It's as if she's never been away.

Her heart beats a little faster as the old blue and white diesel train creaks into the station. She has never travelled on this railway before, but the horror of its construction still scars her mind. As the train grinds and squeaks to a halt beside the low platform, an image comes to her. A half-dug cutting, deep in the hills, glimpsed between the teak trees from a jungle trail. She remembers how she paused, clutching the tree trunk, astonished to see half-naked white men labouring there. Most of them so thin they were little more than skeletons. In the full glare of the noonday sun they worked with hammers, pickaxes and shovels, chipping away at the granite, passing the waste in bamboo baskets down a line of waiting men, to be tipped over the edge of the precipice by the last man. It was a scene of constant movement as men lifted hammers above their heads, slamming them down on metal spikes, repeating the process again and again. Japanese guards strutted about yelling at the workers, prodding them with sticks, lashing out at them with lengths of bamboo. She had stood there staring, aghast, waves of shock passing through her, but she'd quickly turned and gone on her way, afraid that the guards would notice her. Years later she can still hear those sounds. The ringing of metal on rock, the chipping and the hammering, the brutal shouts of the guards. Sirinya shudders and passes a hand over her face now, trying to suppress the memory. She follows the other passengers up the wooden steps and into the stifling carriage. A man turns and helps her up with her luggage. She smiles and thanks him in Thai.

'Kop khun kha.'

Speaking her mother tongue feels strange after all these years, but it is already coming back to her. She knows it's always been there, lying dormant like an old engine, rusting and forgotten in a shed. With a little polish it will soon be in perfect working order again.

She heaves her suitcase onto the luggage rack and settles herself on a wooden bench beside the window. The carriage fills up quickly with passengers and their baggage. Then, with a great blast of the horn the train creeps out of the station and starts on its ponderous journey through the

western suburbs of the city. Sirinya stares out of the window
as they rattle through neighbourhoods of rickety wooden
houses, nestled amongst dense vegetation. People preparing
breakfast on their verandas look up as the train passes. It
rumbles over canals where houses are built on stilts over the
water, past golden temples where saffron-clad monks
parade in single file for their morning alms. Her heart lifts
as she glimpses a giant statue of the Buddha in meditation
pose. How long it has been since she went to the temple, lit
a candle and knelt before the Buddha, felt the peace and
serenity that her faith used to bring.

How different this is, she thinks, from the English countryside where she made her home, with its neat houses and
neat people, the muted greens and browns of the landscape.
She will not miss it, she knows that much. No matter how
long she lived there, she would never feel accepted, would
always be an outsider.

The man who'd helped her has sat down beside her. He
is middle aged, like herself. He looks educated, smart,
dressed in a white cotton shirt and black trousers. The train
rattles over another bridge and the canal below is framed
momentarily like a still photograph. Below, a group of
naked children dive off a floating platform into the murky
water.

'It reminds me of my own childhood,' says the man,
catching her eye as she smiles at the scene.

'Oh yes, me too ...'

'Are you going all the way to Nam Tok?' he asks.

'No. I'm getting off at Kanchanaburi. What about you?'

'I'm going all the way. Visiting my mother. I go every
month.'

She nods and smiles, but doesn't reply.

'Is Kanchanaburi your home?' he asks after a pause.

'It used to be. I was born there. Lived there until I was about

twenty.'

'Where do you live now?'

She hesitates. That is a good question. She is returning, but she doesn't yet have a place she can call home. She shrugs.

'I'm not sure yet. I've been away for many years. Living abroad.'

He raises his eyebrows. 'Really? Whereabouts?'

'England. My husband was English. He died a few months ago.

After the funeral there was no reason for me to stay.'

'Oh, I'm so sorry,' says the man.

He seems kind and well meaning, but Sirinya is in no mood to talk. She just wants to think, to plan, to brood. She turns and stares out of the window as the train begins to gather speed, flashing past banana groves, patches of untamed jungle, and out into open country. Here, emerald rice paddies stretch far into the distance, dotted with the odd coconut palm. Groups of workers in cone-shaped hats, knee-deep in water, bend to their timeless task. It is all so familiar. The years seem to melt away.

In a couple of hours she will be back there. Back in the place where it all happened; the place that has not been out of her thoughts through all these years of exile. And as she has done a million times, she visualises returning to the familiar street, walking past the house where the Kempeitai had their headquarters during the war. She wonders if the building will still be there, and what it might be used for now. Will it be just another hardware shop again, peddling its dusty wares as if nothing extraordinary has ever happened there?

Will she be able to walk past it without breaking down, despite the passage of time? She knows she can do it. She is strong. She will steel herself, hold her head high and walk past that house.

But it is a house further down the same street that she needs to visit first. She has promised herself she will go there before even stopping at her uncle's shophouse, where she knows her cousin will be waiting. She imagines, as she has countless times over the years, knocking on the shabby front door, waiting breathlessly on the step for it to open. Will Ratana still be there? What will the years have done to her? Will she still powder her face and make up her eyes heavily like in the old days? Will her glossy black hair be streaked with grey now, like Sirinya's own? She shivers, despite the heat, and closes her eyes.

'Are you alright?' her companion's voice breaks through her

thoughts. 'You look a little pale.'

'I'm fine, thank you. Just rather tired.'

She turns away and stares out of the window again, not wanting to encourage conversation.

SHE REMEMBERS the day that everything changed; for her and for everyone else in the sleepy, harmonious little community of Kanchanaburi. It was the day that their peaceful existence came to an abrupt end, when the Japanese occupation of Thailand became more than just headlines in the local newspaper.

She recalls it as clearly as if it were yesterday. She and her cousin, Malee, were wandering beside the river; the broad, fast-flowing Mae Nam Khwae. They had grown up on its banks and had never been far from the gentle sound of its voice. It was the lifeblood of the town.

She can still feel the fierce temperature of that afternoon back in 1942. The sun was high in the sky, the air quivering in the intense heat. She knew the monsoon would soon break, and until then any physical activity, virtually any movement at all, was strength- sapping. The two girls had been helping out since early morning in Malee's father's shop. For the past few days at the end of their shift, they had got into the habit of coming down to the river to relax and to wash the sweat and exhaustion of the day from their bodies.

This stretch of land, on the far side of the river from the town, was owned by Malee's father. It was a long walk upriver from the centre of town to the crossing at Ta Mah Kham, where a boatman ferried them across for a few ticals. They had then walked back downriver, down the Bamboo Road, the dirt track that only the locals knew about, which wound along the riverbank, through towering thickets of bamboo, to reach the patch of grassy land where they knew they would be able to bathe in peace. A few buffalo lazed around, dozing in the heat, dried mud encrusting on their bodies, only moving to twitch the flies away with their tails.

The two girls stopped at a little outcrop of rocks on the riverbank and stripped down to their underwear. Then, leaving their towels and clothes on the rocks, they waded into the shallow water.

The pebbles were uneven and slippery underfoot, but they were soon in up to their waists. They stooped to swim. Both gasped and shrieked at the shock of the cold water as they dipped their shoulders under the surface, but once they were in it felt deliciously cool and refreshing. They were both strong swimmers and raced each other up to the place where their favourite casuarina tree leaned out over the water and back again. Then they lay floating on their backs, contemplating the clear blue sky.

When they had cooled off and their skin was beginning to soften and wrinkle, they got out of the water, spread their towels on the grass and lay down, allowing the sun to burn off the droplets of

water.

'That was wonderful,' said Malee. 'What would we do without the river in the hot season?'

'It's a lifesaver,' agreed Sirinya.

They lay in companionable silence for a while, staring up at the sky through the motionless branches of a pine tree. Sirinya closed her eyes and dozed, the light behind her eyelids burning red.

'Oh, by the way, I saw Narong yesterday,' said Malee suddenly.

'He was asking after you.'

Sirinya snapped open her eyes and shifted impatiently. She loved Malee, but wondered why her cousin could not leave this particular subject alone. She turned away.

'Aren't you interested?' said Malee, when Sirinya didn't reply.

'You know I'm not. How many times do I have to tell you that?'

'Oh, I know you are really. How could you not be? Every girl in town's a little bit in love with him.'

'Including you?'

'No, not me. Of course not, silly. I only have eyes for Somsak.

You know that. But Narong really likes you, Siri. You're being very

cruel to him.'

'I don't trust him, Malee. It's as simple as that. He's too

smooth, too sure of himself. I'm sure you know what I mean.'

'I think you should give him a chance. Let him take you out at least. What harm could it do?'

'I don't need a man. I like to be independent.'

Malee laughed. 'You will need a man one day. How will you support yourself otherwise?'

'Don't be ridiculous ...' Sirinya began, turning back to face her cousin, but then she noticed that Malee's expression had changed.

There was sudden fear in her cousin's eyes and her mouth had dropped open. She was staring across the stretch of scrubby grassland towards the gate at the far end of the meadow. Sirinya followed her gaze. Four soldiers dressed in khaki uniform and helmets were marching towards them. Sirinya's heart started beating fast. Her mouth went dry with shock.

She stared at the men, confused. At first she thought they were Thai, but she had never seen a Thai soldier in modern-day khaki uniform. The only ones she had ever seen had been taking part in ceremonial parades at the Grand Palace in Bangkok, dressed in elaborate traditional battledress. Within a few seconds the truth had dawned on her. She remembered the grainy newsreel she had seen at the local cinema a few weeks before. The flickering film had shown Japanese soldiers carrying weapons, advancing stealthily through the jungles and rubber plantations of Malaya. They'd been shown swarming on bicycles down jungle tracks, driving tanks down narrow roads between tall trees, or manning machine guns from behind banks of earth. She recognised the uniforms from that film. They were Japanese soldiers. She knew about the Japanese pact with the Thai government, how the

Japanese had been allowed to enter the country, but she had never seen a Japanese soldier in the flesh before. She knew they were in the south of the country, that Malaya and Singapore had been occupied since February, but she had no idea that they were in this area. What could they possibly want with this little backwater?

There was no time to wonder. Remembering that she was only wearing underwear, she grabbed her clothes and pulled her blouse over her head in a flash, wrapped her sarong style skirt around her waist. Malee was doing the same. To Sirinya's relief, the soldiers were no longer moving towards them. They had stopped a few yards away and seemed to be conferring together. One of them produced what looked like a map from his pack, and the four of them were studying it, gesticulating, deep in discussion.

Sirinya's heart had stopped beating quite so fast.

'Whatever do they want?' Malee whispered.

Sirinya could see from the way Malee bit her lip and was taking quick, shallow breaths that her cousin was afraid. Sirinya was afraid too, but there was also another emotion in her heart struggling against the fear, which was even more powerful. It was anger. Anger fuelled by outrage.

'I've no idea, but I'm going to ask them,' she said. 'This is private land. They can't just barge in here as if they own the place.'

'Siri, be careful ... they've got guns,' hissed Malee, but Sirinya was already striding towards the group of soldiers.

They stopped talking and lifted their heads from the map to stare as she approached them.

'What are you doing here?' she demanded.

One of them stepped forward. He stared straight at her. His face was covered in fine sweat. His expression was stern.

'You must leave at once,' he said. 'You go now,' he said

pointing towards the gate behind him. His Thai was very poor and heavily accented, but Sirinya could just about make out what he was saying.

'This is private land. It belongs to our family,' she said, aware that her voice was shrill with nerves. Her heart was thumping hard again. She knew she was right to challenge the soldiers, but she couldn't help feeling it was a little fool-hardy too. She noticed one of the men move his hands towards a rifle slung over his shoulder.

'Siri, please,' she heard her cousin say under her breath, but she would not be deflected.

'You go!' said the soldier, raising his voice, beginning to move towards the girls.

'Come on, Sirinya!' said Malee, stepping towards her and grabbing her arm. She felt Malee pushing her, trying to propel her forward. But Sirinya stood firm.

'Who own this land?' barked the soldier.

'My father,' said Malee, in a thin voice, addressing them for the first time, lifting her chin and staring the soldier straight in the eye.

'Where is he?'

Malee pursed her lips and carried on staring, remaining silent.

'We will find him anyway. But if you tell us it will save us trouble. Be quicker.'

'We're not telling you,' said Sirinya.

'You will tell us!'

The one next to the speaker suddenly drew his gun and pointed it straight at them. Despite her bravado Sirinya was shaking all over now. She could feel Malee's arm, shivering against her own. The other two soldiers sprang forward and grabbed the two girls by their arms. Sirinya felt rough hands gripping her, the fingers digging into her flesh. She could smell the strange sweaty odour of his body and clothes, the tobacco and alcohol on his breath. The soldier with the rifle came up close and thrust his gun forward, directly at Sirinya, pushing it into her forehead. The cold hard metal dug into her skull. She was beyond fear now. She could hardly breathe. Everything around her became a blur. She could not focus. She wanted to blurt out her uncle's address, but her mouth and throat were paralysed with terror.

'Leave her alone,' said Malee, her voice shaking. 'He lives on Saeng Chuto road in the centre of town. The vegetable shop. Halfway along. Now let us go!'

At a nod from the speaker, the gun was withdrawn. 'We need to see him about this land.'

'He won't talk to you,' said Sirinya.

'Oh, I think he will,' said the soldier with a smile that sent a chill down her spine.

ABOUT THE AUTHOR

Ann Bennett was born in Pury End, a small village in Northamptonshire, UK and now lives in Surrey. Her first book, *Bamboo Heart: A Daughter's Quest* was inspired by her father's experience as a prisoner of war on the Thai-Burma Railway. *Bamboo Island: The Planter's Wife*, *A Daughter's Promise*, *Bamboo Road: The Homecoming*, and *The Tea Planter's Club* are also about WW2 in South East Asia. *The Amulet* was inspired by a recent trip to South East Asia and further research into the fall of Singapore.

Ann has also written *The Lake Pavilion*, set in British India in the 1930s, *The Lake Palace*, set in India during the Burma Campaign of WW2, *The Lake Pagoda*, and *The Lake Villa*, both set in Indochina during WW2. Ann's other books, *The Runaway Sisters*, bestselling *The Orphan House*, *The Child Without a Home* and *The Forgotten Children* are published by Bookouture.

Ann is married with three grown up sons and a granddaughter, and works as a lawyer. For more details please visit www.annbennettauthor.com

PRAISE FOR ANN BENNETT

'A vivid account of a brutal period and a searing exploration of trauma, memory and loss.' The Lady magazine (on *Bamboo Island: The Planter's Wife*)

'[Laura] represents for the author a whole generation of people whose parents refused to talk about the war leaving a gulf in knowledge and understanding. Bennett is primarily interested in how this generation reacts and changes their perspectives once they have a deeper feeling for what their parents suffered. The trilogy .... is the culmination of one such woman's journey of discovery to understand more about her father's past.'

Raelee Chapman, Singapore Review of Books (on *Bamboo Heart: A Daughter's Quest*), which won the Fiction Published in Asia award (AsianBooksBlog, 2015) and was shortlisted for Best Fiction Title (Singapore Book Awards, 2016). Learn more about the author at: www.annbennettauthor.com

facebook.com/Ann-Bennett-242663029444033

twitter.com/annbennett71

ACKNOWLEDGMENTS

Special thanks go to my friend and writing buddy Siobhan Daiko for her constant support and encouragement over the past decade. To Rafa and Xavier at Cover Kitchen for their wonderful cover design; to Johnny Hudspith for his inspirational editing, to my sisters for reading and commenting on early drafts; and to everyone who's supported me down the years by reading my books.

OTHER BOOKS BY ANN BENNETT

Made in United States
North Haven, CT
07 January 2024

47146266R00211